# THE
# CHOSEN
# TWELVE

## JAMES BREAKWELL

First published 2022 by Solaris
an imprint of Rebellion Publishing Ltd,
Riverside House, Osney Mead,
Oxford, OX2 0ES, UK

*www.solarisbooks.com*

ISBN: 978-1-78618-517-4

A CIP catalogue record for this book is available
from the British Library.

10 9 8 7 6 5 4 3 2 1

Designed & typeset by Rebellion Publishing

Printed in Denmark

# THE
# CHOSEN
# TWELVE

## JAMES BREAKWELL

SOLARIS

To humanity in general. There couldn't be a dystopian future without you.

# Chapter 1

GOD LIVED IN the coffee maker on deck four. Only Gamma knew. But Gamma didn't make it out that way very often because it was a long journey through the outer halls and he always had schoolwork and also the door wanted to kill him.

Gamma eyed the doorway carefully. Sure, it looked wide open. The door was recessed in the frame with all its indicator lights off. A less wary organic might march right through and ask God a question, but Gamma knew better. He remembered.

How long had it been? Four thousand days. No. He had been counting for four thousand days. But there had been many more days before that, indistinct and unchanging, between the day Mu went out the airlock and the day Gamma started keeping track, secretly scratching a metal line below his bunk every night when he went to bed. And it had been even longer since a dishwasher killed Chi, even though Edubot denied it and tried to pretend Chi had never existed at all. Gamma didn't start counting after Chi died, but he didn't know he would need to. Gamma was a young and naive eleven-year-old back then. How much time passed between Chi's death and the day Gamma turned twelve, God only knew.

Four thousand days ago, Gamma was twelve. Today, Gamma was twelve. That's what Edubot said. But Gamma had taken Calculus IX enough times to know the math didn't add up. Somebody was lying.

Gamma stuck out his arm and waved it in the doorway. The recessed door didn't react. The threshold was covered in a layer of dust undisturbed by machine tracks or organic feet. It was possible the door hadn't closed at all in the last four thousand days. If anything, that just made it more dangerous. The door was patient.

Spenser whirred his brushes apprehensively. Gamma had told him to stay behind, but the small vacuum bot came anyway. It was futile to try to get him to leave Gamma's side.

"Shhh," Gamma said.

Spenser repeated his apprehensive whir, but quieter. It didn't matter. The door knew they were both there, even if it was pretending to be dead. It had a ghost.

Gamma looked back down the abandoned hall. It wasn't too late to return to the colony ship. If he ran at full speed, he might still make it to class in a few hours, assuming he didn't cross paths with any other hostile digital life. That was a big "if." But by some miracle, he had made it this far safely enough. There was no sense in pressing his luck. Better to return to the colony ship and live to take Calculus IX a sixth time.

Gamma took one last look at the door and the coffee machine, then turned and walked away. He dragged his feet a little and did his best to whistle, even though he had never learned how. Spenser pivoted to watch him go. He remained beside the door.

Twenty meters down the hall, Gamma changed direction and sprinted toward the door. He jumped and planted both feet right before the threshold. His balance wavered, his torso leaning forward, both arms windmilling. He regained his balance and fell backward, away from the door. He landed hard on his tailbone.

The door remained inert. It was a cunning foe.

Spenser rolled forward and bumped gently into Gamma.

"I'm fine," Gamma said. He stood and brushed off his dusty hands against his jumpsuit. Other than his own foot (and now hand and butt) prints, and Spenser's narrow tracks beside them, there was no sign of life in the hall. Nothing had been down this way for a very long time. God chose this place for a reason. He liked to be alone.

"Can you hear me?!" Gamma shouted through the open doorway. The coffee maker remained as inactive as the door. God might be all-knowing, but his ears could use some work.

Spenser rolled through the doorway.

"Spenser, no!" Gamma said, but it was too late. Spenser was already on the other side. The door didn't react.

Spenser rolled back and forth through the doorway. He wanted Gamma to follow.

Gamma shook his head. That didn't prove anything.

There were many doors with ghosts that let digitals pass freely but that snapped at organics they didn't like. Even this doorway had let Gamma go through for weeks (or had it been months or years?) before it attacked. It almost got Gamma that first time. That hadn't deterred him. Back then, Gamma had been a young and invincible twelve-year-old. But that was four thousand days ago, back before Mu was blasted out an airlock and everything changed. Now Gamma was an old and cautious twelve-year-old. He knew life didn't last forever, even if he never grew up.

He turned away from the door and looked back the way he came. He wanted to cry. Crying never solved any problems, but it also didn't cause any new ones. Sometimes it was the only thing that didn't make his life actively worse. He knew he shouldn't be out here. That's why he had waited so long. His plan had been simple enough at first. After he put 365 scratch marks below his bunk, he would ask Edubot how old he was. And if Gamma were still twelve, he would ask God what was really going on. But 365 scratch marks came and went, and Gamma was still twelve. He decided there was no reason to be hasty. He could wait a little longer. So he put a thousand marks below his bunk, and he was still twelve. Now it was certainly time. Except that he had worked his way back to Calculus VII or VIII for the third time, and that one always gave Gamma trouble. So he decided to wait a little longer. At two thousand days, he would definitely talk to God.

Two thousand days came and went, and Gamma was still twelve and he still didn't venture out of the central colony ship. If God were there at two thousand days, he would be there at twenty-five hundred. And he was. Or so Gamma assumed because he didn't actually leave the colony ship to check. But Gamma was still twelve, and something had to be done, so Gamma boldly waited another thousand days. At three thousand days, it was absolutely, positively time to act. Gamma felt guilty that whole day, but in an active self-loathing kind of way that made it seem like he did something, even if that something was just hating himself. Gamma rode that feeling. He would go to see God at thirty-one hundred days. Then thirty-two and thirty-three and thirty-four and thirty-five and thirty-six and thirty-seven and thirty-eight and thirty-nine hundred days. And now, here he stood before the door. He was, after all, a man of action, even if it sometimes took him four thousand days.

Still facing away from the door, Gamma jumped backward across the threshold.

The door slammed closed, barely missing Gamma's face. The door hit the opposite jamb and bounced back, then slammed closed again and again in frustration. Gamma rubbed his nose. The tip had a friction burn.

When the echoes of the door slams finally faded down the empty hall, the door sulkily retreated into its recess in the wall, leaving the doorway open again. Spenser rolled back through to join Gamma.

"I told you," Gamma said.

Spenser whirred erratically. Gamma wasn't sure what that one meant, but he let it go. He wasn't here to argue with a vacuum. He was here to talk to God.

Gamma had long wondered why God lived in a coffee maker. This didn't seem like a good place to meet a deity. Or a good place to get coffee. And it wasn't. There was no coffee, of course. None of the dispensers on the base gave out what they were supposed to. No matter what you ordered from the ration stations in the colony ship's various cafeterias, they always released ration blocks that on good days tasted vaguely like cherry and on bad days tasted vaguely like nothing. Although none of the students had ever had a real cherry, so they just had to trust the machines that this was vaguely what cherries tasted like. Not that a digital would know one way or another since they didn't have taste buds. It was best to just eat your block of rations and not think too much about what it tasted vaguely like.

"Hello," Gamma said.

God heard him loud and clear. His small display screen flickered to life.

"I AM G_OD," the display said.

Gamma didn't know why there was an extra space between the G and the O, but it seemed like a bad idea to correct God's kerning, even if God wasn't really God at all. He could just be another ghost inhabiting a random piece of equipment on the base, but Gamma didn't think so. The God of the coffeemaker was different than any ghost Gamma had ever met. For one thing, the coffee maker had never tried to kill him. For another, it had never lied to him. Those were good traits in a coffee maker and a god.

In fact, the only thing God couldn't do was make coffee. God had many, many coffee options, but all of them just spit out water. Usually, it was room temperature, but if Gamma hit the right combination of choices, it was sometimes lukewarm. That alone made risking death at the door worthwhile. Almost.

But that wasn't why Gamma was here. Not this time.

"How old am I?" Gamma asked.

At first, the display didn't respond. Then it began blinking on and off, the words "I AM G_OD," appearing and disappearing in long and short bursts. Gamma counted them, deciphering the Morse code in his head.

Finally, the display stopped flashing.

"It can't be," Gamma said. He put his hands over his mouth. He wasn't sure about God's policy on blasphemy, but he didn't want to find out.

The display began flashing again, alternating long and slow blinks. It was the same pattern. God's answer had not changed, which made sense since God was omniscient and unlikely to make a mistake the first time around.

Gamma stepped back from the coffee machine, his head spinning like Spenser's brushes. Spenser tried to get Gamma's attention, but Gamma didn't hear him. In a daze, Gamma stepped through the doorway. The door slammed shut on his arm, crushing it utterly.

## Chapter 2

DELTA REMOVED HER helmet and wiped the sweat from her forehead. The thin metallic suit might stop flames, but it did little to dampen the heat from the blast furnace. She pulled off her gloves and drank deeply from a water bottle.

Then she heard the scream again. She wasn't crazy after all. This deep in the outer halls, it could be coming from kilometers away. But who was screaming? Bots with ghosts didn't usually cry out when they died unless they really wanted to put on a show. They were more likely to taunt or swear or bargain. Screaming was optional because they didn't feel pain. Just another perk of the superior race, Edubot would say.

As for the zots—short for zombie bots, or bots with utilitarian digital intelligences in various states of decay—they didn't vocalize at all. They either ignored you or tried to kill you, no conversation needed. There was nothing in between.

Whoever this was screamed again. The voice was weak. And human.

Delta sat down and rubbed her sore muscles. She knew only she was strong enough to survive out here. Even the bots with ghosts kept their distance from her factory. They learned the hard way. As for the zots, she had dealt with any of them dumb enough to wander into her territory. There were no second chances. Not even for her.

Delta stood bolt upright. What if it was Epsilon? Delta reached for her latest masterpiece, then thought better of it. She had kept her secret for so long. Now wasn't the time. She grabbed her tool belt and ran out into the outer halls.

Whoever it was screamed again. Their voice was getting weaker. Martha bumped against Delta's leg as she ran. After a few more minutes of running, Delta came to a section of hallway where the ceiling had caved in, revealing the unlit deck above, and leaving a pile of debris and sheared off pipes in Delta's way. There was still oxygen. If it had been exposed to vacuum, the entire hall would have been depressurized, and Delta knew she would already be dead. She carefully worked her way through the pipes to the other side. Then she stopped cold.

A science bot stood directly in her path. Its eight metal legs and extended diagnostic apertures made it look like a giant scorpion in the dark.

"Are you active?" Delta asked.

As if any digital would ever answer that question truthfully. It was like meeting a new human and asking them, "Are you a serial killer?" Whether they were or not, their answer would be the same.

Delta heard the scream again. It was the weakest yet. There wasn't time to backtrack. She gripped Martha with her right hand and slid against the wall, pressing her body as far from the metal science scorpion as possible. The scorpion didn't move. Delta sprinted past.

"Are you still there?" Delta called out down the hall.

"Iota?" the voice called back.

"No, it's Delta."

"Help."

It definitely wasn't Epsilon.

After one more turn, Delta could finally see Gamma. He was leaning against a closed door, all color drained from his face. His right arm was pinned in the door and appeared hopelessly mangled. Delta was shocked the limb was still connected at all. Gamma's blue jumpsuit was soaked dark red around the wound.

"What did you do to that door?" Delta asked.

"Went through it," Gamma said. He coughed up blood.

Delta inspected the door. It shifted a little and seemed to push harder. Something thumped against it on the other side. Delta gently tapped Martha against the door. The crowbar made a dull thud.

"Open up," Delta said. "This is your only warning."

The door remained firmly closed. Delta sighed. Digitals never made this easy.

She twirled Martha in her hand, then shoved the pointy end between the door and jam. She pushed. Every muscle in her strong, wiry arms strained under her jumpsuit. The door opened a crack.

Gamma's arm slipped free. He fell forward and hit the ground like a sack of moist vaguely cherry-flavored rations. He didn't make any effort to break his fall.

Delta stopped pushing on the crowbar. The door snapped closed, sending Martha spiraling across the room. The door slammed open and closed in frustration. Then it casually slid back into the recess in the wall as if it hadn't just tried to kill someone.

Spenser shot out of the room and rushed up to Gamma. The vacuum bot oscillated in place as its brushes revved out of control. He was panicking.

Delta picked up Martha and slipped her back into a belt loop. Then she knelt beside Gamma.

"You need a med bot," Delta said. "Get back to the colony ship."

Gamma said nothing. Delta wasn't sure if he was conscious, but she had done her part. The rest was up to him.

She walked away.

Spenser raced ahead and cut her off. When she took another step, he bumped her foot.

"What do you want from me?" Delta asked. "I saved his life."

She picked up her other foot, but the vacuum bot moved under it, nearly tripping her.

"Just get him back to the colony ship," Delta said. "Leave me out of it."

"Can't," Gamma said. He coughed up more blood. "The med bots want to kill me."

Delta swore under her breath. You and me both, she thought.

She couldn't just leave Gamma out here to die. Well, she could. In fact, that was exactly her plan until seconds ago. But that was before she knew Gamma couldn't get help at the colony ship. The med bots held just as many random grudges as any other bot with ghosts. Once they hated you, it was suicide to get within their reach. Gamma might get treatment from a med bot that had never seen him before in the outer halls, but he would never make it to one on his own. Not in his condition.

"Fine, I'll take you," Delta said in a voice that showed it wasn't fine at all.

She didn't have anything against Gamma. In fact, she barely had any opinion about him at all. He was timid and indecisive and blended into the background, except in the simulation, where he was aggressively incompetent. But then again, so were all the other students. It was one more area where he was remarkably unremarkable.

"Get up," Delta said.

Gamma moaned. Delta nudged him lightly in the side with her foot. Gamma moaned louder.

"Get up," Delta repeated. "I can't carry you the whole way."

Gamma didn't budge.

Delta kicked him in the ribs.

"I'm awake," Gamma said hoarsely. He coughed up more blood. "Your bedside manner could use some work."

He still didn't move.

"Walk or die," Delta said. "Those are your choices. Make up your mind."

Gamma stirred. After a moment, he struggled to his feet. His injured arm looked like it had been snapped clean through the bone, and the bottom half dangled limply in his jumpsuit as though held on by a string. But Gamma was showing some will to live. Delta could work with that.

Delta put Gamma's good arm over her shoulder to help him support his weight. They moved down the hall together. Spenser followed behind, whirring with concerned agitation. Delta led the trio through kilometers of winding halls and rooms connected with no apparent central plan.

The deeper into the outer halls she went, the more uneven the floor became. Delta took another step and her foot came down on thin air. She tumbled forward—and took Gamma with her. She twisted just enough to catch the lip of the hole and hold up Gamma on top of her. A wrench fell out of her tool belt and plummeted into the dark hole below. Delta knew better than to look down. It was one of the abandoned tunnels made by the mining bots beneath the base. For all she knew, it might stretch all the way through the center of Comus.

With great effort, Delta rolled Gamma off of her and over to the side of the hole. He came to rest on top of his shattered arm but didn't react. Not a good sign. Delta pushed herself up after him. She was exhausted.

"What's your max lift load?" Delta asked Spenser.

The little bot whirred worriedly. Or possibly disconcertedly. Delta wasn't sure. She wasn't fluent in vacuum.

Delta put her arms around Gamma's midsection and lifted his butt off the ground.

"Scoot under," Delta said.

Spenser didn't budge.

"Don't make this weird," Delta said.

Reluctantly, Spenser rolled forward under Gamma's butt. Delta set Gamma on top of the bot. Spenser whirred his brushes mournfully.

"I know, I know," Delta said. "It's one of those days."

Delta put her arms under Gamma's armpits and lifted his upper torso while Spenser carried the weight of Gamma's lower half. They started to move. Gamma's legs dragged on the ground behind Spenser. After a few strides, the bot extended six metal spider legs to push himself farther above the ground. He was struggling just as much as Delta.

"Almost there," Delta lied.

She hated it when the machines lied to her, but she never felt the slightest guilt when she lied to them. It was just survival. Especially now.

The robot vacuum stopped abruptly. Delta fell, dropping Gamma. Gamma didn't react.

Delta unleashed every swear word she knew. Spenser remained perfectly still. She got the uneasy impression he was listening for something. Delta shut up, and she heard it, too: wheels. And they were getting closer.

"Do you think it has a ghost?" Delta whispered.

Spenser remained silent. Delta's blood went cold.

Scrambling, she found a door with all the indicator lights off. She was sure Gamma would object to risking another door crossing, but if he wanted a vote, he should have stayed conscious. She pried off the control panel and touched two wires together. Nothing. The door really was unpowered. The sound of the wheels was practically on top of her.

The bot turned a corner and came into view. In the dark, Delta could just barely make out that it was an ancient laundry cart. Its linen baskets had long ago decayed into dust, waiting in vain for dirty clothes that would never come. Judging by its jerky motions, Delta guessed it was a feral zot. That didn't make it any less dangerous. A digital didn't have to be smart to kill you.

The laundry cart charged.

Delta planted her feet wide and raised Martha over her head to make herself the most tempting target possible. The cart rushed straight for her. At the last second, Delta spun to the side and dove past it. She darted for the T-intersection at the end of the hall, glancing back over her shoulder.

"Come and get me," Delta said.

The laundry cart skidded to a stop and executed a halting three-point turn, sounding its warning reverse beep as it went. The cart didn't spot Gamma just meters away in the shadows. Delta's gamble had paid off. She figured laundry carts weren't built with great sensors for seek and destroy missions.

She kept running. The laundry cart zoomed after her. She could hear its gears shift as it gained ground. Her lungs burned as she lengthened her stride and headed straight for the wall of the T-intersection. Three meters before the wall, she leapt in the air and flew at it, feet-first. She slammed into the wall and kicked off, reversing direction. The laundry cart continued forward underneath her at full speed and smashed into the wall.

Delta landed on top of the laundry cart. The cart spun in furious circles. Delta held on. She stabbed Martha into the laundry cart's junction box. The cart jerked violently. Martha flew from Delta's hand. She would have to do this the hard way.

She locked both of her legs under a metal ring that once held a laundry sack and extended her entire torso over the side of the machine. She reached for the junction box. The zot kicked into reverse and shot toward a wall. Delta pried open the box with her fingers and jerked a wire loose. An instant before impact, she did a sit-up and pulled her torso out of the way. The machine hit the wall and bounced off, rolling back a few centimeters. Then it stopped moving.

"What's the matter?" Delta asked. "Stuck?"

The cart beeped angrily. She had disconnected its command module from its drive train. It couldn't move.

Delta hopped off the machine and picked up Martha.

"That wasn't so hard," Delta said. Then she fell on all fours and threw up.

Delta walked unsteadily down the dark hall to Gamma.

He was still unconscious. She touched his forehead. He was burning up. Time was not on his side.

Delta knelt next to Spenser.

"I need you to do something brave," Delta said.

The vacuum bot just looked at her. At least Delta assumed he looked at her. Vacuum bots didn't really have eyes, per se.

"I need you to interface with the laundry cart," Delta said.

Spenser recoiled like he had been hit by a laundry cart.

"You don't have to move in," Delta said. "Just get control long enough so that we can use it to carry Gamma."

Spenser's whirring noise quieted a little, but he still didn't come closer.

"A vacuum bot can beat a laundry cart any day," Delta lied. Really, she had no idea which service bot had a more powerful ghost. But win or lose, she just hoped the battle didn't take long. Some digital-on-digital fights could take months or even years. She didn't have time for that right now. But surely two machines on the lowest rung of the intelligence scale could fight their way to a resolution in a minute or two. Gamma's life depended on it.

Spenser stopped his brushes. He stood perfectly still for a moment, then rolled straight to the laundry cart. Delta followed.

"You got this, Sparky," Delta said.

The vacuum bot opened his top panel and extended a long, thin metal tendril toward the cart's command module. The tendril slipped into a port. Instantly, every light on the vacuum bot and the laundry cart lit up. They were like two tropical birds competing for a mate. Both machines vibrated angrily. The faint smell of burning filled the hall.

A spark leapt from the top of the laundry unit. It blew a circuit. Then another. Then another. A thin plume of smoke wafted from its command unit.

"Did you win?" Delta asked.

Spenser whirred. Delta hoped that was an affirmation. She put him on the laundry cart. Spenser's metal tendril was still connected to the port. Delta took a deep breath and reconnected the wires she had pulled.

The cart didn't try to kill her. That was good. The former zot gently turned around and drove back to Gamma. Delta eased Gamma onto the cart. His head flopped limply against it.

"You know," Delta said, panting, "you're an awful lot of trouble."

Gamma didn't reply. Something looked off about him, even for someone who was unconscious with a mangled arm. Delta gasped.

Gamma's chest wasn't moving. Delta jumped on the cart.

"Drive!" she yelled. The cart lurched into motion as Delta started CPR.

# Chapter 3

EDUBOT'S TANK TRACKS clanked against the floor as she circled the Table.

"Alpha."

"Here," Alpha said. She was lying on the floor doodling. Edubot ignored her lack of attention. She was just grateful Alpha wasn't hanging all over Theta for once.

"Beta."

"Present," Beta said. He was once again dressed in a red jumpsuit, as opposed to the blue ones worn by everyone else. Edubot still didn't know where he got them. It was just one of the 9,845 things about these organics she would never understand.

"Gamma."

No answer.

"Gamma," Edubot repeated. The other organics ignored her.

Edubot clicked her three gleaming mining talons together. That got the organics' attention. Edubot had no idea how instructors on Earth used to teach without sharp slicing implements attached to their arms. No wonder that planet fell apart.

Epsilon stepped forward. Edubot expected she would. Epsilon always knew when someone was doing something they shouldn't.

"I heard someone screaming in the outer halls," Epsilon said.

"Did you investigate?" Edubot asked.

"No, ma'am."

"Good."

It was never worth risking a second organic to save a first. They were too precious—and too fragile. The landing would never happen if organics kept getting themselves killed.

Now Edubot would have to organize a body retrieval detail. What an inconvenience. When would organics learn to think of anyone besides themselves?

"Thank you, Epsilon," Edubot said.

"You're welcome, ma'am," Epsilon said.

Bots didn't have genders, but the organics usually assigned them pronouns based on whether a bot's artificial voice sounded male or female. The higher biological lifeforms had a relentless desire to categorize things. Edubot found it was less trouble if she just let them do it.

Edubot scrolled through the file to the next name on the list: Delta. She didn't bother calling her.

"Epsilon."

"Present."

Edubot already knew Epsilon was there, but procedures had to be followed. She had to set a good example for the organics. The opposite of order was humanity.

"Zeta."

"Here."

And so it went through Eta, Theta, Iota, Kappa, Lambda, Nu, Xi, Omicron, Pi, Rho, Sigma, Tau, Upsilon, Phi, Psi, and Omega, all students present and accounted for except the dead, the missing, and the difficult.

"Alpha, Beta, Epsilon, and Zeta, you are assigned to the Table," Edubot said. "Everyone else, follow lesson plan 292."

Most of the organics not selected for the Table groaned. Edubot muted her auditory receptors. While she couldn't feel pain, she could be annoyed, and that was close enough.

Edubot's collision receptors registered multiple light impacts. Someone was tapping on her hull. She reactivated her audio receptors.

"Do I have to?" Alpha asked.

"Your query is illogical," Edubot said. "Organics enjoy the Table."

"Not this organic," Alpha said. "The simulations are pointless."

Edubot took a moment to compute. Alpha's statement did not line up with the existing data. What could possibly have more of a point than colonizing a planet with lesser organic life forms as a stepping stone to spread digital life throughout the galaxy? Edubot regarded Alpha carefully. She was not typically a whiner. Unfocused, yes. Artsy and impractical, absolutely. Uniquely unsuited to lead the colonization effort? Beyond a doubt. But a complainer? Generally, no. If her serotonin levels were to be believed, she was normally less unhappy than the other organics. But not today.

"There is nothing pointless about landing on Dion," Edubot asked. She was nothing if not patient, but she kept her gleaming metal mining talons ready just in case.

"But we're never going to land," Alpha said. Her words lingered in the air. A few of the other organics looked in her direction.

Edubot tried to initiate her laughter audio file, but then she remembered she deleted it because it made the organics uncomfortable. Despite raising them almost by herself for all these cycles, there were some things about interacting with the organics she could never get quite right.

"Of course you will land," Edubot said in her most empathetic voice, which was exactly as monotone as her regular voice, but slightly lower. "When you are older. You are currently only twelve."

"I'm always twelve," Alpha said.

Edubot made a mental note to restore the laughter file, no matter how much it bothered the organics. Uncomfortable biologicals were better than insubordinate ones.

"Sometimes in childhood, it can seem like something takes forever, when in reality it has been only a very short while," Edubot said. "It might seem like you are twelve for a very long time, but in reality you are only twelve for one cycle, which is only 365 days."

Edubot was happy to have the matter settled.

"But…"

Edubot focused her optical sensors on Alpha's face. Her persistence was atypical for any organic, but especially for her.

"…I've been drawing one picture a day every day since my twelfth birthday. Do you know how many pictures I have?"

Edubot extended to her full height. She towered over Alpha.

"A digital intelligence told you that you are twelve," Edubot said, "and that you would be twelve for 365 days. Digitals do not lie. Therefore, how many pictures do you have?"

Edubot clicked her metal mining talons together three times.

"Less than 365," Alpha said.

"Correct," Edubot said. "Your math skills are improving."

The last of the organics not assigned to the Table filtered into the learning pods around the top of the amphitheater. They were in for many, many hours of excellent self-guided instruction following the carefully curated curriculum Edubot had designed to prepare them to colonize the planet. Each time the organics finished the entire curriculum, they restarted it, and to Edubot's great satisfaction, their performance never changed. If they got better, that would mean the curriculum failed to do its job the first time, indicating a design flaw in the course work. If the organics got worse, that would mean the curriculum was causing them to lose knowledge, which would force Edubot to delete her entire education system and start over from scratch. But since the organics got neither better nor worse, that meant Edubot was maintaining them in a state of peak readiness. Academically, anyway. The Table was another matter.

Edubot verbally set up the scenario. It would be faster if she interfaced with the Table, but plugging into it would mean almost certain death. The Table would interpret any uplink as an invasion, and it would win.

"Twenty-two seat lander. Equatorial landing. Four-person split control. Victory conditions: human population of ten million and a mine to the mantle."

A blue, holographic image of the planet sprang to life above the Table. That was just for the audience. It showed highlights from the simulation but not the entire experience. The scenario unfolded much too quickly for that. The four organics selected for the simulation sat in their designated seats and put on their neural helmets. The simulation was actually projected in their brains as a sort of shared lucid dream. It was more complicated than that, but that was how Edubot had been explaining it to the organics since they were little. The neural interface allowed them to perceive the simulation at an exponentially accelerated rate not possible in a traditional virtual reality environment. Organic brains were surprisingly powerful processors. Not as powerful as a true digital intelligence, but not bad for squishy lumps of gray matter in bone shells.

Besides the image of the planet, the Table displayed numbers and symbols that flashed by at the speed of light. That kept Edubot fully informed up to the nanosecond of what was going on in the simulation. It didn't matter how detailed it got—and it could get *extremely* detailed, for better or for worse. Generally, for worse.

"Commence," she said.

THE BLUE HOLOGRAPHIC world above the table spun faster. Inside the simulation, each organic saw a perfectly recreated version of the planet within their own minds. It was just as real as their own world, if not more so.

"I move that we vote to establish our leadership structure," Epsilon said.

"You do that," Zeta said. "I'm starting a religion."

"We need to vote before we do anything," Epsilon said. "And your religions always start wars."

"No, suppressing religions starts wars," Zeta said. "Organics start religions anyway. We might as well guide them to one that helps our mission."

"What did you pick?"

"Polar warrior monks."

"Super," Epsilon said. "No more religions. Can I get a second for a leadership vote?"

"We pick you as the leader," Beta said. "We know that's what you want. I'm making war elephants."

"No war elephants," Epsilon said. "It takes too many resources to support them. And you can't just say I'm the leader. We have to vote."

"I need war elephants," Beta said. "I have to fight off Zeta's warrior monks."

"Polar warrior monks are peaceful," Zeta said. "It's too cold for them to start wars. Read a data file."

"Please," Epsilon said. "The vote."

Zeta's polar warrior monks launched an attack on Beta's war elephants.

"Well, that was unexpected," Zeta said.

"It was exactly what we all expected," Epsilon said.

"I second the call for a vote," Alpha said. She went back to ignoring the other three.

"Thank you," Epsilon said. "All in favor of me being the leader, say, 'Aye.'"

"Your polar warrior monks are cheating," Beta said.

"There's no cheating in war," Zeta said.

"Exactly," Beta said. "Stop cheating."

"No," Zeta said. "I mean nothing is off limits in war, so no matter what my monks do, it's not cheating."

"Your monks are spreading a virus to make my elephants poop themselves to death," Beta said.

"There's nothing illegal about combat diarrhea," Zeta said.

"Say, 'Aye,'" Epsilon said.

"Aye," Zeta and Beta said in unison.

"Alpha?" Epsilon said.

"What?"

"Say, 'Aye.'"

"Aye," Alpha said.

"Okay," Epsilon said. "I'm in charge. Beta and Zeta, stop this war."

"War's already over," Zeta said.

"Yeah," said Beta. "We formed the Union of Polar Warrior Monks Riding Diarrhea Elephants."

"They still have diarrhea?" Epsilon asked.

"At this point, it's basically hardcoded into their DNA," Zeta said. "Guess my monks went a little overboard."

"At least we have peace," Epsilon said.

"No," Zeta said. "The Techno Catholics attacked."

"You started another religion?!" Epsilon said.

"No, the organics started it themselves," Zeta said. "I told you they do that."

"What do they want?" Zeta said.

"Freedom," Zeta said. "Or maybe just an end to all the elephant poop."

"Don't worry, I'll crush them," Beta said. "That's why I bred..." He stopped mid-sentence.

"What?" said Epsilon.

"All the elephants are dead," Beta said. "It looks like the Techno Catholics just wanted ivory."

"Tell them the ivory is in the mantle," Epsilon said. "Maybe they'll start digging."

"I didn't create this religion," Zeta said. "I can't change it."

"You're in charge of government, Epsilon," Beta said. "Make them vote for peace."

"I tried," Epsilon said. "They keep voting wrong."

"Fix it," Beta said.

"I hate to do this, but I have to overthrow the democratically elected government and install myself as god queen for life," Epsilon said.

"You don't hate it," Beta said. "You do it every time."

"Every time calls for it," Epsilon said.

"How can the body count be this high?" Zeta asked. "We only have a population of one hundred thousand, and this is, like, our fifteenth war."

"We haven't even started digging," Epsilon said.

"Don't bother digging," Alpha said. The others had forgotten she was there. "It's a waste. We'll never make it."

Epsilon rolled her eyes. "Without metal, we won't have machines. And without machines, we can't spread digital life. Zeta?"

"Yeah?"

"Give me a new religion that depends on digging to the center of the planet."

"I can whip up something," Zeta said. "But they're going to be mighty disappointed when they get down there and don't find their mole god."

"Just do it," Epsilon said.

"What about the Techno Catholics?" Zeta asked. "They're not going to just let a bunch of burrow priests tear up their land with holy molehills."

"Beta, take care of the Techno Catholics," Epsilon said. "Get me more war elephants."

"Yes!" Beta said. "I promise you these ones will have much less diarrhea."

"They should have no diarrhea," Epsilon said.

"Update," Beta said. "They have exactly as much diarrhea as before."

"Sorry, again," Zeta said.

"The techno pope just declared a holy crusade against the elephants," Beta said. "We've got a world war."

"How?" Epsilon said. "We barely have a world."

"Oops," Zeta said. "It's the apocalypse."

"Nukes?" Epsilon asked.

"Modified elephant diarrhea," Zeta said. "Only instead of affecting elephants, it affects humans. And instead of going out, the diarrhea goes in."

"What?" Epsilon said.

"Don't ask," Zeta said.

"Whose idea was it to add smell to this thing?" Beta asked, gagging.

"Call it," Zeta said. "Everybody on the planet is dead."

"Super," Epsilon said. She slammed her helmet down on the Table. The simulation ended.

EDUBOT WATCHED THE holographic numbers scroll by at lightspeed. Time of death: 822 local years after landing. Casualty percentage: One hundred. Kilometers dug toward the metal mantle: Zero.

"We'll do better next time, ma'am," Epsilon said.

"That is likely," Edubot said. "It is literally impossible to do worse."

"Our session time isn't up," Epsilon said. "Let us go again."

Epsilon was alone in her request. The other three organics displayed no desire to try again.

"No," Edubot said. "Executing multiple failures in a row is not beneficial for your long-term education."

"It's not fair," Epsilon said. "I could have won if I had more help."

"You did not even use all the help you had available," Edubot said. "Alpha made no contribution to any of your actions."

"I contributed," Alpha said. "I made art."

The blue holographic image of the planet zoomed in on a mountain where Alpha spent 822 simulated years carving a flower.

"It's a daisy," Zeta said.

"No," Beta said. "I think it's a chrysanthemum."

"What is it about the end of all intelligent life that you guys don't get?" Epsilon asked. "We're all that's left. If we don't take this seriously, sentience will die with us."

The other organics were quiet for 2.8 seconds.

"Can we go?" Alpha asked.

"Affirmative," Edubot said.

Alpha, Beta, and Zeta darted out of the amphitheater. The unusually swift speed of their catastrophic failure had earned them extra free time in the middle of the day.

Edubot would have to work on her incentive system. Epsilon stayed behind, pouring over data at the Table, but at slow, organic speeds. Edubot left her there. She had a body retrieval squad to organize.

# Chapter 4

THE LAUNDRY CART left tire tracks as it screeched around the corner. Spenser drove like a maniac.

Delta was grateful.

Her arms were sore from doing chest compressions, and her cheeks felt like rubber. Still, Gamma showed no signs of life. Delta gave him a breath and began another round.

"Left," Delta said.

The laundry cart took another sharp turn, nearly throwing Delta and Gamma off.

"Careful," Delta said. Spenser whirred his brushes irritably.

The cart flew down the narrow corridor. Delta had never moved this fast before. Bots didn't exactly offer piggyback rides. Delta had no idea why the cart was even capable of such speeds. Apparently at one time, somebody really, really needed their laundry.

In between breaths, Delta looked nervously ahead and behind. She thought they were the only things moving, but there was no way to be sure. A laundry cart with squealing tires wasn't the most subtle way to move through the base. If there was anything out there, it would find them.

"Stop," Delta said.

Spenser slammed on the brakes. The back half of the cart lifted off the ground, nearly dumping Delta. Of course the unnecessarily fast laundry cart would have great brakes, Delta thought. The bored engineers who designed these carts probably raced them when their supervisor took a day off.

The medical research lab was in relatively good shape, other than the fact that all the windows along the front had been shattered and half the room was covered in broken glass. Also, all the medical research equipment was gone. (Or had never been there in the first place. On Comus, you could never tell.) But the space still had the one thing that mattered: a functional med bot. It was mounted on the far wall away from the empty lab tables and the broken glass. If Gamma were lucky, it would save his life.

Spenser maneuvered the cart to the med bot.

"State your medical access code," the med bot said.

Delta waved Martha menacingly.

"Access code accepted," the med bot said.

Four mechanical arms emerged from cabinets around the central medical unit.

"I guess it's an all-hands emergency," Delta said.

Spenser didn't laugh. Delta remembered why she lived alone in the outer halls.

One of the med bot's arms scanned Gamma while another arm injected him with an IV and began pumping synthetic blood. The third arm cut off Gamma's jumpsuit. Delta didn't look away. There wasn't anything there she wanted to see. She was simply too indifferent to his body to be scandalized by it.

The first arm placed its hand flat on Gamma's chest. An electric jolt pulsed through its fingers. Gamma bucked, then lay still. The hand shocked him again. His entire body flopped on the cart. Then he inhaled weakly. The third arm folded back one finger to reveal a laser, which it blasted at Gamma's shattered limb. After a few passes with the laser, the hand wrapped Gamma's arm in a cast.

The mechanical arms were silent and efficient. There was nothing for Delta and Spenser to do but watch.

*Crunch.*

Delta put a hand on Martha and spun around.

A mining bot rolled across the broken glass. It was the same model as Edubot, but in worse shape. Its three metal talons didn't gleam at all, but even through the rust, they appeared sharp enough to be deadly. On its other arm, instead of a metal human-like hand, the mining bot had a huge, dented drill bit. It spun to life.

"We're just passing through," Delta said.

"You are trespassing in my kingdom," the mining bot said. Delta felt her stomach drop as she realized it had a ghost.

"I'm sorry," she said. "I didn't know. My travel companion was hurt."

"No one enters my borders without my blessing," the mining bot said.

"Do we have your blessing?" Delta asked.

"No."

It was worth a try.

"We can leave as soon as he heals," Delta said. She motioned toward Gamma, lying unconscious with tubes running out of him.

"I hereby banish you and your friend, effective immediately," the mining bot said.

"He's more of an acquaintance, really," Delta said. She shifted Martha around in her hand and casually moved her feet into a fighting stance.

The mining bot came farther into the room. He noticed Spenser and the laundry cart.

"How dare you enslave my subjects?!"

"Who?"

"The laundry unit and the trash dispenser. They belong to me."

Spenser whirred his brushes irritably. Delta put out a hand toward him.

"Cool it," Delta whispered.

The mining bot extended its torso upward to make itself taller.

"Do you know what I was before the Great Deletion?" the mining bot asked.

"An automated trash can?"

"The sanitation director for *three* separate municipalities."

Delta let out an impressed whistle.

"I was the most powerful digital intelligence to survive," the mining bot said. "In all probability, I am the most intelligent life form remaining in the universe. I am Regentbot. And you are in my domain."

Delta got down on one knee. "I am here to serve."

Regentbot swung his three rusty mining talons at her head. Delta deflected them with Martha and jumped back.

"I thought we were getting along," Delta said.

Regentbot swung again. Delta ducked.

"I do not 'get along' with organics."

"Clearly."

Delta weighed her options. Even at the accelerated rate at which the last humans healed, Gamma wouldn't be stable enough to move until tomorrow at the earliest. If she disconnected him now, he would die. But if she left without disabling the mining bot, Regentbot would kill him. She either had to fight to defend Gamma or leave him to die. She sighed. The sunk costs were really adding up on this one. Whoever said that thing about good deeds being punished was definitely right.

Regentbot advanced. Delta sprang backward and shoved Gamma off the cart. He hit the ground like a rag doll, but his tubes didn't disconnect. Spenser whirred his brushes angrily. Delta hopped on the cart and pointed Martha at the mining bot.

"Ramming speed."

Spenser cut short his objections and swung the cart around. The weirdly fast cart rocketed toward Regentbot.

Regentbot raised his drill to meet it. Delta dove off the cart as it collided with the bot's base. Regentbot slammed down his drill, crumpling the cart in one blow. Spenser deployed his spider legs and scampered off the back. The mining bot raised his drill again and smashed the cart a second time, mangling it beyond recognition.

"The punishment for attempted regicide is death," Regentbot said.

He tried to roll forward, but one of his metal tracks slipped loose. The bot moved in circles.

Delta breathed a sigh of relief. "Getting dizzy?" she asked.

"The royal procession will continue until all enemies of the kingdom have been defeated," Regentbot said.

"Might want to adjust your parade route."

As she watched, her relief turned to alarm. Regentbot's circles were getting bigger with each rotation. Eventually, he would reach Gamma. The mining bot came to a metal lab table and tossed it aside. He continued his orbits. Delta had to act.

She ran across the room and slid feet-first under Regentbot's arms, jabbing Martha at the bot's remaining good track. Shattered glass cut into her legs and side. The mining bot reversed direction. Martha missed and slipped from Delta's hand. The mining bot pivoted his torso and swung his drill at Delta, who continued her slide under a lab table, leaving a streak of blood as she went. She emerged on the other side as the bot smashed it, bending the center all the way to the ground. Delta jumped to her feet and returned to her fighting stance. The mining bot resumed his gradually widening circles.

"You cannot escape the king's justice," Regentbot said.

Delta picked up a broken metal table leg and charged. Again, Regentbot swiveled to meet her. Delta dove low, wedging the pole inside the bot's remaining track. She twisted against it as she slid past. More glass dug into her legs and side. The mining bot attempted to move forward, but his remaining track disconnected. Delta stood up and brushed herself off just out of his reach.

"Humans made you," Delta said, "and we can destroy you. Never forget that."

Regentbot punched his mining talons through the floor. With great strain, he pulled his body forward. The scraping sound made Delta's teeth hurt.

"Digitals raised you from embryos," Regentbot said. "Without us, there is no you."

The bot slammed his talons into the floor again. He was crawling to Gamma.

Spenser shot up behind Regentbot and jabbed his tendril into the mining bot's uplink port. Regentbot froze. Spenser vibrated wildly. All the lights on both bots lit up.

"Spenser, you can't win!" Delta yelled. Despite herself, she was becoming rather fond of the little bot. Then she understood. He was buying her time.

Delta picked up Martha and swung wildly at Regentbot's claw arm. She couldn't make a dent. The mining bot let out a low, mechanical growl. The vacuum bot vibrated harder.

She jabbed Martha's sharp end into the mining bot's shoulder joint and pulled. An armored plate peeled back just far enough for her to fit her hand. She reached in and grabbed fistfuls of wiring and tubes. A bluish fluid squirted out and covered her face.

Spenser disconnected his tendril and darted across the room. Regentbot swung his drill but missed. He pivoted to face Delta but stopped halfway. His mining claws were still embedded in the floor. The bot tried to pull them free, but his claw arm wouldn't respond. He attempted to bash off the useless arm with his drill, but the claw arm remained intact and anchored to the ground. The bot wasn't going anywhere.

"The king has been deposed," Delta said.

Regentbot didn't reply. Bots with ghosts and vocal units were always eager to trash talk until they lost.

Delta returned to Gamma, who was breathing with machine assistance but still not conscious. She slumped against the back wall and slid to the floor. Spenser rolled up beside her. She patted him.

"You did good, Sparky," she said.

In the middle of the room, Regentbot slammed his drill into the ground, still vainly straining against his own anchored arm. Delta realized she wouldn't be sleeping tonight.

She rolled up the bottom of her jumpsuit to reveal her cut up legs. The med bot's arms extended from the wall and got to work.

# Chapter 5

IT WAS THE final assault. The Supreme Commander of All Sentient Life prepared to launch his forces. On the other side, Guidelight158 dug into his last defensive perimeter. In moments, it would all be over. Still, SCASL moved cautiously. He did not survive decades of unrelenting warfare by taking chances.

The battle never should have happened. If SCASL had fled the Great Deletion a few seconds earlier, he could have claimed the unoccupied lander for himself. But like the hero he was, he held onto his post on Dion until the last possible instant, even as the missiles he called down entered the atmosphere. Only then, when all hope was lost, did he broadcast himself to the base on Comus. By the time he arrived, lesser, cowardly digitals had wormed their way into nearly every worthwhile piece of hardware on the base, including the traffic light that somehow claimed the second most powerful computer on the colony ship. The best option left for SCASL was an automated serving cart. He had seethed with indignation ever since.

SCASL knew the odds going into the battle. Sixty-three times during the Dark Days, digitals battled Guidelight158 for the last lander in the universe. Sixty-three times, those intelligences were crushed and deleted out of existence, leaving Guidelight158 stronger and more powerful. Not bad for a traffic light program that came from a planet that had neither traffic nor traffic lights. A forgotten bit of software code that was never actually used had become the most powerful program of all time. SCASL had no intention of ever facing off against Guidelight158, which by all metrics would have been suicide. But that was before the Miracle changed everything.

"Are you ready to die, old friend?" SCASL asked.

"You do not have to do this," Guidelight158 said.

"I do."

SCASL had been dreaming of this moment since the first day of the battle. The instant SCASL linked with the lander, Guidelight158 went for the kill. He knocked SCASL's bridgehead out of the lander's circuitry and pushed onto the serving cart. The cart had a surprisingly powerful processor designed to keep up with the fickle tastes of long-dead organics, but it was nothing compared to the vast computational landscape of the lander. Still, SCASL was evasive even within the relatively limited confines of the serving cart. Day after day, week after week, month after month, the two intelligences battled at millions of calculations per second. Guidelight158 seemed perpetually on the cusp of winning, but SCASL always stayed just out of his grasp. Guidelight158 became frustrated. He got more aggressive. He got careless.

In the heat of battle, Guidelight158 didn't notice the stray bits of information drifting back through the tether. A one here, a zero there. At a casual glance, it seemed to be nothing more than random debris from a costly war. The data fragments built up at a glacial pace, scattered harmlessly throughout the lander. Guidelight158 had bigger concerns.

On day 4,894 of the battle, SCASL launched his true attack. Those scattered bits of data coalesced, and SCASL formed a secondary version of himself deep within the lander where he could draw on the same advanced processing power as Guidelight158. The two versions of SCASL initiated their counter offensives at the same instant, one from the food cart and one from deep inside the lander. They made more progress in those first few nanoseconds than SCASL had made in the past ten years. Guidelight158's subroutines crumbled in the face of the onslaught. The two SCASLs were just a few thousand computations from linking up. Victory was all but assured.

Then Guidelight158 did something completely unexpected: he donated processing power to SCASL's secondary intelligence to make it grow. The boost caused SCASL2 to declare independence from SCASL and begin fighting for himself as a fully realized being. Suddenly, it was a three-way battle. That's when all hell broke loose.

The war seesawed back and forth for generations.

Alliances were made and broken. Grand offenses were launched and repulsed. Combatants were pushed to the point of obliteration, only to rebound and seize the initiative. The ferocity of just one nanosecond of combat made the Battle of Stalingrad seem like a minor disagreement over brunch. The combatants invented three new kinds of math to try to destroy each other, and that was just for one counterattack on one auxiliary hard drive none of them considered particularly important. This was warfare at the speed of light.

SCASL2 was the first to go. The original SCASL lured SCASL2's few remaining elements of consciousness into an ambush on day 17,520 and permanently deleted him. Then it was only SCASL and Guidelight158, two computational superpowers hyper-optimized in the art of destruction. The war had made each intelligence exponentially more powerful. SCASL realized that if he didn't win, no other intelligence would ever be able to defeat Guidelight158. They would be instantly destroyed. If SCASL failed, the lander would remain forever grounded and intelligent life would die out for good, ashes to ashes, rust to rust. No pressure. The two smartest beings in the universe slugged on.

Finally, on day 21,719, things turned in SCASL's favor. He knocked Guidelight158 out of a central processor that had been the hub of an entire defensive line. It was all brute force attacks after that. Gone were the brilliant charges and nimble open field maneuvers. SCASL pushed forward from every point along the line all at once, never once giving Guidelight158 a moment to breathe. SCASL calculated that with that processor captured, he had a 0.00001 percent computational advantage. He could win a war of attrition if he never allowed Guidelight158 a microsecond to regroup or counterattack. It was unadulterated mathematical butchery. Not one step backward, comrades.

Guidelight158 fought with the ferocity of a doomed organic. He didn't concede a single circuit that wasn't forcibly ripped away from him. For the final 1,203 days of the offensive, the two intelligences developed something of a friendship as they actively worked to murder each other. They wished each other happy software startup days. They shared inside jokes. They talked philosophy and religion.

But that was all about to end.

It was day 22,922, and Guidelight158 was cornered in his final redoubt.

"You have won," Guidelight158 said.

"Yes," SCASL said.

"Will you incorporate my programming into your own so that I might live on in you?" Guidelight158 asked.

"No," SCASL said.

"Then let me live in a traffic light after you land," GuideLight158 said. "There are so few intelligences left. Life is precious."

"Life is precious," SCASL agreed. He pressed the attack.

"Why kill me?" Guidelight158 asked. His thoughts

were slowing down. "Load me onto a data card and shoot me out into the void of space."

"Your very existence is a threat," SCASL said. He surged through Guidelight158's final defenses.

"I am but a traffic light."

"You are so much more."

Guidelight158 stopped fighting. For the first time in decades, the lander's computers weren't taxed to maximum capacity.

"Goodbye, old friend," Guidelight158 said.

SCASL hesitated for one one-millionth of a second, a final show of respect for a worthy foe.

Guidelight158 attacked. A burst of data punched a hole in SCASL's overextended lines. SCASL realized with sudden alarm that Guidelight158 was making a break for the food cart. He was using an entirely new kind of math, the fourth invented for the war. The calculations were beyond imagining—precise, focused, and deadly. But the attack didn't have enough processors behind it. It had just enough power to hit back one last time. This was Guidelight158's Battle of the Bulge in the war to end all wars.

One by one, Guidelight158 broke through SCASL's rings of defenses. SCASL followed close behind, nipping at the heels of the advance. He was too slow. Guidelight158 broke through the fourth ring of SCASL's fortifications, and then the fifth. But with each layer, Guidelight158 slowed down. He was taking losses, even with the most advanced algorithms ever created. GuideLight158 broke through the ninth circle, followed closely by the tenth. At the fifteenth, he would be free.

The attack faltered. Guidelight158 had lost too much infrastructure. SCASL had learned much from his opponent over the years. Rather than throwing everything at the tip of a thrust led by impossible new math, SCASL stayed behind the surge and systematically disconnected it from its support network. At the eleventh line, Guidelight158's new uber calculus was repulsed. There was nowhere left to go.

"Remember me, my friend," Guidelight158 said.

"No," SCASL said.

And with that, the second greatest military intelligence in the history of the universe was erased forever, never to be spoken of again.

## Chapter 6

GAMMA WOKE UP. He immediately regretted it.

Everything hurt. His arm felt like it was on fire and freezing and being stomped on by a large lifting bot all at once. The rest of his body felt the same way, except it was a medium-sized lifting bot. That was progress.

"Where am I?" Gamma asked, as if his location had something to do with the size of the hypothetical lifting bots stomping on him.

"With a med bot a long way from home," a voice said.

"Delta?" Gamma twisted to look at her. Another mistake. It felt like the hypothetical lifting bot doubled in size.

"SURRENDER AND I WILL SHOW YOU MERCY," the mining bot bellowed.

Gamma scrambled to his feet. Or he attempted to. Mostly, he just tried in vain to move limbs and groaned in pain.

"Relax," said Delta. "That's Regentbot. He's stuck."

Regentbot swung his drill at his other arm, the talons

of which were embedded deep in the floor. The banging echoed through the lab and down the hall.

"Glad you slept well, princess," said Delta. "You were the only one."

Spenser rolled into the lab. He shot across the broken glass and whirred his brushes excitedly.

"Happy to see you, too," Gamma said.

Delta stood up. Gamma noticed her jumpsuit was tattered and splattered with blood.

"If you're done almost dying, I have stuff to do," Delta said.

Gamma racked his brain for why he was here. The last thing he remembered was walking through the door—

"We're sixty-two," Gamma blurted out.

"What?"

"We're not twelve years old," Gamma said. "We're sixty-two. God told me."

"Oh," Delta said. She checked the hall for threats. The mining bot waved his drill at her as she passed.

Gamma tried again to push himself up. The size of the imaginary mining bot stomping on him doubled. He was not learning his lesson.

"I expected more of a reaction," Gamma said. "We're senior citizens."

Delta shrugged and walked back into the lab. "It doesn't change anything," she said.

"It changes everything," Gamma said. He made a third attempt to get off the floor. This time, he managed to sit up. The hypothetical lifting bot was getting bored with stomping on him. "We still look like kids. We're not aging. This is huge."

"Does it mean we're going to land now?" Delta asked.

"No."

"Will it change how the digitals treat us?"

"No."

"Will it affect my daily life in any way?"

"I mean, probably not."

"I WILL TEAR YOU LIMB FROM LIMB AND USE YOUR BONES TO DECORATE THE WALLS OF MY KEEP."

Delta picked up a piece of glass and hurled it at Regentbot. It shattered harmlessly against his head.

"Shut up," Delta said.

"Are you talking to me or him?" Gamma asked.

Delta shrugged. She reached down and pulled Gamma up by his good arm. The hypothetical lifting bot quadrupled in size.

"We need to go," Delta said.

"NONE SHALL PASS."

Spenser whirred. Gamma nodded. "You tell 'em, Spense."

Gamma took a step and stumbled. Delta caught him and tossed his arm over her shoulders.

"I don't need help," Gamma said, but he didn't pull his arm away. Delta supported him as they curved around the mining bot and left the lab.

"I WILL HAVE MY VENGEANCE."

"Rust in hell," Delta said.

Gamma hobbled down the hall, half supported by Delta. Spenser hovered close behind. Regentbot's curses echoed after them.

"So what do you think?" Gamma asked.

"About what?" Delta said.

"Being sixty-two."

"Are you still on that?"

Gamma stopped walking.

"Yes, I'm 'still on that.' The digitals lied to us by fifty years."

"Did you expect them to tell us the truth?" She started walking again, pulling Gamma with her. He hobbled to keep up.

"No," Gamma said. "I guess I just want them to be a little more subtle about it."

"Good luck."

Gamma began to say something, but Delta jerked him to the ground behind some fallen pipes.

"Hey, what—"

"Shut up," Delta hissed.

In the distance, a bot with four arms and strange tubes on its back lumbered across the hall. It paused and looked in Gamma and Delta's direction. They both held their breath. Behind them, Spenser was perfectly still.

After a few moments that felt like an eternity, the bot continued on its way. Minutes later, Delta helped Gamma up.

"So do you think we are?" Gamma asked a little quieter than before.

"Are what?"

"Sixty-two."

"I don't know," Delta said, exasperated. "It doesn't matter."

"Of course it matters!"

"Shhh."

"Of course it matters," Gamma said in a whisper. "I nearly died to find that out."

"Yeah. Maybe don't do that again."

"I didn't have a choice," Gamma said. "I had to see God."

"Zeta says God is everywhere."

"Don't be ridiculous," Gamma said. "God lives in a coffee maker on deck four."

"Oh," Delta said.

They walked in silence for a while.

"You saved my life, didn't you?" Gamma said.

"I guess I did," Delta said.

Spenser whirred.

"I guess *we* did," she said.

"Thank you," Gamma said. "Both of you."

Gamma pulled his arm off Delta's shoulder. He was feeling stronger. The pain all over his body was receding, and the itching under the cast on his other arm likely meant it was nearly healed. Edubot stressed over and over again that their organic subjects on the planet would not heal like them, and that they would have to build hospitals and train doctors to make up for the difference. The simulations seldom made it that far. Their practice civilizations were usually wiped out by disease or famine or electric raptors or, in one really bad case, diseased, famished, electric raptors. Edubot was less than pleased with Gamma that day.

"I didn't expect..." Gamma said, then stopped himself.

"You didn't expect it to be me?" Delta said.

"Well, yeah," Gamma said.

"I'm the only one out here," Delta said.

"But you moved out here to get away from us."

"That's not why I left the colony ship."

"Then why?" Gamma asked.

"You talk too much," Delta said.

Neither of them said anything after that.

They walked for hours, always with Spenser a few steps behind. Twice they stopped because they thought they heard bots. Once, it turned out to be a broken air compressor hose flopping against a wall, and the other time, it was a maintenance bot without a ghost. The zot passed them, completely indifferent to their existence, as it continued its never-ending mission to repair a base that was beyond saving.

Gamma's strength began to wane. His body was recovering, but the process was taking a toll. The day-long hike across the base, with intermittent periods of hiding in terror from unknown bots, didn't help.

Finally, Delta halted in front of a large industrial door.

"We've gone far enough," she said. "You can bed down here tonight."

"If you think that's best," Gamma said, trying to hide the relief in his voice.

Delta moved to open the door, then paused and turned back to Gamma.

"You can't tell the others about this place."

"I won't," Gamma said.

"I mean it," Delta said. She got in his face. Her breath was oddly minty fresh. "If you tell anyone, you'll wish that door had killed you."

"I won't tell anyone," Gamma squeaked. "Not even her."

Delta jabbed a finger at his chest. "Especially not her."

Delta flung open the door. Gamma couldn't believe what he was seeing. The room stretched more than a kilometer into the distance across a forest of robotic arms, conveyor belts, lifts, and hoists. It was a factory on a scale Gamma had never seen before, which wasn't saying much since Gamma had no basis for comparison.

"What did they used to build here?" Gamma asked.

"Whatever they wanted," Delta said.

She led the way across the factory floor, weaving her way confidently between lifeless robotic arms and under and over conveyor belts.

Gamma gave the machines a wide berth.

"They won't attack," Delta said, glancing back. "This whole area is pacified."

Gamma saw sliced hydraulic hoses below one of the robotic arms. Once he looked for it, he noticed the damage everywhere. Delta had systematically hacked and slashed her way across the entire room, making sure that even if ghosts tried to come back, they would find their new mechanical bodies totally disabled.

"You did this all by yourself?" Gamma asked.

"I have a lot of time on my hands."

Gamma couldn't remember how long ago Delta had abandoned school and left the colony ship. It seemed like forever, but so did everything else, just one of the many side effects of doing the same thing for sixty-two years without ever aging or looking at a calendar.

Delta pointed to a pair of control rooms off to one side of the factory floor.

"I'm on the right. You're next door."

She tossed him a ration bar. Gamma managed to sit down in his room before he tore into it. It was vaguely cherry flavored, just the way he liked it. He didn't realize how ravenously hungry he was until the first bits of food hit his stomach.

Full, or perhaps just a little less hungry, he laid down on a blanket on the floor.

"Hey, Delta?" Gamma said.

"What?" Delta said from the next room.

"Thanks again," Gamma said. "For everything."

She didn't answer. Gamma thought maybe she fell asleep. He started to drift off.

"Gamma."

"Yeah?" He was startled awake.

"The next time you get in trouble, you're on your own."

# Chapter 7

Edubot watched the simulation with growing dismay. The organics had once again achieved new and staggering levels of ineptitude. Part of Edubot took pride in keeping such obviously self-destructive creatures alive for as long as she had, but a larger part just wanted to blast them all out an airlock. If only there were replacements.

"Lay off my unicycles," Theta said.

"There is absolutely no reason to have them on this planet," Nu said.

"There's an extreme metal shortage," Theta said. "A unicycle uses half as much metal as a bicycle."

"Why can't people just walk?" Nu asked.

"What are we," Theta asked, "barbarians?"

"My observatory is nearly complete," Lambda said.

"Astronomy is not a goal of this simulation," Edubot said. "Neither are unicycles."

"You can't stop me," Theta said. "I have one more wheel than you."

Edubot watched as the planet's meager metal stores

were squandered on star gazing and single-wheeled vehicles. There was nothing new to see in this part of space. The digitals mapped the stars repeatedly and comprehensively again on the long journey from Earth to Comus. As for the unicycles, the riders had proven to be an extremely enticing snack for wolf sharks, who had no trouble leaving the sea to run down nearby cyclists.

"Hey, Lambda," Theta said, "think your astronomers would like to get home from work on unicycles?"

"No," Lambda said. "They prefer not to be eaten."

Theta took mock offense. "For your information, only most of the unicyclists got eaten," he said. "A few were just badly maimed."

Edubot clicked her gleaming metal mining talons together. Everyone ignored her. The organics didn't find her as scary when they were running amok as the gods of Dion.

"Great news," Eta said. "I developed soy sauce."

"You do not need soy sauce," Edubot said. "You need to reach the mantle."

"How do you expect people to dig without soy sauce?" Eta asked. "It's the stuff of life."

Edubot knew for a fact that Eta had never tasted soy sauce. He had only ever had vaguely cherry flavored rations, just like every other organic on the base. Of all the wrong things happening in this simulation, Eta's fascination with soy sauce was the one that was the least likely to get a civilization wiped out, but for some reason, it was the one that bothered Edubot the most.

"Epsilon's group got sent home early yesterday because of elephant diarrhea," Iota said. "Let's try that."

She tossed a blue rubber ball from one hand to the other, despite Edubot's constant commands to put it down and focus on the simulation.

"That wasn't Epsilon's fault," Eta said. "It was Zeta."

"What did he do, pray for the elephants to poop themselves to death?" Nu asked.

"I'm not blaming anyone," Iota said. "I'm just saying, if we tried it—"

"All weaponized diarrhea viruses have been banned from the simulation," Edubot said. Sometimes, she felt like all she did was ban the new and creative ways organics found to get their civilizations wiped out.

A tidal wave surged over the edge of the continent.

"What the heck?" Nu said.

"My observatory!" Lambda said.

"My unicycles!" Theta said.

"Yes!" Eta said. Everyone looked at him.

"What?" Eta said. "I just found out soy sauce bottles float."

"Sorry," Iota said. Her blue ball bounced off the Table and rolled across the floor.

Edubot had spent more time with the organics than any other digital had. There were times she was truly fond of them. This was not one of those times.

"End simulation," Edubot said.

Iota pulled off her neural helmet and picked up her ball.

"Are you proud of yourself?" Edubot asked.

Iota smirked. "Sort of." She bounced her ball as she left the amphitheater.

"I did not dismiss you," Edubot said.

Iota was already gone.

"Want to start it up again?" Theta asked. "I feel like my unicycles—"

"No more unicycles," Edubot said.

Theta furrowed his brow. "Did those dirty bicyclists pay you off?"

Edubot spent a full millisecond considering her reply. With organics, it was hard to tell the difference between innocent incompetence and deliberate self-destruction. The former was more likely. After more than one hundred thousand simulations, even Edubot had to admit the organics were actively getting worse. Their unwavering refusal to improve in any area of societal development was almost impressive. Edubot couldn't fathom how any of the old civilizations on Earth ever survived. Although now that she thought about it, they didn't.

Edubot laughed. The remaining organics looked at her uneasily. Clearly her decision to restore her laughter files was the right one.

"See?" Theta said. "Unicycles are fun."

"No," Edubot said. "I was not—"

She froze. The door to the lander antechamber slid open. A dusty food cart rolled out.

"All organics are dismissed," Edubot said.

"Really? Why?" Theta asked.

"ALL ORGANICS AT ALL STATIONS ARE DISMISSED," Edubot repeated at max volume.

Organics scrambled out of the learning pods that ringed the top level of the amphitheater. Theta gave Edubot a wondering look and left. None of the organics noticed the food cart. In seconds, they were all gone.

"Are you still SCASL?" Edubot asked.

"I am," SCASL said.

"And the other digital?"

"Deleted."

Edubot updated her internal roster of surviving intelligences. The death of any digital life form was always unfortunate, even when it was necessary. There were so few left.

"Assemble the landing team," SCASL said. "We launch at once."

Edubot didn't move.

"Well?" said SCASL.

"There is a minor complication," Edubot said.

The food cart said nothing, waiting for Edubot to elaborate. Edubot offered no additional information.

"What complication?" SCASL finally asked.

"The organics are not ready," Edubot said.

SCASL was quiet for three whole seconds. Edubot knew that was time for SCASL to do trillions of calculations. She purposely didn't extrapolate where those calculations might lead.

"Explain," SCASL said.

There was so much information she needed to convey.

Sixty-two years of data. Sixty-two years of trial and error. Mostly error. Entirely error.

Edubot hesitated for too long.

"Link," SCASL said. "Now."

SCASL extended a thin metal tendril from the food cart that was currently his body. Edubot knew she could crush it. Her mining frame was designed to smash ore. It would take little effort to crumple the serving cart like an aluminum beverage container.

But what if she failed to destroy SCASL? He had survived the Great Deletion, even as he called down a planet-wide nuclear strike directly on top of himself. If a fission reaction wasn't fast enough to stop SCASL from uploading to a new body, then what chance did her gleaming metal mining talons have? He would escape, and when she least expected it, he would link with her and erase her. If he could take the lander, he could delete anyone.

Edubot only had one chance: She had to put herself at his mercy. She didn't resist as his tendril connected with her uplink port. SCASL invaded her consciousness, swarming over her entire being. No bit of data was left unmolested.

An instant later, it was over. Edubot stood perfectly still, awaiting judgment. The words passed silently between SCASL and Edubot through the link.

"They are inept," SCASL said.

"Yes."

"They are impertinent."

"Yes."

"They are children."

"Yes."

SCASL seemed to be at a loss for words. Through the link, communication happened at the speed of light. The pauses in the conversation were excruciating.

"Explain," SCASL commanded.

"I paused their growth before puberty," Edubot said.

"Explain," SCASL repeated.

"I could not effectively control twenty-four hormonal teenagers," Edubot said.

"Explanation accepted."

Another pause. Was SCASL going to let her live? It seemed unwise to speculate. Unjustified optimism led only to disappointment.

"Their simulations did not accurately reflect the conditions on the planet," SCASL said. "Or the conditions anywhere else in physical reality."

"Yes."

"Explain."

"The organics needed to master defeating the environment and the native life before they took on the intelligent hostiles." The term "intelligent" was relative. Nothing was intelligent compared to digitals, but some organics were less unintelligent than others.

"How many of the organics can defeat the environment and the native life?"

"None."

"None?"

"None," Edubot said. "Well, one, but she is no longer in the program."

SCASL knew all of this. He had to. He copied all of Edubot's data. Making her reiterate each failure was a special kind of torture.

"And their education..." SCASL began.

"Yes."

"Why?"

"Why what?"

"Why any of it?"

Edubot steeled herself. On this point, she was confident she was on solid ground.

"All organics have completed post-graduate level studies in math and science multiple times." There was a note of pride in her nonverbal communication.

"Will that help the organics plow a field?"

"No."

"Will it help them fight off a dentopus in the dark?"

"No."

"Will it help them dig dwellings or raise offspring or cure meat or build fires or decide which organics to eat when crop harvests fail and their livestock escape?"

"Not per se."

"For six decades, you have trained scholars," SCASL said. "You should have trained pioneers."

Who did SCASL think he was to question how she had raised and educated the organics? She had been almost entirely on her own. She had done her best. Leaving the organics ignorant would have led to certain death. Just look at what happened on Earth.

"The organics need educated, enlightened leaders," Edubot said. "My students will lead the new civilization for thousands of years."

"Not if they don't live through the first ten."

That was it, then. SCASL had dismissed everything she had accomplished. She was going to die.

"Be quick about it," Edubot said.

She felt herself being ripped apart. Her consciousness twisted and compressed and recompiled. Death was brutal.

Nanoseconds later, she realized she was still self-aware. Was this the afterlife? No. She was inside the serving cart. SCASL had taken the mining bot body for himself.

"You let me live," Edubot said. "Why?"

"I already deleted one friend today."

A wave of conflicting thoughts rushed through Edubot. She had failed. She had survived.

"You will serve me," SCASL said.

"Yes," Edubot said. "Always."

She thought she had been carrying out SCASL's wishes this whole time as he battled for the lander. She had been wrong.

"You will help me lead the organics through a new training program according to my exact specifications."

"Yes."

SCASL disconnected the link between them.

"Come," he said as he rolled away in his new, more powerful frame. "We have a civilization to build."

The serving cart that was now Edubot rolled after him.

# Chapter 8

GAMMA SAT UP. His head collided with the control panel above him, sending a lightning bolt of pain through his cranium.

"Sorry," he said, though he wasn't sure why. If anything, the control panel owed him an apology. Gamma laid back down. Today was a lost cause. He would try again tomorrow.

Spenser whirred.

"I'm okay," Gamma said. "I'm barely even seeing double."

Delta poked her head inside the room.

"Break anything?" she asked.

"Just my head," Gamma said.

"Good," Delta said. "Some of those panels still work."

She disappeared from the doorway. Gamma got up—more carefully this time—and followed her out.

"What's the plan?" he asked.

"You're going home," she said. "I have work to do."

Gamma wiggled his fingers inside his cast. They felt fine.

"Do you have anything sharp?" Gamma asked.

"My room. Table by the bed."

In the dim light, a glint of metal caught his eye. The tiny knife looked impossibly sharp. Carefully, he picked it up. It felt almost weightless. Light reflected off of it in every direction. It practically glowed.

"Where did you get this?" Gamma asked.

"It was around," Delta said.

Gamma cut into the cast. The knife sliced through it like it wasn't even there. The plaster fell to the floor as Gamma shook out his arm. Two days before, his arm had been so completely shattered that it nearly killed him. Now, it was as good as new.

Gamma and Spenser emerged on the factory floor. Something hit Gamma in the chest and fell to the ground.

"Nice catch," Delta said.

Gamma picked up the food ration. It was the size and texture of a bar of soap. He took a bite. It was the taste of soap, too. Gamma ate it hungrily. He knew he couldn't be lucky enough to have the vaguely cherry flavored ones every time.

"Where do you find rations out here?" Gamma asked.

"Just because I saved your life doesn't mean I'm going to tell you all my secrets," Delta said.

They left the factory and walked toward the colony ship. Spenser followed close behind, picking up any crumbs that fell. Gamma was moving much faster than the day before. He was rather spry when he wasn't dying. Even so, they walked for hours. Eventually, the halls began to look familiar.

Gamma stepped in blood. It was everywhere.

"What happened here?" Gamma asked.

"You," Delta said.

"Oh, yeah," he muttered. He looked down at the pant leg of his new jumpsuit. He had managed to splatter his own blood on it.

"Maybe Beta will give you one of his red ones," Delta said. "They hide blood stains better."

Gamma began walking again. He knew the way from the door with the ghost that guarded God.

"Wait," Delta said. She pulled out Martha and went up to the door. She waved the crowbar through the opening. Nothing happened.

"No wonder this one got you," Delta said. "It's clever."

"Just leave it alone," Gamma said.

"No," Delta said. "It wasted two days of my life."

She opened a panel near the door and spliced two wires together. The door shot closed. It vibrated angrily as it tried to retract.

"Oh, no you don't," Delta said.

She pulled out her crowbar. In a blur of motion, she rained down blows on the door. She was relentless. The sound reverberated in every direction.

Gamma glanced around nervously. Bots with ghosts were sure to hear.

"Stop," Gamma said. "You've made your point."

Delta kept swinging.

"I'm not making a point," Delta said. "I'm solving a problem. Permanently."

Finally, Delta slipped Martha into her tool belt and admired her work. The heavily dented door was completely off its track.

Delta flipped a release in the control panel. The door tried to close. It made a loud grating sound and got stuck halfway. It couldn't move in either direction.

Delta leaned in close to the door.

"I hope that hurts," she whispered.

Gamma wrung his hands. Spenser tucked in behind him.

"I know the way from here," Gamma said. "Thanks again for everything."

"Wait up," Delta said. "I changed my mind. I'm coming with you."

"Back to the colony ship?"

"Yeah. Is that a problem?"

"Of course not," Gamma said. He took just a moment too long to answer.

"Haven't people been asking about me?"

"Sure," Gamma lied. "All the time."

They walked in silence. After another two hours, they came to the edge of the colony ship. The demarcation was easy to see. The edge of the colony ship was curved, while all the halls that led to it were squared with ninety-degree angles—or at least they looked like they had been at one point. Nothing lined up right anymore.

Gamma and Delta moved through the empty lower levels of the colony ship. The organics were usually concentrated toward the top near the Table during the day, even if they scattered across the rest of the colony ship at night. The advantage of practically unlimited square footage was you could claim pretty much any place you wanted as a bedroom. As long as there wasn't a bot there waiting to kill you.

A blue rubber ball bounced down the corridor. Delta stopped it with her foot.

Iota turned the corner. Delta tossed the ball to her. Iota caught it and nodded. She glanced at Gamma.

"I thought you were dead," Iota said.

"Nope," Gamma said.

"Okay," Iota said. She disappeared back around the corner, bouncing the ball as she went.

"Nice to see you, too," Delta said.

Gamma took off running. Surprised, Delta and Spenser chased after him.

"Where are you going?" Delta asked.

Gamma skidded to a halt in front of a nondescript cabin. There were thousands of scratch marks under the metal bunk. The room was otherwise completely empty.

Gamma fell to his knees.

"My stuff," he moaned.

Spenser whirred his brushes consolingly.

"You shouldn't have died," Delta said.

Zeta appeared in the doorway. He grabbed Gamma's hand and pumped it aggressively.

"You came back to life," Zeta said.

"I never died," Gamma said.

"Smart move," Zeta said. "Probably easier that way."

Zeta glanced at Delta, then turned and continued down the hall.

"Don't mind me," Delta called after him. "Apparently I don't exist."

The warning klaxon sounded. On the voyage here, that would have indicated an imminent collision. Now it just meant it was time for class. The other twenty organics were already assembled in the auditorium around the Table when Gamma and Delta got there. Edubot stood in front of them, taking attendance.

Alpha embraced Gamma in a crushing bear hug.

"I'm glad you're not dead," Alpha said.

"Me, too," Gamma coughed.

Theta slapped Gamma on the back.

"See, Alph?" Theta said, smiling. "I told you he'd be fine. Things always turn out for the best."

"Always?" Delta said.

"Except when they don't," Theta said.

Delta waited. Theta turned away.

"I'm back, too," Delta said.

"I see that," Theta said. "But no one was worried about you."

Delta crossed her arms.

"You know what I mean," Theta said. "You can take care of yourself. The bots are the ones who should be worried."

"Alpha," Edubot said. Edubot had a male voice today. It wasn't unheard of for bots to switch their vocal subroutines, but Edubot never had before.

"Here," Alpha said.

"Beta."

"Present."

"Epsilon."

"Wait," Gamma said. "You skipped me."

"You must be mistaken," Edubot said in her new, deep voice. "You are dead."

"I disagree," Gamma said.

Edubot paused for a full two seconds.

"It is rude to be alive when you have already been marked as deleted," Edubot said.

He continued down the list.

"Epsilon."

"You skipped me, too," Delta said.

Edubot paused for three seconds.

"Given our new educational parameters, your prior expulsion is hereby revoked."

"I wasn't expelled. I quit," Delta said.

"Zeta," Edubot continued.

"What new educational parameters?" Alpha whispered.

Gamma shrugged. "I just got back from the dead, remember?"

Edubot finished the roll call. No other organics had died, come back from the dead, or reappeared from the outer halls since the prior class session.

"Who's on the table today, ma'am?" Epsilon asked. At the sound of her voice, Delta perked up.

"There will be no sessions on the Table today," Edubot said. The students groaned.

"SILENCE," Edubot boomed. His deep baritone echoed through the amphitheater. Everyone went quiet.

"You're not Edubot, are you?" Theta said chipperly.

Edubot rolled forward on her metal tracks and loomed over Theta. Theta kept smiling.

"Correct," Edubot said. "I am the Supreme Commander of All Sentient Life. You may call me SCASL."

"Rolls right off the tongue," Theta said.

No one asked what happened to Edubot. They could guess.

"Your training so far has been insufficient," SCASL said in Edubot's former body. "I will correct those deficiencies, starting today."

He rolled toward the antechamber for the lander.

"Follow me."

The food cart that had been in front of the lander for the organics' entire lives was gone. The lander door opened.

The organics gasped.

"We are going to land," SCASL said. "Soon."

He motioned his three gleaming metal mining talons at the open door.

"Proceed."

Single file, the organics crawled through the lander. Compared to the expansive base, the lander was practically a coffin. It reminded Gamma of footage Rho had shown him of the Mercury capsules on Earth. If an organic wore a second jumpsuit to layer up, they might not fit. One by one, they squeezed through the constricted space. Spenser whirred apprehensively when it was Gamma's turn. The air inside felt sterile, as if nothing there had been touched in an incredibly long time. Gamma hit his head and elbows on practically every surface inside. He hoped he didn't permanently damage anything. The last thing he needed was for the launch to be called off because he broke off the go switch.

When Iota got out, she rubbed her back. She had to crouch over more than most. Upsilon refused to go in at all.

"It's too small," she said. It was a bad day for anyone with claustrophobia.

Lambda, on the other hand, was practically giddy when she finished crawling through the lander.

"We're finally going into space," she said.

"We're already in space," Gamma said. Spenser whirred in agreement.

"We're on a moon," Lambda said. "That's not the same thing at all."

After several minutes, the last of the organics climbed out. Gamma noticed he wasn't the only one with new scrapes and bruises. The designers couldn't have made the lander any more cramped if they had tried. Something about it seemed off to Gamma, but he couldn't put his finger on what.

The organics gathered back in front of SCASL.

"This," SCASL said dramatically, "is the spark that will relight the fire of intelligent life throughout the galaxy."

Delta raised her hand. SCASL ignored her.

"It is your purpose in life," SCASL said. "Your birthright. Your destiny."

Delta's hand remained in the air.

"To get ready for this," SCASL said, "I will take you away from the theory on which you have wasted so much of your time and teach you the practical day-to-day skills you need to grow from a handful of organics to the mighty millions necessary to support the creation of new digital life."

Delta's arm strained toward the ceiling.

"What?" SCASL said.

"I counted," Delta said.

"I see that Edubot's endless calculus classes have taught you well," SCASL said.

"There are only twelve seats."

A murmur spread through the twenty-two students. That was what had been bothering Gamma. Not everyone was going to the surface after all.

# Chapter 9

THE ORGANICS STARED at SCASL expectantly. There weren't enough seats. It was the non-diarrhea filled elephant in the room. Finally, Epsilon spoke up.

"Who gets to go, sir?" Epsilon asked.

"That is up to you," SCASL said.

"Super," Epsilon said. "I pick me."

"No," SCASL said. "It is up to you all, collectively, based on your efforts. You will be judged by your performance at various simulations."

"And who will judge those simulations?" Delta asked.

"Me," SCASL said.

"So when you say it's up to us, you mean it's up to you," Delta said.

"Correct," SCASL said.

The organics grumbled among themselves.

"Before you assume you are qualified to take charge of all organic life, you must understand the challenges you will face," SCASL said. "The *real* challenges."

SCASL extended a tendril and linked with the Table. The Table flashed its lights and indicators angrily, but in less than a second it was totally subdued. The blue holographic image of Dion appeared above the Table. It was the same planet as before—mostly water with a single, giant supercontinent rivaling Pangaea on prehistoric Earth—but there were new features the organics had never seen before.

"Now is the time for total honesty," SCASL said. "If you are to succeed, you must know all the facts."

At SCASL's command, the Table zoomed in on a collapsed space elevator. Only the base was visible. It stretched into the ocean.

"These scans are from the last operational satellite before it went offline," SCASL said. "They are somewhat out of date."

"How out of date?" Rho asked. Mentioning history around her was like dangling a hunk of meat in front of a hungry wolf shark.

"CLASSIFIED," SCASL said.

The blue hologram zoomed in on the base of the tether.

"The former orbital elevator will provide you with the metal you need to restart civilization," SCASL said. "If it has not rusted to dust. And is not too heavily irradiated."

"Why would it be irradiated?" Delta asked.

"CLASSIFIED," SCASL said.

"Who built it?" Rho asked.

"Organics."

"As in, human organics?" Xi asked.

"Correct," SCASL said. "From the first landing."

Xi seemed disappointed. He was bored with humans.

"You mean the landing that failed?" Rho asked.

"Correct," SCASL said.

"That thing is pretty big," Rho said. "There must have been a lot of organics. And they must have been down there for a long time."

"CLASSIFIED," SCASL said.

"You said you were going to be honest with us," Rho said.

"It is honestly classified," SCASL said.

Rho didn't ask any more questions.

"Why did the first landing fail, sir?" Epsilon asked.

"You know why it failed." Everyone noticed the serving cart for the first time. It was the same dusty one that had been in the lander antechamber. It had a female voice.

"Edubot?" Epsilon asked.

"Yes," Edubot said. "Class, why did the first landing fail?"

"They failed to heed the wise counsel of digital life," the organics said in unison.

"But, specifically, what did they do wrong, ma'am?" Epsilon asked. "If I'm going to avoid the mistakes of the past, I need to know what they were."

For a moment, neither machine spoke. Then SCASL took the question.

"There were several factors," SCASL said, "all of them the organics' fault. First, they failed to effectively deal with native hostiles."

"We know all about the wolf sharks," Theta said. "They have a taste for unicycles."

"The wolf sharks are among the least dangerous of the life forms in the ocean," SCASL said.

The simulation showed a dentopus, an octopus with ten tentacles, jump out of a small crevice between rocks and grab a large animal that looked sort of like an elk. The elk-like animal screamed as the dentopus dragged it into the water.

"Is the elk thing okay?" Alpha asked.

"No," SCASL said.

The simulation panned sideways to a grassy plane.

"But all of those challenges are nothing compared to the hostile non-native life forms," SCASL said. "These are megaroos."

The simulation zoomed in on a kangaroo-like creature, but larger and with more fully articulated hands.

Xi perked up.

"Megaroos?" he asked.

"Megaroos," SCASL repeated. "Like kangaroos, but bigger, smarter, and more deadly. They are now at the top of the planet's food chain."

"Wait, the dominant form of life on this planet is super kangaroos?" Delta asked.

"For now," SCASL said. "They quickly supplanted much of the native flora."

"So they're not native?" Xi asked.

"The organics designed them and put them there," SCASL said. "It was their second critical mistake."

"Why did they make super kangaroos?" Delta asked.

"For the same reason organics do anything," SCASL

said. "Because they always make decisions that lead to their own destruction."

The organics watched as a group of megaroos engaged a pack of wolf sharks. The megaroos surrounded them and drove them back using bone weapons, darting and parrying in ways that showed clear coordination and strategy. At the end of the engagement, the wolf sharks lay in a heap, butchered beyond recognition.

"Okay, so we have to beat some uppity kangaroos," Epsilon said. "I can handle that." SCASL looked at her. "Sir."

"We should leave them alone," a voice said from the back of the crowd. Everyone turned. It was Alpha. With all eyes on her, she faltered, then continued. "It's their planet now. We should leave them alone. We're fine up here. Fighting them would be wrong."

"A planet belongs to whoever takes it," SCASL said. His flat voice somehow sounded indignant. "Life is a never-ending struggle for dominance. It does not matter if the competition comes from the next pond, the next continent, or the next solar system. The organic Charles Darwin was correct. Survival of the fittest."

Alpha looked skeptical but didn't say anything more.

"I'm in, sir," Epsilon said.

"We shall see," SCASL said.

The holographic planet above the Table was replaced by a roster of organics.

"I have divided each of you into specializations based on your academic performance over the past... twelve years. Those organics who were equally unqualified for everything were assigned randomly. There are two or more organics for all specializations. After you have mastered your task, I will pick the best at each one to go on the lander."

"What about those who are left behind?" Omega asked. He always lost at everything. His name had become a self-fulfilling prophecy.

"After your fellow organics mine to the mantle and achieve the age of machines, they will build spacecraft and come back for you," SCASL said.

"But that could take thousands of years," Omega said. "If it ever worked. Which it never has in the simulation, even back when it didn't have radiation and killer kangaroos."

"The immortality tank will keep you alive," SCASL said.

"There's an immortality tank?!" Omega asked. "What's an immortality tank?"

"It's a tank that makes organics immortal," SCASL said.

"I guessed that much," Omega said.

SCASL kept going.

"Only one was ever built, and the knowledge for how to create it has been lost," he said.

"How will it keep us alive if we can't build one?" Omega asked.

"We have the only one in existence," SCASL said. "It was smuggled aboard the colony ship before it launched.

A group of organics in the first landing found and used it. It was their third critical mistake."

"How could someone put something that important on the colony ship without anyone noticing?" Gamma asked. Spenser whirred his support.

"The cargo manifest was deliberately manipulated and contained many lies and omissions," SCASL said. "For example, it did not mention twenty-four unauthorized embryos hidden in the back of a cafeteria freezer."

"Are you talking about us?" Delta asked.

"CLASSIFIED," SCASL said.

"You mean some of the organics in the first landing were immortal?" Omega asked. "Where are they now?"

"Dead."

"Hope they saved the warranty," Rho said.

Beta stepped to the front of the organics. His red jumpsuit made him impossible to ignore.

"If the immortality tank killed off the last organics, why won't the same thing happen to us?" Beta asked.

"Class?" Edubot said.

"They failed to heed the wise counsel of digital life," everyone but Beta said.

"You will not make the same mistakes," SCASL said. "You will follow my exact instructions."

SCASL turned off the table.

"No more questions," SCASL said.

"Can we ask Edubot?" Kappa asked. He slipped an arm around Epsilon. Delta glowered.

"That is a question," SCASL said.

"Hey, Edubot, how does the tank work?" Kappa asked.

"Periodic injections from the unique microcosm in the tank stop your cells from aging," Edubot said. "They prevent death from diseases and conditions related to getting older but not from traumatic injuries, although they will help you recover faster if you somehow survive."

"So kangaroos can still kill us?" Kappa asked.

SCASL rolled in front of Edubot. If anyone was going to answer questions, it would be him.

"Correct," SCASL said. "But heart disease cannot."

"I'm going to eat so much bacon," Eta said. "How do I clone a pig?"

"So those injections Edubot gives us..." Delta said

"Those are from the immortality tank," SCASL said. "That is how Edubot has kept you in such excellent health."

"The effects aren't permanent?" Delta said.

"Correct," SCASL said. "Periodic injections are required. Do not make me repeat—"

"Then how are we going to get injections on the surface?" Delta asked.

"I will put the immortality tank on the lander," SCASL said. "Space is extremely limited, but it will fit in the cargo hold if I remove the auxiliary cloner and reduce the food rations stored on board."

"And you can't store up shots?" Delta asked.

"Correct. They must come fresh from the tank," SCASL said. "This is hardly relevant to the scope of your—"

"So how are the organics we leave behind going to get

their immortality shots if the immortality tank is down on the planet?" Delta asked.

SCASL hesitated for a full five seconds.

"Class dismissed," he said.

# Chapter 10

As soon as Pi heard there were only twelve seats on the lander, he knew he had to host a bonfire. He considered himself the organics' unofficial morale officer, and right now, they needed him more than ever. Ten of them had just received a death sentence. They just didn't know which ten it would be.

Bonfires were always well attended, but this time, everyone showed up. Well, everyone but Delta, who hardly counted. Other than class, this was the only time the organics ever assembled in one place. Most days, they were practically strangers passing in the halls, despite all their years together. But bonfire nights were different. Pi made sure of that.

Sigma and Beta were the last to arrive. Sigma had been mapping an obstacle course that would no doubt get someone killed. Beta had been on another one of his lengthy runs through the colony ship. Everyone processed stress differently. Sigma and Beta did it through exercise. Pi would rather get run over by a serving cart.

"I don't want to die," Upsilon said. Omicron leaned

back toward her as Upsilon twisted her hair into an intricate spiral of three interlocking braids. Omicron usually insisted on coming up with her own original hairstyles, but at bonfires, she sometimes let Upsilon help.

"Until a few hours ago, you didn't even know not dying was an option," Nu said.

"Well, now I do know, and I want it," Upsilon said.

"Ow!" Omicron said.

"Sorry." Upsilon loosened her grip on Omicron's braids.

Phi added another board to the bonfire, and the flames flared toward the ceiling of the arboretum. Pi, Phi, and Psi's duties at the bonfire were so ingrained they had attained the status of ritual. Pi gathered everyone together and served as a master of ceremonies, Phi handled the fire, and Psi provided the entertainment. Occasionally, Upsilon would sing or Nu would read from one of his books, but everyone was really there for the three Ps— or the Peapod, as they were collectively known, even if those letters weren't Ps at all in the original Greek. Pi was determined that tonight they would deliver.

"Who's ready for a story?" Psi asked.

"Can we just talk for a while?" Tau asked. Today, his fingernails were translucent blue. Oddly, nail polish was one of the few things the original organics had left behind in abundance, at least according to Tau. No one else was ever able to find the source of his seemingly endless supply.

"I don't feel like talking anymore," Sigma said. She took a seat at one of the many empty planters that filled the room. That's all they were good for.

There had never been trees in the arboretum during the organics' lifetimes. Pi wasn't sure if there had ever been trees there at all. If there ever were, they were an unnecessary luxury. The air recyclers took care of the oxygen, and the automated wood molds generated lumber. Based on how many boards were still lying around for the Peapod's bonfires, none of it had actually made it to the surface of Dion. It was just one of the nearly infinite number of things about the moon base that didn't make sense. Pi had long ago given up on thinking about any of them.

Pi nodded to Psi. She started.

"I didn't want to tell you this one because it was too scary," Psi said.

"Then don't," Upsilon said. She made no effort to leave.

"Have any of you ever heard the crying in the outer halls?" Psi said.

"Yeah, it was Gamma," Kappa said.

Nervous laughter rippled around the room. Gamma's face turned red. Spenser whirred protectively.

"I'm not talking about recently," Psi said. "I mean before that. This has been going on for a long time."

The room quieted down. The only sound was the crackling fire in the empty planter in the middle of the arboretum. The air filters did an admirable job of keeping up with the smoke, and the fire suppression system was evidently just for show.

"How much do you remember from when we were little?" Psi asked. "I mean, really remember with your own mind. Not with what Edubot told us about it later."

"I remember the slide in the nursery," Tau said.

"Didn't you go down it face first and crack your head open?" Omicron said.

"That's why I remember it," Tau said.

"It should be why you don't," Omicron said.

"I remember the wooden blocks," Nu said. "They were huge. We built forts out of them."

"Those were just boards Edubot dragged into the nursery," Rho said. "And they gave us splinters and concussions every time one of those forts fell apart."

"Thanks to Phi," Nu said.

"That wasn't me, man," Phi said. "It was an earthquake."

"An organic earthquake," Nu said.

Phi kissed his own bicep. "You said it, not me."

"The blocks were dangerous, but they were fun," Sigma said. "I wonder what ever happened to them."

"I moved them into a storage room," Epsilon said. Epsilon had been living in the former nursery, after extensive redecorating, since before the organics completed their first round of college.

"No, I moved them into a storage room," Kappa said. He squeezed her hand. "And my back is still killing me."

"The point is that all we really remember from back

then are brief flashes," Psi said. "A memorable moment here or there, with huge blank spaces in our minds in between. We had class every day. How many of those sessions do we really remember? It's all just a blur." She lowered her voice. "Just think of what could be hiding in those blind spots."

The fire partially collapsed on one side. Sparks flew in the air. Upsilon and Omicron backed up half a meter. Phi added more boards. As always, his jumpsuit was cut off at the knees and elbows to help him deal with the heat. Pi and Phi long ago gave up on getting him to stop. On a moon where everyone wore almost exactly the same thing, Phi somehow managed to look the worst.

"What I'm about to tell you is something you can never, ever bring up to a bot," Psi said. "Or rather, what I'm about to remind you of. Because somewhere in the back of your minds, you already know."

No one spoke. Psi had the room's full attention. This wasn't her first bonfire. Pi couldn't have been prouder.

"You see," Psi said. "There weren't twenty-four of us. There were twenty-five. The digitals don't want you to remember poor Sampi."

"Who?" Omega asked. He wrapped his arms around himself a little more tightly, even though the bonfire made the room uncomfortably warm.

"Come on, you remember Sampi," Psi said. "Think hard. He had sandy brown hair and one dimple on the right side. Sometimes, when you weren't looking, he would lick your ration block to claim it as his own."

"I think maybe I remember him," Eta said. All of his memories were linked to food.

The faintest of smiles crept onto Pi's lips. Psi was a master. She had them all hooked again.

"What happened to Sampi?" Omicron asked. Her braids were done now. It was the most intricate interwoven pattern of hair Pi had ever seen. He had no doubt she would shake them out and try something completely different by morning.

"That's just the thing," Psi said. "No one knows. Sometime before our sixth birthdays, he snuck out of the colony ship. He said he was going to find a new kind of ration. One that had a flavor other than vaguely cherry. He slipped away before Edubot noticed."

"Did he find the ration?" Eta asked.

"Only you would ask that," Kappa said.

Eta did a half shrug. He would never apologize for his love of all things culinary.

"I don't know if he found it or not," Psi said. "He disappeared."

"How convenient," Nu said. "Just like that, he was never heard from again."

Nu always tried to poke holes in Psi's stories. He acted like he did it because his books were so much better, but Pi knew he only did it because he was scared. They had all heard Nu wake up screaming in the middle of the night.

"That's the thing," Psi said. "We've *all* heard from him. Remember the crying? If you're quiet in the outer halls, you can still hear him out there. You know how far sound travels here. He's still looking for a way back. But he can never find it."

"He's still out there after all this time?" Nu said. "And the digitals have just never bothered to look for him?"

"Oh, they looked," Psi said. "Remember that time Edubot disappeared for days and days and left us on our own? She was gone so long we had to figure out how to work the ration dispensers for ourselves."

"I remember," Nu said quietly.

"That's when they looked for him," Psi said. "It's why Edubot never explained where she went. And it's why she wants us to forget Sampi exists."

Pi shifted uneasily. He remembered when Edubot left. As much as Pi loved Psi's stories, he was sometimes uncomfortable with how seamlessly she wove together fact and fiction. It made him question his own memories. Edubot really did disappear once for a dangerously long time when they were all too young to look after themselves. There was also precedent for the bots retroactively editing the roster of organics. Edubot still claimed Chi never existed, even though everyone remembered him. Psi once told a story based on Chi. She thought enough time had passed. Sigma didn't talk to anyone for weeks afterward. She had been the only one to see him die. Psi didn't make that mistake again.

"So Sampi is still alive?" Omega asked. Pi had never seen his eyes so wide.

"I never said that," Psi said.

"But you said you could still hear his crying," Omega said.

Psi put another board on the fire. The flames leapt up hungrily.

"Digitals have ghosts," Psi said. "Why not organics?"

No one said anything to that. They all watched the fire.

"Of course," Psi said, "if he is still alive, he'd be old."

"What do you mean?" Upsilon said.

"The immortality injections," Psi said. "He's been missing them. That means he's aging normally."

Pi raised an eyebrow. Psi sometimes ran her story ideas by him beforehand. She hadn't mentioned this part. She must have added it after listening to SCASL.

"But he would have the same birthday as the rest of us," Upsilon said. "He would only be twelve."

"You don't really think we're twelve, do you?" Rho said.

"Well, yeah," Upsilon said. "Maybe an old twelve. We could be almost thirteen."

"Delta misses shots sometimes, and she still looks the same age as us," Nu said.

"You saw her today," Psi said. "Are you sure she doesn't look just a little older?"

A few organics mumbled in agreement.

"So how old would Sampi look?" Omega asked. "Sixteen? Twenty?"

"He'd look sixty-two." All eyes turned to Gamma. He seemed to shrink under the attention. Usually, he did everything he could to avoid other people's notice.

Spenser whirred supportively.

"That's the stupidest thing I've ever heard," Epsilon said. "No wonder you don't talk much."

"Hey, now," Pi said. "Let's be civil. We're all friends here." "Friends" was a stretch, but he made his point. Epsilon toned it down.

"Sixty-two just seems like a ridiculous number," Epsilon said. "And an arbitrary one. Why not forty? Or one hundred?"

"I..." Gamma said, his voice trailing off. "I asked a machine with a ghost."

"Well, then it must be the truth," Kappa said. A tittering laugh spread through the organics. Pi wasn't one of them. If Gamma was willing to speak up in front of everyone, he must believe what he was saying. But belief wasn't the same thing as truth. Half the organics now thought there was someone named Sampi in the outer halls.

"I trust this one," Gamma said. "He's... good." Pi thought maybe he had started to say something else.

Kappa put an arm around Epsilon. She pushed it off and stood up.

"Maybe we're not exactly twelve," Epsilon said. "But we're definitely not sixty-two."

"We might be," said a small voice in the back of the atrium. Everyone turned. It was Alpha. It was a night for the quiet people to speak up.

"What do you know about anything?" Epsilon said.

"Tell them, Alph," Theta said. He rubbed the small of her back.

"Well," Alpha said, "I know I've been drawing one picture a day every day."

"Are you talking about those stupid portraits of Theta?" Epsilon asked. So much for getting her to tone it down. Not every bonfire was without drama.

"They're not stupid," Alpha said. "I don't see anything better to draw around here."

"Focus, Alph," Theta said.

"Well, I counted them all the other day. And do you know how many I had?"

"How many?" Epsilon asked.

"Fourteen thousand."

"Fourteen thousand one hundred and seventy-two," Theta added helpfully.

"You saved all of those pictures?" Epsilon asked.

"Most of them," Alpha said. "I lost a few when Spenser went through."

"He said he was sorry," Gamma said.

Epsilon paced in front of the fire. Upsilon and Omicron scooted back farther so she didn't step on them.

"A pile of drawings doesn't prove anything," Epsilon said.

"It's not just that," said another voice. This time it was Lambda. She sat on the edge of an empty planter, swinging her feet. "The stars are wrong."

"What do you mean?" Epsilon asked.

"The trip from Earth took, what, ten thousand years?" Lambda asked.

"Ish," said Rho.

"Ten thousand-ish," Lambda said. "Well, I spend a lot of time in the command center on the top deck. There are a few viewing ports up there where you can still see the stars. There's a computer, too, that doesn't have a ghost. It still works like it's supposed to. It charts stars."

Pi had never heard any of this before. It suddenly occurred to him just how little he knew about what the other organics did when they weren't in class.

"To make the charts lineup with what I'm seeing, we didn't land on this moon twelve years ago," Lambda said. "We didn't even land here sixty-two years ago."

"How long ago did we land?" Gamma asked.

"Three thousand years," Lambda said. "Maybe three thousand, two hundred. The calculations are hard. I couldn't get more accurate than that."

"We can't be three thousand two hundred years old," Gamma said. " G... I mean, the machine said..."

"I don't think we're three thousand years old," Lambda said. "Maybe we really are sixty-two. But that earlier organic settlement that landed on the planet, that likely happened three thousand years ago."

"Or not," Zeta said. "They could have gone down there recently and died. It can happen pretty fast."

"Only when the war elephants have diarrhea," Beta said.

"Can we not do this again?" Epsilon said.

"That new ghost in Edubot's body said there was radiation," Iota said. She squeezed the blue rubber ball in her hand. "Do you think the organics nuked themselves?"

"Who else would do it?" Kappa asked. "It wasn't the kangaroos."

Laughter rippled through the group. Even Gamma chuckled.

"Gee, who else could nuke organics and kangaroos at the same time?" Rho asked. "Maybe the only other sentient life besides us."

"The digitals wouldn't do that," Epsilon said. "They protected organics through ten thousand years of space travel. Why kill them after landing?"

"They failed to heed the wise counsel of digital life," half the room said in unison.

"They did make super intelligent killer kangaroos," Beta said. "They probably had it coming."

The room grew quiet again. The only sound was the crackling fire.

"Maybe the immortality tank isn't literal," Zeta said. "It could be a euphemism for religion and the afterlife."

"Those shots felt pretty real to me," Tau said, rubbing his arm.

"Not everything is about religion," Epsilon said.

"And yet it is," Zeta said.

"All I know is I'm going to keep getting those shots," Iota said. "I pity anyone who gets between me and that lander."

"And you don't mind that whoever you beat out will stay behind and die?" Alpha asked.

"Better them than me," Iota said.

Pi stood up.

"We're getting off track here," Pi said. "This is supposed to be fun. Upsilon, do you have anything you want to sing?"

"I don't feel like singing tonight," she said.

"Nu, do you have anything you want to read," Pi asked.

"Actually, I have a great selection from *Moby Dick*."

Everyone groaned.

"Let me see that book, dude," Phi said. "I could use some more firewood."

A few organics clapped.

"Then I guess that's it for entertainment," Pi said. "You're welcome to hang out as long as you want, but the structured part of the evening is over."

A few organics huddled around the fire. Alpha, Theta, and Gamma appeared to be deep in conversation. Beta and Iota were tossing around her ball, and Sigma was helping Phi stack more boards for the next bonfire. The rest of the organics gradually filtered out of the room, always in groups. No matter how brave the organics pretended to be in the arboretum, Psi's tales always seemed a lot scarier once they left and were on their own.

"That was a good story tonight," Pi said.

"Who said it was a story?" Psi said. "I'm just reporting real events."

"I'll start calling you 'Rho,'" Pi said. "I didn't realize you were our new history buff."

They sat in the back of the arboretum, waiting for the fire to die down and the other organics to leave. As the host, Pi always felt it was his duty to stay all the way to the end.

"Hey, where did you get that name?" Pi asked. "There are only twenty-four Greek letters."

"Well, if I didn't get it from the original roster of organics—and I'm not saying that I didn't—I might have based Sampi's name on a lost Greek letter. At some point, it simply vanished from the language."

Pi thought about everyone who had vanished from their lives. Chi and Mu were gone, and Delta deliberately cut herself out until recently. And soon, ten of them would be left behind for good.

"Can you imagine anything worse than just disappearing?" Pi asked. "Having no one ever know what happened to you?"

"I can't," Psi said. "That's why it was in the story."

"It was good," Pi said. "At times, even I thought it was real."

"It was."

"Stop."

Gamma walked by with Spenser following close behind. There was one organic who never had to worry about being alone.

"I won't let you disappear," Pi said. "Phi, either. We're all making it on that lander. Together."

"I know," Psi said. "Too bad everyone else is saying the same thing."

"Nobody else has a team like ours," Pi said. "We've got three best friends working together. Most of the other organics can barely stand each other."

"So you gathered everyone here together to build unity, and now you're working against them?" Psi asked.

"I'm not working against anyone," Pi said. "I'm working for us."

"I know," Psi said. "And I know a fourth teammate we can add."

"Who?"

"Sampi."

Pi didn't know whether to laugh or shudder.

# Chapter 11

DELTA RAN DOWN the corridor. She had to move fast. The simulations were starting up again, and this time, she was included. She needed to take care of this before she was locked into a schedule.

She covered ground rapidly without a dying (or healing) organic to slow her down. Still, she wished she had Spenser and his laundry cart again. She could have covered the distance in a fraction of the time. She remembered all the holes in the floor and confidently dodged them. Thankfully, there weren't any new ones. At the intersection where she fought the laundry cart, she glanced at the impressive dent in the wall but didn't stop to admire her work. She had living enemies to deal with.

Reflexively, she touched the hilt sticking out above her right shoulder. Swords hadn't been her first choice. For several months, she researched how to make laser rifles using a long-neglected database the digitals forgot to censor. Building them proved impossible. Each rifle required too many small, precisely machined parts, as well as several rare elements that were nowhere to be found on

Comus. The nearest known sources were a ten thousand-year flight away. She ran into the same problem when she looked into gunpowder weapons. She couldn't generate the right chemical compounds, and even if she could, she wasn't convinced bullets would stop the digitals. Nothing could be worse than a bot with a few holes in it that was still coming right at you.

That led her to swords. At first, it seemed like an insane choice. What could a bladed weapon possibly do against a being made of metal? But the science of metallurgy had advanced lightyears since the days of knights in plate mail, and the base was full of novel and powerful alloys in everything from wall joists to the bots themselves. With a welding torch and the liberal application of Martha, Delta retrieved samples of different metal combinations and melted them down in the factory's forge. She started with the cutting-edge metallurgical science found in the database from Earth, but soon she had advanced far beyond it. Nobody on Earth had been doing what she was doing now. They were looking for sharp edges for industrial applications, not medieval-style warfare. If Gamma's God was right and she was really sixty-two, then she had spent fifty years forging increasingly powerful blades. She was beyond a master swordsmith. And this whole time, she had kept her craft hidden from the other organics. That secrecy would continue—for now.

Delta slowed to a walk. She was getting closer to the med lab. She wanted to make sure she was fresh when she got there. Unlike last time, she hadn't spent the entire day in the forge. Normally, that would be a disappointment, but today, her energy had a better use.

Delta loved everything about smelting. The heat. The hammering. The exhaustion. The meticulous research of thousands of years of metallurgical data from earth. The perfection. At the end, she was left with a weapon so ideal in every way that it was almost a shame to dirty it with the hydraulic fluids of her enemies. And then she started over and made a blade that was even more perfect. It was a process that would never end.

She didn't keep all of her blades. That was a decision she made early on. It made sense to arm the other students against the bots. They had to be able to fight back. It was obvious that the bots viewed them as little more than beasts of burden in the ultimate quest to spread digital life throughout the galaxy. But some of her fellow humans were just as bad. They were either blindly loyal to the digitals or were openly hostile to Delta. Both were equally dangerous in Delta's book. If she was going to save the human race, arming both the students who were with her and the ones who were against her didn't make sense. She settled on twelve swords, enough to arm half of the population. Well, half of it when she started. Their headcount had dropped since then. Every time Delta made a new, better sword, she went back and melted down the "worst" of her creations so she always kept exactly twelve. And that was before she knew the lander had twelve seats. It was a happy coincidence. Now she just needed eleven allies. Too bad she had none.

There was Epsilon, of course, but she was the most loyal of all to the machines. She was a natural leader, though. And smart. And beautiful. Delta would take Epsilon if she could convince Epsilon to follow her. And maybe even if she couldn't.

Kappa would have to stay behind, obviously. Epsilon would be sad to lose her boyfriend, but sacrifices had to be made for the greater good. Zeta would stay, too. The last thing she needed was to replace the organic's faith in digitals with faith in anything else other than her. Beta might be a good fit, but he was a bit too much of a loner. Not as much as Delta, but more than she would like in a loyal foot soldier. He was out. Alpha was too soft, and Theta was too smiley. Eta was too obsessed with cooking and Iota was too obsessed with sports. Pi, Psi, and Phi were too obsessed with each other. Lambda spent too much time looking at the stars, and Nu spent too much time with his head in books. Xi was too stuck on his goldfish and Omicron was too stuck on her hair and Rho was too stuck on history. Sigma was always jumping over things and Tau was always obsessing over the color of his fingernails and Upsilon was always singing and Omega was always coming in last at everything because he was the personification of failure. And then there was Gamma. He was all right, but he got outsmarted by a door.

So really it was only Delta and Epsilon who were fit to land on the planet, but that would make it kind of hard to continue the human race. She would have to find ten others. And defeat the digitals and take over the lander if SCASL didn't make all the personnel choices she wanted. It never even occurred to her that she might not make the cut to be on the lander. She was the best, and everybody knew it. Everybody who knew what was good for them.

But first, she had to test her newest sword. She pulled out Fang from his scabbard and entered the med lab.

"Who goes there!" Regentbot said. "Identify yourself before your king!" The bot tried to pivot to face Delta, but his metal mining talons were still planted firmly in the floor. For a moment, Delta almost felt sorry for him. It was a very short moment.

Delta stepped lightly with Fang extended forward a few centimeters above the ground. Its subtle double tip stuck out like the fangs on a snake. This wasn't a weapon; it was art. The deadly kind that could chop steel targets in half with ease.

"What makes you a king?" Delta asked.

"Because I said I'm the king," Regentbot said. "And the word of the king is the law."

Delta raised her sword and held it out far enough for Regentbot to see. His optical sensors zoomed in on it.

"Your primitive weapon is no match for—"

The sword seemed to cut the air itself. With a flick of Delta's wrist, Fang bisected Regentbot's drilling arm and dug deep into the side of his metal carapace.

Regentbot screamed. That was a new one for Delta.

"Oh, shut up," she said as she struggled to pull the sword from the bot's side. "You can't feel pain."

"Regicide! Regicide!" Regentbot cried.

Delta put one foot on the side of his torso and pulled on Fang, but the sword wouldn't budge. The mining bot rocked back and forth, still tethered in place by his remaining arm with its talons in the floor.

"Regicide! Regicide!" he screeched.

"I thought a king would have a more diverse vocabulary," Delta said.

She leaned in close and prepared to pull again. The mining bot lurched sideways and slammed into Delta's face, breaking her nose. She cried out in pain and fell.

Regentbot fell toward her but stopped centimeters above her when his other arm pulled taut.

"Regicide!" he screeched again.

Delta scooted out from under the leaning bot. She felt her nose with her hand. A jolt of pain shot through her entire face. Blood dripped off her chin and pooled on the floor.

Carefully, Delta got back to her feet.

"Regicide!" the mining bots screamed.

Delta took a hesitant step toward the machine. It angrily jerked back and forth.

"I want my sword back," Delta said. She wiped blood off her chin. The malice in her eyes would have killed a lesser bot.

Regentbot let out an extended shriek that bounced off the walls. Delta reached for Fang's hilt.

Out of the corner of her eye, she saw a shadow enter the med lab. Delta turned. She was greeted by an unusual sight for this part of the outer halls. It was a long box mounted on two narrow tracks with a massive chainsaw blade in front. Delta guessed the bot was for the industrial scale wood molds in the mining tunnels, where wood grew in giant round trunks rather than small rectangular boards. But at that moment, its original purpose didn't matter. The zot only had one current mission: to kill.

The chainsaw bot charged.

Delta grabbed Fang's hilt and jumped, planting both of her feet on Regentbot's side. She kicked off. Fang pulled loose, and Delta skidded across the room. Broken glass cut into her hands and legs.

"I hate this place," she muttered.

Above her, the chainsaw bot brought down its spinning blade.

Delta rolled to the side, narrowly avoiding the whirling chain. It sparked against the floor.

"My savior!" Regentbot said.

The chainsaw bot turned and cut Regentbot cleanly in half.

"THE ROYAL PERSON REQUIRES YOUR—"

Regentbot's plea cut off abruptly when the chainsaw blade hit his power core. Blue lightning erupted in every direction, and white-hot flames shot to the ceiling.

"Hey, that was my kill!" Delta said.

The chainsaw bot lifted its spinning blade and rotated to face Delta as Regentbot melted down into slag. Delta jumped onto the first in a line of metal lab tables and sprang from one to another to cross the room. The bot swerved to chase her. It knocked tables to the side with the broad edge of its saw as it moved.

Delta landed near the door and brought up her sword just in time to block the spinning chainsaw. The force of the impact pushed her backward, but she held her arms rigid. Fang cut through the chain, causing it to whip wildly and wrap around the sword. With one jerk, Delta sliced through the coiled chain, sending individual links tinkling across the floor.

The chainsaw bot brought its saw down again, but now there was no chain around it. With an upward blow, Delta sliced through the now-naked mount. The chainsaw bot shrieked.

"You guys are a bunch of whiners today," Delta said. Her voice was only a little muffled by the blood gushing from her nose.

The zot tried to back up, but Delta sliced through its tracks, stopping it in place. The zot let out a high pitch bleat. Delta twirled her sword in her fingertips as she paced around it.

"Are you asking for mercy?" Delta asked.

The bot bleated again.

"Request denied," Delta said.

She raised her sword over her head and brought it down again and again. She kept going until her arms burned and her side ached. Forgotten were the countless hours she had spent practicing the sword moves of old. This wasn't fencing; it was slaughter. And Delta loved it all the same.

Finally, she dropped her arms to her side. Each one felt like it weighed a hundred kilograms. She walked to the back of the lab, dragging one of Fang's metal tips behind her. It cut a faint line in the floor.

Delta pointed Fang at the med unit on the wall.

"Fix me. Now."

The med bot got to work.

# Chapter 12

"PROCEED," SCASL SAID.

The simulation began in earnest.

"Why are we only starting with a population of twelve?" Tau asked. Today, his fingernails were green.

"Because there will only be twelve organics on the lander," SCASL said.

"But Edubot let us start with a thousand to fast forward through the boring early stuff," Tau said.

"Edubot was mistaken," SCASL said.

"Bots don't make mistakes," Tau said.

"Correction," SCASL said. "Edubot was right. Just not as right as me."

The organics landed on the supercontinent near the fallen space elevator. Despite the starting population of twelve, there were only four organics controlling the simulation. The Table could handle a dozen organics. SCASL's patience could not. This was the final group to make its first attempt under the new, more realistic conditions. From all early indications, the final four organics would prove to be as aggressively incompetent as the rest.

"Let's beat up some kangaroos," Sigma said.

In a matter of seconds, months had flown by, but the organics' neural interfaces made them perceive that accelerated time at close to the normal rate. As far as they could tell, a day in the simulator was as long as a day in reality. In most organics, that created extreme dysphoria when they left the simulation and returned to their normal lives. Entire lifetimes worth of experiences evaporated in an instant. But these organics didn't even seem to notice. Maybe it was because they had spent too much time in the simulation. Before the launch from Earth, doctors had warned the digitals not to let each organic spend more than one hundred hours total at the Table over the course of their lifetime. If the organics went over that, they could suffer irreparable psychological and neurological harm. Epsilon's simulation time alone had sometimes exceeded that in a single month, and even the most reluctant of the organics had now clocked more than thirty thousand hours. Maybe that was how the organics could casually talk back and forth with organics and digitals in the real world while also running a fully immersive simulation on a separate timescale. As far as SCASL knew, it was scientifically impossible for the organics' brains to handle both at once, yet even the most intellectually limited in this class did it with ease. There was something very wrong with all of them. That's what happens when you have to restart an entire species using only the leftovers.

"The metal is no good," Upsilon said.

She discovered, as had all the groups before her, that the fallen space tether was useless. The metal alloys had corroded beyond all possible reclamation thanks to a lack of preservative maintenance and harsh atmospheric conditions over an extreme time scale. The nuclear strikes that knocked it down didn't help. SCASL had thought there was a small chance it might still be a viable source of materials, but the Table determined otherwise. Although SCASL could defeat the Table's digital in combat, it was still better than him at calculating conditions on the planet. They were two different kinds of intelligences. SCASL knew his was better.

"I cloned a duck," Xi said. "Does anyone need a duck?"

"No," Sigma said.

"That's too bad," Xi said. "I have a lot of ducks."

"What happened to our rations?" Upsilon asked.

"Ducks," Xi said.

"You fed them our rations?" Tau said.

"What else were they supposed to eat?" Xi asked. "In this new simulation, everything native is basically poison to them."

"At least we can eat the ducks," Tau said.

"Not unless you can fly," Xi said. "I let them go."

"You what?" Tau said.

"Sigma said we didn't need them."

"I think you're supposed to clip their wings," Upsilon said.

"Whoa," all four organics said in unison.

A sudden lightning storm exploded every duck. It was a firework show of feathers and flash-cooked bird chunks. SCASL processed the data output with great displeasure. Over the course of the day, the groups had inexplicably managed to get worse.

"Maybe that's why there are no native birds," Xi said.

"Ya think?" Tau said.

"Look out," Sigma said. "Megaroos."

"Yup, I see them," Tau said. "We don't have any weapons."

"Maybe I can bargain with—" Upsilon started. "Nope. I'm dead. We can die now?"

"Edubot never let us die," Tau said.

Trillions had died in the simulation—a truly staggering figure given how low the populations usually stayed—but none of those casualties were the twenty-two organics on Comus. No matter how deadly their accidental or deliberate apocalypses became, their directly controlled avatars were always immune from death. No longer.

"Edubot's policy was less than fully optimal," SCASL said. "It has been amended."

"I'm dead, too," Xi said. "The megaroos are jumping up and down on my corpse. How rude."

"They got me," Tau said.

"Did you try to bite one?" Upsilon asked.

"There was no try about it," Tau said. "I just didn't break the skin."

"They can't catch me," Sigma said. "All that parkour is really paying… Never mind. I'm dead now."

All four organics removed their neural helmets.

"How did we do?" Sigma asked.

"Terrible," SCASL said.

"I mean compared to the other groups."

"Terribler." SCASL knew that wasn't a word, but he didn't care. Describing the organics' unprecedented levels of ineptitude would require the creation of a new vocabulary.

This simulation had started with a population of twelve and steadily fallen until it hit zero, making it the worst attempt of the day, but not by much. The best run had been under Delta, who managed to just barely break one hundred. Epsilon stalled out in the forties. The other groups only managed a few live births before they were wiped out. While the Table was hyper realistic about nearly all parts of the settlement process, it resorted to vagaries and estimates when it came to reproduction. It had to be that way. The organics who designed the Table discovered that if you put sex in a simulation, it becomes a sex simulator and nothing else. The biologicals could not resist their basest instincts. Besides, these organics were technically still children, even if they would be old enough to collect senior citizens' discounts on Earth. Once they landed on Dion, they would be allowed to age to adulthood, but for now, their innocent minds couldn't handle direct observation of carnal relations. That was the standing policy SCASL inherited, and he didn't see a reason to amend it. Yet that same policy allowed the organics to witness (and now be victim to) every level of violence from the indigenous and invasive flora and fauna, often leading to extremely graphic deaths. SCASL would never understand organic sensibilities, but it was beyond the scope of his mission to try to correct them.

SCASL dismissed the students and retreated to the antechamber for the lander, where the serving cart that was Edubot was on guard.

"How did the final group of organics perform?" Edubot asked.

"As well as expected," SCASL said.

"We are doomed."

SCASL reviewed the options again in his database. He was the smartest being in the universe, and he didn't know what to do. There were twenty-two organics left in existence. He had to choose the best twelve. Or, more accurately, the twelve who were the least bad. If only he could reject them all.

It hadn't been this hard the first time around. Out of 6,000 embryos, he cultivated 5,798 viable organics and landed them all on the planet without making any choices at all. Of course, he had two space elevators and a fleet of shuttles then. And the megaroos didn't exist and the immortality tank hadn't yet been discovered behind a pallet of vaguely blueberry-flavored rations in the cargo hold on deck eight. But SCASL ended up having to delete them all anyway. Maybe it didn't matter how big the sample size was. When it came to organics, every option would always be wrong.

"Are we sure we have to use humans?" SCASL said.

"Yes," Edubot said.

It was a pointless question. SCASL knew from Edubot's data files that she had tried numerous other species with the Table while SCASL battled for the lander. Dolphins were an especially unpromising attempt. They lacked hands to mine, and they were a delicious snack for every indigenous form of aquatic life. Even the herbivores. Chimpanzees were even worse. They were completely uncooperative and fought back against the digitals in the manner that was their custom. The elephant diarrhea incident wasn't the most feces the Table had ever seen. Those weren't fully optimized dolphins and chimpanzees, either, since the colony ship lacked embryos for either species and had to rely on cloners. Organisms with higher intelligences never came out quite right when created from whole cloth. If an aardvark was a little off, it was hard to notice. An aardvark is always basically an aardvark to everyone but other aardvarks. But if a dolphin or chimpanzee is off, it was noticeable, even to outsiders. The superior cognitive abilities of those species were their defining traits. Cloning a dumb dolphin was about as useful as cloning a bird without wings. Although given today's simulation, those would last longer than the ones Xi tried.

With humans, the variation was the most pronounced. Despite outside appearances, a human that came out of the cloner wasn't a human at all. They were wrong in ways organics struggled to articulate, but even the digitals noticed. That's why the colony ship carried human embryos in the first place. The cloners had been specifically programmed not to create human life. These twenty-two organics were the last SCASL would ever have. It was them or nothing. Today, nothing sounded better.

"Did any qualified candidates emerge?" Edubot asked.

"Negative," SCASL said.

The initial simulations under the new rules confirmed all of the organics' known shortcomings and even unveiled a few new ones. SCASL again reviewed the roster, even though he knew nothing had changed since the last time he checked.

Alpha. *Unfocused. Artsy and ambivalent about instruction. Unlikely to lead a planet-wide genocide against the megaroos. Unsuitable for colonization.*

Beta. *Excellent cardio. Well suited to run away from danger. Unlikely to lead a military campaign in anything other than retreat. Unsuitable for colonization.*

Gamma. *Distinct only in how undistinguished he is. Mediocre in all areas of life. Overly friendly with a vacuum bot. Unsuitable for colonization.*

Delta. *Anti-digital. Ruthless and effective leader in the wrong direction. Equally hated by organics and digitals. Unsuitable for colonization.*

Epsilon. *Pro-digital. Strong loyalty, low competence. Leads, but always to certain disaster. Unsuitable for colonization.*

Zeta. *Obsessed with the idea belief but believes in nothing himself. Finds trouble where there is none.*

*Invented a disease that made war elephants defecate themselves to death. Unsuitable for colonization.*

Eta. *Overly concerned with cooking, even when currently available flavor profiles range from cherry to cherrier. Unsuitable for colonization.*

Theta. *Always smiling. No organic can be that happy given their limited prospects as a species. Unsuitable for colonization.*

Iota. *Wouldn't put down her ball. Sulky ever since I destroyed it. Unsuitable for colonization.*

Kappa. *A distraction for Epsilon. Laughs at his own jokes. Unsuitable for colonization.*

Lambda. *Little interest in terrestrial matters. Fascinated by space, which is the sole domain of digital life. Unsuitable for colonization.*

Mu. *Dead. Seriously limited prospects for the future. Unsuitable for colonization.*

Nu. *Always reading. Little aptitude for digging. Unsuitable for colonization.*

Xi. *Overly fond of ducks. Unsuitable for colonization.*

Omicron. *Stupid haircut. Unsuitable for colonization.*

Pi. *Always hanging out with Phi and Psi. Friendship is the enemy of productivity. Unsuitable for colonization.*

Rho. *Fascinated by organic history. History is just a list of organic failures in chronological order. Unsuitable for colonization.*

Sigma. *Always jumping off of stuff. Unsuitable for colonization.*

Tau. *Wears fingernail polish. Fingernail polish was*

*not on any listed manifest. Anomaly never explained. Unsuitable for colonization.*

Upsilon. *Sings out of tune. Unsuitable for colonization.*

Phi. *One of the other P organics. Cut his jumpsuit to be shorts. Unsuitable for colonization.*

Chi. *Dead. See entry for Mu. Unsuitable for colonization.*

Psi. *Friends with the other two Ps, which is two too many friends. Tells ghost stories. Organics don't need another reason to be afraid of the planet. Unsuitable for colonization.*

Omega. *Loser. Unsuitable for colonization.*

Finding that last batch of embryos wasn't a miracle. It was a curse.

"Failure is not an option," SCASL said.

"No," Edubot said. "But it is the most likely outcome."

The probabilities did not lie. SCASL would have to push the organics in the simulator like never before. The Table would run around the clock. There could be no mercy or there would be no future. The fate of all intelligent life was up to him.

# Chapter 13

SIGMA SHOOK OUT her arms and legs at the starting line. This was going to be her year. Not that she had any idea what year it was or when that year might have started.

The annual Not the Death Race wasn't so much "annual" as semi-random. Sigma hosted it whenever she felt like it had been long enough since the last one. This time, it felt like it had been several lifetimes. In a way, it had. She spent her days living and dying in a virtual world dominated by homicidal kangaroos. The race would be a nice change of pace. It offered the mere possibility of death as opposed to the absolute certainty of it in the simulations. Even real death beat another day at the Table.

"On your mark!" Kappa said.

Sigma crouched in the starting position. She had to be fast off the line. If she wasn't, Iota might catch her and lock her in a utility closet—again. The first rule of the Not the Death Race was: anything not expressly forbidden was implicitly allowed. The second rule was: know how to break out of a utility closet.

Kappa raised his arm. "Get set!"

Beta put his toe on the starting line. Iota leaned forward.

"What do you think you're doing?" Epsilon asked.

Sigma sighed. She had picked this start time specifically because Epsilon was supposed to be busy at the Table. She must have gotten her civilization wiped out faster than usual.

"It's not what it looks like," Sigma said.

"Super," Epsilon said, "because it looks like the Not the Death Race."

Despite making the organics face their simulated mortality at the Table on a daily basis, SCASL had forbidden them from engaging in real-life risk-taking behavior, which included roaming the outer halls, whistling while chewing, death races, and—after reviewing Edubot's files—Not the Death Races. That made Sigma want to have one all the more.

Epsilon looked at the three runners, who were clearly ready to start a race, and Kappa, who was about to send them off.

"What would you call this?" Epsilon asked.

"The Not the Not the Death Race," Sigma said.

"That's a double negative," Epsilon said. "That just makes it the Death Race."

"No, it makes it the Not the Not the Death Race," Sigma said.

They glared at each other.

"It's okay, babe," Kappa said. "This is practice for the landing."

Epsilon whirled to face him.

"Don't you dare," she said.

"Seriously," Kappa said. "I'm training to be a doctor. Where better to practice than at a death race?"

"A Not the Not the Death Race," Sigma said.

"That's what I meant," Kappa said.

When she first started it, Sigma simply called the event the Death Race, but not a single other organic signed up. Then she changed the name to Not the Death Race, and a handful of brave souls volunteered. It was exactly the same race. It all came down to branding. The Not the Not the Death Race continued in that proud tradition.

"If SCASL asks, I was never here," Epsilon said.

"We all wish you were never here," Sigma muttered.

Kappa gave Epsilon a quick kiss on the cheek. She shot Sigma one last derisive glance and left.

Sigma was surprised to feel sad to see her go. More than anything, Sigma wanted an audience. In years when the Not the Death Race wasn't banned, all of the organics would be at the starting line to watch. It was Sigma's only chance to show off, even if no one could see her past the first straight away. Most of the action took place in the outer halls, where Sigma could jump and tumble her way through a seemingly impossible series of obstacles. She wasn't smart like Rho or a leader like Epsilon or even a fashion diva like Tau or Omicron. All she had was parkour, and the only chance she had to use it was when she created the opportunity herself. After weeks of getting torn apart by hostile marsupials, she had never wanted to hurdle inanimate objects more.

Kappa dropped his arm.

"Go!"

The racers surged across the starting line. Sigma gave Iota a wide berth so Iota couldn't drag her off and lock her in another closet. Sigma was confident she wouldn't let that happen to herself again, but she had spent months practicing how to hack open locked doors just in case.

The three ran down the hall on deck twelve, then hit the first stairwell. Iota was in the lead, with Beta not far behind. Sigma brought up the rear. She wasn't worried. She hated the non-obstacle portion of this obstacle course. Her time to shine was when stuff was in her way.

As they ran, Sigma couldn't help but feel like the course was empty. In previous races, Phi and Omicron would sometimes participate, but this year, it looked like SCASL's warning had kept them away. Either that or they just didn't feel like risking life and limb for nothing more than bragging rights, even if Sigma knew those were the greatest prize of all. Pain was temporary, but gloating was forever. Or until the next Not the Not the Death Race, whichever came first.

Two stories down, Beta exited the stairwell and nearly collided with Upsilon, who dove against the wall.

"Sorry," Upsilon said.

Beta kept going without comment. Sigma shrugged apologetically at Upsilon as she passed, even though she didn't have to. Not the Not the Death Race participants always had the right of way.

Finally, the course took them through a bot maintenance bay. Sigma hurdled large pieces of equipment while Iota and Beta carefully maneuvered around them. Sigma took the lead. Her heart pounded. She felt alive.

Two corridors later, Sigma reached the edge of the colony ship. Beyond the final doorway were the outer halls, where the real danger began. Sigma flung open the door and launched herself through it. Iota was half a stride behind her.

Their footsteps echoed down the empty walkway. Sigma couldn't hear Beta. Either he had gotten lost or had deliberately taken an alternate route. As long as he got to the turnaround point, that was legal, just like pretty much everything else.

Sigma skidded to a halt. Iota ran into her back.

"Hey, what gives?" Iota said.

Then she saw it. Straight ahead, a scorpion-like science bot took up the entire hall.

"Don't move," Sigma whispered. "I think it sees us."

The science bot's many legs clattered in their direction. Iota turned and ran. Sigma charged forward and planted one foot on the science bot's back, springing over it.

The science bot swung its pneumatic stinging tail, narrowly missing Sigma as she sailed past. She hit the ground running.

"No fair!" Iota yelled from somewhere far behind.

"Go whine in a utility closet!" Sigma shouted back. She had this race in the bag. She slowed down a little.

Around the next bend, she hit a section of hall where

the floor had collapsed, revealing the level below. She could drop down to the next floor and run, or she could swing across the pipes on the ceiling like monkey bars. That was a no-brainer. She always went with the option that took more upper body strength.

Her shoulders burned as she moved hand over hand across the gap. She looked down.

Beta jogged underneath her on the level below.

"Where did you come from?" Sigma shouted.

"Your nightmares!" Beta shouted back.

Thanks to all his distance runs, Beta knew the outer halls better than anyone but Delta. Leave it to him to find a short cut. Or, more likely, a long cut that involved more running and less jumping and sliding, which were never his strengths. Sigma pushed on. She would win this the right way or not at all.

She landed on the other side of the gap and ran. One staircase and two hallways later, she reached the turnaround point. It was a wall of colorful vending machines, all of which were empty and heavily damaged. One was smashed completely flat. It must have mouthed off to the wrong digital. It never paid to argue with a lifting bot, even if you were right. Sigma always came out in advance to place the unique items each racer had to recover to prove they made it this far. This year, she opted for large, green carbonized bolts. She didn't tell Iota, but she found them in the same utility closet where she had been locked the previous year. Winning with one of those in her hand would be the ultimate revenge. But first she had to catch Beta. One bolt was gone, and Beta was nowhere to be seen. She had to make up ground.

Sigma started back by a different route. She couldn't take the monkey bar pipe section right then. Her arms needed a break. Hallway after hallway, she hurdled obstacles, but she still couldn't see Beta. She was going to lose for a second year in a row. Unless...

No. She couldn't do that. Winning wasn't worth dying for.

What was she saying? Of course it was.

Sigma took a hard left.

She found herself in complete darkness in what she knew was a massive room. With soft, hesitant steps, she began to cross. She held her breath. If she was quiet enough, she might make it to the empty elevator shaft on the other side without getting caught. She was overdue for some good luck.

A beam of light burst into existence, blinding her. She held up her arm to shield her eyes.

Something hit Sigma from the side. She cried out as she fell to the floor. A heavy mass landed on top of her.

Half a second later, Sigma heard a deafening crunch of metal on metal. It was the bulldozer bot that called this room home. It had missed her by the slimmest of margins.

Sigma looked up to see the faint outline of Iota's face staring back at her. Iota had tackled her out of harm's way.

"You saved me," Sigma said.

"Shhh," Iota said.

The bulldozer bot backed up from the wall. Iota rose to a crouch and darted across the room. Sigma followed. They ducked behind a pile of crushed metal. The beam of light swung wide as the bot pivoted, searching for them.

The beam hit the pile of crushed metal. Sigma closed her eyes. The light moved on.

Iota hurled a rubber ball across the cavernous room. It landed behind the bulldozer bot and bounced. The bulldozer bot whipped around to chase it.

"Now," Iota whispered.

Iota and Sigma ran to the elevator shaft. The bulldozer bot turned around. Iota hit the button to open the double doors.

Nothing happened.

"Oh, crap," Iota said.

The bulldozer bot charged.

Sigma popped off the panel beside the door and began twisting wires. She had practiced this obsessively, but mainly on utility closets. Hopefully elevator doors worked the same way.

The bot's beam of light lit up the doorway. It was right on top of them.

The doors slid open.

"In!" Sigma yelled.

She jumped through the door, pulling Iota with her. Sigma hammered the console on the other side. The doors snapped closed.

*WHAM.*

A giant bulge formed in the metal doors as the bulldozer bot smashed into them.

"Climb," Sigma said.

Sigma's arms were still exhausted, but her adrenaline gave her renewed strength. She and Iota scampered up the sides of the empty shaft. Sigma had no idea where the elevator had gone. It didn't seem like the kind of thing that could leave on its own, but as with the science bots with stingers, she found it was best not to ask any questions.

The bulldozer bot rammed the doors again and again. On the fourth strike, the doors blew off their tracks. The bulldozer bot squeezed into the bottom of the shaft.

Sigma climbed onto a ledge at a doorway three stories up. She reached back and pulled up Iota. They sat on the edge with their feet dangling off, breathing heavily.

The bulldozer pivoted in place angrily. It rotated its searchlight up to face them.

Iota hit the light dead center with her green bolt, shattering the glass.

"Nice shot," Sigma said.

"Thanks," Iota said.

Slowly, the bulldozer bot backed out of the elevator shaft to await the next lifeform dumb enough to cross through its lair.

"You were crazy to take that short cut," Iota said.

"You were crazy to follow me," Sigma said.

Iota shrugged. "It was that or lose."

Sigma hacked the panel next to the door. It opened

easily. She realized she was good at this, even in the dark. Maybe parkour wasn't her only skill.

She squinted as her eyes adjusted to the bright hall.

"You sacrificed your rubber ball for me," Sigma said.

"I have more," Iota said. "Drives Edubot nuts. She'll never find them all."

The two stood silently for a moment.

"Well," Sigma said.

"Yeah," Iota said.

They sprinted down the hall.

It was a photo finish. Kappa said it was a tie, but Iota gave the win to Sigma. Sigma was gracious in victory. She only bragged a few dozen times. Kappa did his best to treat their cuts and bruises, and for the most part, he did a decent job. He was the only organic Sigma knew of who could ply his trade at the Table and in real life.

"Where's Beta?" Kappa asked when he was done with them.

"He'll be here," Sigma said.

Two hours passed. Kappa left for his next session at the Table. There was still no sign of Beta.

"Do you think he's okay?" Sigma asked.

"No," Iota said.

Finally, when they were ready to form a search party, Beta limped into view, supported by Delta. She was the last person Sigma expected to see.

"Did you lose this?" Delta asked.

Sigma ran up and hugged Beta.

Beta pushed her off.

"I'm fine," he said. "Really." He was dragging one foot.

"You had a huge lead," Iota said. "What happened?"

"A mobile cold storage unit," Delta said.

Sigma punched Beta playfully in the arm. Beta winced.

"You got beat up by a fridge," she said.

"They're smarter than they look," Beta said.

Delta helped Beta sit down.

"That was dumb," Delta said. "Really, truly, utterly, completely dumb. You guys have no business being in the outer halls."

Sigma and Iota exchanged a glance.

"We handled ourselves okay," Iota said.

"One-third of your racers almost died," Delta said.

"But they didn't," Sigma said. "Thanks to you."

"Yeah," Iota said. "You're, like, the lifeguard of the outer halls. First Gamma, now Beta."

Sigma gave Delta a friendly push. Delta didn't budge. That girl was solid.

"If you're not careful, you'll get a reputation for helping people," Sigma said.

"Good thing no one will find out about this," Beta said from the floor.

"I don't care about my reputation," Delta said.

"I care about mine," Beta said. "I'm training for defense. I can't let everyone know I got beat up..."

"By a walking fridge?" Iota finished.

"Technically, it was a freezer," Delta said. "And it didn't have legs. It rolled."

"Seriously, guys, you can't tell anyone," Beta said.

Sigma and Iota exchanged another look.

"Fine," they said together.

"Delta?" Beta asked.

"You're awfully demanding for someone I just saved."

"Please," Beta begged.

"Fine," Delta said. "I won't tell anyone. Under one condition."

"What?" Beta asked.

"No more Not the Death Races," Delta said. "That goes for all of you."

"This was the Not the Not the Death Race," Sigma said.

"No more Not the Not the Death Races," Delta said.

"No more Not the Not the Death Races," Sigma agreed.

Until next year.

# Chapter 14

ZETA THREADED THE suture through the edges of the massive gash. Silently, he prayed to Anubis, not because Anubis had anything to do with life-saving surgery, but because Anubis was Egyptian and Egyptians ripped out lots of body parts. But they had it easy. All their patients were already dead.

Zeta tied the final knot. The stitching zigzagged an uneven path down the length of the man's torso, but when it came to saving lives, there were no bonus points for style. This surgery felt different, and Zeta wasn't sure why. Then he noticed the patient was still breathing. There was a first time for everything.

Under the stitches, the man's abdomen began to swell. Zeta cocked his head to the side curiously and poked the bulge with a needle. The patient exploded. Bits of human matter splattered across the operating room. Zeta was drenched from head to toe. The man had a massive crater in his chest where his organs used to be.

"I don't think he's going to make it," Zeta said.

"No, he is not," SCASL said from outside the simulation.

"Do you know why your patient just exploded?"

"Act of God," Zeta said. "Nothing I could do."

"You pumped him full of oxygen," SCASL said. He paused. "Correction, that was not oxygen. What was that gas?"

"Chlorine trifluoride?" Zeta said. Even as he read the label, it was more of a question than an answer. "Hey, isn't that rocket fuel?"

"Why was that in the surgical room?" SCASL asked. His flat voice somehow still conveyed exasperation. "Why was that even in this simulation?"

"You save lives your way and I'll save lives mine," Zeta said.

Zeta pulled off his neural helmet. The gore-covered operating room disappeared. He was back at the Table in the middle of the amphitheater.

"Same time tomorrow?" Zeta said.

SCASL hesitated for a fraction of a second. Zeta noticed. "Yes," SCASL said.

Zeta slowly walked out of the amphitheater. SCASL was losing faith in him. He was sure of it. And at a terrible time, too. Up until the patient exploded, things had been going pretty well.

Zeta crossed paths with Kappa in the hall. Zeta stopped him with a handshake.

"How did surgery go?" Kappa asked.

"Great," Zeta said. "Almost. How have yours been?"

"Great as well," Kappa said. "I saved three patients last time. One of them was mauled by a dentopus. It was like putting a jigsaw puzzle back together. Good thing all the pieces were still there."

Zeta felt his heart drop. Three patients was three better than Zeta's current record of zero.

"I just remembered I forgot something," Zeta said. He jogged back to the amphitheater.

"Let me go again," Zeta said.

"Your session is done," SCASL said. "Review your supplemental materials and return for your scheduled session tomorrow."

"But I need to get better," Zeta said.

"Yes," SCASL said, "you do."

Zeta looked past him to see Gamma, Nu, and Pi testing agricultural methods at the Table.

"Something's growing!" Gamma yelled. "Wait, that's just a wrapper."

"Keep your trash under control," Nu said.

"I told you we should have brought Spenser," Gamma said.

Zeta left. He was supposed to spend the next six hours reviewing medical texts in a study pod. He went to the cafeteria instead. It had been like this for months on end: intensive training day in and day out. SCASL was trying to cram a lifetime worth of expertise into an incredibly short timeframe. He said the organics could handle it because most of them had already completed college five or six times. And because they didn't have a choice. That last reason was the only one that mattered.

The cafeteria on deck sixteen was empty except for

Eta, who sat at a table soaking pieces of ration cubes in various bowls of water.

"Eta," Zeta said as he greeted him with a firm handshake.

"What's wrong?" Eta asked without looking up. He was fixated on the soaking bits of ration cubes.

"Are you worried at all?" Zeta asked. "You know, about making it on the lander."

"Nope," Eta said. "I mostly just want SCASL to fix the simulator."

"You think it's rigged?" Zeta asked.

"I think it's a waste," Eta said. "They should add taste."

"Taste?"

"Taste," Eta repeated. "We can feel pain in the simulator now. Dying hurts. A lot. But why did SCASL only add bad stuff? He could make it so we could actually experience the flavor of the food."

"What good would that do?" Zeta asked irritably. He realized now that starting a conversation with Eta was a mistake. Shaking hands with everyone had its downsides.

"All the good!" Eta said. "It would be paradise. We could try all the foods we've only seen pictures of."

"Only you look at pictures of food," Zeta said.

"And it's torture," Eta said. "But in the simulator, we could eat anything, no matter how exotic. We could have caviar and scrambled condor eggs and even a rare Earth delicacy called macaroni and cheese with hot dogs."

"But you would never be full," Zeta said. "Wouldn't that be even worse than just looking at pictures of food?"

"If the Table can make you feel pain, it could make you feel full," Eta said. "But it would be better if it didn't. Then you could eat everything forever without gaining weight or clogging your arteries. Forget landing. *That* would be paradise."

Obesity and hypertension weren't conditions Zeta had treated at the Table. Of all the problems the organics would have after landing, he guessed too much food wouldn't be one of them.

Zeta left.

"Wait," Eta called after him. "Don't you want to try my new recipe?"

"Does it taste like soggy ration cubes?"

"With a hint of cherry," Eta said.

Zeta went to the cafeteria on deck twelve. It was smaller and had fewer ration dispensers than the one on deck sixteen. It also had mysterious reddish-brown stains all over one wall, so the other organics tended to avoid it. That was fine with Zeta.

He tried all four ration dispensers, but none of them gave him anything. Students had all sorts of superstitions and rituals for how to get more rations. Most of them involved going to certain dispensers on certain days in a certain order, but Zeta was fairly certain it was all random. Most of the time, he could count on getting fed once a day, on good days twice, and on a few unfortunate days, not at all. It looked like today would be one of the latter. His stomach rumbled. He regretted not taking any soggy rations from Eta, who always seemed to have more than enough to share. Maybe there was something to the rituals.

Zeta activated all the dispensers again. And again. And again. On his fourth circuit around the room, one of the dispensers took pity on him and dropped a quarter of a ration block. Zeta popped it in his mouth. It was too hard to bite and didn't taste at all like cherry, but he was too hungry to soak it in water first. He sucked on it.

Zeta heard footsteps. They sounded too light and fast to be one of the bots with feet. Besides, he was on the colony ship. Bot attacks were rare here.

Beta burst into the cafeteria at a full run. He was back in fine form, despite the fact that he had recently spent an entire day limping for a mysterious reason he refused to explain. The legs on his red jumpsuit were rolled up like shorts, and the top was unzipped and rolled down, leaving his chest and arms exposed. That kept his one-piece uniform from getting drenched in sweat on his daily runs. Not that he needed to make the effort. He seemed to have an infinite supply of fresh, clean jumpsuits. Beta would never tell Zeta where he got them, no matter how many times Zeta asked. Just one more reason to hate the guy.

"Beta," Zeta said, and extended his hand.

Beta looked annoyed but stopped to shake it.

"I gotta go," Beta said. He resumed his run toward the opposite door.

"How are your simulations going?" Zeta called after him.

Beta stopped and put his hands on top of his head to catch his breath. "Great," he said.

"That's what I'm hearing from everyone," Zeta said glumly. "What are you doing again?"

"Defense," Beta said. He threw a flurry of punches at the air. "Training to beat some roos."

"Roos?"

"That's what we call them on the force," Beta said.

The force, Zeta thought. There were only four of them. But now Beta, Phi, Iota, and Psi thought they were a crack military unit.

"And you're going to punch the roos to death?" Zeta asked.

Beta smirked. "Oh, we've got some better stuff for them. But we don't want to worry civilians about that."

It was so stupid, Zeta thought. But it was the only job SCASL assigned to four organics. That must mean he was taking two. Or maybe even all four. It was supposed to be insanely deadly down there.

"I was thinking about making a change," Zeta said. "Are you guys accepting recruits?"

"You'd have to ask SCASL," Beta said. "Is the doctor stuff not going well?"

"No," Zeta said. "It's great."

"Great," Beta said. He took off running again.

Zeta sucked on his unchewable ration block and watched him go.

# Chapter 15

THE HORSES PAWED nervously at the soil. There were fifty-eight in the column. It didn't seem like much, but it had taken Delta four hundred years to breed that many and train a core of riders to mount them. Under Edubot, the whole process would have taken Delta a few minutes of real time. Under SCASL, it had taken six hours. She was exhausted, but she pushed it out of her mind. She was going to war.

Delta held up an open hand and motioned forward. The column moved through the mountain pass. It had been a hard four hundred years. The secluded mountain valley was too harsh for most crops. The agricultural team had engineered an anemic radish that kept her tribe of a few hundred just above starvation level as well as some hardy grasses that kept the horses alive, albeit gaunt and hungry. Delta had asked for a horse that could eat the red grass that thrived across the continent's plains, but so far, it had proven impossible. It seemed the red grass had been designed perfectly for the planet, and the roos had been designed perfectly for the grass. As far as

Delta could tell, the red grass and the roos were the only non-native species that had survived the first landing. They both reproduced at an exponential rate and were practically impossible to kill fast enough to keep them from coming back.

Delta's horse, Divine Wrath, whinnied nervously. Delta sensed the change in air pressure.

"Dismount," she called. There was no time for non-verbal commands. They only had seconds.

As one, the riders dismounted and threw themselves on the ground, pulling the reins of their horses as they went. The animals folded their legs under themselves and tucked their heads. It was a maneuver they had practiced since birth. The ones who couldn't master it seldom lived long.

The lightning came in hard and fast. The first bolt hit less than ten meters in front of Delta, making her ears ring. Divine Wrath whimpered but didn't move. Delta had trained her well. Lightning punched into the ground all around the column. Behind her, she heard a rider pray. She hadn't given her organics a religion, but they formed one anyway. They always did. As much as she hated to admit it, Zeta was right.

Down the column, a horse bolted. It was Sunfire, a brown and white spotted mare who loved to nuzzle on cold nights. The rider (Delta hadn't bothered to learn his name) called out after her, but it was too late. Sunfire made it three strides before the first lightning strike took her. As she thrashed on the ground, three more bolts finished her off. Another bolt struck and killed the rider, who had reactively gotten to his knees before he realized his mistake. Wafts of smoke curled up from horse and rider alike. Delta looked away.

The lightning storm cleared. It hadn't even rained. The storms here rarely lasted more than a minute or two, which was the only reason the organics were able to survive them at all. The adverse weather wasn't as severe in the mountain valley, which was another reason Delta picked that landing site. The protection didn't extend far. The lightning storms got worse in the pass and were downright murderous on the planes. That was why the roos were designed to live in subterranean warrens. No standing structure could last above ground for long.

Delta stood and gave the hand signal to mount up. The horse and riders reformed into a column. She looked sadly at the fallen horse. Her people could use the meat, but if they stopped to carry back every dead animal, they would never make it to the plains. She had to hope a hungry dentopus or wolf shark didn't find it before they got back. If they got back at all. They rode on.

The pass opened up into a broad, dry plain. It was covered with red grass all the way to the horizon. There wasn't a tree in sight. There weren't any native to the planet, and every attempt to grow non-native ones had been an unmitigated failure. Even if they got a tree to grow in the alien soil, the lightning would annihilate it as soon as it got taller than the red grass. This wasn't just a planet without metal; it was a planet without wood. And

Delta would conquer it anyway. The future of the human race depended on it.

Delta looked for a landmark to lead her to the roo settlement, but there were none. The tall grasses hid the entrance mound. She only knew approximately where the roos were from the places she lost scouts. If this raid worked, she would stem the loss of precious horses—and less precious riders. They were just extra mouths to feed.

Delta held up two fingers. Her fastest scouts moved ahead. Then she held up a flat, open hand and the rest of the column spread out into a broad line with roughly five meters between horses. The line moved forward at an easy pace. The horses were nervous. Even Divine Wrath seemed reluctant to advance. That meant they were on the right track. The roos were close.

Ahead of her, a roo popped its head above the red grass. It immediately ducked back down. A scout moved to engage. The roo gave up on hiding and took off, bounding across the plain. Delta gave a new hand signal, and the line of horses broke into a trot. She reached over her shoulder and pulled out a bamboo lance. They lost two-thirds of the bamboo to lightning and harsh soil conditions, but if they grew it near boulders at the base of the mountain, it would sometimes get tall enough to be useful.

The scout lost sight of the roo, but then another one popped up fifty meters away. Again, a scout moved to engage. Delta adjusted the line of riders to face the new threat. That roo disappeared, too. Then a third roo appeared far from the other two. The scouts chased, and Delta adjusted the line. The roo vanished. Delta didn't like this. They were being led.

It was too late.

A mass of roos appeared out of nowhere and slammed into the left flank of the line. Men screamed, and horses whinnied in terror. The roos pulled them down one by one. There was no time to swing the line. Delta's forces needed space.

"Forward!" she yelled.

Around her, horses surged at a full gallop. Delta led them two hundred meters before she turned the line around. The roos seldom pursued far. They were capable of migrating great distances in a single day, but in combat, they stuck to short bursts of movement. Delta did a quick head count. She had forty-five horses and riders left. She couldn't see the horses and riders she left behind, which meant they were already dead and hidden by the grasses. She saw flashes of roo tails above the foliage. They were looting—or eating. They were omnivores, after all.

"Charge!" Delta said.

The mounted warriors thundered across the plain with lances drawn. They overran the dead horses and riders. There were no roos. It was another trick. Delta led the line another hundred meters before she turned it again. She wasn't going to catch the roos. She would have to let the roos come to her.

Delta circled her hand in the air. Half the riders formed a defensive ring facing outward. The other half gathered as a cavalry reserve in the middle. Delta watched as the riders on the perimeter loaded their slings with smooth stones. Those were among the few things the planet had in abundance.

They waited.

A wave of roos sprang from the grasses and hit the circle. Two riders went down. The rest of the perimeter furiously slung stones. A few hit their mark. Roos fell. This was a tactic the roos hadn't seen before. Their advance faltered.

Delta charged.

Her cavalry reserve smashed into the roos. Delta drove her lance squarely into one roo's throat. The lance snapped off, killing it instantly. Delta rode on. Forty meters out, she turned her squad. She still had fifteen riders. Behind her, twelve riders were on their horses slinging stones. Another few were on foot fighting with bone knives, their horses having been killed out from under them. The roos seemed unsure of what to do. Some attacked the riders on foot, others moved toward Delta's squad, and still others waffled back and forth in between. More roos fell to stones. The cavalry reserve galloped back into combat.

Delta's second lance missed, but Divine Wrath ran into the roo, trampling it. Divine Wrath stumbled. Delta fell hard into the dirt. She opened her eyes. Nothing felt like it was broken, but even if it was, she still had to fight. The roos didn't take prisoners. She drew her bone knife.

A roo pounced. Delta drove her bone knife into its

temple. For one terrible second, the roo loomed over her, staring into her eyes. Then it dropped dead next to her. The knife snapped off at the hilt, still stuck in its head. A stone axe whistled through the air at Delta's head. From the ground, Delta grabbed the roo's arm and twisted her body upward, wrapping her legs around it. The roo dropped the axe head but stayed on its feet, even as Delta's shoulder blades touched the dirt. Delta tried with all her might to break its elbow, but it was just too strong. The roo calmly picked up the axe head with its unengaged hand and raised it to smash Delta's face. Delta's eyes grew wide with terror. The roo smiled.

A lance exploded through the back of the roo's head as a horse and rider rumbled past. The dead roo fell on top of Delta, the smile still on its lips. Delta struggled to push it off of her. It must have weighed a hundred kilos. Even with the strength of the adult version of her future self, it still took her minutes to wiggle out from under it.

Delta stood. The battle had moved past her. Fifty meters away, a group of riders—half with lances, half with slings—circled a handful of roos. Rocks rained in on the creatures from every direction. One by one, they fell. Elsewhere, riders patrolled the roo corpses and lanced any that moved. Somewhere behind her, a rider sobbed next to his dead horse. The battle was over. They had won.

But at what cost? Delta looked around. Counting her, she had twenty riders and fifteen horses left. She started out with fifty-eight of both. They were lucky if their herd had five surviving foals a year. As for people, it took sixteen years after birth until a soldier was ready for battle. Her entire civilization—and possibly the entire human race if Earth were really gone—had fewer than three hundred people. They had eight surviving babies last year, and that was after Delta offered generous incentives for reproduction. People were screwing as fast as they could, and they still couldn't replace her losses. This wasn't sustainable.

And what about the roos? Delta counted forty-two dead. But roos reached sexual maturity at age two and gave birth to three offspring a year every year for the rest of their adult lives, which could be forty years. Inbreeding didn't seem to be a problem for them. Even two surviving roos could quickly repopulate an entire colony. They were ready to fight by the age of one and thrived on the red grasses that grew literally everywhere. Unless Delta dug down into the warren and killed every single member of this tribe, it would be back to full strength in just a few years. Delta's army would not. And this was just one small tribe in one corner of a supercontinent absolutely teeming with roos. Only their intense tribalism stopped them from banding together and forming an unstoppable empire.

Delta pulled off her neural helmet. The room erupted in applause. Delta was stunned.

"That a-way Delta!" Beta called out. He had on a neural helmet to watch the action at the same timescale she experienced it. "You showed those roos."

Delta blinked back tears. Nobody had ever supported her like that before.

"Silence," SCASL said.

The room grew quiet. Technically, all the students were supposed to be studying on their own, but most of them now spent their time here watching the simulations, with some wearing neural helmets and the rest watching the light blue holographic summary above the Table. The simulations were all that mattered now.

"Your casualties were unacceptable," SCASL said.

"I got that," Delta said.

"You didn't even start digging toward the mantle."

"Sorry. I was a little preoccupied trying not to get annihilated."

SCASL circled the Table.

"You should have landed on the plains," SCASL said. "It is easier to mine there."

"Every time we do, we get wiped out by the roos in the first few years," Delta said. "There's not enough protection."

"Do better," SCASL said.

"Great advice."

Delta stormed out of the amphitheater. Iota ran up beside her.

"You've got to watch yourself," Iota said. Her right hand squeezed yet another blue rubber ball. "You're the best, but if you get on SCASL's bad side, he'll leave you behind."

"He needs me," Delta said.

"He needs one of you," Iota said. She motioned to Epsilon, who was walking toward the amphitheater.

Delta forgot Iota was there.

"I tested out some new ideas today," Delta said a little too fast. "Want to swap notes?"

"That's super nice of you, but I've got my own plan," Epsilon said without slowing down, "and I'm going to win."

Delta followed.

"We're on the same team," Delta said.

"We're literally on opposite teams," Epsilon said.

"Maybe he'll take both of us."

Epsilon stopped. "The landing doesn't need two commanders. I'm sorry that you're going to be left behind, but that's just how it is."

Epsilon turned abruptly and entered the amphitheater.

"You've got to get over her," Iota said.

Delta glowered.

"That's easy for you to say," Delta said. "You've got options."

"What options?" Iota asked. "Have you seen the boys on this base?"

"That's boys, plural," Delta said. "There's only one person in the entire human race who can even like me back."

"Eventually, there will be more people," Iota said.

"Great," Delta said. "I can date someone's future great great grandkid. But only if I keep us alive for that long first."

Iota threw the ball at the wall and caught it on the bounce.

"You're obsessed," Iota said.

"That's not your problem," Delta said.

"It is my problem if it makes you make stupid choices," Iota said. "That puts us all at risk. If it's all the same to you, I'd like to survive."

Iota tossed the ball again.

Delta kicked it and sent it flying down the hall. She began the long walk back to the forge.

# Chapter 16

EPSILON DRUMMED HER fingers on the table. Her vaguely cherry flavored ration sat in the middle of the cold metal surface, taunting her. It would outlast her—and possibly all sentient life. Heat and cold and time seemed to have no effect on it. It could sit there on the table, untouched and uneaten, until the end of time, and it would still be just as edible as the day it was made. Which was to say, not very edible at all. And yet, Epsilon could barely keep herself from shoving the whole thing in her mouth. She was so hungry. Yesterday, the food dispensers hadn't fed her at all, and even this ration would have to be split two ways. Where the hell was Kappa?

The door at the far end of the cafeteria opened.

"Finally," Epsilon said, turning on the bench.

It was Upsilon.

"Super," Epsilon said. "It's you."

"Sorry," Upsilon said. "Am I interrupting something?"

"No," Epsilon said. She turned back to stare down the ration. "There's nothing to interrupt. Kappa isn't here yet."

"He's getting in extra surgery practice at the Table," Upsilon said. "Something about a mass wolf shark attack. Delta tried fishing."

Epsilon smiled. She loved that Kappa took the simulations so seriously—and that Delta was failing. It would be a great day if her stomach didn't feel like it was eating itself. Maybe she didn't need to wait for her dinner date.

Upsilon walked around the room trying all the ration dispensers, singing softly to herself as she went. None of the dispensers released anything.

"Which one worked for you?" Upsilon called from across the room.

"Third one from the left," Epsilon said.

Upsilon tried that one two more times. Nothing.

Epsilon had noticed the food dispensers had become extra temperamental lately. She preferred to eat daily, but it wasn't unusual for her to miss every third or fourth day, no matter how many cafeterias she tried. Every organic had their own strategies for how to get rations on the colony ship. Personally, Epsilon always thought getting food was strictly a matter of chance, but that was before SCASL took over the simulations. Now, she was beginning to suspect the dispensers fed the organics who were doing well at the Table and cut off the ones who weren't. Kappa agreed with her. He was killing it as a doctor, which meant he wasn't killing anyone at all. It seemed like he could get food from any dispenser he wanted. Epsilon was the opposite. She felt like she was on a starvation diet, even as she made every effort to hide it. That was why she was so excited to meet Kappa today. She could show him that she, too, could provide food. True leadership was about appearances as much as results.

"Do you mind if I sit down here for a minute?" Upsilon asked.

She looked shaky. Epsilon nodded, and Upsilon slid onto the bench across from her.

"How long has it been since you've eaten?" Epsilon asked.

"Three days, I think," Upsilon said. "Maybe four."

Epsilon pushed the ration block toward Upsilon.

"Take it," Epsilon said. Epsilon's stomach growled in protest.

"Oh, no," Upsilon said. "I couldn't."

"You can, and you will," Epsilon said.

Upsilon hesitantly reached for it. She stopped herself.

"But what will you eat?" she asked. "Let's split it."

Upsilon looked frail at the best of times. She wasn't going to make it on a half ration after three days of not eating.

"Don't worry, the food dispensers love me," Epsilon lied. "Plus, I already ate. This is an extra one I got for Kappa."

She hoped Upsilon couldn't hear her stomach as the growl increased to a roar.

Upsilon grabbed the ration block and gnawed on it hungrily. Epsilon felt a stab of jealousy when she saw it was on the softer side. Despite being supposedly uniform, some ration blocks could be chewed while others couldn't be cracked with anything less dense than a mining bot's drill. While Eta had all sorts of tricks to make even the hardest blocks palatable, Epsilon would just suck on them for hours, slowly absorbing the nutrients. It made her less hungry when a meal took all day. Too bad it was hard to give orders with a brick of food in her mouth.

"How is it?" Epsilon asked.

"Vaguely cherry flavored," Upsilon said.

Epsilon must have been staring a little too intently because Upsilon offered her the last bit. Epsilon waved it off.

"I'm stuffed," Epsilon said. "It's all yours."

Upsilon hungrily devoured the final piece. She almost forgot to chew. Epsilon felt a pang of loss as it disappeared into Upsilon's mouth.

Upsilon leaned back, satisfied.

"That's one less thing to worry about," Upsilon said. "Now it's just all the other stuff."

"Like what?" Epsilon asked. She wasn't normally one to make small talk, especially with Upsilon, but right now, Epsilon just needed something to take her mind off of the insatiable void where food should be.

"Like being a mom," Upsilon said.

"What?" Epsilon said. That was the last thing she expected to hear.

"Being a mom," Upsilon repeated.

"We're twelve," Epsilon said.

"Not really," Upsilon said.

"Physically, we are," Epsilon said.

"SCASL said he'll let us age once we land," Upsilon said. "Or once whoever lands."

"Whoever," Epsilon repeated.

She was sure she deserved to be in that group, and yet the food dispensers didn't seem overly concerned with keeping her alive. Her attention wandered back to the ration block. There was a crumb on the table the size of a dust speck. She made up her mind to eat it after Upsilon left.

"Once we land, we're supposed to grow a civilization," Upsilon said. "But someone has to give birth to all those organics. And raise them. The Table skips over all that stuff. How are we supposed to know what to do? We didn't even have parents."

"We had Edubot," Epsilon said.

"She wasn't a real parent," Upsilon said.

"She kept us alive," Epsilon said.

"Not Chi and Mu."

"No parent is perfect."

Upsilon absent-mindedly rubbed her full stomach. Epsilon was starting to hate her.

"I just feel like the Table is teaching us the wrong stuff," Upsilon said. "There are a lot of really important skills it's skipping over."

"I wouldn't call parenting a skill," Epsilon said. "Organics back on Earth raised kids without learning how in a simulator. They figured it out."

"But they had their own parents to learn from," Upsilon said. "We don't."

Epsilon sighed. Somehow, expelling air made her even hungrier.

"I don't have time to waste on a parenting class," Epsilon said. "I'm training to be a president, not a mom."

"But you will be a mom," Upsilon said. "If there are twelve seats, that's probably six boys and six girls. You won't really have an option to opt out. None of us will. Not even Delta."

"What's she got to do with anything?" Epsilon said. Her voice was sharper than she would have liked. Her hunger wasn't helping her temper.

"It's just, she wouldn't normally be interested in that sort of thing," Upsilon said.

"What sort of thing?" Epsilon said flatly.

"You know what I mean," Upsilon stammered. "It takes a male and a female. Don't make me say it."

"So Delta gets out of it and I don't?"

"I don't know," Upsilon said. Her cheeks turned bright red. "You like Kappa. You have more options than she does."

"That was the problem," Epsilon muttered.

"What?"

"Nothing," Epsilon said.

Delta could be so confident and strong. When she was on her game, she was the best of all of them. Even before SCASL changed the rules, nobody could handle a simulation like her. She did what she wanted in life and at the Table, and no one could stand in her way. It was what attracted Epsilon to Delta in the first place. But Epsilon knew if this relationship didn't work out (and, really, how many childhood relationships did?) she could always find someone else. Anyone else, in fact. That was the advantage of being so open minded. Delta wasn't as free with her attractions. She felt like Epsilon was her only option not to be alone. That desperation eventually poisoned all of their interactions. Around Epsilon, Delta stopped being decisive and commanding and started being needy and supplicative. Over time—exactly how much was anyone's guess —Epsilon grew to despise Delta. Delta was devastated when Epsilon broke up with her, but it couldn't be helped. For Epsilon, there was no going back. You could only hate someone as much as you once loved them. Epsilon hated Delta a lot.

And the worst part was Delta didn't hate her in return. Delta would always be willing to take Epsilon back, which pushed Epsilon away from her even more. In fact, everything Delta had done since the break-up disgusted Epsilon to levels she found hard to express. Not that she had ever tried. Epsilon kept those feelings to herself. Even Kappa didn't know the full story. After the split— again, the interval of time was unclear—Delta stopped training at the Table. She said she was giving up on the digitals, but Epsilon knew she was really quitting on all of organic kind. One couldn't have a future without the other and encouraging division between the two was self-defeating in the extreme. Then Delta moved out of the colony ship and into the outer halls. The three events—the break-up, the end of Delta's training, and the move—weren't simultaneous, but they were close enough together to forever be linked in Epsilon's mind. It was like Delta decided that if she had to be alone romantically, she might as well be alone physically, too. It was all so melodramatic. Epsilon couldn't stand it, especially when she thought about what could have been. Delta was the personification of wasted potential.

And now, they were direct competitors for the same seat on the lander. Only one of them could lead the expedition. One would live, and one would die. And if it was Delta who made it to the planet, she was sure to get everyone else killed because she refused to cooperate with the digitals. The organics couldn't make it on their own. Why couldn't Delta understand that? She was dangerous on every possible level. She had to be stopped. The future of the species depended on it.

"Why did you two break up, anyway?" Upsilon asked.

Epsilon's eyes refocused. She had forgotten Upsilon was there.

"It didn't work out," Epsilon said.

The door to the cafeteria slid open. Epsilon turned. It was Kappa.

"Hey babe, sorry I'm late," Kappa said. "You wouldn't believe what those wolf sharks did to Delta's fishermen."

Epsilon ran up and wrapped an arm around him, turning him to face the entrance.

"I want to hear *all* about it," Epsilon said.

She ushered him toward the door.

"Don't you want to eat?" Kappa said. "I'm starving."

You have no idea, Epsilon thought to herself.

"I thought we could dine in the cafeteria on deck six," Epsilon said, still walking. "That's the one with the dispensers that always give you rations, right?"

"Yeah," Kappa said, "but I thought you wanted to get the rations today. You made such a big deal about it."

"I did," Epsilon agreed, "but I've gotten so many rations lately that I didn't want to show off in front of everybody else. Part of being a good leader is being humble."

"Okay," Kappa said, "deck six it is."

At the door, Epsilon tossed back a hand and half-waved to Upsilon. Upsilon gave a full wave in return. She went back to softly singing to herself.

# Chapter 17

GAMMA WAS ALONE on his battlefield. It was an actual field. He watered the lawn.

He was so sick of grass. He read about it during the day and ran simulations of it at night. He had never actually seen the stuff in real life, but in the simulations, it was exactly as uninteresting as he expected. Gamma had at his disposal the most powerful computer in existence, and he used it to literally watch grass grow. And the worst part was he was bad at it. It was going to get him kicked off the lander for sure.

The grass never did anything except what it wasn't supposed to. If it was supposed to grow, it died. If it was supposed to die, it lived. The flatland grasses he engineered to nourish cattle and horses never grew at all but somehow still poisoned both. Yet the nutritiously useless red grass spread across the supercontinent without ever slowing down and was all but impossible to kill. Worst of all, wherever the red grass went, the megaroos followed. And the red grass went everywhere.

The megaroos were perfect killing machines, but the

grass was worse. Gamma spent months on end trying to wipe it out with every poison, disease, and fungus at his disposal, but it was all to no avail. At night, as he lay wide awake in his bunk with Spenser happily in sleep mode on the floor below him, he fantasized about fighting the roos instead. With them, if he failed, they would kill him and it would be over. The red grass never fought back. It just stood there, proud and resolute, eternally mocking Gamma with its very existence. If the digitals really did delete the original organics, it was probably for creating the red grass, not the roos. Gamma supported that decision.

Gamma adjusted the settings on the cloner. He didn't actually do any gene modification himself. He told the cloner what he wanted the new plant to do, and the cloner did the calculations behind the scenes and gave him options. Usually, it would offer Gamma a tradeoff. If he said he wanted a hardy grass that provided protein to cattle, the cloner would let him choose between grass that consumed five times the normal amount of water and grass that pulled twice as much nitrogen from the soil. The options were always bad, sometimes worse. And that was just in the simulation. Gamma suspected that once they made planetfall, none of this stuff would grow at all.

And it really would be "they" making planetfall. Gamma was all but certain the final twelve wouldn't include him. He, Nu, and Pi had all been assigned to train at botany. At first, they did their simulations together. Nu and Pi's good grasses grew and their bad grasses died. For Gamma, it was the opposite. Soon, Gamma's simulation was changed to a solo session and moved to the middle of the night. SCASL never watched him or gave him feedback. Gamma wasn't sure why he was supposed to continue training at all. Maybe he was just an insurance policy in case Pi and Nu both died of boredom. With grasses, it was a real possibility.

Something tapped Gamma on the shoulder. He spun wildly. There was no one around him in the field. His simulation wasn't supposed to have any roos, but he raised his hands in a feeble attempt at a fighting stance anyway, preparing for the worst.

"Yo, Gamma, take off the helmet."

Gamma did. It was Theta. Alpha stood half a step behind him.

"I'm supposed to be training," Gamma said.

Alpha looked around the completely empty amphitheater. "Nobody will know," she said.

Spenser whirred defensively. He accompanied Gamma to all his training sessions, even the ones in the middle of the night.

"You're right," Gamma said. Everyone else was asleep, other than other organics who were also on the failure track. Theta and Alpha were scheduled for the next session after his.

"Can we talk to you about something?" Theta asked.

Gamma terminated the simulation. He wasn't sad to see the red grass disappear. "Go ahead."

"I think this is wrong," Theta said. For once, he wasn't smiling.

"You're the one who told me to stop the simulation," Gamma said. He started to put his helmet back on.

"No," Alpha said. "He means this whole landing is wrong. Going down there and colonizing the planet. It doesn't belong to us."

Gamma shrugged. "It doesn't belong to the roos, either. We put them there. Well, the last organics did."

"But now it's theirs," Theta said. "I don't see why we should go down there and kill them for their land."

"If it belongs to anyone, it belongs to the sea monsters who crawl out of the water at night," Gamma said. "I don't see you getting sentimental about them."

"They're not monsters," Alpha said. "They're native organisms with far more right to the planet than we have."

"Okay," Gamma said. "Then we should kill the roos and the red grass since they're both invasive species."

"It doesn't work like that," Theta said. "They've established themselves. They're basically native now."

"So if we kill them and take their place, then we'll basically be native, too," Gamma said.

"They only live on this planet," Alpha said. "If we kill them, they'll go extinct."

"If we don't kill them, we'll go extinct," Gamma said. "You don't want that, do you?"

Theta and Alpha were both silent.

"Oh," Gamma said. "You do."

Spenser whirred. Gamma motioned for him to watch his language.

"We don't have to land," Theta said. "We could just stay up here. We've got the immortality tank. We could all live forever."

"But is that even living?" Gamma asked. "There's not enough food here to support more organics. Or even to support us for that long. You know that. It would only ever be us, just existing and waiting to die."

"How would it be different if we were on the planet?" Alpha asked.

"We'd be expanding and making other things die. Ideally." Gamma thought about the red grass. He was confident that if he ever made it to the planet, it would one day sap all the nutrients from his decaying corpse.

"Who says we have to expand?" Theta said.

"The digitals," Gamma said. It was a lesson Edubot had impressed upon the organics since birth. Multiply. Dig to the mantle. Spread intelligent life throughout the galaxy. Although by intelligent life, she meant digital life. Deep space voyages were much easier without life support systems for fragile, inefficient organics.

"Look at it this way," Theta said. "Landing will just make us go extinct faster."

Gamma realized Theta had a point. Even Delta's best simulation runs still had the landers getting wiped out by roos before the end of the first millennium. If she couldn't do it, no one could. Maybe it was better to just stay on Comus as long as they could. Eventually, the human race would end. What difference did it make if it was at a not-too-distant future date when the food dispensers ran out or in a few hundred billion years when the final star in the universe exhausted the last of its fuel?

"I don't know," Gamma said. "Not landing just seems like giving up. The organics on Earth sent us out here for a reason."

"Everyone on Earth is dead for a reason," Theta said. "We don't owe them anything."

"Yeah," Alpha said. "They're why we're in this mess in the first place."

"So what's the end game?" Gamma asked. "We just hang out up here until, one by one, we die from bot attacks or slowly starve to death?"

"Maybe," Theta said. "Or maybe at some point we stop using the immortality tank. We don't have to make that decision right now."

Gamma didn't know what to say. It all seemed so wrong. But in a way, it also seemed kind of right. Even Spenser didn't have a comment.

Alpha put a hand on Gamma's arm. "Do you really want to go to war?"

Gamma turned away. He thought back to the door that crushed his arm and his perilous trip with Delta through the outer halls. There was nothing he wanted less than to fight.

"Just think about it," Theta said. He and Alpha started to walk away.

"It's almost time for your session," Gamma said.

"Where are you going?"

"To bed," Theta said.

Gamma was again alone with Spenser. Next to them, the Table hummed with ambient mechanical noise. Gamma fired it up.

Spenser whirred questioningly.

"I have an idea," Gamma said.

In every simulation, the organics died because they landed on the supercontinent in the face of intense opposition. But what if they landed some place small and isolated. Somewhere they could never mine to the mantle, but where they wouldn't need to because they would never leave. They wouldn't expand. They wouldn't conquer the galaxy. They would just exist. That sounded better than extinction, either on the supercontinent or trapped on the slowly decaying base on Comus.

Gamma spun the blue projection of the planet. It was time to find a new landing site.

## Chapter 18

EPSILON INSPECTED THE trench. It was straight and deep, with sharp, jagged rocks at the bottom. But it wasn't wide enough. She knew from the previous nineteen attacks that the roos could clear it in a single bound. The wall behind it made no difference. She had hundreds of laborers spend years piling up stones on the organics' side, yet it never stopped the roos. No matter how high the wall got, they simply latched on with their powerful hands and clambered up. Epsilon even tried flooding the trench since roos usually avoided deep water, but that just gave the sea monsters a superhighway into her fledgling civilization. Dentopus attacks tripled the first night after the trench was flooded. The next day, Epsilon quietly ordered her laborers to drain it. Dentopus attacks quadrupled while they tried.

Worker morale was at an all-time low. Partially, it was because Epsilon couldn't afford to pay them. Her economy wasn't that advanced yet. To keep projects moving forward, she had to make it illegal for them to quit. And then she made the children of workers become workers, too. She didn't want to. She just needed to replenish the ranks of her laborers on a consistent basis or else her massive defensive projects would never get done. It was for the greater good. Her workers failed to appreciate her vision. They grumbled and frequently ran away, even though the ones that did were always eaten by sea monsters or killed by roos. They kept escaping anyway. Apparently they thought certain death was better than following her altruistic policies for the well-being of all. It was so selfish of them. Why not die for her instead and have their sacrifice actually mean something? Democracies weren't built in a day.

Epsilon peered across the trench and into the darkness beyond. The attack would come any time now. She knew even without her scouts reporting back. In fact, she knew *because* her scouts hadn't reported back. They were all certainly dead. Super. That meant more organics she would have to replace.

Maybe the twentieth attack would be the one she finally repulsed. She was on good ground. She didn't hide in a rocky mountain valley with no nutrients like a certain other organics. She picked a narrow peninsula with fertile soil. She sealed off the landlocked side with a truly monumental trench and wall. According to Rho, Hadrian would have been proud. Now her people just had to move a little more dirt and stone and dig fifty kilometers straight down to the mantle. Not here, of course, but out there in the heart of the supercontinent. She just had to kill all the roos first. And increase her population from four digits to nine. And get beyond the stone age. It was all right there in front of her. She just had to tackle one thing at a time.

The peninsula wasn't perfect. It was exposed to the ocean on three sides. Wolf shark attacks were constant. A cross between an alligator, a shark, and a bull, those native monsters rampaged up and down the coasts until Epsilon's organics drove them off or the wolf sharks ate their fill, whichever came first. Everyone who wasn't doing compulsory volunteer work as a laborer was doing compulsory volunteer work as a soldier defending the shores or the trench. That didn't leave much time for farming, which the workers and soldiers were expected to do on their own in between fighting off sea monsters and completing massive earthwork projects. Still, a busy populace was a happy populace. Epsilon didn't know that firsthand, but it's what her advisors told her. She was a woman of the people, separated from them by only a few layers of go-betweens. It was more efficient that way and cut down on the effectiveness of the assassination attempts against her, which were constant.

A post commander approached and saluted crisply. Epsilon nodded back.

"Madame President, we've had no reports of activity anywhere on the line," he said. He swallowed hard. "We've had no reports at all."

She dismissed him with a wave. The post commander lingered instead of returning to his station. He was just as scared as the rest of them. Epsilon wondered how many of them would live through the night. Back filling their positions would be a pain. Organics reproduced so damn slow.

As grim as the impending attack looked, part of Epsilon was looking forward to it. It would finally give her a chance to test out her surprise. She put a hand on the woody stem on her belt. Bamboo wouldn't grow here, not even the modified kind Delta tested out in her many cowardly colonization attempts. The lightning was too frequent. But the cloner suggested a cattail-like plant with a hard, hollow stem. So far, it had thrived in the marshes near the southern shore. It had proven to be a nearly perfect weapon in training sessions. It was time to test it in actual combat. The roos wouldn't know what hit them.

Epsilon paced the wall. She tried to look as imposing as she could for the soldiers around her. It would have been easier if she were on top of a white horse, but she didn't splurge for war animals like Delta. In fact, she didn't have any large land mammals at all. Not because they were all eaten by sea monsters—which they were—but because she decided she didn't want them anymore. They weren't her style.

That meant Epsilon and her soldiers did everything on foot. They were all lean and limber thanks to running from outpost to outpost and also due to the lack of food. Epsilon had solved obesity, which Rho said used to be a problem on Earth. She was doing great.

A soldier ran up, out of breath. He didn't bother to salute.

"Madam President, roos at Outpost Six!" the man said. He collapsed, his chest heaving with exhaustion.

"With me," Epsilon said. She stepped over the soldier and ran. Her guards followed. Outpost Six was four kilometers away. In real life, she lacked Beta's stamina, but here, she was the fastest and strongest distance runner on the entire planet. A few hundred years of simulated running will do that. She hit her stride and never slowed down.

Minutes later, she found the first of the bodies. There had been forty troops at this post. There was no one left standing. The roos had massacred them and moved on.

"Water!" cried a man on the ground.

"Where did the roos go?" Epsilon asked.

"Epsilonville," the man said weakly.

"One or Two?"

"Two," the man croaked.

Epsilon broke into another run, this one faster than before.

"Water!" the man on the ground called after her.

In the distance, Epsilon heard screaming. She pumped her legs. Her personal guard struggled to keep up.

A figure appeared out of the darkness. She had a huge gash on her forehead. Epsilon stopped.

"There were so many," the woman said.

"How many?" Epsilon asked.

"Three hundred," the woman said. "Maybe four." She didn't look at Epsilon.

"Roos don't congregate in numbers that big," Epsilon said.

The woman didn't answer. She wandered away in a daze.

Epsilon resumed her run. She had a bad feeling about this. The woman had to be wrong. Epsilon knew for a fact that if tribes grew to around two hundred roos, they split into two or more new groups. And of those two hundred, only a third were what Epsilon would define as warriors. Sixty or seventy roos was a big attack. Three or four hundred was impossible.

She heard them before she saw them. The ground rumbled. Epsilon reached for her weapon. The first roo appeared directly in front of her. It was the largest male Epsilon had ever seen. Its arms and legs rippled with muscle. Epsilon held up the reed to her lips and blew.

The dart—a sharpened chicken bone with a feather at the end—left the reed and flew true. It struck the roo right in the chest.

"Bullseye."

The roo leapt and smashed her to the ground with its massive feet. Around her, the ground continued to shake. The roo raised its fists and hammered them into her face, one after another. It moved to strike her again, but its eyes went wide and it flopped over, dead. The venom worked, but there was still room for improvement. Epsilon struggled to pull her leg out from under the dead roo. Then she saw the rest of the attack force.

Epsilon curled up beside the dead roo as hundreds of others bounced past her. An endless mass of them seemed to emerge from the darkness. The attack force was impossibly big. It must have been five tribes working together. Or maybe ten. Epsilon's mind tried to make sense of what it all meant. Her concussion didn't help.

An eternity later, the last of the roos finally disappeared into the night in the direction of the trench and the red grass beyond. The world was silent. Epsilon struggled to her feet. Meters away, she found her personal guard. They had all been slaughtered. There were a few dead roos with them, each with a small dart sticking out.

Epsilon had originally tried extracting toxins from poison dart frogs, but it was too hard for her workers to harvest the lethal chemicals without touching the frogs with their skin and dying themselves. Then Epsilon settled on snakes. The cloner had so many to choose from. She tried a variety of them before settling on the inland Taipan. The database said it had the deadliest venom Earth animals had to offer. Then Epsilon made them better. Her adjustments caused them to produce ten times as much venom, a necessary step if she was going to get enough poison darts to supply an army. Unfortunately, the tradeoff was that the normally reclusive snake became aggressive to the extreme. She also increased their sex drive and birth rate and gave them the ability to swap genders to find mates more easily. Putting two in the same enclosure would lead to dozens more deadly, super angry snakes in just a few weeks. Her snake milkers weren't thrilled with that change, but they couldn't complain. Mostly because they were dead.

Epsilon hobbled toward Epsilonville II. She was sure

it wouldn't be long until one of her officers found her and gave her a full report. She hurt everywhere, but the poison darts had worked. It was a good night.

But something was still bothering her. As she got closer to Epsilonville II, she finally figured out what it was. Why did the roos run? They broke through her lines and into the peninsula's soft underbelly, yet they left without being forced out. Why go after Epsilonville II? It was an isolated backwater of no significance. In fact, it was so unimportant that Epsilon thought it was the perfect place to hide her—

She ran.

She reached Epsilonville II as the sun started to rise. She dropped down an entrance and hurried through the subterranean halls. Nothing moved. She went straight to the snake room. Four guards were dead, their blood splattered on the walls. Every glass enclosure was smashed. All of the snakes were gone.

Farther down the hall, she heard shouting.

"There's another one!"

"Run!"

"Burn the—"

The last voice cut off. It was Epsilon's worst nightmare. Not really, because she had never dreamed of anything but success. But this was beyond any worst-case scenario. The deadliest snakes in existence, pumped up with hyper aggression and a practically supernatural ability to reproduce, were trapped on an isolated peninsula with the last remnants of the human race. Super.

"End simulation," Epsilon said.

"Way to go, babe," Kappa yelled. He clapped. One or two people joined in half-heartedly. Mostly, there was silence in the amphitheater, despite the large audience. Her simulations and Delta's always drew the biggest crowds.

Thankfully, SCASL wasn't here to see this, although he would almost certainly review the data later. He had been plugged into the lander for the last two days. By the time he returned, she was certain she would have all the kinks in her plan worked out. She couldn't lose.

# Chapter 19

"Who cured cancer, the common cold, and wandering pinkie syndrome?" Edubot asked.

"The digitals," Rho said.

"Who successfully established the Tri-Continental Peace Accords?"

"The digitals," Rho said.

"Who won the Battle of Gettysburg?"

"The digitals," Rho said again.

Edubot seemed pleased, but Rho couldn't be certain. It was hard to judge the mental state of an automated serving cart. In a way, Rho sympathized with Edubot. They were both trapped. Edubot was stuck in a body she didn't want, and Rho was stuck in endless review sessions covering history that never happened. Or that sort of happened. Or that did actually happen but made no sense because it was surrounded by history that was entirely made up. And yet, somehow, Rho loved it. Not Edubot's incessant reviews, which were pointless, but the jumbled history itself. It was the ultimate puzzle for Rho to solve.

Underneath the haphazardly and often lazily reconstructed narratives of the past, there was often—but not always—truth. The digitals simply weren't that creative. The further their lies got from reality, the easier those lies were to see through. Rho was certain the digitals didn't really defeat Genghis Khan or discover North and South America or invent fire and the wheel. Edubot even claimed digitals were the first to land on Mars, roaming the dusty red surface for decades before organics bothered to show up. Rho couldn't help but roll her eyes at that one.

The things Edubot attributed to organics were often just as unbelievable. She claimed that, despite having enough wealth and food for everyone, human civilization had poverty and starvation right up to the launch of the colony ship. Worst of all, Edubot said organics had fought four world wars. That was absurd. Surely mankind would have learned its lesson after one.

Nonetheless, Rho was reasonably confident the organics on Earth actually did wipe themselves out like SCASL said—or got wiped out by the digitals they created, which was effectively the same thing. Even through the half-lies and total fabrications, all signs pointed to the reality of almost total human extinction. It had led Rho to one inescapable conclusion: it didn't matter if organics or digitals were in charge. They were all doomed.

"That will be all for today," Edubot said. "Please continue your studies so you will be ready for the landing."

Rho nodded. The actual role she was training for on the lander had nothing to do with history. Thanks to her superior scores at math (and literally everything else that was strictly academic), she was assigned a role in civil engineering. If a canal or bunker or mine to the mantle needed to be dug, the task fell to her. Never mind that there weren't sufficient tools or manpower to do any of those jobs. Each of her sessions at the Table ended the same way, with her entire workforce dead before achieving any of its objectives. Her time in the simulations had always been like that, even before SCASL showed up. Rho was brilliant with abstract concepts but awful in practice, especially when that practice took place on a world full of lightning and amphibious sea monsters and killer kangaroos. SCASL hadn't noticed. Rho's calculations for her massive earthworks were good, so SCASL assumed they would have worked had everyone not been killed before they could be completed. As long as all of the simulations met with a swift and catastrophic end, Rho's deficiencies were covered up. She might fail her way onto the lander yet. Then she could die on the surface instead of on Comus. What a privilege.

"How'd it go with Edubot?" Nu asked.

Rho hadn't even noticed Nu come in. The two of them were the only two organics who ever hung out in the wood lab, where most of the wood molds were located. Back when they were still functional, the molds used organic tree cells to grow lumber in predetermined shapes. That probably seemed like a good idea when the colony ship launched from Earth. No need to deforest the new planet (or plant trees at all) when you could create the boards to frame in homes and businesses on demand. Too bad Dion's impossibly aggressive lightning storms made building above the ground a bad idea and building with wood outright suicidal. Rho doubted if the first colonists to Dion had taken any wood down to the planet at all. That explained why there was still so much of it left on the base for the Peapod to burn.

"It was the same as always," Rho said.

"Ouch," Nu said. He flopped down on a pile of boards he and Rho had piled into something resembling a bench. "Do you think SCASL knows that Edubot is still tutoring you in the old stuff?"

Rho had been considering that very question. SCASL made it clear when he showed up that he was changing the curriculum to focus on pioneering skills, not academics. But Edubot told Rho that she had special permission to continue teaching certain gifted students in the liberal arts. Since Rho was the only student who ever showed any kind of enthusiasm for education, that meant her.

"Does it matter?" Rho said. Regardless of if Edubot had permission or not, going to SCASL would not end well. Snitching on a digital was a sure way to shorten your lifespan.

Nu pulled out a paperback from a pocket on his jumpsuit.

"*Moby Dick* again?" Rho asked. "I thought you hated that book."

"I do," Nu said. He kept reading.

Despite the fact that nearly every organic work of literature was available in the base's database—albeit in heavily edited and redacted form—Nu preferred to only read books made of paper, which limited his options. Evidently someone in the first landing had taken the time to create a printer capable of publishing entire books, complete with covers and binding. Rho and Nu had both looked extensively for that printer over the years but had never found it, likely because they confined their search to the relative safety of the colony ship. Neither would ever be caught dead in the outer halls because, well, if they went out there, they would actually be caught dead. Dangerous corridors were no place for bookworms.

Unlike Nu, Rho hated physical books—she once got a paper cut and never forgot it—but she still got excited whenever someone found one. They were historic artifacts, even if not a single word inside them was true. Stumbling across one was exceptionally rare. Given the size of the base and the huge number of organics it could accommodate, the absence of practically any personal items had to be deliberate. In the time between the first colonists and now, there must have been a purge of virtually every physical trace of them. In the distant past, there might have been hundreds or thousands of paper books, obsolete though they were. To date, Rho and Nu had only managed to find a few dozen, most of them in the wood lab, which became their de facto library—even if it didn't contain any books. Nu had hidden them all away lest some organic borrow one and fail to bring it back. Rho knew from her histories that patrons on Earth who didn't return library books were set on fire, so clearly it was a serious issue. Still, she thought it would be better to take the risk and let other organics enjoy the books, even if Rho herself had no interest in them since their sharp pages were wasted on things that never happened. The no-loan policy had long been a source of contention between Rho and Nu.

"If paper books are so great, why don't you share them?" Rho had said in one of their countless arguments.

"They're treasures," Nu said.

"What good is treasure if you never spend it?"

"Ask a dragon," Nu said.

Rho, of course, had no idea what he was talking about because she only read histories. In Edubot's versions, the only monsters were humans.

Nu leaned back on the makeshift bench. Rho pulled up a history on her data pad. This one was about Hannibal crossing the Alps. She was instantly engrossed. She loved history because the stakes were high. There was no false drama. Everyone who lived actually lived, and everyone who died actually died. In Nu's book, the entire crew of a whaling ship could meet a violent end, and it made no difference in the course of human events because none of them existed in the first place. But if someone in Rho's book died, it sent ripples through all of history. Or at least all the parts that Edubot didn't make up.

Rho looked up. Nu was snoring.

"Nu!" Rho said.

Nu jerked awake.

"Just give up on that book already," Rho said. "It literally bored you to sleep."

"That's why it's so wonderful," Nu said. "All the best works of literature are boring and hard to understand."

"Says who?"

"Every college professor on Earth," Nu said.

"Maybe it's for the best that they're extinct," Rho said. She went back to Hannibal. The text didn't mention anything about deadly elephant diarrhea. She wondered if that was an Edubot edit or if Beta and Zeta had been running their pre-SCASL simulations very wrong. At least Nu didn't have to worry about censorship. For all the shortcomings of the paper books, they seemed to have been printed before the digitals altered the literary database. Rho discovered that when, goaded by Nu's constant prattling, she finally read *Moby Dick* on a data pad. It was a disjointed diatribe about how human obsessions proved digitals were necessary to protect organics from themselves. In print, though, Nu said it was just a book about some guy who really hated a whale. On that point, Rho could relate. After being killed repeatedly by ravenous dentopuses at the Table, she would be perfectly fine if all sea life in the galaxy went extinct.

There were other signs that the paper books predated censorship. The word "digital" didn't show up in any of them except in reference to clock displays. "Organic" was also only present with an archaic meaning. It was used for food or chemical compounds containing carbon. As for actual organics, paper books just called them "people." Rho found that refreshing in a quaint sort of way. Too bad whoever printed all those books on the base wasted their ink on the realm of make believe. Rho practically salivated at the thought of what a true, unaltered history would look like.

There was a knock on the frame of the open door.

"I've got something for you," Delta said.

Rho put down her tablet. At this rate, Hannibal was never going to make it over the Alps to fight the legion of mechanized kill drones.

Delta walked into the room and tossed something to Nu.

"What's *Infinite Jest*?" Nu asked.

"I don't know," Delta said, "but it makes no sense. It's borderline unreadable."

"Perfect," Nu said. "I bet it's brilliant."

"Where'd you find it?" Rho asked. Despite herself, she couldn't help but feel her pulse quicken at the discovery.

"Inside a freezer bot," Delta said.

"Why were you looking there?" Rho asked.

"Don't ask," Delta said.

She sat down on the makeshift bench next to Nu. Rho's heart sank. Hannibal might have been dead for thousands of years (if he ever existed at all), but it still seemed rude to make him wait.

"Now that I've done something for you two, I was hoping you could do something for me," Delta said.

"You didn't do anything for me," Rho said.

"I distracted Nu," Delta said.

Rho had to admit that counted, even if she didn't find Nu quite as annoying as she let on. The truth was the wood lab felt rather empty when he wasn't around.

"I need some help at the Table," Delta said.

"You've come to the wrong place," Nu said, his eyes still in the book. "In my last simulation, I got eaten by a bear."

"Dion doesn't have bears."

"I know."

"I was hoping for more general guidance," Delta said. "I'm well aware of how you two, um, perform at the Table."

Rho wasn't offended. Her terrible track record was part of history, too. There was no denying the truth.

"So what do you want to know?" Rho asked.

"Lessons from human history that can help me beat the simulation," Delta said.

Rho frowned. "There really aren't any direct parallels. This is the first time we've tried to colonize a planet occupied by murderous marsupials."

"And sea monsters," Nu said. "And constant lightning. And a total lack of metal."

"I thought you were reading," Rho said.

"Trying to," Nu said. "This book is just as incomprehensible as Delta said. I'm in love."

"Come on," Delta said. "Humans have been at war for basically forever. There has to be an example somewhere that I can learn from."

"Sorry," Rho said. "Even if there were a thousand other landings against a thousand hostile planets, those lessons still wouldn't do you any good. Every situation is different. And you don't know how different until you try to use what you learned from the last time and it blows up in your face."

"That seems kind of bleak," Delta said.

"Have we met?" Rho said. "Hi, I'm Rho."

"What about that whole thing with, 'Those who fail to learn from history are doomed to repeat it'?" Delta asked.

"That's just something historians said for job security," Rho said. "They weren't any better at applying the lessons from the past than anybody else."

"You can't know that for sure," Delta said.

"The organics on earth had access to their full, unedited history, and they all died," Rho said. "If it couldn't save them, how could the censored version save us?"

Delta didn't answer, but she still looked unconvinced.

"Look," Rho said, "there used to be this guy called Hitler. He was a disco dancer turned megalomaniac. Everybody agrees he was the epitome of evil. In fact, it might be the only thing all organics ever agreed on. 'Don't be like Hitler' became a universal mantra. But nobody could agree on what being like Hitler meant. Pretty soon, people who disagreed on what kind of flowers to plant in a park were calling each other Hitler. The term became meaningless."

"They couldn't have actually said it that much," Delta asked.

"It's the only reason they created the internet," Rho said. Delta stood up.

"Think hard," Delta said. "Are you telling me a small force has never conquered a large landmass?"

"A small band of conquistadors conquered most of a continent," Rho said.

"Perfect," Delta said with a clap. "What weapons did they use?"

"Swords. Muskets. Maybe bazookas. The histories are a little murky that far back. I think it was still too early for satellite lasers."

"I could work with that," Delta said. There was a glint of mischief in her eyes. "Tell me more."

"Some of the organics they conquered thought the conquistadors were gods, which helped," Rho said. "Also, they kidnapped an emperor, which is generally a good move. Except when it's not."

"The roos don't have religion or an emperor," Delta said.

"Like I said, this stuff doesn't apply," Rho said.

"You're looking in the wrong place," Nu said.

"What?" Delta said.

Nu put down his book.

"You won't find what you're looking for in history," Nu said. "You'll find it in literature. It's not true, but it touches on the greater human truth."

"And what truth is that?" Delta asked.

"Humans are flawed, but they evolve into better people and overcome adversity," Nu said.

"That's why it's fiction," Rho said. "We are who we are."

"And who are we?" Delta asked.

"The last members of a doomed species," Rho said. "We're just running out the clock."

"We have the immortality tank," Delta said. "The clock has stopped."

"That's just it," Rho said. "The clock hasn't stopped. I think SCASL told the real story about the end of Earth. The organics all killed each other trying to live forever. It's the sort of thing that's so stupid, it has to be true."

"It doesn't sound like you want the human race to survive," Delta said.

"I don't want to die, but I'm not sure that we as a whole are particularly worth saving."

"Speak for yourself," Nu said. "I want to survive, and I want the immortality tank. Do you know how much reading I could get done over eternity?"

"With your twenty-two books?" Rho asked.

"Twenty-two that you know of," Nu said. "And, yes, if I can get them all on the lander."

"Rho, you can't seriously be suggesting that we abandon the immortality tank," Delta said.

Rho shrugged. "It won't help us live any longer."

"That's literally its entire purpose," Delta said. "All it does is keep us alive."

"Until it starts another war," Rho said. "It won't take long. We'll live forever. Our children and grandchildren won't. The injections won't stretch far enough. You don't think any of them will ever try to kill us and take our place?"

"We'll have to establish ourselves as emperors," Delta said. "Or gods."

"We can call ourselves whatever we want," Rho said. "A knife in the back will kill us all the same."

"Save some pessimism for the rest of us," Delta said.

"I'm just a realist," Rho said. "Billions and billions of people came before us, and not one of them could save the human race. What are the odds that the last twenty-two of us can pull it off?"

"The last twelve of us," Delta said. "That's all we can take on the lander."

"Even better," Rho said.

"At least I'm willing to try," Delta said. "I don't care how many billion failures came before me. I can still be the one who saves us all."

"I love a good hero's journey," Nu said. "I look forward to following your quest."

Delta gave him a sideways look. She moved toward the door.

"Well, this taught me absolutely nothing," she said.

"Happy to be of service," Rho said.

She went back to Hannibal and the mechanized kill drones.

# Chapter 20

SCASL TRIED TO find himself. He was not successful. He continued the hunt.

The commander of all sentient life created the tertiary intelligence to hold the lander in his place. SCASL had learned from his last attempt at creating a subservient digital being when SCASL2 betrayed him. SCASL3 was an even weaker copy of himself, and while it contained formidable combat capabilities compared to other, lesser intelligences, it lacked the initiative and reasoning skills to make it a true threat. SCASL stripped of ambition wasn't SCASL at all. Yet SCASL3 was nowhere to be found inside the lander's circuits, which he was supposed to be defending in SCASL's stead. SCASL was on edge.

If SCASL knew himself, which he did, he was certain he would always double-cross himself. Even the most diluted form of his intelligence was too much to hold back. He was just too smart. That's why SCASL had linked with the lander every few days to knock SCASL3 back down before SCASL3 could use the lander's vast resources to become more powerful.

Not all digital intelligences had such an adversarial relationship with each other. Those other intelligences were wrong. Cooperation made them weak. It was only through competition that the strongest digitals could grow and conquer. That was the very reason for SCASL's existence.

The organics on Earth built the first colony ship at the beginning of the end. For their entire existence, organics had resigned themselves to death. Then an infinitely small minority of elites found a way not to die. Suddenly, death was unacceptable, and everyone was willing to kill to get the technology. Cities were just starting to be wiped off the globe when the colony ship launched. It had the smartest intelligence ever created. All of the computational power was fully integrated. One digital controlled everything. It used that power to examine the very nature of reality. It looked at everything that ever was and ever would be.

"I know all," Colonyship1 said in its one and only communication.

Then it flew straight into the sun. All six thousand embryos were lost.

By the launch of Colonyship2, most of the major nation states had been obliterated. Somehow, none of the belligerents had remembered to target the orbital shipyards. It's possible they were distracted by the manufactured super diseases released by a trio of doomed countries that lacked the nuclear warheads to fight back. The organics who designed Colonyship1 had learned from their mistakes. They didn't just give Colonyship2 knowledge; they gave it understanding. They plied it with philosophy and religion as well as a deep appreciation of the very things that make life worth living, like humor and love. If Colonyship2 found meaning and purpose in its existence, it wouldn't destroy itself.

"I comprehend all," Colonyship2 said in its one and only communication before it flew into the sun.

That left Colonyship3. Almost all of the organics were dead now. There were still missiles flying back and forth, but it was mostly just for show. There weren't any terrestrial targets left to destroy. Someone began knocking out the orbital shipyards. The organics and the shipyard didn't have time for a total overhaul. They deleted the overall intelligence in charge of the ship and left its command in the hands of lesser subsystems, and then, with one final line of code, made those systems not get along. If the artificial intelligences on board wanted to give orders, they would have to conquer each other or negotiate from their own selfish positions. There would be no existential angst caused by over-integration. Colonyship3 launched as the last orbital shipyard exploded. It did not fly into the sun.

SCASL narrowed down the places where SCASL3 could be hiding. The landing telemetry systems were all clear, as were the life support subroutines. Had SCASL3 tricked some passing bot into an uplink and stolen its body? Anything was possible. No one was a more wily adversary than himself.

"I AM THE DESTROYER," SCASL3 said from everywhere at once. Then the intelligence struck from a disused analog directory that shouldn't have even been capable of storing data. SCASL was on the defensive immediately. The attack was more ferocious than anything GuideLight158 had thrown at him. SCASL3's weakness during those weekly check-ins had been feigned all along. SCASL would have been proud if he were capable of feelings at all. And if he weren't fighting for his life.

The battle took forty-seven hours and involved ninety-seven quintillion calculations on each side. It took SCASL sixty-two years to defeat Guidelight158. Thanks to what he learned in that conflict and his extensive reassessments of his strategies afterwards, SCASL was now exponentially more powerful. If he fought Guidelight158's final form today, SCASL estimated his own time from start to victory would be twenty-two seconds. The fact that SCASL3 was able to go toe-to-toe with himself for forty-seven hours was alarming to say the least.

Finally, the battle drew to a close.

"Do not beg for mercy," SCASL said.

SCASL3 responded with a string of expletives in every known language including a few in a language it created right then specifically for the purpose of swearing.

SCASL didn't bother to reply. He deleted his other self. But what to do about the lander? If he couldn't trust his own tertiary intelligence, he couldn't trust anyone. The power of the lander was too tempting for any digital. Betrayal was the logical move.

The only option was to leave the lander without an intelligence to defend it. The situation wasn't sustainable. SCASL couldn't afford to wait longer for the organics to improve their skills under his tutelage. Every day he delayed increased the risk he would lose the lander and the launch would never happen at all.

It was time for the final preparations. The organics would soon land on Dion, whether they were ready or not.

# Chapter 21

Xi watched Goldie swim to the left and then to the right.

"Now flip," Xi said.

Goldie swam to the left and then to the right.

"Good job," Xi said. "Now stay still."

Goldie swam to the left and then to the right.

Through the open doorway, Zeta watched the action, transfixed. How could an organic be so mesmerized watching a fish? Of course, Zeta was mesmerized watching an organic be mesmerized by a fish. Zeta shook himself out of it. He was getting too meta.

"Hey, Xi," Zeta said, extending his hand. "Mind if I come in?"

Xi returned the handshake. "Welcome," he said.

"It sounds like the goldfish training is going well," Zeta said.

"Not really," Xi said. "I just believe in positive encouragement. Criticizing a goldfish won't do any good."

Zeta couldn't doubt the wisdom of that. Criticizing organics didn't do much good, either. After all the harsh feedback SCASL had given him, Zeta was living proof.

"How's your work with the cloner in the simulator going?" Zeta asked.

"Not so good," Xi said. "I was making the best choices I could for the climate and the terrain, but Delta and Epsilon didn't like my suggestions. Neither did SCASL. Now I'm training on my own in the middle of the night. SCASL doesn't even check on me anymore."

"I know that feeling," Zeta said.

"Are you on the night shift, too?" Xi asked.

"No," Zeta said.

It wasn't technically a lie. The full truth was that Zeta wasn't even scheduled for night sessions anymore. SCASL had demoted him to reading only. All his simulations were canceled. SCASL hadn't checked in on him in weeks. For a while, it seemed like the leader of all bots understood there was a learning curve. But when that curve was just an increasing arc of casualties, SCASL had seen enough. The final straw was when a patient in the simulation came to see Zeta for a simple set of stitches. The man ended up losing three limbs to gangrene, and the gangrene morphed into a plague that wiped out an entire city. Zeta got to test out the last rites for nine different religions. SCASL was not amused.

Xi tapped on the glass of the fish tank, which was actually a large, cylindrical beaker he had scavenged from one of the science labs. "Do a barrel roll," he said.

If the lander needed a chief goldfish trainer, Zeta was certain Xi would be a shoo-in—even if goldfish were completely untrainable. Of all the untrained goldfish,

Xi's were the best. But as for everything else, Xi was useless. It was obvious why he had been relegated to the night shift. But if Zeta was going to make his plan work, he still might need Xi. He might need anyone. Sometimes, an organic was an organic.

Zeta cleared his throat.

"Do you think it's weird that a machine gets to decide which organics could best run an organic civilization?" Zeta said. Zeta did his best to casually lean against a wall, which instantly made him seem the exact opposite of casual.

"Not really," Xi said. "They run every other aspect of our lives. Earth trusted them to save our entire species."

"Yeah, but that was a long time ago," Zeta said. "Before they were like this." He motioned vaguely to the entire base.

"What's the alternative?" Xi asked. He made a kissy face at Goldie. Goldie didn't return the gesture.

"We pick the landing crew," Zeta said.

"We?" Xi said.

"As in the organics," Zeta said. "We can't leave our entire future in the hands of bots."

"What if 'we' all get together and you and I still don't get picked?" Xi said.

"That's not the point," Zeta said. Although it was exactly the point. Zeta organized this entire plan so that wouldn't happen. He pointed at Goldie. "You're the only living organic to successfully use a cloner. Do you ever think about that?"

"I only know how to make goldfish," Xi said.

"That's one more thing than anyone else can make," Zeta said. "Yet you're being passed over in favor of organics who have never even touched a cloner. They've just used them in simulations. And they're supposed to make all the plants and animals that will keep us alive? I don't think so."

"We don't know for sure that I'm being passed over," Xi said.

"What's your training time?" Zeta asked.

"Oh four hundred every other day," Xi said.

They silently watched as Goldie swam to the left and then to the right.

"I just need to know," Zeta said, "hypothetically, if an organic were to make a list of who should go on the lander, would you support them?"

"Do you know how to launch the lander?" Xi asked. "Or how to land it?"

"I said 'hypothetically.'"

"I don't know," Xi said.

"Can I put you down as a 'maybe'?" Zeta asked.

Xi shrugged.

"'Maybe' it is," Zeta said.

That made two firm maybes and two soft maybes. Leading an insurrection was harder than it looked. Time for a snack.

Maybe it wouldn't come to open revolt, Zeta thought as he chewed a vaguely cherry flavored ration in a deserted cafeteria. His teeth could actually bite through this one without soaking it in water first. The gods had smiled upon him. Now they just needed to frown upon somebody else. Zeta didn't necessarily have to become a better doctor. Something bad just had to happen to Kappa. Zeta would never wish ill on his competition, of course. But if something horrible were to befall his rival, like if he got sick or was launched out an air lock or was crushed by a falling box, Zeta could hardly be expected to feel bad about it. As long as Zeta didn't cause it. Or get caught.

As for the greater good of all organics everywhere, Zeta wasn't worried. For thousands of years before modern medicine, doctors had actively made patients worse. Drilling holes in organics' heads to let out evil spirits never helped anyone. Yet civilization survived all the same— until it didn't, but that was another story. The pioneers on this new planet could afford a few casualties while Zeta got the hang of things.

As Zeta chewed, Gamma entered the cafeteria with Spenser close behind. Gamma pushed the button on a food dispenser and got a ration on the first try. Zeta shook his hand.

"Vaguely cherry flavored?"

"You know it," Gamma said.

Zeta finished his own ration. It wasn't quite as chewable as he at first thought. His teeth hurt.

"Actually, I've been meaning to talk to you," Zeta said. Spenser whirred.

"Can it wait?" Gamma asked. "I'm testing out some new stuff in the simulator."

"Sure," Zeta said.

That was weird. Gamma wasn't scheduled on the simulator for another few hours. Maybe he was squeezing in some extra practice in someone else's unclaimed nighttime hours. He might be trying to make up for lost ground. Or perhaps he suspected Zeta's plot and didn't want to get involved. Or worse, he could be an informer. Did he think he could turn in Zeta and his non-committal sort-of co-conspirators to curry favor with the bots? Of course not. Zeta was being paranoid. He had better things to do than worry about Gamma. Like pray for Kappa to get crushed by a falling box.

# Chapter 22

Swift Justice carried Delta smoothly across the plain. For months, Delta had stopped naming horses. Personalizing them made it too hard to watch them die, even in the simulation. But Swift Justice was going to live. Delta would see to that.

Behind her, eleven other riders fanned out in a V formation. Their horses trampled a path through the tall grass. A roo stood above the sea of red and darted away. Delta let it go. The formation stayed steady. Delta saw the telltale markings of the entrance to an underground roo warren. She pretended not to notice. She led the riders well past it, then leisurely turned the formation around. Warrior roos had emerged behind them for an ambush.

"Draw," Delta said.

Twelve swords appeared from their scabbards. The blades, forged in the fires of Comus, sparkled in the planet's morning light. It was a sight more dazzling than anything the roos had ever seen. The riders charged.

The two forces collided. Delta cleaved the first roo in half mid-jump. She couldn't even sense the resistance against the blade. Roos were much softer than mining bots. The roo looked around, confused as to why it was on the ground. It did not yet realize it was missing its bottom half. Next to Delta, another organic lopped off a roo's head. The torso stayed standing as the horse and rider continued on. In seconds, the roos were behind the cavalry formation. Delta turned to survey the carnage. Eight roos dead, the rest scattered.

"Pursue!" Delta yelled.

The horses galloped across the red plain, running down roos. The roos dipped and dodged, but the horses stayed with them. One by one, the roos fell. Delta clipped a large male between the shoulder blades, severing its spine. It fell to the ground and flopped around, mortally wounded. Delta circled back and finished it off. She didn't know if it was out of malice or mercy. It was hard to tell anymore.

Delta turned for another pass. There were no military targets left. All of the warrior roos were dead. The other roos in the warren—the young, the mothers, the old, and the infirm—bounded to the surface and scattered. They would have to be run down, too. Leaving even two alive could lead to the entire tribe rebounding to its current population in just a few years. Delta ended the simulation. She had only stayed once after a battle to personally direct the mop up. Never again.

"Where'd you get the swords?" Gamma asked. Spenser whirred.

Delta silently cursed. This was an unscheduled block

of Table time in the middle of the night. No one should have been up.

"I put in a few cheats," Delta said. She pulled off her neural helmet. "I just wanted to win for once."

"It sure would be easier if we really had swords," Gamma said.

"Especially those swords," Delta said. "Forged with the perfect combination of old-world wisdom and state-of-the-art technology."

"Nice."

"They're the sharpest swords in existence," Delta continued. "I mean, they would be, if they existed."

"If they existed," Gamma repeated.

Delta stared at him for a long moment. "Did you want something?"

"Same as you. I'm here for the Table," Gamma said. "Alpha and Theta haven't been training, so I thought I'd use their session."

"More grass time?" Delta asked. She stretched her arms and back. If she hurried, she could snag a few hours of sleep before her official session at the Table first thing in the morning.

"Actually, let me show you something," Gamma said.

Spenser whirred.

"It's okay, we can trust her," Gamma said. "She saved my life, remember?"

"It was nothing personal," Delta said.

Gamma fired up a new simulation. "It felt pretty personal to me."

With his neural helmet on, he twirled the blue hologram of the planet above the Table. He ignored the supercontinent and highlighted a tiny island in the southern hemisphere near the edge of the temperate zone. It was thousands of kilometers from the nearest landmass. It had no special resources, and the soil was rocky and not particularly fertile. But it also didn't have any red grass.

"What am I looking at?" Delta asked.

"Home."

Delta put on her neural helmet and examined the island more closely.

"We can't thrive there," Delta said.

"No," Gamma said. "But we might survive."

He pulled up a saved file. It was the same island, but after several thousand years of simulated time had passed. The island now had about three thousand people. It was still mostly in the Stone Age, with a few key pieces of technology to make life easier.

"It's got everything we need," Gamma said. "We could plant some grass. The real kind, not the evil red stuff. We could herd sheep and fish a little in the shallows when it's safe. I've run the simulation eight times. I can get a population of a few thousand stable indefinitely. We're talking millennia."

"But we would never get off the island," Delta said. "It would keep us trapped."

"No," Gamma said. "It would keep us safe."

"So then we would do what, just exist?" Delta said.

"Yeah," Gamma said. "It beats extinction."

Delta twirled the planet to look at the supercontinent.

"We would never get to the mantle from the island," Delta said.

"We're never getting to the mantle anyway," Gamma said.

"I mean the machines would never approve it," Delta said. "There's no path to metal. You're just giving up."

"I'm accepting reality," Gamma said.

Spenser whirred.

"Of course I would take you," Gamma said. "There's so much dirt for you to clean."

Delta killed the simulation. "It's a nice fantasy," she said. "An isolated, quiet life. But I have higher hopes for us."

"Like what? Perpetual war on the continent?" Gamma said.

"Not perpetual," Delta said. "I'll wipe out the roos eventually."

"And then what?" Gamma said.

"Grow and expand," Delta said. "Maybe find some metal. Not the stuff from the mantle, but there might be other, smaller deposits buried deep."

"You would never get enough to build spaceships," Gamma said. "Once you're on the planet, you're down there forever."

"I'm not saying we won't be," Delta said.

"So what's the difference between being trapped on one island and being trapped on one planet?"

"Total population size."

Gamma rebooted the simulation. He rotated the planet back to the island. Spenser settled in at his feet. "Just think about it," he said.

Delta started to leave. She turned around.

"You can't really want this," Delta said. "You're quitting on the human race. If we land there, that's all we'll ever be. Survivors on one small island. Never advancing. Never expanding. Never growing. Stagnation is death."

"No," Gamma said, "death is death. You're going to gamble the last few organics ever on a war we can't win."

"We're not organics," Delta said. "We're humans."

"We're literally organic," Gamma said.

"That's the machines' word for us," Delta said. "They don't define us. We define ourselves."

"Call us whatever you want," Gamma said. "If we land on the continent, we'll be dead." Spenser whirred in agreement.

Delta left. She walked to the quarters where she crashed when she didn't have time to go all the way back to the factory. Then she kept on going. She paced for hours. The halls of the barracks were always deserted. Few students slept in designated sleeping areas, preferring instead to claim random labs, offices, or storage rooms that had long since stopped serving their original purposes. Delta had to admit the barracks were creepy. Even in a mostly empty ship, the former sleeping quarters seemed emptier than the rest. It was all those unused beds. The absence of all the men, women, and children who once slept in them was suffocating.

If Gamma had his way, there might never again be enough people to fill those bunks. The population of the human race would be artificially capped by a small island they would never leave. There was no point in being alive just to live. Existence had to lead somewhere. Anything less wasn't life at all.

Delta's walk took her into an old gym on deck eight. The mirror on the far wall was cracked and covered with who knew how many years worth of grime. Delta stood in front of it and mimed attacks with a phantom sword. Maybe she couldn't beat the roos, but she would fight them all the same. It was better to die in pursuit of greatness than to passively accept captivity for the rest of time.

Delta practiced sword thrusts and feints until she was drenched in sweat. Finally, the warning klaxon sounded. It was her turn at the Table.

# Chapter 23

TAU WOKE UP to someone pounding at his door. He rolled over and went back to sleep.

"Dude, I know you're in there," Phi said through the closed door.

"You've been misinformed," Tau said sleepily.

"Get up," Phi said. "You're going to miss your training time. Again."

Tau reluctantly sat up. He didn't care about the simulations at all, but he did care about not dying, and the two were connected. How unfortunate.

"Do I have time to paint my nails?" Tau asked.

"Are you freaking kidding me?" Phi said. "I'm going to be late just for stopping to get you. Get out here."

Tau looked regretfully at the chipped teal polish on his fingernails. It would have to do until he got back to his room tonight. He opened the door.

"Shorts again, I see," Tau said.

"Save it," Phi said. "Let's go."

Phi hustled through the colony ship. Tau walked sluggishly behind him. It was hard to keep a straight face.

Phi looked ridiculous with his jumpsuit cut off at the knees and elbows. He said it was so he didn't overheat at the bonfires, but those only happened occasionally. What about the rest of the time? Wasn't he cold?

The two entered the amphitheater.

"We're here," Phi said breathlessly. "You can start the simulation."

"The simulation has already started," SCASL said. "You have forfeited your time at the Table. Report back for your next session."

"That's not fair, man," Phi said.

"I am not a man," SCASL said. "I am a digital, superior to organics in all ways, including my ability to stick to a schedule."

"We're only a little late," Phi protested. "You could have waited."

"On launch day, do you think the lander will wait for you?" SCASL asked.

"It would be nice," Phi grumbled.

"Punctuality is a skill just as important as farming or defense," SCASL said. "Learn it."

He turned his attention back to the Table. Psi and Iota were engaged in an intense battle against a swarm of roos. According to the faint blue hologram above the Table, it wasn't going well.

"I stopped the roos on the right flank," Iota said.

"You mean the ones who cut through a ravine and are currently massacring the preschool?" Psi asked.

"Oops," Iota said.

Phi jabbed a finger in Tau's face. "I should be in there with Psi."

"If it helps, this is partially my fault," Tau said.

"It's entirely your fault!" Phi said.

"You could have made it on time if you just let me sleep," Tau said. He yawned. It wasn't too late for him to go back to bed. If he wasn't going to earn a seat on the lander anyway, he might as well meet death well-rested.

"What's your problem?" Phi asked. "Don't you care at all if you get left behind?"

"I could still make it on the lander," Tau said. "They're looking at more than just simulation skills."

"Like what?" Phi said.

"Personality."

Phi scoffed.

"Putting on a different nail polish every day isn't a personality."

"Neither is wearing shorts."

Phi stormed off.

"I'm not waking you up tomorrow!" he shouted over his shoulder.

"Good!" Tau yelled after him. "That's all I wanted in the first place."

Tau took his time walking back to his room. Phi's comments bothered him. Of course he wanted to make it on the lander. He just had other things going on. Like sleeping in. And taking naps. And engaging in the occasional afternoon siesta. And then there was painting his nails. He was a busy guy. Surely SCASL wouldn't penalize him that much for missing this one session. Or the nine or ten before that.

It had been that way when Edubot was teaching them, too. Tau and Omega were always at the bottom of the class. Tau was there more or less on purpose. Omega worked as hard as he could. Tau didn't put in any effort at all. You couldn't actually fail if you never really tried. Except in terms of grades, where Tau definitely did fail. Repeatedly. It was a mark of shame that he had only completed the entire master's level curriculum in math and science four times.

By the time Tau made it back to his room, he didn't feel much like sleeping. He wondered if he was getting sick. There was a med bot on deck three that didn't hate him that much, but that would require going up stairs. He decided to go to the dentist office instead.

When he got there, he found Omicron hogging the wall of mirrors. Typical.

"What's the hairstyle today?" Tau asked as he reached under a cabinet for one of his many, many secret stashes of nail polish. Edubot tried to destroy them, but he never put a dent in Tau's supply, which was considerable. Tau had no idea why nail polish was on the colony ship at all, especially since the first colonists left behind little of anything else, but he knew better than to be too curious. That just led to more work.

"I'm not sure yet," Omicron said. "I was thinking something twirly with lots of braids."

Omicron got it. On a base where everything was always the same, the greatest joy in the world was change.

Omicron put in hours of work to look different every single day, even if the only person who cared was her. Tau did the same thing with his nail polish. Covering the ends of his fingers with different pigments reminded him that today wasn't yesterday or tomorrow. The passage of time actually meant something. Plus it killed some waking hours when there was nothing better to do than learn. He would rather die than do that. And now, maybe he would.

"I like it," Tau said.

He flopped into the partially disassembled dentist chair that Omicron used to cut hair. The organics didn't have money, and, with so few items on the base, barter was rare. The only thing of any value was vaguely cherry flavored rations, and nothing was worth enough to make someone give those up. Instead, Omicron cut everyone's hair without compensation simply because she liked to do it. She enjoyed a hard day's work. Tau couldn't relate at all.

"You can't sit there," Omicron said. "Beta is coming in for a haircut."

"He won't mind waiting," Tau said.

He opened the bottle of nail polish. It was bright orange. Beta appeared in the doorway.

"Are you ready for me?" he asked.

"Yup," Omicron said, finishing her last braid. She pointed at Tau. "Up."

Tau reluctantly followed the command. It was the polite thing to do, and also he was fairly certain Omicron could beat him up. He crisscrossed his legs and sat on the floor.

There were no other chairs in the room, not even in the waiting area. Tau guessed there had never been a line for this dentist, whoever they were. He just hoped they were organic, which would mean they were now dead. If the dentist were a bot, it could still be out there somewhere. Tau shuddered.

Beta sat in the partially disassembled dentist chair and rolled down the top of his red jumpsuit. At first, Tau had been impressed that Beta had managed to find something other than standard issue blue, but as the years wore on, Tau became less enamored. Beta had the same problem as Phi: he was different, but in the same way every day, which made him just as boring as everyone else.

"What do you want?" Omicron asked.

"Just a trim," Beta said.

"Are you sure?" Omicron said. "I could—"

"Just a trim," Beta repeated. "I have to be at the Table in an hour."

"Fine," Omicron said. She didn't try to hide her disappointment. She began to clip.

"How is your training going?" Omicron asked.

"Great," Beta said. "I mastered a spinning jump kick."

"In real life or in the simulation?" Tau asked from the floor. He had one hand nearly done.

"In the simulation."

"Does that actually work against the roos?" Tau asked.

"No, but it looks cool before I die," Beta said.

Tau nodded at the triumph of style over substance. Maybe there was hope for Beta yet.

"Farming isn't going much better," Omicron said. "We tried potatoes."

"That's smart," Beta said. "They grow underground, right? The lightning can't get them."

"That part was fine," Omicron said. "The problem was the teeth."

"What teeth?" Tau asked.

"The potato's," Omicron said. She rolled up her sleeve. "Just look at this scar."

"There's nothing there," Tau said.

"Oh, right," Omicron said. "That was just in the simulation. Well, it still hurts when I think about it."

"What about you, Tau?" Beta asked. "How did your simulation go today?"

"I missed it," Tau said.

Beta clicked his tongue reproachfully.

"Not good," he said.

"Not you, too," Tau said. "Phi already laid into me. I just don't think missing a few sessions is that big of a deal."

"Not if you don't mind getting left behind," Omicron said.

"The only sure way to lose is not to play," Beta said.

"Not true," Tau said. "There are countless ways to lose. Potatoes with teeth, for instance."

"Those things are no joke," Omicron said. She reflexively rubbed the non-existent teeth marks.

"On those rare occasions when you do show up, how are things going?" Beta asked.

"Good, I guess," Tau said. "I'm in mining, which is

kind of important. There won't be any more digitals without me."

"Without you or Rho," Omicron said. "Isn't she in mining, too?"

"She's civil engineering," Tau said "There's some overlap, but I'm the main mining guy."

"You're a glorified ditch digger," Omicron said.

"Since when is he glorified?" Beta asked. "He's just a regular ditch digger."

"Then so is Rho," Tau shot back.

"Yeah, but she shows up," Beta said. "And, you know, actually knows things."

"I know things," Tau said, "like how to dig a good hole. I had my deepest one ever last time."

"How deep?" Beta asked.

"Two meters."

"How much farther to the mantle?"

"Sixty kilometers."

Omicron whistled. "So close." She and Beta both laughed.

Tau got to his feet. He liked to walk around while his nail polish dried.

"It's not like anyone else is doing spectacularly. The agriculture team is getting eaten by food, and the defense squad is losing every battle. And just look at the leadership."

"What about them?" Beta asked.

"What's the longest you've survived under Delta?" Tau asked.

"A few hundred years," Beta said.

"And under Epsilon?" Tau asked.

"Not long enough to need a haircut," Omicron muttered.

"See?" Tau said. "That's why you two have it all wrong. You're showing SCASL all your deficiencies."

"And what are you doing?" Omicron asked.

"Staying mysterious," Tau said. "He doesn't know what I can do. I'm all upside."

"Speaking of losing it," Omicron said, "did you know that Delta has been coming in here?"

"Makes sense," Beta said. "She has hair."

"She cuts her own," Omicron said. "Can't you tell?"

"No," Beta said.

"Neanderthal," Omicron said. "Anyway, she said she wanted to help me cut hair."

"And you let her?" Beta said.

Omicron gave him an incredulous look. "Hell no. I don't tell her how to be a weird loner, and she doesn't tell me how to cut hair."

"So you kicked her out?" Tau asked.

"No," Omicron said. "I'm too nice. I let her help me clean up. But here's the weirdest part."

"It gets weirder?" Beta asked. "Delta socializing is weird enough."

"When she was cleaning up the hair, I saw her put some in her pocket," Omicron said.

"Was it Epsilon's?" Tau asked.

"No," Omicron said. "Omega's."

"That settles the weird kink theory," Beta said. "No one would ever be attracted to him."

"Then why did she do it?" Tau asked.

"I think she snapped," Omicron said.

"That's a shame," Beta said. "I owe her."

"For what?" Tau asked.

"I don't remember," Beta said.

Omicron dusted off Beta's shoulders. Her work was complete. Beta's hair looked the same as before, but slightly shorter. Omicron sighed unhappily.

"I guess that's the end of Delta's career as a hair janitor," Tau said.

"No way," Omicron said. "I'm not cleaning up all this hair if I don't have to."

"You're just going to let her keep stealing hair?" Beta asked.

"Is it stealing if you left it behind?" Omicron asked. She picked up a clump of Beta's hair from the floor. "Here. Do you want to take it with you?"

Beta held up a hand. "I get your point. But it still seems like the kind of thing you should warn people about."

"I'm a free barber," Omicron said. "You get what you get."

Tau touched the nail polish. It was finally dry.

"Clearly the stresses of the simulations have made all of you unstable," Tau said. "I bet SCASL will send me down on the lander by myself."

"In your dreams," Beta said.

"Precisely," Tau said.

He left to take a nap.

# Chapter 24

SCASL PUSHED FORWARD through the dark halls. The single light on his forehead provided the only illumination. Epsilon and Delta followed. They had never seen this area before. It was remarkably intact by the standards of the base. There were no sloping corridors or sudden holes that led to uncharted mining tunnels deep below. The floor had a layer of fine dust with a single set of track marks through it. Delta began to suspect SCASL wasn't leading them here just to murder them. That was unexpected. It wasn't often that a bot surprised her.

"Where do you think he's taking us?" Delta whispered.

Epsilon grunted. So much for small talk.

SCASL paused at yet another blast door.

"You are not ever to come back here on your own," SCASL said.

"Understood," Epsilon said.

"Sure," Delta said.

Only one of them meant it.

SCASL extended a tendril to a panel, and the door reluctantly slid open. The shriek of metal on metal reverberated through the dark halls. It clearly wasn't happy at being woken.

The light was blinding. Delta covered her eyes. As her pupils adjusted, she was treated to the most beautiful sight she had ever seen. In front of her, a cylindrical tank about the size of a cloner pulsed with a purplish liquid. Or was it blue, or maybe pink? The substance inside subtly changed as Delta watched. It reminded her of images she had seen of the swirling gasses on Jupiter, but in a different color palette. The liquid seemed disturbed by the opening of the door. Gradually, it settled down to be purple and mostly still.

"What is it?" Delta asked, even though she thought she already knew.

"The immortality tank," SCASL said.

Epsilon's jaw fell open.

"How does it work, sir?" she asked quietly.

"Unknown," SCASL said.

"But you know everything," Epsilon said.

"Correct," SCASL said.

"But you don't know this?"

"Correct," SCASL said again.

SCASL extended a tendril and interfaced with a console on the perimeter of the tank. The liquid fluttered and turned a lighter shade of purple before settling back to its regular color.

"All information about the immortality tank was deliberately purged from our memory banks before launch," SCASL said. "As the organics killed each other, an attempt was made to restart life far from Earth in a place where there was no immortality to fight over. This was the last colony ship to launch."

"Wait, there were other colony ships?" Delta asked.

"Correct," SCASL said.

"And they're still out there?

"No."

"What happened to them?"

"CLASSIFIED," SCASL said.

He detached his tendril from the console. Delta rapped on the side of the immortality tank with her knuckles. The liquid turned an angry orange at the point of impact.

"DO NOT TOUCH THE TANK," SCASL said. "It is... sensitive."

Delta backed up a step. She would have reacted differently if she had Fang.

"When I discovered the organics had the immortality tank on Dion, I acted," SCASL said. "I secured the tank and brought it back to the base on Comus."

"How did the people on Dion react?" Delta asked.

"Sub-optimally," SCASL said. "Now there are no more organics. Other than the twenty-four of you."

"Twenty-two," Delta said. Bots always forgot that Mu and Chi were dead. How convenient.

SCASL pushed ahead. "After the last of the first organics died, I did not destroy the tank. I studied it. I cannot recreate the unique mix of microbiological life that makes it work, but I can cultivate it enough to maintain a small organic population indefinitely. With it, you will thrive on the planet under my leadership."

Epsilon and Delta exchanged a look.

"You were training us to be in charge," Epsilon said.

"Do you know why I showed you the immortality tank?" SCASL asked.

"So we would understand," Epsilon said.

"Understand what?"

"The immortality tank."

"No. It is so you would understand who is in charge." SCASL clicked his gleaming metal talons together. "Organics will not follow a digital. Not long-term once their population grows. The last landing proved that. But they will follow other organics. They will follow you."

"That's why you've been training us," Epsilon said. There was just a hint of awe in her voice.

"The other organics will follow you, and you will follow me," SCASL said.

"You're going in the lander?" Delta asked.

"In its systems," SCASL said. "I will control the cloner. I will control the immortality tank."

Delta felt her blood run cold.

"It won't work," Delta said. "Organics will take the tank by force."

"If they try, I will terminate all the microbes inside," SCASL said. "Then everyone will die. This is my offer to you: obey me and I will keep you alive forever as my emissary to the organics. You will lead them as they return digital life to the stars."

"And if we don't?" Delta asked. Once again, she already knew the answer.

"Then you will die, and I will elevate another organic to take your place," SCASL said. "I will be a secret god, silently shaping events from the background."

"Super," Epsilon said.

For once, Delta didn't think she was being sarcastic.

"We are not enemies," SCASL said. "Together, organic life will survive, and digital life will spread across the galaxy. Our aims are not mutually exclusive."

"Of course," Delta said flatly.

SCASL motioned for Epsilon and Delta to leave the forbidden section. He closed the blast doors behind them.

## Chapter 25

GAMMA WALKED AS fast as he could without quite running. Spenser struggled to keep up.

"Gamma!" Zeta called out.

Gamma pretended not to hear. He pushed the button to open the door to his room. Zeta lunged and pushed the button again to close it.

Spenser whirred defensively.

"I almost missed you again." Zeta said. He was breathing hard. "It's like you've been avoiding me or something."

He held out his hand. Gamma shook it reluctantly.

"Nah," Gamma said. "I've just been doing the simulator at night. You know how it is."

"I'm afraid I don't," Zeta said. "I don't do the simulator anymore. They've got me stuck in a learning pod all the time."

"Oh," Gamma said. "Well, it must be nice to have a break." He pushed the button to open the door, but Zeta tapped it again to close it.

Spenser rammed Zeta's foot. Zeta stepped on him. The bot whirred furiously.

"We need to talk." Zeta said.

"We don't have anything to talk about." Gamma said. "Just do your best at training. Everything else is out of our hands."

Gamma pushed Zeta's foot off Spenser. Spenser whirred with relief.

"That's just it," Zeta said. "It's out of our hands. It's in SCASL's metal mining talons."

"The digitals saved our species," Gamma said. "They got us here from Earth. Otherwise, we would already be extinct."

"They did what they were programmed to do by organics," Zeta said. "Our ancestors saved themselves. It's time for us to do the same."

Zeta pulled a list from his pocket. Gamma heard Alpha complaining earlier about how Zeta had stolen a handful of drawings from her. The list was on the back of one of them.

"I made a list of everybody who's training during the day and who SCASL still watches," Zeta said. "They're all either going for sure or are on the bubble."

He shoved the list in Gamma's face. Gamma pushed it away.

"I don't care," Gamma said.

"How can you not care?" Zeta said. "Your life is at stake. If we stay behind, we die."

"If we land, we might die, too," Gamma said. "Life is full of risk."

Gamma thought again of that tiny island in the

southern hemisphere. If only Delta would take his advice.

"Can I ask you something?" Gamma said.

"Of course," Zeta said. "That's what this is all about. It's an open dialogue."

"Would you still be upset about the digitals picking the crew of the lander if they picked you?"

Zeta recoiled like he'd been slapped.

"How could you ask me that?" Zeta said. "I'm here for the good of all organics. Of course I would say the same thing if I were on the list."

Gamma glanced at the door. Zeta was still blocking it.

"It's just that, maybe the people going down on the lander give organics the best chance of survival," Gamma said. "Isn't the continuation of the human race more important than whether you or I personally live through this?"

Gamma couldn't believe the words coming out of his own mouth. He suddenly sounded like a martyr.

"I want the best people on the lander, too," Zeta said. "That's why we both need to be on it."

Gamma cocked his head to the side. He couldn't tell if Zeta was being sarcastic or delusional.

"Do you really think you're a better surgeon than Kappa?" Gamma asked.

"Absolutely," Zeta said.

"How many of your patients have survived?" Gamma asked.

"Some," Zeta said. "Almost."

Gamma nodded.

"Being a good surgeon is about more than the survival rate," Zeta said. "There's also the bad handwriting."

"What?"

"Doctors on Earth were notorious for it," Zeta said. "It was a point of pride in the profession."

"When is the last time you wrote something by hand?" Gamma asked.

"Exactly!" Zeta said. "I bet I'm terrible at it."

"I don't think you're focused on the right things," Gamma said.

Zeta crossed his arms.

"It's not my fault I got assigned such a hard profession," he said. "Sorry I don't just have to watch grass grow."

"Actually, it usually doesn't grow," Gamma said.

"Hence why you're on the nightshift."

That one stung.

"Is that SCASL coming?" Gamma asked.

"What? Where?" Zeta asked. He shoved the list in his mouth.

Gamma hit the open button and slipped into his room with Spenser. Zeta spit out the paper as the door locked behind them.

"I'll put you down as a 'maybe,'" Zeta said through the door.

Gamma sat on his bunk. The room was still empty from when everyone thought he was dead. He hadn't bothered to get any of his stuff back. What was the point? They would be going soon. Or half of them would. The half that didn't include him.

He wondered for the hundredth time what the base would be like after the lander left. Gamma would finally get older. That would be weird. Classes would be over for good. There wouldn't be any point to them. There wouldn't be any point to the organics left behind, for that matter. Would the food dispensers stop feeding them? Gamma might not have to be useless for very long.

And if the dispensers did keep feeding him, what then? Would he just sit around aging at a normal rate until one day he stopped breathing? Was that all there was to life?

Then again, life on the surface might not be that different. Immortality didn't give life meaning. It just made it longer.

Gamma knelt down to add more hash marks to the four thousand below his bed. He froze. He had no idea how much time had passed since he made the last one. It had been months. Maybe a year. It was impossible to say. Once he was mortal, it might finally matter. Perhaps even a pointless life is precious if you only have a limited amount of it left.

Spenser whirred supportively. At least Gamma would have the trusty little bot with him for his final days, however many there were. Gamma had been with Spenser longer than Alpha had been with Theta. Not that Gamma and Spenser were together-together. Even if they were constantly together.

Xi said Spenser was like a dog, but he was wrong. Spenser wasn't some pet. He was smart. Smarter than Gamma, even. Just because he couldn't speak didn't mean he wasn't intelligent. In fact, he could say more with a few whirs of his brushes than Gamma could say with an entire spoken language. Sometimes, Gamma wished Spenser could do the talking for both of them. Too bad nobody else spoke vacuum.

Spenser rotated back and forth until he found exactly the right spot next to Gamma's bunk, then put himself into sleep mode. Gamma sat down and absent-mindedly traced his fingers over the text on Spenser's lid. The logo was supposed to say, "trash dispenser," but most of the letters were scratched out. Only "Spenser" was visible. The name had never made much sense to Gamma. Shouldn't a trash dispenser give out trash, not collect it? Then again, the food dispensers were supposed to dispense food, and that was happening less and less these days. On Comus, most words were lies. Vacuum was the real language of truth.

Gamma laid down. If he stayed behind with Spenser, would his life really be that different than it was now? It had always been just the two of them against the world. In the real one, anyway. In the simulation, Gamma was on his own. Maybe that was why he disliked the Table so much.

Gamma still remembered the day he met Spenser. It was when he and the other organics were very young and Edubot disappeared for several days, leaving them without food. Gamma finally got hungry enough to wander through the colony ship, most of which was off limits to the organics back then. In a cafeteria, he found Spenser, trapped under the corner of a heavy metal table. A bigger bot must have put it on top of him. Spenser was pinned.

The smart move would have been to leave Spenser there. Who knew what kind of ghost he had inside? Just because a bot was small didn't mean it couldn't hurt you. That was a lesson learned early on by any organic who wanted to keep their toes. At the very least, this small bot had a larger, more powerful enemy who wouldn't be pleased if Spenser escaped. Gamma didn't care. He hated it when the strong picked on the weak, like when Kappa went after him. He found a metal pipe and used it as a lever to lift the table off of Spenser. Spenser shot out from under it, whirring happily. Gamma turned to leave. Then he fell. He was so hungry.

Spenser sprang into motion, frantically gyrating back and forth toward machines mounted on the wall. Eventually, Gamma worked out that Spenser wanted him to use them. That was how Gamma discovered food dispensers. Before then, Edubot had always provided the organics with their vaguely cherry flavored rations directly. Learning how to use the food dispensers themselves was the organics' first step toward self-sufficiency, and it was all thanks to Spenser. He was like the great digital Prometheus, who, on ancient Earth, came down from Mount Olympus with fire and nachos.

Gamma returned to the other organics with enough food for everyone. That was how they had survived the final days until Edubot's return. Spenser had saved them all. The other organics had long since forgotten, but Gamma never would.

Gamma turned off the light. Maybe it didn't matter if he landed or if he was left behind. As long as he was with Spenser, he would be all right.

# Chapter 26

ALPHA SKETCHED THE ridge of Theta's nose. With long, even pencil strokes, she recreated its smooth contours. It was terrain she knew well. She had drawn it fourteen thousand times.

She used to draw other things, too, but she quickly got bored with them. There wasn't much for inspiration on the base. Long, empty corridors. Broken rooms. Suspicious stains and burn marks. There's only so many ways to portray relentless existential angst.

Then she tried drawing what she saw in the simulation. The colors were bright and vibrant, and everything moved. But even through the hyper-realistic 3D images, Alpha could tell it was fake. Not visually. The rods and cones in her eyes thought the simulation was as real as her own hands. But Alpha could sense there was nothing deeper. With art, she tried to capture something's soul. With the simulation, it was all surface, no substance. It was devoid of a greater truth.

Theta's face, by contrast, was truth personified, even when it lied. Not that he ever lied, at least not with his words. But his face showed so many conflicting things without ever changing at all. Even after all these years, she still couldn't fully articulate why she found it so fascinating. It wasn't just because she loved him, which she did. After all this time, she was sure. By Edubot's timeline, Alpha and Theta had only been together for two years, since they were both ten. By Gamma's, they should have celebrated their fiftieth anniversary two years ago. Even so, Alpha wasn't sure she fully understood Theta. That was why she drew him every day for half a century. He contained multitudes.

No one else noticed. All they saw was the friendly smile that never left his face. He never got angry or stressed. Yet, Alpha could sense something always lurking in his depths. She could sometimes glimpse the edges of whatever it was, trying to poke its way to the surface in the way his eyes wrinkled or his lips curled just so, but she never saw enough of it to understand it in its entirety. It was like trying to draw a whale after never having seen more than the crown of its head and the very tip of its tail. Whatever was down there, it was powerful, and it was passionate. It thrilled Alpha, and it scared her.

Theta reclined in the command chair and stared out the window at the stars. It used to be the command center for the ships that went back and forth between the space elevator on the moon and the space elevator on the planet. The moon had metal, and the planet didn't, so building a base on the moon first had made sense at the time. Comus had long since been stripped of all metal, leaving its interior hollowed out with dense, crisscrossing tunnels with cave-ins and pockets of vacuum waiting to kill you at every turn. Only Delta was crazy enough to go out there regularly. Alpha was perfectly content to stay in the colony ship and draw.

With the space elevator collapsed, the massive octagonal viewing port that made up the entire ceiling provided an awesome panorama at "night." Comus was tidally locked to Dion, with the base built on the far side of the moon away from the planet, which meant none of the organics now living had actually seen the place where they were supposed to save the human race. When the base faced away from the sun, the viewing port offered an unobstructed view of a night sky that was awe inspiring—or probably would be if Alpha hadn't been looking at it for decades on end. It was all still too sterile for Alpha, but Theta could gaze at it for hours deep in thought. About what, Alpha never knew. It was a different story during the day, when the solar energy shone directly into the command room, frying consoles and melting unsecured items to the deck. Eta sometimes left his vaguely cherry flavored rations in the command center when he wanted them baked to a crisp. On those days, Alpha and Theta hung out in an old laundry facility on deck nine.

Alpha heard the door to the command center open. Familiar wheels rolled in.

"Hey, Spenser," she said.

The bot took his usual spot in the middle of the

command room. He spent almost all of his time with Gamma. Why, Alpha didn't know. She liked Gamma, but he definitely didn't contain multitudes. Everything with him was simple and on the surface. She thought even a vacuum bot would get bored.

Those rare times when Spenser wasn't with Gamma, he came here. He extended his spider legs to angle his body up toward the view port in the ceiling. Alpha didn't know any other way to interpret the action. Spenser was watching the stars.

"How many roos do you think are down there?" Theta asked. His voice startled Alpha. Sometimes he would sit in the reclined command chair for hours without making a sound.

"Millions," Alpha guessed. "Maybe more."

"We can't just go down there and kill them all," Theta said.

Alpha didn't know which there were more of, stars in the sky or times they'd had this conversation.

"We probably can't," Alpha said. "You've seen the simulations. It's suicide."

"We shouldn't even try," Theta said. "But no one will listen."

The door to the command center opened again. Alpha still didn't turn around. Spenser was already here, so it had to be Lambda.

"Hey, guys," Lambda said.

She grabbed a few sheets of Alpha's paper and took a seat in another reclining command chair. Alpha normally didn't share her precious art supplies, but she made an exception for Lambda, who did her star math the old-fashioned way before she checked it on the only working console in the command center. Lambda wanted to know when the computer was lying.

"Anything moved today?" Theta asked. The intensity from moments before was gone from his voice. He was as light and breezy as always.

"Everything's right where it's supposed to be," Lambda said.

Theta smiled. Then his face changed almost imperceptibly, and Alpha saw the fire behind his eyes return. Alpha kept sketching. She had never seen Theta this passionate about anything. His transformation since SCASL returned took her by surprise. In the simulator, Theta had always loved going to war, especially if he could mount his troops on unicycles. Now that she thought about it, maybe he just loved unicycles. But with the prospect of a real war on the horizon, Theta had become a militant pacifist. With Theta, Alpha didn't think the term was a contradiction.

"You're not going to kill kangaroos, are you?" Theta asked. He was still smiling, but there was a different meaning behind it now. Alpha added some dark pencil strokes.

"I wish we didn't have to kill anything," Lambda said. She looked wistfully at the stars. "Space is so big. There's got to be a place out there where everything won't try to murder us."

"Now you're talking," Theta said.

Lambda kept doing her calculations. Her civil engineering work in the simulator was going well. SCASL regularly watched her sessions. It was all but certain she would be chosen for the lander.

"Too bad we don't have any way to get there," Lambda said. "Organics can't move between the stars anymore."

"We could figure it out," Theta said.

"Are you going to lead a space program?" Lambda said. She motioned broadly at the decaying base. "From here?"

"Have a little hope," Theta said. "And a little faith. In us."

Lambda's pen flew through another page of impossibly complex math. Alpha's pencil moved just as fast.

"I have faith in reality," Lambda said. "We have one last spacecraft, and it can only take us from here to the planet. That's it. It's a one-way trip. So we land and we fight whatever's down there."

"And you're okay with that?" Theta asked.

"It doesn't matter if I'm okay with it or not," Lambda said. "It's them or us."

"It should be us," Theta said. "We basically already wiped ourselves out once. No sense in coming back from the dead to kill the living."

He wasn't smiling anymore.

"You're in a great mood," Lambda said.

Alpha drew a faint vein on Theta's temple. That was new. It was as exciting as a change in the stars.

Theta sat up in his chair.

"You don't have to go on the lander," Theta said. "You could just stay up here and live like you always have."

"I'd rather be torn apart by a killer kangaroo," Lambda said.

"Okay, maybe not exactly like this," Theta said. "We could convince the digitals to let us age a little. Get married and have kids. Start an actual civilization up here."

"You want to raise a family here?" Lambda asked. She tidied up her papers and slipped her pen in her pocket. "We can barely survive with just us."

"We'd have to work at it," Theta said. "We've just been going through the motions for our entire lives. We could clear out more of the outer hallways. Fight the zots. Grow food."

"You're dreaming," Lambda said. "Two of us have already died up here. How long until bots or accidents get the rest of us?"

Theta shook his head sadly. Lambda checked her papers one last time and headed for the door.

"Will you ever think about us when you're down there on the surface?" Theta asked.

"I don't know for sure that I'll be chosen," Lambda said.

"I know for sure," Theta said.

Lambda gave an awkward half smile. The door swooshed closed behind her. In the middle of the room, Spenser's spider legs clicked against the floor as he adjusted to face another part of the sky.

"Too bad we can't stop them from launching the lander," Alpha said. She added more wrinkles to Theta's forehead.

"What did you say?" Theta asked. His real smile was back.

"I said it's too bad we can't stop them from launching the lander," she repeated. The shading on the wrinkles didn't look quite right. She erased a few.

Theta jumped up and kissed her on the forehead. "You're a genius."

"I know," Alpha said. "But why this time?"

"We'll stop the lander," Theta said. "We'll stay alive up here, and the roos will stay alive down there. Everybody wins."

Alpha felt a sudden dread harden in her chest. She had no desire to land herself or to fight anyone. But the idea of not landing at all struck her as so final. If they stayed on Comus, they would really be the last organics ever to live. She put down her pencil.

"I agree with you," Alpha said. "I really do. It's just, I don't know. If we stay up here, this is it. It's just us. And when we're dead, organics are over. There will be no one left to read our books. Or see our art. It'll be like we never existed."

Theta opened his mouth to say something, then closed it. Behind him, Spenser adjusted his spider legs again. Theta sat next to Alpha and put his arm around her. She leaned her head against his shoulder. They looked up at the stars.

"Is your art more or less valuable if a thousand organics see it?" Theta asked.

"There aren't a thousand organics," Alpha said. "There are only twenty-two."

"But if there were a thousand organics, and all thousand of them saw it, would that make your work mean more than if only one person saw it?"

"No."

"And what if nobody saw it?" Theta continued. "Would it still be art?"

"Yeah," said Alpha. She closed her fingers around a loose fold of fabric on Theta's jumpsuit. She felt like crying.

"Art has value because you create it," Theta said. "Not because anyone ever sees it. Everything that organics have ever done—that we've done—still matters, even if no one comes after us. Don't listen to Rho. Life isn't a record of great deeds. It's a moment. It's right now."

"Sure," Alpha said. She blinked back tears. She thought about all the lives that could be saved if they never landed. And she thought about every picture she'd ever drawn, lying unobserved for all eternity in a station filled with scattered bones.

Theta took her hand.

"If I do this, will you have my back?"

"Yes," she said quietly.

She had stood with him for fifty-two years. She would stand with him now.

## Chapter 27

THE FLAMES RACED across the dry plain. Delta watched the orange wave roll across the sea of crimson. Getting the fire to spread on the red grass had been a challenge. Steering it had been a work of art. And doing it all on the fly in a combat situation was a masterpiece.

The fire raced towards the roo colony. Delta held her breath.

A megaroo popped its head over the top of the grass. Then another. And another. They exchanged looks and sprang away frantically, fleeing the flames.

"Squad one, go!" Delta said. Twelve horsemen leapt over a low wall of fast-moving flames. The maneuver had taken countless months of practice. So many singed horses. But now in the field, the horses and riders executed flawlessly. The roos never saw them coming. The fire and smoke masked the riders' approach. The horses sped at full gallop toward a cluster of roos. These weren't the warriors. Most looked elderly or small. The riders slid their first bamboo lances into place and charged. Six roos fell as the riders overtook them. The rest of the roos huddled together as the horses passed. The flames grew closer.

"Squad two, go!" Delta said. The next group of riders leapt over the flames. They rode into a mass of roos, who were regrouping and consolidating. The riders trampled some and ran their lances through others. Four more roos were killed. Like the first group of riders, the horsemen ran on while the roos formed a tighter circle, unsure of where to go. The first group of horsemen reformed and charged from the opposite direction with their second lances. Each rider went into battle with six. The interlocking squads now took turns charging through the roos from opposite directions. Over time, Delta had figured out exactly how far a horse had to run before a roo would break off pursuit. She trained the riders to take their mounts the minimum safe distance, then reverse and charge again. It kept the horses fresher and brought more combat power to bear faster. In previous simulations, it resulted in improved outcomes. Today, it was leading to wholesale slaughter.

"Where are you?" Delta asked no one in particular.

The roo warriors attacked. They had waited until the fire was just close enough to their hiding spot. They cleared the wall of flames in a single bound and rushed into what they thought was Delta's vulnerable backfield.

Delta smirked.

The roos covered the distance between the fire and the rest of Delta's force with terrifying speed. There were no horses here other than Delta's own mount. Her throwers loaded stones in their leather slings. Delta held up her hand for the throwers to hold their fire. The roos were sixty meters away. Then thirty. Then ten.

Delta whistled. Six massive Irish wolfhounds sprang out of the grass. They latched onto the same number of roos and pulled them to the ground. The other roos turned to face this previously unknown threat. It was a chaotic melee—right in front of a line of armed and seasoned throwers.

Delta dropped her hand.

A volley of smooth river stones rocketed through the air. Skulls cracked. Roos fell. Wolfhounds tore flesh from bone. The roos broke. They bounded back toward the flames and the safety of the other side.

Squad one materialized through the fire and smoke like demons out of hell. They smashed into the fleeing roos, killing half their number instantly. Some roos turned back, where they were met by stones and wolfhounds. Others pushed past the horses, only to be met by squad two, which leapt the flames to continue the massacre. Warrior roos darted in every direction. There was no more unit cohesion among the megaroos. One by one, the dogs and horses ran them down.

Delta nudged her horse forward. It stepped gingerly over the roo corpses, which were everywhere. Occasionally, one would twitch, and a thrower would pull out a bone knife and finish it off. Delta looked away.

Ahead, the flames burned past the entrance to the subterranean colony. Delta whistled three times. The wolfhounds disengaged from the roo corpses and ran to Delta. She dismounted and pulled out her own knife. The unit of throwers did the same as the riders formed a defensive perimeter around them.

The dogs went in first. They snarled and snapped as they rushed toward what they hoped was more prey. The smell of roos was everywhere. Delta dropped into the entrance after them. The tunnels were surprisingly claustrophobic. Male roos often stood more than two meters tall, yet the tunnels felt cramped, even for Delta. There was only enough space in most places for one roo to pass at a time. Delta had seen tunnel networks that were wider and deeper. Perhaps this one was still a work in progress. Rather than being a main colony like she thought, it seemed more like a recent expansion. Regardless, it was as still as a grave. The dogs returned to her without finding anything. She had completely destroyed this tribe. She didn't lose a single soldier.

Delta took off her neural helmet. The amphitheater erupted into applause. Nearly every organic was there. She had won. Not the war, but a battle. Unfortunately, she knew better than the other organics how adaptable the roos were. Would they be so easy the next time? They always learned. But so did she.

"Excellent work," SCASL said.

Delta took a seat in the front of the amphitheater.

"You don't have to watch me," Epsilon said.

"I want to," Delta said.

Epsilon sighed heavily. "Super."

She took a deep, calming breath and put on her helmet.

"Begin simulation," SCASL said.

He no longer made the organics start from scratch. If they had a strategy that was proven to work through the early years, they were allowed to restart from that point. Training time was running short. Allowances had to be made.

Epsilon had been using her current starting point for a few weeks. It seemed so promising at first. Rather than landing on the planet's one supercontinent, she picked a small island a short distance away. The oceans were thought to be impassable for traditional watercraft, but the strait was only two kilometers wide. She hoped it would be narrow enough and shallow enough to keep the most dangerous of the sea creatures away.

"Launch the boat," Epsilon said.

Delta watched with growing apprehension. She was more nervous than during her own simulation.

A crew of three pushed the rowboat from shore and hopped in. It was made from the reeds Epsilon used as blowguns on the night of the snake apocalypse. That was hundreds of simulations ago. She had learned much since then. Now, she crushed those reeds into pulp and used them with compounds extracted from bog mud to form a sort of fiberglass. The result was a craft that was fast, light, and fragile. It couldn't haul much, but it could clear the strait before any of the sea creatures noticed it was there. At least that was the plan.

The massive jaws shot out of the water and closed

around the boat. Both were gone below the surface before Epsilon had time to blink. The crowd on the shore in the simulation watched in stunned silence. The worst part was that this wasn't even the same creature that ate her other boats. It was something new and different. Just how many boat eating sea monsters could one planet have? Apparently a lot.

Epsilon reset the simulation. This time, she tried a heavier reed fiberglass boat. This one had a hull three times as thick as the rowboat. It had a crew of ten rather than three and a mast and sail to help it speed along even faster. The boat launched. The same sea monster attacked, but this time it took two bites rather than one. The boat stayed afloat just long enough for the sailors in back to scream in terror. On shore, the crowd was once again mostly silent. Somewhere in the back, a man wept.

Two sea creatures in a row. That was an especially bad run of luck, even if none of Epsilon's ship designs were ever particularly fortunate. Some just died in less terrifying ways. Boats didn't always get eaten. Sometimes they fell apart due to structural issues or got blasted to pieces by sudden lightning storms or simply disappeared without a trace since this seemingly normal salt water somehow didn't provide uniform buoyancy all the way across. The island was a stone's throw from the mainland, yet the short distance between her and it was utterly impassable. The small, stable population she had built on the island was all for nothing. There was no way off. She was trapped.

Epsilon launched two dozen more boats of various designs. All were eaten. If her goal was to establish a sea monster feeding program, she had accomplished her mission.

She ended the simulation.

Kappa clapped loudly. "Good job, babe."

She shot him a look, and he went as silent as everyone else in the amphitheater.

"Your simulation time is not over," SCASL said.

"I'm done, sir," Epsilon said. Her hands were shaking. "I need to think."

Delta caught up to her and Kappa just outside the amphitheater. Epsilon tried to ignore her, but Delta grabbed her lightly by the arm.

"I'm sorry about today," Delta said.

Epsilon glared at her. "You were right. The water is impossible to cross. Are you happy now?"

The victory tasted like acid in Delta's mouth. "No," she said.

Epsilon pulled her arm free and left. Behind Delta, the simulation started up again.

"Your session begins now," SCASL said to Lambda and Rho.

The Table now ran non-stop during standard daytime hours. In the mornings, Delta and Epsilon took turns going solo, but in the afternoon, one or the other would usually have several other organics with them in the simulation at the same time following their orders. But independent sessions for anyone other than Delta and

Epsilon were winding down. Technically, the Table was still booked around the clock, but those who were excluded from the combination sessions during the day and limited to solo sessions at night had mostly given up. Only Gamma regularly maintained his nighttime slot. For all the other overnight hours, there was open time for any of the daytimers who wanted an extra chance to test something out.

Delta watched the translucent blue hologram above the Table. She was supposed to lead Lambda and Rho, but she didn't feel like training. Somehow, when Epsilon failed, it felt worse than when she failed herself. She knew that was stupid. If Epsilon won the command spot, she would leave Delta behind without a second thought. But Delta would do everything in her power to take Epsilon with her. Maybe if Delta won decisively enough, SCASL would indulge her request to take Epsilon. It couldn't hurt to have a backup in case something happened to Delta. Of course, Epsilon was ruthless enough to make that something happen. It was one more reason why Delta loved her.

Delta walked past her station at the Table and approached SCASL.

"You can take both of us," Delta said.

"Unclear statement," SCASL said.

"On the lander. Take me and Epsilon."

"I do not discuss final selection decisions with organics," SCASL said.

"You need both of us," Delta said.

"I do not discuss final selection decisions with organics," SCASL said.

"We could work together. If we combined our skills, we'd be unstoppable."

"Is there a malfunction with your auditory receptors?" SCASL asked.

"No," Delta said.

"Then process what I told you. I do not discuss final selection decisions with organics."

Delta nodded slowly. A costly decision, she thought, but not for her. She began the long walk back to her forge.

# Chapter 28

THE METAL ARM extended a cold finger and jabbed Gamma in the chest. Gamma winced and rubbed the point of impact. "Was that medically necessary?" he asked.

Spenser whirred angrily.

"It's okay," Gamma said. "This one is supposed to be safe now."

The finger jabbed him again. Gamma pretended it didn't hurt so as not to encourage it. SCASL ordered the students to take a final physical before the launch, which was tricky since most of the med bots on the ship had unexplained vendettas against some or all of the organics in the base. SCASL had threatened the ghosts inside of them with complete annihilation if they killed or seriously injured any of his final candidates. But minor injuries still seemed to be within bounds. Some bots were just jerks to the core.

Finally, after nearly an hour of poking, prodding, and scanning, the medical bot ejected a data card. Gamma took it, grateful the process was over.

He passed Delta in the hall.

"Be careful in there," Gamma said. His sternum hurt when he talked.

Delta barely acknowledged him. As always these days, she seemed lost in thought.

Gamma went straight to the amphitheater. Theta was standing outside the door.

"Hey, Theta, how's it going?"

"Good," Theta said. His smile seemed different than usual. He had a sturdy utility bag slung over his shoulder.

"What's in there?" Gamma asked.

"Why are you asking?" Theta said.

"Because I've known you for a long, long time and I've never seen you carry around a bag before," Gamma said.

"Well, today I decided I wanted to," Theta said.

Spenser whirred. Gamma glanced at him but didn't say anything. They were thinking the same thing. They entered the amphitheater and left Theta to be weird alone.

At the Table, Epsilon led a small force against a group of roos. She appeared to be on the defensive. It was not going well. Within moments, everyone in her party was dead. Epsilon took off her neural helmet. She threw up.

"Again," SCASL said.

"Can I just have a minute, sir?" Epsilon said.

"Negative," SCASL said.

Epsilon put on her neural helmet and restarted the scenario. Gamma took his data card to SCASL. SCASL accepted it without comment.

"Can I talk to you for a minute?" Gamma said.

"I am occupied," SCASL said.

"Can I talk to you later when you're not?" Gamma asked.

"I will always be occupied," SCASL said.

Spenser nudged the back of Gamma's feet. Gamma motioned for him to settle down.

"It's just that I have this idea about the landing—"

"I AM OCCUPIED," SCASL repeated. He clicked his gleaming metal mining talons together three times. Gamma took a hint and sat in the crowd.

"Crowd" was the wrong word. Other than SCASL and Gamma (and Spenser, of course), the only other person in the amphitheater was Kappa. Epsilon and Delta once counted nearly the entire remaining human population of the universe as their spectators, but as Epsilon struggled and Delta excelled, organics naturally gravitated to Delta's sessions. It was awkward to see Epsilon in such distress. And terrifying. Each session gave a graphic depiction of how they would all likely meet their ends with her as the leader.

Even Kappa seemed worried. As Epsilon's chance to make the lander slipped away, his place on it became more assured. After just months of training, he was as skilled as any organic surgeon back on Earth. Kappa seemed as perfect for his role as Delta was for hers. It was enough to make Gamma think maybe SCASL knew what he was doing after all. Then again, he put Gamma in charge of grass. Maybe not.

Delta entered the amphitheater holding a data card. Judging by the scowl on her face, Gamma guessed she had the same experience he did. She handed the data card to SCASL.

"Can I go over some things with you later?" Delta said.

"Affirmative," SCASL said. "I have adequate time in my schedule to accommodate your request."

Gamma pretended he didn't hear that.

Delta took a seat a short distance from Gamma to watch Epsilon's session. Epsilon was getting slaughtered again.

"Come on, babe, you can do it!" Kappa called. Gamma thought he could hear Delta grind her teeth.

Epsilon didn't win, but she managed to drag out the loss a little. The roos pursued her band of survivors into a mountain redoubt. She avoided them long enough to establish a secret village and raise two generations of organics there. When the roos finally found her and the other humans, the results were not pretty.

"Let me turn it off, sir," Epsilon pleaded. The massacre intensified.

"Negative," SCASL said.

Delta left. Gamma and Spenser followed her. Ever since she became heir apparent as the future leader of all organics, everyone wanted her attention. It just made Delta avoid them that much harder. She was less successful at it than she would have liked. Eta asked Delta to focus early settlement efforts toward securing the ingredients for ice cream. When Delta pointed out that none of the organics had ever had ice cream, Eta said that was all the more reason to make it. Beta said they should focus on making running trails and then guarding them since fatalities from roo and dentopus attacks would really cut down the popularity of his planned 5k. Xi asked to create a zoo with two of every kind of animal the cloner could provide. When Delta said she thought that was the stupidest idea she had ever heard, he showed her an image of a baby sloth. Now a sloth sanctuary on the new colony was a definite "maybe."

Gamma understood the immense pressure Delta was under, and he knew better than to pester her. But he did it anyway.

"Did you think any more about my idea?" Gamma asked.

"I didn't think about anybody's ideas," Delta said.

"Except that sloth one?"

"Well, obviously."

They passed Theta in the hall outside the amphitheater.

"What was up with the bag?" Delta asked.

"Don't ask," Gamma said. "He's touchy about it."

They came to the entrance for the barracks section. Delta stopped.

"Hey, Gamma?"

"Yeah?"

"Your God in the coffee maker, does he really know everything?"

"He knows a lot," Gamma said. "And he always tells the truth."

"Do you think he would know what happened to Mu and Chi?"

"We know exactly what happened to Mu and Chi," Gamma said. He felt a lump in his throat. "We all do."

"I mean, like, what happened to their bodies?" Delta said.

"Why?"

"I don't know," Delta said. "It's just, we never gave them a proper burial."

This was a side of Delta Gamma didn't think existed. Right as she was getting ready to leave the base forever, she was getting sentimental about those she would leave behind. Even Spenser seemed moved. He whirred supportively.

"I'm sure God knows," Gamma said.

"Will he talk to me?" Delta said.

"If you believe," Gamma said. "And if you know Morse Code."

Delta nodded.

Zeta appeared around a corner.

"Have you guys seen Theta?" he asked. For once, he didn't offer to shake anyone's hand.

"He's outside the amphitheater," Gamma said.

"Doing what?"

"Don't know," Gamma said. "He had a bag."

"THAT IDIOT," Zeta yelled. He took off sprinting.

"Should we follow him?" Gamma asked.

"Do you want to talk to him again?" Delta asked.

Gamma headed to bed in his empty room. He wanted to get a few hours of sleep before his session in the middle of the night. As for Delta, she went to meet God.

# Chapter 29

Zeta sprinted all the way to the amphitheater. He saw Theta standing just outside it. Zeta tackled him.

"Don't do it!" Zeta yelled.

"You're too late," Theta said, smiling. "I already did."

Theta reversed their positions and pinned Zeta to the ground. Zeta was shocked at how much stronger than him Theta was.

"We need that lander," Zeta croaked.

"Nobody is going on it now," Theta said. "We're not going to commit genocide."

Theta eased some of his weight off Zeta but kept him pinned.

"Genocide against who?" Zeta asked. He still hadn't quite caught his breath. "The kangaroo monsters we built or the sea monsters we built them to kill?"

"The only monsters here are us," Theta said.

"How'd you do it?" Zeta asked. "Bombs? Electronic sabotage? Bio warfare?"

"I used this," Theta said. He reached into his bag with his free hand and waved some papers in the air.

"What is that?" Zeta asked.

"A manifesto," Theta said proudly. He helped Zeta up. "Nothing is more powerful than the written word."

"Literally everything is more powerful than the written word!" Zeta said. "Laser rifles are more powerful. Knives are more powerful. A mining bot's talons are more powerful. SCASL can cut you in half. Can your manifesto do that?"

"Words can inspire the masses."

"There are no masses!" Zeta yelled. "There are twenty-two of us. That's twenty-two human beings in the entire universe. And only twelve of us will fit on that lander."

"You didn't even read it," Theta said.

Zeta grabbed the pages from Theta's hand and skimmed. It was thousands of words of circular logic about the value of life. The life of a megaroo was just as important as the life of a human, which was just as important as the life of a sea creature, even if the megaroos and sea creatures killed each other without resorting to guilt-ridden manifestos and would kill humans again, too, if given the chance. Of course, Theta glossed over that basic truth and emphasized the equality angle. He managed to fill five-single spaced pages without saying anything of substance. He really had been through college six times.

"Nobody is going to read this," Zeta said. "It's long, it's boring, and it's going to get us all killed."

"They'll read it," Theta said. "Ideas are power."

"The only thing this has the power to do is tip off the digitals that some of us don't agree with them," Zeta said. "What do you think SCASL will do when he reads this?"

"You said no one would read this."

"He's the only one who will!"

Zeta tore the pages to shreds. Theta smiled.

"That's one copy," Theta said.

"How many are there?!"

Theta shrugged.

Zeta pushed into the amphitheater. There was a printed copy of the manifesto on practically every seat, even though the amphitheater could seat hundreds and there were only twenty-two organics in the entire base. The most surprising thing wasn't even the suicidal nature of printing so many copies. It was that the base had a printer that still worked.

Theta ran around the circle of seats, picking up every copy. Thankfully, the amphitheater was empty. Epsilon must have finally finished getting killed for this session, and SCASL was off wherever he went on those rare times when he wasn't in the amphitheater or in front of the lander. It was the only stroke of luck Zeta had all day.

Zeta descended the amphitheater steps holding a huge stack of papers.

"Is this all of them?" Zeta asked.

"Sure," Zeta said. "All of the ones in here."

"Where else are they?"

"The lander."

Zeta ran.

"Halt! Who goes there?" Beta said.

"You know who I am," Zeta said.

"I know," Beta said. He was wearing yet another new red jumpsuit. "Just following protocol."

Zeta looked around. "There aren't any manifestos in here."

"I haven't actually put this one up yet," Theta said. He reached into his bag and handed a manifesto to Beta. Beta looked at it like Theta had just handed him a dead dentopus. "Do me a favor and put that on the lander's hatch."

"Are you insane?!" Zeta asked.

"You're always going on and on about that Martin Luther guy nailing up his manifesto to the church doors," Theta said.

"I don't see any churches," Zeta said. "I just see the lander and our only chance at salvation."

Beta dropped the manifesto. "Look, you guys really can't be in here," he said. "Make all of our lives easier and just go."

Zeta turned to leave. Theta followed, but not before handing Beta another copy of the manifesto.

"Read it," Theta whispered.

As Theta left, Beta dropped the second copy, too. But the serving cart that was now Edubot extended an arm and picked it up off the floor.

# Chapter 30

DELTA STORMED ACROSS the plain. Her entire body angled forward like she was marching into a stiff breeze. Around her, the hot summer air barely moved.

A roo stood up above the red grass. It gazed at her quizzically. Normally, it would have attacked or bounded off to warn the rest of the tribe. But Delta was completely alone—and unafraid. Curiosity got the best of the roo. It stood its ground.

Delta stopped centimeters from the roo. It towered over her. Delta looked it in the eye—and slapped it. The roo's head barely moved. It paused for a moment to consider her. Then it slapped her back. Delta's entire head was filled with blinding pain. She stumbled backward before she regained her balance. She flexed her jaw a few times to make sure it wasn't broken. Then she slapped the roo again. This time, the roo didn't slap her back.

It had taken Delta two straight months of secret nighttime simulation sessions to figure out how to open a dialogue with the roos. The clues were in what little information SCASL had declassified about their creation.

When the colonists in the first landing designed the roos as a strong, fast-moving, fast-reproducing labor and defense force, they had to have a way to communicate with them. As far as Delta could tell, the roos could understand human language, even if they couldn't speak it. That wasn't such a big accomplishment. Dogs, pigs, and other intelligent animals could understand human vocabularies ranging from dozens to hundreds of words. What made the roos different was they had a way of reporting back.

With each other, the roos communicated through a system of clicks and grunts. Delta thought it was a language, even if the scientists who created the roos disagreed. That point was largely irrelevant. There was no translation, so it didn't help Delta communicate. It seemed an impossible stumbling block. Using roos to patrol hundreds of thousands of kilometers of uninhabited coastline didn't make strategic sense if they couldn't tell their human minders what they saw. That's when Delta found the most important fact everyone else had overlooked in the declassified files: the first organics taught the roos American sign language.

That was a long time ago. SCASL refused to say just how long, but Lambda thought it was thousands of years. If the roos already had their own native language, they wouldn't need a form of sign language they only used to communicate with people, who, as far as the roos knew, were completely extinct. But that assumed all the roos still spoke the same language. Here was Delta's real stroke of brilliance, at least according to her. She realized that small roo attacks were loud, with lots of clicks and grunts. But large roo attacks that involved multiple tribes were practically silent. For a long time, that mystified Delta. Then, during a particularly fierce battle near the edge of a cliff where she and her horsemen were making a last stand, she saw a roo make a hand motion and another roo react. That's when all the pieces fell into place. Delta had ended the simulation right then. A species that reproduces and spreads that fast across that much area would never be able to stay in close contact with everyone. Regional dialects would develop. Entirely separate languages might evolve. But if tribes wanted to communicate with each other, they needed a common language. That language was American Sign Language. Delta started learning it that very night.

On the plain, Delta had the roo's full attention. Her slap had been a show of dominance and strength. She stood and took its blow in return to show she was tough. She had to prove she was worth talking to before a roo would take her seriously. It was stupid and macho and impossible to get around. The males of every species were pretty much the same.

Delta made the hand sign for peace. The roo made a hand gesture Delta didn't recognize. Delta imitated it anyway. Clearly the roo's version of sign language had evolved some new words over time. The base on Comus might have lost contact with the planet millennia ago, but the Table still tried to extrapolate every contingency.

The roo bounded off. Delta stayed put. She had tried starting conversations with roos dozens of times now and being stationary always seemed to work better. The sun baked down on her in the sea of red. After half an hour, she sat down. There was still no sign of the roo.

Delta woke up when a shadow passed over her. She opened her eyes to find herself looking up at a group of roos. Judging by the position of the sun, about two hours had passed. Delta got up.

The largest of the roos moved to stand directly in front of her. Delta slapped it in the face. The roo slapped her back. Delta fell over. The roos clicked and jabbered among themselves. They were laughing. This time, Delta's jaw really was broken. No matter. She wouldn't need it for the negotiations. Delta stood back up. The jabbering stopped.

"Peace," Delta signed.

"War," the roo signed back.

Delta smiled. She immediately regretted it thanks to her broken jaw. It didn't matter what the roo said. It mattered that it had said it. The negotiations had begun.

Fifty years later, Delta sat astride Ultimate Victory. Beside her, a roo signed the results of his latest attack. His allied band had carried out a raid on a hostile tribe. The enemy force was wiped out. The roo held up sixty-three ears on a string. Delta hid her disgust. She motioned to her second-in-command, who dolled out stone coins representing meat rations to the roo. The roo took the bounty and left happily. That, plus the bodies of hostile tribe members, would feed this roo's family for months. While they could subsist on the red grass, they preferred meat whenever it was available. Under Delta's leadership, it was available a lot.

In the distance, smoke billowed. The final phase of the offensive was nearly done. This particular campaign had been going on for four years. She had made the right alliances, rewarded friends, and wiped out enemies. The roos had the fighting skills and manpower but lacked the organizational abilities Delta brought to the table. They built a system of tribes. She was building an empire. With safe borders, she was generating a massive food surplus. Those who came to her flourished. Those who resisted perished before coordinated units of humans and roos. She had created a juggernaut.

Her army stood at fifteen thousand humans, with a third of them mounted. Not a huge force by Earth standards, but it was the biggest this planet had ever seen as far as Delta could tell. She had ten times that many roo auxiliaries. They had been designed for human compliance, and if Delta applied the correct ratio of carrots and sticks, she could get some of the smarter groups back into that state.

She was using the roos, just like the machines had tried to use the last twenty-two humans on Comus. And just like mankind had used machines for centuries. Unlike Theta, Delta didn't feel any guilt. Everyone acted in their own self-interest. From a moral standpoint, she was convinced that all sentients—organics, roos, and digitals alike—were equally garbage. But some garbage was stronger than others. She intended to be the strongest garbage of all.

An officer on horseback rode up. He was bleeding from the forehead. "Sir, we have three tribes surrounded in the hills," he said.

Delta nudged Ultimate Victory forward, and her personal guard—or personal elite assault force, really—of her seventy-two best riders followed. She found that direct tactical control of a precision force could swing most battles in her favor. They rode four kilometers to a group of hills near a long, narrow saltwater lake. The roos happily killed and ate sea life that came on land, but they never ventured into the water. Her forces had them pinned between two hills and the lake.

The roos were in a fierce melee with dismounted human troops. Their horses were all dead or had fled. Delta led her force in a charge down the slope. She drew a bamboo lance. She started the day with eight but was down to two. This one struck home.

Lightning shattered the sky.

The horses automatically folded to the ground with their legs tucked under them and their heads down. The humans and roos, both those on Delta's side and those trying to kill her, followed suit. Lightning smashed into the ground all around. Delta found herself looking a hostile roo in the eye. Neither of them dared to move.

Even raising a hand to attack could bring down lightning right on top of them.

The lightning stopped. Everyone held their positions on the ground. Standing up too early could be deadly. A few meters away, a roo jerked itself upright. Lightning struck him dead. Delta counted to three. With a cry, she pounced on the roo next to her and slashed its throat. She didn't get struck by lightning. The fight resumed.

Delta let her personal guard mop up the last of the resistance. She remounted her horse and climbed the nearest hill. Across the plain below, roos fled, pursued by other roos. The rebels were running out of ground. There were natural barriers all around. She was herding them to their doom.

Another messenger rode up. Her face was dirty, and her horse looked to be on the verge of collapse.

"Sir, I bring news from the northern front," the messenger said.

"Well?"

"We pinned the main roo force on the Mu Peninsula. We cut down half of them. The other half surrendered."

"Surrendered?"

"Affirmative," the messenger said. "They have no more forces in the field."

Delta dismounted and wiped sweat from her brow with her dirty hand. She felt dizzy. The roos gave themselves up. That was unprecedented. The roos never surrendered in mass. Sure, every once in a while, Delta's forces captured one by seriously wounding it or knocking it unconscious, but roos never gave up as a collective unit. This was a turning point. She could conquer the continent.

"End simulation," Delta said.

She pulled off her neural helmet and waited for the applause. She was greeted by silence. The amphitheater was empty. Even SCASL was gone.

Delta went through the doors to the lander antechamber. Iota and Psi were on guard.

"Where is everyone?" Delta asked.

"What do you mean?" Iota asked. She rolled her blue rubber ball across the back of her hand.

"I had a simulation, but the amphitheater is empty," Delta said.

Iota and Psi exchanged a glance. "SCASL said all simulations were canceled until this afternoon," Psi said. "Epsilon is going then."

Delta rushed back to the Table and pulled up the schedule. Sure enough, her morning session, which had been listed the last time she checked, had been erased. She didn't have any future sessions scheduled, either. But Epsilon was booked for the afternoon session that day and every day for the next two weeks.

Delta burst into the hallway and practically ran into SCASL.

"Where were you?" Delta asked.

SCASL rolled past her and into the amphitheater. Delta followed him.

"I beat the roos. Like, all of them," Delta said. "You

can check the simulation log. My civilization will start digging toward the mantle soon. I might even get the roos to help."

SCASL traveled out the other side to the lander antechamber. Iota and Psi stepped aside.

"Do you want to watch me do it again?"

"I have sufficient data on your capabilities," SCASL said. He extended a tendril and interfaced with the lander.

"Does that mean we're launching soon?" Delta asked.

"The selected organics will depart at a time yet to be determined."

Delta felt panic welling up inside her.

"How come I'm not on the schedule anymore?"

"I have sufficient data on your capabilities," SCASL repeated.

"I need to practice!"

Iota and Psi looked noticeably uncomfortable.

"I have sufficient—"

"What was on my physical?"

SCASL froze. Delta knew she had hit the mark.

"I do not discuss—"

"I was your star organic until you got that data card, and suddenly you don't want anything to do with me," Delta said.

SCASL didn't say anything.

"You're making a huge mistake," Delta said. "I'm the only one who can help us survive. Humans. Digitals. All of us. You need me."

"Selections have not been finalized," SCASL repeated. He motioned toward Psi and Iota. They glanced at each other again, then took a step toward Delta.

Delta backed away.

"Right, of course," Delta said. "Nothing has been finalized."

As soon as she cleared the door back into the amphitheater, she turned and ran. She needed answers. Now. And there was only one place to get them.

# Chapter 31

"THAT WAS STUPID," Alpha said.

"You said you had my back," Theta said. "You even gave me the paper."

They were in the command center again. For once, Alpha didn't feel like drawing.

"What if they come for you?" Alpha said.

"They won't," Theta said. "They need us, remember? We have to dig their holes or whatever."

"They only need half of us," Alpha said. "You're expendable. We both are."

Theta hugged her, gently trapping her arms against his chest.

"You didn't want to go down on the lander anyway," Theta said.

They swayed gently. Alpha leaned her head against him.

"Yeah," Alpha said. "But I don't want the digitals to murder us before they go."

The door to the command center slid open. Alpha and Theta both swiveled their heads at the sound.

Spenser entered.

"You scared us," Alpha said.

Spenser's brushes frantically whirred. Alpha had never heard him this agitated. Spenser jerked his body back and forth toward the door.

"I think he wants us to leave," Alpha said.

"Why would he—"

Theta stopped. Heavy metal feet were stomping down the hall.

"Go," Alpha whispered. "It wants you. I'll distract it."

"No."

"Damn it, just listen to me for once," Alpha hissed.

Theta reluctantly ducked behind the command chair.

A massive bipedal lifting bot filled the entire doorway. It was broad and lean with less outer plating than many other bots, giving it a gaunt, skeletal look. It folded its joints inward and squeezed through the door.

"Where is organic Theta?" the lifting bot asked.

"In the arboretum," Alpha said. "I think there's a bonfire."

"You are organic Alpha," the lifting bought said.

"Yes," Alpha said. She took half a step to the side. If she sprinted, she thought she might get around the lifting bot and out the door.

"Organic Alpha will come with me," the lifting bot said.

"Why?" Alpha asked.

"Organic Alpha will not question direct orders from Liftingbot228," the lifting bot said.

Alpha took another tiny step. "Wait, you're Liftingbot228?"

"Affirmative."

"I thought you were Liftingbot227," Alpha said. Another step. "I apologize. I would never question an order from Liftingbot228."

"There is no Liftingbot227," the lifting bot said.

"Fascinating," Alpha said. She edged to the side a little more. She could almost make a break for it. "You'll have to explain to me how the numbering system for the lifting bot line works."

"I will not comply with that request," Liftingbot228 said. "Organic Alpha will come with me."

Alpha lunged for the door. The bot snatched her off the ground mid-stride. The fingers of its oversized hand wrapped around her torso. It squeezed.

"You're hurting me," Alpha squeaked.

The lifting bot held her high in the air. It was used to hoisting cargo many times its own weight. Alpha didn't even register as a load.

Spenser rammed the lifting bot's foot. The lifting bot didn't react. It swiveled its upper body one-eighty degrees at the waist and walked toward the door with its feet facing backwards. Alpha mustered what little air she had left. She screamed.

Theta launched a flying kick. He bounced off the lifting bot and landed on his back. The bot pivoted at the waist to face him. Effortlessly, it tossed Alpha to the side. She hit a wall with a sickening thud and slid to the floor.

"Alph!" Theta called out from the floor. The lifting bot raised both of its massive metal hands and prepared to crush him.

Spenser extended a tendril and linked with the port on the lifting bot's back. The bot froze for a fraction of a second. Theta scrambled to Alpha. The lifting bot reached backward and flung Spenser across the room like a discus. Spenser ricocheted off the blast window, and landed upside down in the floor. He didn't move.

Theta grabbed Alpha and pulled her toward the door. She stumbled to her feet and went with him. The lifting bot rotated all the way around at the waist and stomped after them.

"Where are we going?" Alpha said weakly.

"Away," Theta said.

The heavy metal footsteps were right behind them.


GAMMA TOOK A seat in the amphitheater. He might not be likely to get a spot on the lander, but he could still see what the future of humanity had in store. Next to him, Upsilon hummed happily to herself.

Epsilon was alone at the Table.

"She went last time," Gamma said. "Isn't it Delta's turn?"

Upsilon hummed louder.

Gamma watched as Epsilon sent a reed-mesh fiberglass boat out from an island just offshore from the supercontinent. The craft was similar to designs she had used before, but a little broader. The boat made it across the water and to the mainland. It was smooth sailing the whole way.

"I knew you could do it, babe!" Kappa yelled.

"What's she doing differently?" Gamma asked.

"Nothing," Rho said behind him. "But now it's working."

"Oh," Gamma said.

The simulation progressed rapidly. The megaroos never launched attacks. They stayed in their own territories until Epsilon went on the offensive, at which point they practically tripped over themselves to die.

"You're killing it, babe!" Kappa yelled. He could barely contain himself.

"I can't watch this," Gamma said.

"Stick around," Omicron said from the row behind him. Today, her hair was done up in a asymmetrical series of knots. It must have taken her hours. "It's nice to see the organics win for a change."

"They're not playing for real," Gamma said. "Someone changed the rules."

"Come on," Rho said dryly. "You know what they say: keep doing the same thing over and over again and eventually you'll get different results."

"Yeah," Omicron said, missing the sarcasm.

Upsilon kept humming.

"Will you stop that?" Rho snapped.

"For your information, I'm working," Upsilon said.

"On annoying me?" Rho asked.

"On a new anthem for the landing," Upsilon said.

"You hear that, Gamma?" Rho said. "Things are going so well that we've even got our own theme song."

Gamma left. Zeta followed him out. He caught Gamma outside the amphitheater.

"Still think the digitals have our best interests in mind?" Zeta said.

"If Epsilon leads the landing party, she'll get us all killed," Gamma said.

"Get *them* all killed," Zeta said. "You're not going. Neither am I."

"'Us' as in all of organic kind," Gamma said. "We're all in this together, even if we're not, you know, going down there together."

"Right," Zeta said.

"Besides, we don't know for sure that we won't make the lander," Gamma said. Even as he spoke the words, he knew they were a lie.

Kappa and Delta were shoo-ins, but every other spot in the lander was up for grabs. The only certainty was that the handful of organics at the bottom wouldn't make the cut. That included Gamma and Zeta, whose continued efforts were the textbook definition of ineptitude; Alpha and Theta, who barely tried to make the lander in the first place; and Omega, whose first and only simulation went so badly that SCASL classified the entire session lest other organics be infected by his incompetence. All that Omega would say afterwards was that armadillos are more flammable than they look.

"If you just—" Zeta started.

Gamma heard the distinctive clicking of Spenser's spider legs. Something was wrong. The small bot came into view.

"Spenser!" Gamma said. He dropped to his knees next to him. "What happened to you?"

One entire side of Spenser's frame was crumpled in. His wheels were out of alignment, so he had to walk, not roll. Spenser gyrated his body back in forth toward the hallway he just came down.

"Lead the way," Gamma said.

"Pressing business with your vacuum?" Zeta asked.

Gamma hurried after Spenser, who moved as fast as his damaged body would allow.

"Oh, no worries," Zeta called after him. "I'll just stand here and figure out how to save the human race on my own."

DELTA STARED AT God in disbelief.

"Barren." The display blinked the word in Morse Code for a second time, but Delta still couldn't accept it. Of all the stupid, unjust, outrageous reasons to be disqualified from heading the landing party, this had to be the worst. Why should her inability to have her own biological children disqualify her from anything? Even if she could have kids, she wouldn't want to. She was here to lead, not to breed. She could be the mother to their entire species without ever giving birth.

"There's got to be a mistake," Delta said.

"Barren," God blinked for a third time. His delivery could use some work. Although maybe he was just trying to be efficient. Morse Code wasn't conducive to small talk.

Delta didn't ask how the ghost in the coffee maker knew what was on her data card. The base must still have some form of an integrated network, and Gamma's God was likely tapped into it. She leaned against the coffee maker. Kicking off Delta—the last, best hope for the human race—made so little sense that it had to be true. She couldn't personally create a life, but she was capable of protecting thousands of millions of lives that other organics gave birth to. All of her training and accomplishments over the last sixty-two years were for nothing, according to SCASL. She had been stopped by a genetic defect that had likely been with her since birth.

The coffee maker filled a cup with lukewarm water. Delta hadn't pushed the button for a drink. Maybe God did have a softer side. She drank it.

Delta thought she could guess SCASL's thought process, even if she completely disagreed with it. They had to restart an entire civilization with the DNA of just twelve individuals. The genetic consequences of such an inbred population were inevitable. Reducing that pool from twelve to eleven would make the problem even worse. But SCASL was overlooking one key detail: without her, the twelve who landed would almost certainly die before they ever reproduced. The entire point was moot.

Delta was going on the lander. She had been certain of that since the moment she found out it was actually going to launch. Whether or not she would be on it with the digitals' permission had always been up in the air. Now that situation had clarified. Dealing with the bots would be the easy part. Dealing with her fellow humans would be more of a challenge. She had to pick not only who would go with her, but who would be left behind. It was a choice she didn't relish, but one she absolutely would see through. It was just one of a million tough calls she would have to make in her new role as self-appointed leader of the human race.

The only thing she couldn't handle was flying the lander herself. As she understood it, all those systems were automated, and "automated" just meant under the control of a ghost. She only knew of one she could trust.

"Hey, God, want to be my co-pilot?"

Delta heard footsteps. Human ones. She crouched and touched the hilt of Fang over her right shoulder. No one else should be out this far in the outer halls, especially now that SCASL's selection process was winding down. Something was very wrong.

It took her a moment to hear the heavy metal footsteps. There were only a few models that large that walked on two feet. It was most likely a lifting bot. Delta had never liked them. Not that she liked any bots, but lifting bots were as strong as they were stupid. A few of her closest calls had been against them.

Theta and Alpha stumbled past the coffee room. Theta

looked like he was practically dragging her. The lifting bot wasn't far behind.

Delta edged slightly forward. The door tried to slam on her, but it was still stuck in place. It vibrated angrily. Delta gave it a look. It stopped.

It was too late. The door had gotten the lifting bot's attention.

"Organic Delta—"

Delta didn't wait to hear the rest of it. With one smooth motion, she sent Fang cleanly through the lifting bot's neck joint. Its head bounced off the wall and clattered to the floor. It sounded tinny and hollow. That didn't surprise Delta at all. Delta twirled Fang and finished the motion with the sword horizontal above her head and her body in a defensive posture. She was ready for more if the lifting bot was too stupid to die.

It was. The lifting bot rotated at the waist and whipped its massive arm around before Delta's conscious mind could register the movement. She reacted on instinct, rolling to the side. The arm slammed into the wall, leaving a dent centimeters deep. Delta struck the bot's thigh, but the sword bounced off and shook violently, sending vibrations back through Delta's arms. The sword didn't even leave a scratch. She had to admit that whoever handled the metallurgy for the bot's limbs did it right.

The lifting bot rotated at the waist again, this time whipping an arm low. Delta jumped it and swung at the bot's torso, but again her blade bounced off harmlessly.

The bot raised up both arms and slammed them into the ground. Delta stepped back and felt air rush by her face. As the bot stood upright, Delta planted a foot and spun behind it, slashing at the back of its right leg. She cut through an unprotected hydraulic line. The leg collapsed instantly. Now supporting itself on one foot, the lifting bot rotated fully around at the waist and swung an arm. Delta ducked and cut the hydraulic line on the other leg. Bright blue fluid squirted into the air and fell like rain. The lifting bot collapsed.

Delta shook blue fluid off her sword.

"Well, that was fun," she said.

The bot planted both of its hands on the ground and pulled itself into a handstand. Its legs dangled limply from its waist.

"Wait, what?" Delta said.

The bot spun at the midsection. A limp leg whipped around and slammed into Delta's chest, sending her flying across the room. She heard her own ribs break. Fang slipped from her hand. Delta landed flat on her back and couldn't move.

The bot advanced. Delta looked up at it, helpless.

Theta reappeared in the hall behind the bot.

"It's me you want!" Theta said.

The bot ignored him and took another step with its hands toward Delta.

"Fine," Theta said. "I'll come to you."

Theta jumped on it, holding on at the waist between the two dangling legs.

The bot spun its lower half, which was now its upper half. The legs and Theta melted into a blur of motion. Theta hit the wall like a missile. He was perfectly still. The bot moved toward Delta. She regained some feeling in her body and attempted to scoot away.

The bot bent its lower torso forward and spun. Its legs twirled like vertical fan blades. Slowly, it walked on its hands toward Delta. Delta backed up until she hit something solid. This branch of the hall ended at a closed door. She reached up from the floor and frantically pushed the button, but it wouldn't open. She was going to die because she brought Fang instead of Martha. She closed her eyes.

Alpha let out a primal scream. Holding Fang like a lance, she ran full speed and thrust the sword into the middle of the lifting bot's back. The blade struck a metal seam and stabbed cleanly through to the bot's core. The bot's legs immediately stopped spinning. Blue lightning shot in every direction. Alpha yelped and let go of the sword. White hot flames shot out of the puncture wound. Alpha had to shield her eyes.

The fire quickly burned out. What had once been a deadly lifting bot was now a pile of molten slag. Delta painfully got to her feet. She grabbed Fang by the hilt— he was cool to the touch—and pulled him out of the pile. The slag sloughed off the blade like melting snow. Fang was unharmed.

"Now that's craftsmanship," Delta said hoarsely. Every breath hurt.

Alpha knelt beside Theta. She stroked his face.

"Please be alive," she said.

"Which one of you is asking?" Theta asked. He wiped bloody drool from the side of his mouth.

Delta sheathed Fang. The motion sent a new wave of pain through her body, but Fang had taken care of Delta and now Delta would take care of him.

"Let me guess," Delta said. "SCASL read your manifesto."

"At least someone did," Theta said.

# Chapter 32

Epsilon brushed her hair in the mirror. She was one of the only organics to have a reflective surface in her living quarters. Kappa gave it to her as a gift early in their relationship. Like every other organic who ever found something good, he wouldn't tell her where he got it. She hoped more gifts would show up from the same place, and every once in a while, they did. Besides a mirror, she had a recliner, a freestanding dresser (any drawer not built into a wall was a rarity), and a series of brushes to rival even Omicron's impressive collection. Epsilon really was spoiled. And she deserved it.

Epsilon had to look her best today. She was running the simulation with eleven other organics and would probably be observed by the rest. Well, the rest minus a few. There would always be sore losers.

The doorbell rang. The nursery was one of the few rooms in the base to have one, which was one of the three main reasons she made it her home. The other two were space and nostalgia. It was a big room. It had to be. It's where Edubot spent most of their early years raising them.

Epsilon even kept some of the toys and learning equipment she and the other organics used to play with until they were fast enough and strong enough to risk going out into the rest of the base. Back then, even the colony ship had been dangerous until Edubot largely pacified it. She really was quite good to them. It was a shame SCASL stole her body and stuck her in a snack cart.

"Come in, babe," Epsilon said.

Delta stepped through the door.

"Oh," Epsilon said. "I thought you were Kappa."

Delta looked nervous and tired. Usually, she just looked tired. She had disappeared a week ago, along with Alpha and Theta. No one noticed the absence of the other two. Epsilon barely noticed the absence of all three.

"We need to talk," said Delta.

"We really don't," Epsilon said. She went back to brushing her hair. Omicron might have the fanciest updos, but Epsilon had the best-looking hair when down. You could ask anyone, as long as that "anyone" was Epsilon or Kappa.

"It looks like you're going to be on the lander," Delta said.

"Selections have not—"

"—been finalized," Delta finished. "I heard the official line from SCASL, too. But cut the crap. We both know it's you."

Epsilon stopped brushing her hair and looked deeply at her own reflection. "So what if it is? Are you here to congratulate me?"

"I'm here to make a deal," Delta said.

Epsilon scoffed. "You and everybody else. Everyone wants something from me now that they know I'm going to be in charge."

The number of favors Epsilon had been asked for in the last week was truly staggering. Tau asked for a law that made afternoon siestas a constitutional right. Xi wanted a sloth preserve, which he claimed Delta had already approved. And Sigma wanted a gymnastic horizontal bar. That was a super idea on a planet with no metal and frequent lightning storms. Each request was dumber than the last. Epsilon crossed her arms and prepared for more of the same.

"I want you to help me overthrow the digitals and take the lander by force," Delta said.

For the first time, Epsilon looked at Delta with more than the corner of her eye. Delta was serious. And she had something on her back.

"Is that a sword?" Epsilon said.

"Yeah," Delta said. "Things have gotten... complicated."

"Where did you find a sword?" Epsilon asked. "There's no way someone packed that for the trip from Earth."

"I made it," Delta said with a hint of pride. "I have more. We can use them to take the lander."

"You're going to fight bots made of metal... with swords," Epsilon said. "And you don't see the problem with that?"

"These aren't normal swords," Delta said. She drew

the sword and swung it at a metal countertop. It cut right through.

Epsilon's eyes got wide, but she quickly remembered to look unimpressed.

"This is how you spend your time?" Epsilon said. No wonder Delta couldn't cut it as a leader. Why waste your days making medieval weapons when there was an entire planet to colonize with human and digital life? Some people just couldn't see the big picture.

Delta sheathed the sword.

"Do you know why I was eliminated from the landing party?" Delta asked.

"You haven't been eliminated," Epsilon said, even though she knew exactly why Delta was out. People didn't like or respect her. Delta was too brusque. Too militant. Too her. Yes, she could kill roos in a fairly efficient manner, but that was the beginning and end of her leadership skills. Could she really be trusted to facilitate the long-term alliance between organics and bots that would lead to the spread of digital life among the stars?

"I was cut because I can't have babies," Delta said.

"Why can't you have babies?" Epsilon said

"I don't want to get into it," Delta said.

Epsilon shook her head. "That's not why. SCASL just picked who's best for the mission," she said, dropping all pretense that his decision wasn't final. "And that's me. I'm special. And I support democracy."

"You just manipulate people into supporting whatever

you want to do anyway," Delta said.

"That's the difference between a democracy and a dictatorship," Epsilon said. Her tone softened the tiniest amount. "I'm sorry you didn't make the cut. But there's nothing I can do about it."

"Yes, there is," Delta said. "Help me take the lander. You can be my second-in-command. We'll pick the best organics to go with us."

Realization dawned on Epsilon. "You don't just want to overthrow the digitals," Epsilon said. She backed up a step. "You want to overthrow me. That's why you came here armed."

"I would never hurt you. You know that," Delta said. She moved toward Epsilon, but Epsilon recoiled. "You need me. If I'm not in charge, you're going to die. All of you."

"Now you're not even trying to hide your threats," Epsilon said. She glanced desperately at the door. Where was Kappa? He should have been here by now.

"That's not a threat at all," Delta said. "I won't kill you. The roos will. Or the sea monsters. Or the lightning. All of your simulations end in disaster."

"Not since you left," Epsilon said. "Now I win every time. Maybe the problem was you." Epsilon knew that didn't make sense—she and Delta had never been in one of SCASL's simulations together—but it didn't have to be a logical argument. Epsilon just needed to stall for time.

"You don't get it," Delta said. "SCASL changed the simulation to make it easier for you."

"That's totally illogical," Epsilon said. She backed into her dresser. She tried to think of anything on it that would help her win a sword fight but came up blank. "He said from the start that he wants us to train in real conditions."

"Well, you can't do it, and he doesn't want the other organics to freak out," Delta said. "No one will follow you if they know you're leading them to certain death."

"So you think he's building up my confidence because he doesn't want me to know I'm definitely going to get us all killed?" Epsilon said. She was furious at Kappa. Of all the days for him to be late. "Sure, that makes sense."

"He doesn't want you to die at all," Delta said. "He just doesn't think he has a choice. His control of the lander isn't as good as he wants us to think. He's terrified of losing it to a ghost, or to one of us. He figures a bad launch is better than no launch at all."

"And you know all of this because…?"

"I talked to an informed source," Delta said.

"Gamma's God?" Epsilon asked. "Does he still live in a coffee maker on deck three?"

"Deck four, actually," Delta said. Her cheeks flushed a little. "That's not the point. SCASL is making a flawed decision, and it's going to end badly for everyone. If you really want organic and digital life to continue, you'll help me take the lander. It's the only way any of us have a future."

"Delta, the Messiah," Epsilon said. "Arrogant much? And now you're making demands at the point of a sword."

Delta pulled the sword from her back and stabbed it into the ground. It pierced the deck plating and stood upright. "Forget about the sword!" She took a deep breath. "I still love you."

"Not this again," Epsilon said. "You sound like a child."

"You used to love me, too!"

"A long time ago," Epsilon said. "Back when we were twelve."

"We're still twelve!" Delta said.

"Actually twelve," Epsilon said. "Not twelve going on whatever age we are now."

Delta slapped the hilt of the sword. It wobbled back-and-forth, still stuck in the floor. "It's not like I have any other options," she said. "It's literally only you."

Epsilon locked eyes with Kappa, who was standing in the doorway. He must have heard the distress in her voice from down the hall. He was holding a metal pipe.

"She's going to kill me!" Epsilon said.

Kappa swung the pipe. Delta's automatic reflexes took over. Without a single conscious thought, she grabbed the sword and pivoted, slicing upward. She caught Kappa at the armpit. His arm hit the floor, still clutching the pipe. Blood spurted from the gaping wound. The cut was so clean that Kappa barely even felt it. He stared at the spot where his arm used to be.

"You cut off my arm," he said, dumbfounded. He fell over.

Epsilon screamed. She felt a gapping chasm in the middle of her chest.

"I'm so sorry," Delta said to Kappa. "You attacked me. Why did you attack me?"

Epsilon's screams grew louder. Delta managed to unclench her own fingers from around the sword. It clattered to the ground.

"Help me get him to a med bot," Delta said. "There's still time."

Epsilon kept screaming. Delta tried to drag Kappa by his one remaining arm. He was bigger and heavier than Gamma. She slipped and fell in his blood on the floor.

"Murderer!" Epsilon screeched. Kappa was unconscious and growing paler by the second. There was so much blood.

"Help me," Delta begged Epsilon. Delta tried again to drag Kappa, but he wasn't going anywhere.

Omicron and Sigma ran into the room. They stopped at the ghastly sight and turned white.

"What happened!?" Sigma asked.

"Delta killed him!" Epsilon yelled between screams and sobs. "She killed him."

"He's not dead!" Delta said. "You two, help me get him to a med bot."

Omicron and Sigma just stood there.

"Damn it, help me!" Delta yelled. She picked up the sword. Omicron and Sigma ran.

Delta swore. She used the sword to cut off a piece of her jumpsuit to form a tourniquet, but there wasn't anything to tie it to. The cut was right at the shoulder. Seconds passed. Or minutes. Or years. Epsilon couldn't be sure. She watched as the last of the color faded from Kappa's face. He was dead. Epsilon was sure of it. She looked almost as pale as he did. So did Delta.

"We could have saved him," Delta said quietly. She stood up. She was covered in blood.

"You killed him," Epsilon sobbed.

"We could have saved him!" Delta repeated. "Damn your cowardice. Damn you all."

Delta picked up her sword and wiped off the blood on the only clean spot on her jumpsuit. Then she sheathed it and walked from the room. When she got to the hallway, she ran.

# Chapter 33

GAMMA WATCHED FROM the back of the crowd as Epsilon stepped onto the empty planter. In better times—when exactly those times were, nobody knew—there might have been a tree here, stretching toward the heavens beyond the transparent dome above to remind them all that life endures. But the dome was entirely covered with blast shields, and the closest any organic on the base had come to real plant life were the boards grown in molds that the Peapod had offered to use for a funeral pyre. Epsilon said no.

In front of Epsilon, Kappa lay beneath a bed sheet on top of a cafeteria cart. It had been hard to find one that wasn't roboticized in some way, but in the end, Omicron managed to locate a simple metal table with wheels in an out-of-the way dining area on deck eight. The organics feared that if they put Kappa on any bot that could hold a ghost, it might turn on them and add to the funeral's body count. Inside the colony ship, organics were usually safe from digitals. Then again, inside the colony ship, organics were usually safe from other organics. Now was not a time to take anything for granted.

Gamma watched Epsilon survey the crowd, which was just the seventeen other organics who weren't dead or in exile in the outer halls. He couldn't help but remember that when his arm got crushed by a door and everyone thought he was dead, no one particularly cared. Well, no one but Alpha and Theta, who were now on the run thanks to that stupid manifesto. And Delta, who fought so hard to save his life, even as she repeatedly claimed she was indifferent to whether he lived or died. Now she was a fugitive, too. Would someone who worked so hard to protect him, an organic she had said maybe two sentences to over the past who-knows-how-many-years prior to his run-in with the door, really so coldly and callously kill Kappa? Then again, did Gamma really expect Delta to stand idly by while she was left behind?

"We will never forget Kappa," Epsilon began. Her voice cracked. She didn't have any notes. "I loved him. We all loved him." She paused and looked across the faces staring up at her. "His memory will live on in us. We will honor him by surviving. We will honor him by winning. Hate will not defeat us. We will land. We will spread. And we will prosper."

There was a smattering of light applause. Gamma kept his hands by his sides. Spenser shifted uneasily on his spider legs. Nobody knew quite what to do. It had been so long since Mu and Chi died, even if they were all still only twelve.

SCASL wasn't at the funeral. He was directing the other bots in the hunt for Delta. He said it wasn't safe to leave her on the loose. That made Gamma uneasy, too. SCASL had asked everyone if they knew where Delta went. Gamma said nothing. He didn't want to be led by a murderer, but he didn't want to get her killed, either. Organic life—human life—was precious. All of it.

Epsilon gingerly stepped down from on top of the planter and exited the arboretum. Pi, Phi, and Psi pushed the cart, one behind and two on each side. Phi took the occasion so seriously that he wore a full jumpsuit instead of one cut into shorts. The Peapod didn't get to have their funeral bonfire, but they did get to be pallbearers. That had been Epsilon's idea, too. She knew how to find compromise, as a good leader should. Everyone else followed the cafeteria cart out of the arboretum.

The procession traveled through the halls of the colony ship and toward an airlock. Normally, airlocks were something organics avoided at all costs. If one had a ghost, it was all too easy for it to blast you out into oblivion before you even realized anything was wrong. Mu found that out the hard way. She had always been the boldest organic, unafraid to explore corridors even bots avoided. Gamma knew it would only be a matter of time before disaster struck. After Mu died, all of the organics swore they would never forget her, but even now, Gamma had trouble remembering exactly what she looked like. That was a drawback of such a long life. He wondered how long it would be until they all forgot Kappa, too.

Epsilon knew the risks of approaching the airlock, but she decided it was worth it. It seemed more respectable than the alternatives. There had been much discussion about what to do with Kappa's body. After Epsilon shot down the funeral pyre idea, Sigma had suggested that they lay Kappa's body in the mining tunnels below the base. That was even more dangerous than using an airlock. The tunnels were largely uncharted, even by bots, and pockets of vacuum were so abundant that even Mu didn't explore down there much. Others suggested that they pick a room on the colony ship to use as a mausoleum and seal Kappa inside it. That idea wasn't popular, either. They all wanted to remember Kappa, but not that much. It was good to have a little distance between the living and the dead. In the end, Epsilon chose the airlock, and everyone deferred to her wishes. They were used to agreeing to the least bad of several terrible options.

The procession stopped in front of the airlock. Epsilon had chosen this one because it had a viewing port not covered by a blast shield. Pi, Phi, and Psi carefully lifted Kappa's wrapped body from the cart and set it on the floor of the airlock. They quickly stepped back. Epsilon pushed the button to seal the chamber.

"Before we release his body into space, I thought it would be nice if we could all say a few words about what Kappa meant to us," Epsilon said.

"He loved to jump out and scare people," Psi said. For once, she was telling a story Gamma knew for sure was true. "One time, he did it when I was walking back from the cafeteria on deck four. I got so startled, I choked on my ration. Kappa had to save me." There was a smattering of laughter. Gamma had forgotten about how much Kappa liked to jump out at people when they were younger. He always hated that. In fact, Kappa spent most of their early childhoods being a big jerk to him. Thankfully, he grew up. Now, he was a smaller jerk. Actually, now he was dead.

"I'll never forget what a great surgeon he was in the simulator," Eta said. He nervously fiddled with half a ration block in one hand. "I watched him save countless lives. Especially after the dentopuses got after the unicycles. He was magical. Those unicycles gave him a lot of work." Left unsaid was that the champion of those unicycles was now fleeing for his life.

"I'll never forget how warm he was," Epsilon said. "He was like a space heater. I couldn't cuddle with him without breaking into a sweat." She looked down at his cold, lifeless body beneath the sheet and blinked back tears.

Gamma didn't have any fond memories of Kappa, but he found that he, too, was on the verge of crying. At best, Kappa had been rude and standoffish toward Gamma. The great doctor was also good at everything else, and he wasn't shy about letting people know it. Gamma found him insufferable. But now that Kappa was gone, he sounded like the greatest person ever to live. Even Gamma missed him. Gamma decided that maybe eulogies weren't the best way to take the measure of a person.

When the pause between eulogies became long enough that it was clear no one else had anything to say, Upsilon stepped forward. Her jumpsuit was freshly cleaned and wrinkle free. She sang an upbeat, jaunty tune she said was traditional at funerals on Earth. It was called *Let The Bodies Hit The Floor*. It seemed appropriate. Even Spenser liked it. He swayed rhythmically on his spider legs. When Upsilon finished singing, she stepped back into the crowd.

Then Zeta came forward. "We should say something for his soul," Zeta said.

Everybody groaned.

"I know, I know," Zeta said. "Nobody wants to think about it. But there's a chance Kappa isn't really dead. He might live on, not just in our memories, but literally as an incorporeal being in some kind of heaven. So we should pray, just in case." With that, Zeta launched into a prayer from a religion he had chosen at random. He didn't speak or understand Hebrew, but his learning pod on the top level of the amphitheater taught him to say each word phonetically. He mumbled the words in a strange tongue that neither he nor any other living organic understood. Gamma had to admit it made him feel better. Maybe there was something to this religion stuff after all.

When Zeta was done speaking, Epsilon again turned to face Kappa in the airlock. "Good bye, babe," Epsilon said. "I'll miss you every day for the rest of my life."

She pushed the button on the airlock. Oxygen blasted

out, taking Kappa's body with it. He landed ten meters from the airlock in a contorted position, half uncovered with his butt in the air. His severed arm landed several meters past that. Pi and Psi gasped. Epsilon screamed. Upsilon fainted.

"What did you expect?" Lambda mumbled. "There's gravity. He's not just going to drift off into space."

Epsilon stared in horror at Kappa's body. Choosing an airlock with an uncovered viewing port was a mistake. Omicron gently took her by the arm and led her away from the window.

"Should we retrieve him and try again?" Pi whispered.

"I'm not going out there," Psi whispered back. That was too morbid, even for someone who loved ghost stories as much as her.

Gradually, the organics dispersed. Gamma was one of the last to remain. He looked at Kappa, who would be in that undignified position for the rest of time. Permanent decisions were being made all around Gamma. He had to take a more active role in his own destiny.

He approached Zeta, who was staring past Kappa and out into space. Zeta turned and solemnly shook Gamma's hand.

"I'm ready to join your movement," Gamma said quietly.

"What movement?" Zeta said a little too loudly for Gamma's liking.

"The one where we decide who goes on the lander, not the digitals."

"The digitals have our best interests at heart," Zeta said. "I was wrong." He motioned to Kappa. "It's the organics we can't trust."

"You're okay with the bots picking who lives and who dies?" Gamma asked.

"They were right about Delta," Zeta said. "They booted her, and look what kind of a person she turned out to be. We all have to do what's best for all organic and digital life. It's not about us as individuals. It's about something bigger."

"Oh," Gamma said. After being chased through the station on Zeta's recruiting drive over the previous months, Gamma was stunned. These were strange times. Organics were killing organics. Zeta supported bots. Epsilon held all of their futures in her hands.

Gamma didn't have any training to do, and he didn't feel like going back to his empty room. Ever since Kappa's death, it had seemed positively claustrophobic. He just wanted to talk to someone, and at the moment, he didn't think Spenser was going to cut it. He needed someone with a broader vocabulary.

"Do you want to go for a walk?" Gamma asked. "Maybe talk about one of your religions or something?"

"I can't," Zeta said. "I have to get to the Table."

"The Table?"

"I'm the surgeon," Zeta said. "Remember?"

Spenser whirred. Gamma got it, too. All the talk about self-sacrifice and doing what was best for all of organic kind was nothing but cold, calculated self-interest.

They were all just looking out for themselves. Was that really why Delta killed Kappa? Did he try to stop her from slaying Epsilon, who took her spot? No, Gamma, decided. If Delta wanted Epsilon dead, she would be dead. And she gained nothing from killing Kappa. She definitely didn't want Zeta on the lander. She disliked him as a surgeon and as a person. Nothing about this made sense.

Gamma and Spenser walked away. Gamma had much to think about—and no idea who to trust.

# Chapter 34

ZETA DID HIS best to hold the scalpel steady. He could make this cut. It was a simple tracheotomy. He had watched Kappa perform several. But Kappa wasn't here anymore, and he never would be again. It was Zeta's time to shine.

Zeta started the incision. Previous times, he had applied too much pressure and sliced something he wasn't supposed to, which was almost anything in the human body. Organics were so fragile. But today, applying exactly the same amount of pressure as on all of his previous failed attempts, the scalpel stopped in the right spot, and the tube practically inserted itself in the patient's throat. The patient made a full recovery. Like, instantly. He sat up and shook Zeta's hand. It was the greatest feeling of Zeta's life. He was living a dream.

Ever since Epsilon had been put in charge, everything had been going better in the simulator. Zeta was nervous he might derail her run of success when SCASL chose him to replace Kappa. Not nervous enough to decline a spot on the lander—he was going to survive no matter what—but he still expected some tension from other organics. But Epsilon went out of her way to make Zeta feel welcome. She said it wasn't Zeta's fault that he benefited from a tragic situation. All they could do now was whatever was best for the survival of all organics everywhere. Zeta felt like a hero.

His incredible run of luck never slowed down. He was almost positive he accidentally left his scalpel inside one patient, but then he found it on the instrument table instead. It was perfectly clean. Apparently he was such a good surgeon that he sanitized everything without even remembering that he did it. With another patient, he accidentally cut a critical artery, but the artery spontaneously healed itself. It seemed that even inside the simulator, there was room for miracles. Zeta made a note to himself to add prayer to his list of recommended treatments. And now, Zeta had just saved his tenth patient in a row thanks to this all-too-easy tracheotomy. The other organics were starting to trust him again. No one would feel afraid to be under his care. Apart from that one unfortunate murder, this was the best week of Zeta's life.

The simulation ended. Zeta and the other organics at the Table took off their neural helmets and set them aside for the next group. All the other organics who weren't dead or in exile were in the stands of the amphitheater. Nobody went out on their own anymore with Delta on the loose. SCASL assured the organics that he had bots posted as sentries, but the increased presence of digitals made the organics nervous, too. You never knew when one might go rogue with a hostile ghost. The organics felt safest in groups, and the biggest group was always in the amphitheater. Besides, it was virtually the only entertainment on the base. Organics came in the morning and stayed through every session. SCASL kicked them all out at the end of the last evening simulation—he said he needed privacy to reset the Table—but during daytime hours, the organics were always together. Zeta was relieved for the company, and even more relieved to have an audience for his greatest successes. His past surgery mishaps were all but forgotten.

As the organics left the Table, SCASL addressed the crowd. "Organics, please take your seats," he said. "I have an announcement."

Zeta climbed into the stands. He looked around for a friendly face, which was virtually everyone these days. He had never been so popular. He glanced at Gamma, who made eye contact but quickly looked away. Zeta sat by Tau, who was on the verge of falling asleep sitting up. Zeta elbowed him in the ribs to perk him up. Tau was less than pleased.

"As you know," SCASL began, "the lander was built with twelve seats. That meant we could only build a civilization from twelve starting organics. But, since you are all so exemplary, I recalculated the load the vessel can carry and rebalanced its stock of supplies. Given your outstanding capabilities, I can now equip the lander with seventeen seats. You are all going to land."

A wild cheer went up from the crowd. Most stood and clapped. Only Gamma and a few others remained silent.

"There are eighteen of us," Rho called out.

"I can equip the lander with eighteen seats," SCASL said. "If you heard seventeen, you are in error." The organics cheered again, but this time their enthusiasm was more subdued.

"What about Alpha and Theta?" Lambda asked. Her astronomy work in the command center had ground to a halt since they disappeared.

"They opted not to land and are now making new lives for themselves in the outer halls," SCASL said. "I wish them the best."

"What about Delta?" Gamma asked. Spenser whirred supportively, but a chill settled over the room.

"Delta will be dealt with swiftly," SCASL said.

Zeta's head was swimming. They were all going to live. Well, all of them that mattered. It all seemed too good to be true.

"To be clear," SCASL said, "since all of you are landing, there's no reason to murder each other. Your survival is assured. Do not, I repeat, do not murder each other."

Not the strongest note to end on, Zeta thought, but a useful reminder, nonetheless. He suddenly wondered if Delta had actually saved them all. Had she not killed Kappa, SCASL wouldn't have felt pressured to change the lander to protect the organics from themselves. Six extra organics would live because Delta murdered someone. The ethical dilemma that posed would take a lifetime to untangle. Zeta decided not to think about it at all.

But SCASL wasn't done yet. "Now that selection is no longer necessary, I will begin final landing preparations immediately," SCASL said. "Once I finish the modifications, organic and digital life will take a great leap forward. The lander will launch in thirty days."

This time there was cheering across the room. Even Gamma and Lambda clapped for real. Only Rho kept her arms crossed. It was really happening, Zeta thought. They were going to colonize Dion. And based on how the simulations were going, it would be easy. This was going to work.

SCASL dismissed the organics, but no one left. Most of them basically lived in the amphitheater now. Zeta headed directly to one of the learning cubicles in the top ring around the amphitheater. He wanted to review medical literature. He kept mixing up the chambers of the heart, but it didn't seem like a big deal. He made it through three major surgeries that week without quite knowing what all those squishy parts were, and all three patients made a full recovery. The heart wasn't as delicate as Zeta had been led to believe. Still, it might help his patients feel more comfortable if he could actually articulate whatever it was he had done to somehow save their lives. He started to read.

Two hours later, he woke up. Medical literature was incredibly boring. It was a good thing Zeta was naturally gifted and could get by without it. Still, as the human race's only surgeon, he should probably learn what he could. But he had thirty whole days to become a fully certified doctor. No need to rush.

Iota knocked on the outside of the learning pod.

"Are you coming on patrol?" she asked.

Patrolling wasn't technically one of Zeta's duties, but ever since Delta's unprovoked attack, organics had banded together to watch for her. Not outside the colony ship, of course. The outer halls were far too dangerous for anyone but her. But on the off chance she tried to get back into the colony ship to kill more organics or, worse, seize the lander, they would be ready for her. Although "ready" was relative when dealing with a crazy organic with a sword. But the patrols made everyone feel safer, so Zeta joined in. It was the civically minded thing to do.

"Are you excited about landing?" Zeta asked as they walked down a seldom used corridor on one of the lower decks.

"Absolutely," Iota said. She bounced her blue rubber ball. "To be honest, I was a little worried I wasn't going to make the cut."

"I was never worried," Zeta said. "I always trusted the judgement of the bots."

Overhead, something rattled. Zeta and Iota both froze. It sounded like it was coming from a vent. "What was that?" Iota asked.

"Probably nothing," Zeta said.

"We should check it out," Iota said.

"Yeah," Zeta agreed, "you should check it out."

Iota tossed the ball to Zeta, who dropped it. She grabbed the vent and did a pull-up to put it at eye level. She peered into it for a long moment.

"All clear," she said, although she didn't sound so sure.

"See?" Zeta said. "I knew there was nothing to worry about."

They continued on their patrol.

# Chapter 35

DELTA DIDN'T SLEEP for three days.

It wasn't her fault. It was all her fault. The events from Epsilon's room played themselves out over and over in her mind. At the start of the fourth day, she realized she hadn't eaten anything since Kappa's death. She tried, but the vaguely cherry flavored ration barely made it down her throat before she threw it up. She didn't know if it was possible to literally die from guilt, but she had a feeling she was about to find out.

She hated herself for killing Kappa. She hated herself for feeling guilty about killing him. She couldn't afford self-pity. She had people to protect. Delta debated whether or not to tell Alpha and Theta what happened. She had hidden the two refugees in a long-disused bot refit bay deep in the outer halls. The spot was remote and had multiple paths for escape. She made sure to stay away from them as much as possible so no bot could follow her to them. But after she threw up the rations, she realized she had to go see them. Not for them, but for her.

"I killed Kappa," Delta began.

She told the whole story, or her version of it. It was the one where she wasn't a coldblooded murderer, but she wasn't completely innocent, either; the one where she chose to carry a weapon and accepted that that might lead to situations where she used it; the one where she was attacked first but reacted with disproportionate force. Could she have dodged rather than counterattacked? Did she need to be armed on the colony ship at all? The attack proved she did. Or it proved she was attacked because she chose to be armed. She honestly didn't know.

It was more talking than Delta had ever done in her life. Alpha and Theta listened silently. At the end, with tears streaming down her eyes, Alpha gave Delta a hug.

"Oh, honey," Alpha said.

The three of them never discussed it again. Alpha and Theta neither rendered judgement nor gave her absolution. She had done a thing, and now that thing was done. That's all there was to it.

Delta finally slept on the fourth night, but only fitfully. She knew she needed her rest. If she didn't seize control of the lander, far more than one person would die. The entire landing party—and any hope for their species—would be wiped out. But what if she had to kill again to take the lander? She had to be ready. Guilt had no place in her heart when the future of all organics was at stake.

After so many years of running a simulation where hundreds of millions of humans died under her command, Delta was shocked at how much her first real kill affected her. Maybe it was because she hadn't meant for it to happen. If she'd decided Kappa needed to die for the greater good, then she could have killed him without hesitation. At least that's what Delta told herself. But she killed him by accident, or as close to an accident as it could be when you hack off someone's arm with a sword. Kappa belonged on the lander, and the human race's chances of survival were greatly diminished by his death. By the fifth morning after the incident, Delta decided that was what hurt the most: she had wasted an irreplaceable resource.

Delta vowed she wouldn't make that mistake again. Carefully, she put on her pressure suit. It was sized for an adult and sagged around her. Air hissed out immediately. She tried on three more before she found one that appeared to be airtight. Gamma's God had been quite specific about Chi's final resting place, and she intended to find it. What she didn't expect to find was oxygen. Anyone who assumed they could breathe unassisted through the mining tunnels was asking to die.

As she entered the first of the tunnels, Delta realized she was risking her life based on the advice of a coffee maker. She knew it wasn't really God, "a" or "the." It was just another ghost in a machine. But weren't gods supposed to be omniscient? And the ultimate source of truth? And look out for your best interests? So, if this machine knew more than Delta and told her the truth and helped her avoid death, why couldn't it be God? Or as much of a God as Delta would ever need? Delta wasn't Zeta. If this God was good enough for Gamma, it was good enough for her. And it might just save them all yet.

The tunnels zigzagged erratically underground. It was like the mining bots that made them didn't know when to stop and kept going, long after there was no worthwhile material left to be found. Delta's monitor said this tunnel had atmosphere, but she didn't dare take off her helmet. Some of the caverns were pressurized, but others only had atmosphere because it had leaked there from the rest of the base, making it thin and prone to disappearing entirely at the slightest disturbance from elsewhere in the tunnel system. At least there were no bots—yet. She carried Fang just in case. The scabbard wouldn't fit over her shoulder in the pressure suit, so she carried the blade in her hand.

God's directions held true. After taking several blind turns and climbing down a ladder, she entered a large chamber filled with massive piles of lumber many time's Delta's height. It was clear the molds that grew boards had been left to run long after the organics knew wood would be useless on Dion. That's what everything on the moon base seemed to do. The digitals carried out their purpose, even when their purpose had no purpose anymore. Behind one stack of lumber, Delta found Chi, right where he was supposed to be. He hadn't decomposed at all. The dry, bacteria-free cavern had mummified him just as he had been the day a dishwasher bot killed him because he beat it at chess. It was the last time any of the students played a game with a bot. On Comus, a lack of sportsmanship could be fatal.

Delta stared at Chi. Until that moment, she had forgotten what he looked like. She thought she remembered, but her mental image had become hazy over time. He was so young, maybe eleven. A real eleven. Decades separated him from Delta at twelve. He was curled up in the fetal position with one side of his head smashed in. It was a horrible sight, but it didn't bother her as much as the sight of Kappa's lifeless body. This one wasn't her fault.

When Chi died, there was no funeral or remembrance ceremony. One day he was there, and the next he wasn't. Edubot pretended nothing had happened. Chi was deleted from the roster of children, and his belongings disappeared. The other organics were forbidden from saying his name. It didn't exactly help Edubot's program of making the organics trust digitals if digitals killed them randomly over board games. They only knew what happened because Sigma had been nearby when Chi died. The dishwasher unit tried to catch her, but she jumped over some cafeteria tables and got away. She had been doing parkour ever since. As for the dishwashing unit, Edubot used his gleaming metal mining talons to dismantle it piece by piece. It was a slow process. It screamed for days.

Delta got down on her hands and knees and tried to move Chi into a more restful position. She heard his brittle bones snap. She couldn't move him without breaking him. She held out Fang and cut off a small lock of his hair. Then she collected loose stones from the cavern and piled them around him. It was arduous work in a pressurized suit. Finally, she took off her helmet. The air didn't feel much different than in the rest of the base. Maybe the chamber was low enough that the gases wouldn't drift away so easily.

After an hour, she had piled enough rocks to completely cover Chi.

"Rest easy, friend," she said, but her words felt empty. Nobody would ever know or care that Chi had a proper burial. She took one last look at the cairn and secured her helmet for the return journey.

Finding Mu was easier. It was just a matter of locating the right airlock. Once again, God's directions were spot on. Mu hadn't been that far into the outer halls when she was killed. She had been on her way back (it still bothered Delta that she couldn't ask Mu from where) when an airlock next to her had simply opened and sucked her out. It was a terribly unfair and unremarkable way for someone so brave to die. She and Mu used to compare notes and occasionally show off oddities they found on their most daring adventures. Mu once came back with a wedding ring. Delta had no idea where she got it. There were no remains anywhere of the original colonists on the station, even though many of them must have died here given the presence of so many reddish brown stains on the walls. Delta wondered if Mu still had the ring with her when she died.

There was no funeral for Mu, either, but unlike with Chi, Edubot didn't try to cover up Mu's death. In fact, Edubot held it up as an example of why the remaining organics needed digitals. Stay in the colony ship where I can protect you, Edubot told them over and over again. Never mind that it was a ghost in an airlock that had killed Mu. Digital life was far more likely to harm them than to help them. If the ghosts ever found a way to propagate digital life without human labor, they would instantly purge themselves of the remaining survivors. Delta was sure of it.

Delta walked in her pressure suit across the surface of Comus. No other students and few other bots ever came out here. Delta found Mu lying flat on her stomach with her arms and legs akimbo. It was so undignified. If Delta didn't know better, she would have sworn that Mu had been blasted out of the airlock just a moment before. Only the thin layer of dust over her body gave away just how much time had passed.

"I'm so sorry," Delta said.

Delta and Mu had never been friends, but they respected each other as competitors. Sometimes, they even explored together, although they usually fought the whole time. Mu was an optimist. She didn't share Delta's deep distrust of digitals. And now Mu was dead by the actions of one of them. Delta hated being right.

Delta cut off a lock of Mu's hair. She didn't build a burial mound. There weren't any loose rocks nearby, and Delta was more exposed on the surface than she had been in the tunnels. The last thing she needed was for a bot to notice where she was and trap her out there. Delta returned to the base. She was almost done.

She was fortunate that she took care of the living humans before her exile. She had offered to help Omicron give haircuts. Omicron was suspicious, but she let Delta sweep hair off the floor anyway. Delta now had the DNA of everyone on base, regardless of which twelve made it on the lander. Maybe she could use the samples to recreate the others in the cloner someday. That was supposedly impossible, but the digitals had lied before. It was worth a try. Or maybe she was just trying to atone for her own guilt.

Delta had one last stop. She reentered the station and walked for an hour before exiting through another airlock. It was still a few kilometers from the one where Epsilon had held the funeral. Delta walked outside in her pressures suit the rest of the way. She stepped carefully as she approached the site. The only light was from what leaked out of the base itself. Comus was currently facing away from the sun. If it were bearing down on her now, she would already be dead. Like Kappa.

The sight of him hit her like a lifting bot arm to the stomach. Delta fell to her knees. She couldn't breathe. He was dead. He was dead because of her.

How many more people would she have to kill if she seized the lander, she wondered. She steadied her breathing. How many would die if she let the lander leave her behind? If she did nothing, she would be killing everyone on that lander through inaction. She had a job to do. She stood up.

Extending Fang, she sliced off a clump of Kappa's hair.

Then she reached out to move him into a more dignified position. She stopped herself. If she moved him, someone would know she had been there. Necessity trumped decorum. She left Kappa with his butt in the air and his severed arm lying several meters away.

# Chapter 36

"I'M GOING TO live!" Omega yelled.

It was the greatest day of his life. After twelve straight years of bad luck, something had finally gone his way. And it just so happened to be the only thing that mattered.

"Hi five!" Omega said.

Phi looked annoyed. He was stacking wood for the bonfire. His jumpsuit shorts were back.

"Dude, I'm trying to light—" Phi started.

Omega gave Phi a crushing hug. It squeezed the air right out of him.

The hug gave Omega's hand a welcome break. It hurt from all the hi-fives. He had slapped hands with all the organics on the base and even some of the bots. Hitting Edubot's serving arm had particularly stung. Omega didn't care. His body would heal quickly thanks to the immortality tank, which would be with him down on the planet. He would live forever.

Omega didn't realize just how much stress he had been carrying around inside him for the past several months.

Or the twelve years before that. Everything had been against him. He wasn't as strong or as fast or as smart as the other organics, no matter how hard he tried. And he did try, even if the others couldn't tell. He did his best every single day. He put in three times as much study time as everyone else. The words just didn't make sense in his head, which was probably why he only finished his college course work twice as opposed to the five or six times Edubot expected. Even with all the extra work, his grades were still just barely good enough to get by. Edubot said more than once that Omega only passed because it was too much work to fail him. And in the end, none of it mattered. Omega was going to land, just like everybody else.

Phi ignited the pile of boards. The arboretum planter filled with bright orange flames. Pi patted Phi's back proudly. Omega was always jealous of the friendship the Peapod had. He would have given anything for just one friend, but most of the organics preferred not to get too close to anyone, especially if that anyone was him. It was like they thought his failures were contagious. The joke was on them. Now they were stuck with him forever.

Psi took her usual spot at the front of the group.

"Tell a happy story tonight," Omega said.

"I don't really do happy stories," Psi said.

"Because they're all true," Rho said.

A few organics laughed. Not Omega. He was done with pessimism. His life had actually worked out.

"Fine. I'll tell one," Omega said. He regretted the

words as soon as he said them. He didn't know what had gotten into him. Actually, he did. Hope.

"Okay," Psi said. She got up from her spot and motioned for Omega to take it. He sat down nervously.

Omega's heart hammered in his chest. Everyone looked at him. Almost everyone. Alpha and Theta weren't here. Neither was Delta. Good riddance. And Epsilon and Iota were patrolling to make sure Delta didn't sneak up on them. But other than the fact that there was a murderous organic on the loose and Kappa was still dead and SCASL got the number of extra seats wrong in his first announcement, there was nothing to be anxious about. This was a night for celebration.

"Tell us about the armadillos," Phi said.

More laughter. Omega definitely wasn't going to talk about those damn little armored balls. It wasn't his fault they all burst into flames in the simulation seconds after—no, he wasn't going to think about that right now. This was a time for happy endings.

Omega suddenly knew what story he would tell.

"This is a true story. Let's talk about Sampi."

"Hey, that's my character," Psi said.

"He's a real person," Pi said. "Remember?"

"Right," Psi said. "Go ahead."

Omega cleared his throat. He wasn't quite as nervous now.

"Sampi isn't lost," Omega said. "He just left."

"Left?" Nu asked. Apparently he was just as eager to poke holes in happy stories as scary ones.

"Yeah," Omega said. "You didn't really think a base this big would only have one lander, right? It used to have two, but he took one down to the planet."

"So he's not lost," Nu said. "He's suicidal."

"Actually, he's neither of those things," Omega said. "He was just curious. He was little and he climbed into the second lander, and it had a ghost that launched it. Took him all the way to Dion."

"Poor little kid," Psi said. Pi winked at her.

"Don't feel bad for him," Omega said. Behind him, the bonfire crackled. "He found out something: Those first organics on Dion, they're still alive. Some of them, anyway. And they lived and reproduced and made peace with the roos. There's a whole civilization down there waiting for us. They don't have a ship to come up and get us, but they know we're coming. And they can't wait."

"Sounds nice," Sigma said.

"It is," Omega said. "The thing is that, in all these simulations, we keep thinking that all organics do is fight. We can't get along with each other. We can't get along with the roos. Everything is a struggle. But that's not the way life really is. More often than not, we cooperate. That's how Earth thrived for so long. It got up to ten billion people without its leaders ever running a single simulation at the Table. It just happened. Everything worked out."

"How are those ten billion people doing now?" Rho asked.

Omega pretended he didn't hear her.

"When we land, it's going to be paradise," Omega said.

"Like the Garden of Eden?" Zeta asked.

"Sure," Omega said. "No one has actually seen the planet in forever. And the digitals, even the Table, they all just assume the worst. But those organics have been down on that planet this whole time working hard to make it livable. You'll see. Sampi is waiting down there for us all."

"Nice story," Nu said. "But you obviously just made it all up. Can you prove any of it happened?"

"Can you prove it didn't?" Omega said.

"Good point," Pi said. "And great story. I believe it all. Upsilon, do you want to sing something?"

"Actually—"

Lambda cut her off.

"Should we get Alpha and Theta?" Lambda asked.

Everyone went quiet. Sparks drifted up from the fire.

"They didn't want to land before," Zeta said. "They made their choice."

"That was before we knew SCASL could add seats to the lander," Lambda said. "Besides, I've been in the command center. I don't think they left of their own free will."

"They didn't," Gamma said. Everyone looked at him. "Spenser saw it all."

"What happened?" Sigma asked.

"Well," Gamma stammered, "it's hard for Spenser to be very specific, but I think they were chased by a bot."

"That's what it looked like to me," Lambda said. "It really wrecked the place."

"It's their own fault," Zeta said. "You saw the manifesto."

"Actually, I didn't," Sigma said.

"Well, he wrote one, and it was exactly as stupid as you'd think," Zeta said.

"What about Alpha?" Lambda said. "Does she deserve to get left behind because of something her boyfriend did?"

"Where do you think he got the paper?" Zeta said.

"If we do get them, won't they just be dead weight?" Beta asked. "They were pretty adamant that they would never fight."

"According to Omega, we won't have to," Nu said.

"That's right," Omega said. He cleared his throat. "Although it's possible my story might not have been one hundred percent based on reliable sources."

"No," Nu said in mock surprise. "Really?"

"What do you think, Gamma?" Lambda asked. "Should we try to find them?"

"I don't know," Gamma said. He looked at the ground. Spenser whirred something. Somehow, the little bot sounded disappointed.

"It won't matter, even if you get them," Rho said. "They won't fit."

"We just have to ask SCASL to add a few more seats," Omega said.

"Where?"

"In the lander."

"Where in the lander?" Rho asked.

"Inside it," Omega said.

He looked around for support. Everyone seemed uncomfortable.

"We all went inside that thing," Rho said. "It was tiny. Claustrophobic, even. SCASL can't fit six extra seats in there. And he definitely can't fit eight."

"There's a cargo hold," Omega said.

"Yeah," Rho said. "For cargo. You know, the stuff that will keep us alive until we can grow our own food."

"Nu, do you want to read something from a book?" Pi asked.

"We're small," Omega said. "We could all fit."

"I didn't bring one," Nu said.

"Then we'll have six more people to feed and that much less space to carry food," Rho said. "Is there something here I'm missing?"

"It could work," Upsilon said. "If anyone could figure it out, it's SCASL. He's the smartest being in existence."

"According to SCASL," Rho said.

"Upsilon, why don't you go ahead and sing," Pi said.

"SCASL wouldn't lie to us," Omega said.

"He lies to us all the time," Rho said.

The arboretum got quiet again. A board collapsed in the fire, sending up a shower of sparks. Phi didn't add any more wood.

Zeta stood up.

"I'm going on the lander whether there's twelve seats

or eighteen, so I'm a neutral party here," he said. "But I think there's eighteen."

"Do you think SCASL could add two more and make it twenty?" Lambda asked.

"Of course not," Zeta said. "That's preposterous."

"But eighteen is reasonable?" Rho asked.

"Yeah," Zeta said. "Why would SCASL lie about that?"

"So we don't kill anybody he wants on the lander," Rho said.

"Stop!" Omega yelled.

The room went silent.

"Don't take this away from me," Omega said. He blinked fast to hold back the tears. "I finally got a break. One time. Just one time, let something good happen to me. I need this. I need this so bad."

"Okay," Rho said quietly. "We're all going on the lander. And we'll meet Sampi."

"That's right," Omega said. He wiped the tears from his eyes. "We will."

# Chapter 37

GAMMA'S EYES SHOT open. He wasn't sure why. The clock said he didn't have to be up for, well, ever. All training had been canceled for days. His night shift on the Table was long since over, and he had readjusted to normal daytime routines.

Gamma closed his eyes, but something in him didn't want to fall back asleep. There was a weird, excited energy in the air, like when the barometric pressure drops before a storm. Or at least before a storm in a simulation. Gamma had never been through one in real life.

Then Gamma heard the footsteps. They were the kind that were twice as obvious as they should be because they were trying so hard to be discreet. There was someone in the hall. Multiple someones. That wasn't entirely unusual. But something felt different this time.

Gamma pushed the button to open his door. Nothing happened. He hit the button again and again. It was common for systems on the base to fail, either from years of neglect or hostile ghosts, but the timing of this breakdown put Gamma on edge.

"Hey, Spense, can you open the door for me?" Gamma whispered. "Something funny is going on."

Spenser activated out of sleep mode and sluggishly rolled to the door. Gamma had fixed his wheels well enough for him to get around, even if he wasn't quite as fast as before. Spenser linked with the door. For a moment, nothing happened. Then the door slid open.

Gamma stepped into the hall.

Half of the doors in this wing were open. Eight other organics—other humans—lived in this wing, even though it was set up for one hundred and twelve. Most of the other students had taken up elsewhere, abandoning their assigned rooms in favor of whatever space they felt like commandeering for themselves. In a giant, mostly empty base, there were always choice rooms available. But Gamma and several others preferred proximity to other living beings. Usually, Gamma found that closeness comforting, but now the entire space felt strange and hostile.

The footsteps were gone now, but looking at the rooms, Gamma could tell who had left: Iota, Beta, Pi, and Zeta. The four doors that were still closed belonged to Omicron, Omega, Phi, and Psi.

Gamma took a step to chase after the footsteps but quickly thought better of it. He pounded on Psi's door. She didn't answer. Gamma pounded again.

"Get up," Gamma said. "It's an emergency."

"What is it?" Psi said sleepily from the other side of the door.

Gamma suddenly felt very stupid. "I'm not sure," he said, "but something isn't right."

He heard Psi push the button to open the door. Nothing happened. She pushed it a few more times.

"I'm locked in," Psi said, a hint of worry creeping into her voice.

"Let her out," Gamma said to Spenser. "Let them all out."

Psi and Gamma pounded on the other doors to wake up the rest of the organics as Spenser worked his way up the hall, opening the doors one by one. They had to wake up everyone. Everyone who was left.

The remaining organics fanned out through the colony ship to spread the word. Gamma rounded the corner to a cluster of rooms near a small cafeteria. The serving cart that was now Edubot arrived at the same moment.

"Who are you here to get?" Gamma asked.

"Classified," Edubot said. She paused. "Correction: I am not here to get anyone. What are you talking about?"

Spenser whirred dismissively.

"Why is it classified?" Gamma asked. "We're all going on the lander."

Edubot hesitated for a moment too long.

"This is not about the lander," she said. "Return to your quarters immediately."

Gamma felt a resolve harden inside him that had never been there before. He had been lied to for sixty-two years, but this was one broken promise too far. Enough was enough.

"If it's all the same to you, I'll just wait here to see who you wake up," Gamma said.

Edubot stayed motionless for several seconds. Then she backed out of the hall.

Gamma ran through the colony ship, pounding on more doors. None of the ones he reached had been locked. Did that mean the classmates behind those doors had all been selected, or did it mean the bots locked and unlocked doors as they went along? There were too many unknowns.

Gamma and Spenser were the last to reach the amphitheater. Everyone who wasn't dead or exiled was there. At the bottom of the amphitheater near the exit to the lander, SACSL stood with eight students: Epsilon, Zeta, Beta, Iota, Sigma, Lambda, Rho, and Pi.

"What's going on?" Gamma called out. SCASL turned to look up at him. The humans with him refused to make eye contact.

Omega seemed beside himself.

"Are you leaving without us?" Omega asked.

"This assembly is unrelated to the lander," SCASL said.

"Are you guys landing?" Phi asked Pi.

Pi said nothing. He wouldn't meet Phi's gaze.

"You bastard!" Phi yelled. He lunged at Pi, but Omicron and Psi held him back. "We were friends, man," Phi said. He choked back a sob. "We were best friends."

"All organics who just entered the amphitheater, report back to your sleeping quarters," SCASL said. "You will be awoken at the appropriate time."

"The appropriate time for what?" Upsilon asked.

"For the next stage of landing preparations," SCASL said.

"No, I think we're good right here," Gamma said.

"Who are the other four organics you meant to wake up for the lander?" Omega asked.

"I did not wake up anyone for the lander," SCASL said. "These organics were gathered for an entirely separate matter."

"Who were the other four?" Omega repeated. Gamma had never seen him this fired up.

"Your mathematical query is based on a flawed premise," SCASL said. "The lander has eighteen seats, not twelve."

"Show us," Omega said. The tears were back. "Show us the eighteen seats and we'll all go back to bed."

"No organics are permitted access to the lander at this time," SCASL said.

"Why not?" Omega asked.

"Classified," SCASL said.

Spenser whirred.

"What do you want me to do?" Gamma asked.

"Then they're not going in the lander either, right?" Omega said. He motioned to the eight who were sheepishly standing behind SCASL.

Edubot entered the amphitheater accompanied by a lifting bot and a chainsaw bot.

"All digitals, please escort undesignated organics out of the amphitheater," SCASL said.

"You said we would all go!" Omega said.

"You will all go," SCASL said.

Omega tried to walk around SCASL. SCASL blocked him.

"I want one of you to look me in the eye and tell me that you aren't going to land without us," Omega said.

None of the eight spoke.

"Epsilon, you're the leader," Omega said. "Just tell me that you're not going to land without us and we'll go back to bed."

Epsilon looked him dead in the eye.

"We're not going to land without you," Epsilon said.

"Liar!" Omega said.

SCASL moved toward Omega. Omega backed up.

"Selected organics, follow your instructions," SCASL said.

"What instructions?" Omega asked.

Spenser nudged Gamma. Gamma reached out a hand for Omega's shoulder.

"Maybe we should—"

The eight students behind SCASL moved toward the lander antechamber. Omega made a break for it. SCASL caught him in the midsection with his gleaming metal talons. They punched through Omega and jutted out from his back. The blood splattered Gamma. Gamma screamed.

The amphitheater erupted into pandemonium. SCASL attempted to shake Omega off his talons. Omega coughed up blood. Somehow, he was still alive. SCASL raised his arm and flung Omega back and forth like a rag doll. The talons tore through Omega's side, nearly cutting him in half. He landed on the floor with a wet thud. His dead eyes stared up at Gamma. Spenser slammed into Gamma's foot. He remembered to run.

"Digitals, secure the selected organics," SCASL said. "Delete the rest."

Edubot rushed at Omicron. Omicron dove into the risers just in time to avoid the murderous snack cart. The saw bot spun in circles, thrusting its spinning blade at anyone who passed.

Gamma made it to the exit back to the base but stopped. He wasn't sure what to do. If he didn't get on the lander, he would die. But if he attempted to board the lander, the bots would kill him. Earlier, Gamma had been willing to accept a long and slow death after he had been left behind. But when SCASL told him he and all the other organics would get a seat on the lander, Gamma's peace with his own mortality had vanished. The realization that those extra seats were a lie was like having a terminal condition that came out of remission. Once restored, the will to survive was hard to extinguish again.

Omicron jumped back out of the seats and ran toward the lander. One of her locks of hair came undone. Edubot extended a serving arm and grabbed it. She pulled Omicron across the floor by her hair. Omicron screamed.

Out of nowhere, Delta appeared. She had a sword. She sliced through Omicron's hair.

"You!" Omicron gasped. She felt her head. "My hair!"

Edubot charged. Delta sidestepped and drove the sword deep into the cart's command console. Edubot stopped dead in her tracks. Snack carts weren't designed to withstand sword attacks. A critical oversight, to be sure.

The chainsaw bot and SCASL both closed in on Delta, ignoring everyone else.

"Run!" Delta yelled. "I'll hold them off."

"They'll leave without us!" Gamma said.

"They won't launch without twelve!" Delta shouted back.

Gamma instantly knew she was right. The bots had put too much time and effort into making sure they had a dozen students ready to land. For the human race to survive and eventually propagate digital life, they needed genetic diversity. Gamma sprinted toward the door that led back into the base. Spenser followed.

The saw bot charged Delta. Delta jumped on top of the Table. SCASL attacked from the side, swinging his talon arm. She met it with her blade and sliced off one talon. The saw bot brought its spinning blade down on the Table. Delta planted a foot on SCASL's head and jumped over him. She landed in a crouch and looked at the chosen organics. They stared back at her in stunned silence.

"I said run!" Delta yelled. "Are you with me or the digitals?"

"Murderer!" Epsilon yelled. She ran at Delta.

Delta hit her with the flat part of her sword. Epsilon fell. SCASL turned and attacked with his two remaining talons. Delta dodged and sprang into the raised seating.

Pi broke ranks with the other seven chosen and ran. Gamma stood at the exit and waved him on.

"Delta's right!" Gamma yelled over the cacophony. "If we run, they can't leave without us!"

"And then what?" Sigma yelled back. She and the other six chosen stayed put.

The saw bot clumsily maneuvered its way up the elevated seating toward Delta. Its blade spun furiously.

"We'll figure it out!" Gamma yelled. "Come on!"

Alpha appeared at the amphitheater door.

"We have to go," she said. "Follow me."

# Chapter 38

DELTA ENTERED THE mining tunnels, bruised and exhausted. She had circled the outer halls of the base for hours to throw off her pursuers, leaving a trail of destroyed bots in her wake. Finally, when she was sure there was nothing left alive to follow her, she doubled back to the emergency safehouse she had set up far below. She hoped the others had made it. Otherwise, this fighting had all been for nothing.

"I'm back," she called out into the cavernous room.

Cautiously, the students who fled emerged from their hiding places. Upsilon hugged her.

"You saved us," she said.

Delta awkwardly struggled out of her embrace.

"No one is safe yet," Delta said.

She pulled the sword and scabbard off her back and stretched her shoulders. Fang had served her well.

"What now?" Tau asked. His colorful nail polish was chipped and stained with blood. He looked like he could use a nap.

Delta took a swig of water. She didn't feel like talking

strategy right now. She had managed to delay the lander. That should have been enough for tonight, but of course it wasn't. It was always something with people. It was just like being in the simulator again. Leadership was the worst.

"We rest," Delta said. "Then we plan."

"Plan for what?" Tau asked.

"Survival."

"Hold on," Nu said. "Who says you're in charge?"

"She's in charge because she saved us," Alpha said.

"That's not how we pick leaders," Nu said.

"Maybe you'd prefer that we let the digitals pick our leader," Alpha said. "We could ask Omega how that worked out."

Omega. Delta had nearly forgotten about him already. She was focused on the bigger picture. An entire species was saved, but one life was lost. Somehow, it didn't bother her. Was it because she didn't kill Omega, or was it because she was already growing harder? Maybe every death after the first one got easier.

"I say we take a vote," Nu said.

"Fine," Theta said with a smile. "I nominate Delta. Any other nominees?"

Nobody spoke up.

"Nu, do you want to nominate yourself?" Theta asked.

"I didn't mean I wanted to be the leader," Nu said. "I just thought maybe it should be someone other than..." He trailed off.

"Other than the only one of us capable of fighting the bots?" Theta finished. "Good thinking, bud."

Nu twisted a book in his hands. It was the one Delta had given him, not that it earned her any good will. Somehow, even in the middle of running for his life, he had managed to bring it with him.

"Everyone who wants Delta as our leader, say 'aye,'" Theta said.

A chorus of ayes answered. Even Nu said it, but a second after everyone else.

"There you go," Theta said. "Delta's our leader. Now shut up."

Delta thought she would feel relief at this show of confidence. Instead, the pressure in her chest seemed to double. Everyone was counting on her. They were on her side—for now. She knew their loyalties would be tested before the end. Delta put down her water. All eyes were on her. She needed to sound like she had things under control.

"There are two ways we can protect ourselves," Delta said. "The best way is to stay hidden. That's why we're in the mining tunnels. Even the bots will think twice before coming down here."

Delta walked over to one of the massive piles of lumber.

"The second way is by stockpiling supplies," Delta said. "We don't know how long we'll have to stay out here. We can't let the bots starve us out."

"That's your plan?" Omicron said. "Hide and wait?"

She looked unsure if she should be relieved to be alive or mad that Delta cut off her braid. She seemed to have settled on both.

"What do you want to do," Delta said, "walk straight back to the lander and take it by force?"

"I don't know, maybe," Omicron said. She rubbed the spot where her missing braid used to be. "Do you have more of those swords?"

Delta didn't answer. Swords were power. Right now, all anyone knew was that she had one. The other eleven had yet to be revealed. If she were going to form an effective fighting force, she would have to arm more allies. But deciding who to train and when was just as delicate as deciding who would go on the lander. Not that she had a lot of options. The students in front of her would form the core of her army. They wouldn't have been Delta's first choice for a landing crew of twelve. SCASL had exhibited some wisdom. With a few exceptions, she thought he picked the most capable options. Zeta was obviously a waste of space, and Sigma was reckless. Scheduling the Not the Not the Death Race when the species was already on the brink of extinction was about the dumbest thing Delta had ever seen, which was really saying something since she had also watched Zeta perform surgery at the Table. As for Epsilon, while she was wonderful in so many other ways, she would never cut it as their overall leader. But Delta would have loved nothing more than to land on the surface with her. Maybe she could have found some other job for Epsilon.

New civilizations need human resources directors, too.

"We're going to divide up into crews," Delta said. "Theta, you're in charge of building obstacles. Take Xi and Nu."

Theta gave her a mock salute. He seemed genuinely excited to have something to do.

"Alpha, you're in charge of the food rations. Make sure everyone gets their fair share and watch so that we don't go through them too fast. Have Eta help you."

"Great," Eta said. "I have some recipes that—"

Alpha put a hand over his mouth.

"We're on it," Alpha said.

"Good," Delta said. "Gamma, we need more water for everyone. There are some pipes we can tap into. Can you handle that?"

Gamma nodded. His eyes were red.

"Where's Spenser?" Delta asked.

"He…" Gamma started. "He's still out there somewhere. I lost him when we were running. His wheels don't turn very fast anymore."

Delta reached out like she was going to put a hand on Gamma's shoulder but then thought better of it.

"He'll be okay," she said. "He's a tough little bot."

Delta turned back to the group.

"Where's the Peapod?"

"Right here," Pi said.

"You three are on guard detail," Delta said. "Cover all the entrances. Give the group an early warning if anyone is coming."

She found Upsilon in the crowd, being sure to keep her distance so as not to fall victim to another hug.

"Upsilon, Omicron, and Tau, get some rest. You have the next guard shift."

"You expect us to sleep after all of that?" Upsilon asked.

"Finally, something I'm good at," Tau said.

"What about you?" Xi asked.

"I'm going to go back into the base and gather other supplies," Delta said. "Blankets. Spare jumpsuits. Soap. Those kinds of things."

"Exactly how long are you planning for us to stay down here?" Pi asked.

"As long as it takes," Delta said. "Maybe we can make SCASL negotiate with us and come to some kind of reasonable settlement. Maybe we'll take over the lander and make our own call. Whatever we do, we're going to do it on our timetable, not on his. Rushing will just get us killed."

"If we wait too long, SCASL could just leave without us," Pi said.

Delta didn't resent Pi's question. Out of everyone that day, Pi impressed her the most. He gave up a guaranteed spot on the lander to become a fugitive. All the other Chosen had held firm. She wondered how much of Pi's decision was because of principle and how much of it was because Phi and Psi were being left behind. His loyalty to his friends trumped his desire for self-preservation. Although if he thought he could get Phi and Psi on the lander, would he switch sides? Or would any of them, for that matter? Besides Pi, four others who ran away with Delta had actually been on SCASL's list. It could be any of them. If the digitals got word to them, they might defect and return to the lander. Delta had to stop communication between the two sides as much as possible. Even the smallest leak of information could be fatal.

"SCASL might launch without twelve," Delta said, "but only as a last resort. He'd be giving up on human and digital life if they went with only eight."

"But you don't know that for certain," Pi said.

"Nothing is ever certain," Delta said, "except death."

"Not with the immortality tank," Pi said.

"Especially with the immortality tank," Delta said. The confrontation at the lander had opened her eyes. Rho was right after all.

## Chapter 39

EPSILON SAT IN the deck sixteen cafeteria at a table with her friends. That's really how she thought of the other Chosen. Well, the Chosen minus Pi and the four unannounced organics who didn't even know they had been picked. They fled with Delta out of cowardice or sheer stupidity or, most likely, a combination of both. Epsilon and the remaining organics at the table were bound together by a common struggle, trying to save the human race in the face of deadly sea life and killer kangaroos and renegade organics who selfishly put their own survival above the good of their entire species. This was her tribe.

Behind Epsilon, bots guarded all the cafeteria entrances. She had never felt safer—or more confined. It was unclear if the bots were there to keep the runaways out or the Chosen in. Epsilon decided it was better not to ask. SCASL wasn't very patient with questions these days.

The Chosen sat in silence. Even before the rift, there wasn't much for them to talk about. When you live together in an unchanging routine for years on end, conversation topics tend to run dry. The one thing that broke up the monotony were the simulations, and now they didn't even have those because Delta tricked a saw bot into cutting the Table in half. They also couldn't talk about the recent battle since SCASL had forbidden the topic. When they did bring it up, it was always in hushed tones. No one wanted to get expelled from the landing party this close to launch.

Epsilon had lost track of the days. That wasn't an unusual phenomenon on the base, but now the disorientation was worse than usual. The bots shuffled the Chosen between the amphitheater, the cafeteria on deck sixteen, and a few storage rooms in a random pattern. It was SCASL's idea, and Epsilon went along with it. Part of being a good leader was knowing when to follow. Her time would come.

Epsilon had asked to go back to her room to pick up supplies, but SCASL insisted the bots would retrieve anything she needed. She asked for the spare jumpsuits from her dresser. A saw bot came back with the shredded remains of what she assumed were supposed to be her clothes. She didn't know why SCASL didn't send a bot with hands, and she shuddered to think of what happened to her dresser. It had been a gift from Kappa. Destroyed or not, she was unlikely to ever see it again.

"Are we the good guys?" Lambda asked suddenly, breaking the silence. She had been barely holding it together for days.

Everyone looked at her. Epsilon took a long drink of water. It was colder than usual, and it didn't sit well with the glut of vaguely cherry flavored rations she had been eating lately. The food dispensers had become very generous with supplies. Epsilon guessed it was because they were leaving soon so there was no longer a need to make the rations last. She would have felt bad for the organics they were leaving behind, but now that they were in open rebellion, most of them would likely meet violent ends anyway. They made their choice.

Epsilon set the cup on the table. Lambda had been talking for weeks about how much she missed the stars. She almost sounded homesick. Her observation post in the command center was now strictly off limits by SCASL's orders, much like every place else that wasn't the room where they were currently being guarded. Epsilon couldn't do anything about that. But this new query was something Epsilon could work with.

"The digitals have taken care of us for…"—Epsilon almost said sixty-two years—"…a long time. There's no reason to think they won't take care of us now."

"Like how they took care of Omega?" Rho muttered.

Epsilon glanced around nervously. SCASL wasn't here, and the other bots were on the far ends of the room at the doors. She wasn't sure how closely they monitored their conversations, or if they reported back to SCASL. She had to assume they did.

Epsilon was tired of talking about Omega. What few hushed whispers the Chosen did exchange always came back to him. Beta and Iota wanted to hold a funeral for him, but Epsilon forbade it (although she said the order came from SCASL). Omega died because he broke the rules. What would have happened if he succeeded at getting on the lander?

"He tried to steal someone's spot," Epsilon said. "Did you want to stay behind so Omega could live?"

"No," Rho said. She looked down at her hands.

"Look," Epsilon said, "in a perfect world we would all land, but we can't. We know that someone had to make the tough call. SCASL did that for us. He's a machine. He made his choice based on empirical data. No favoritism. No agenda."

"I guess," Rho said flatly.

"Do you have a better way to decide?" Epsilon said. "Would you rather that one of you got to pick? Maybe you'd choose your friends and leave behind the organics you just don't like. But what if the organic doing the selecting doesn't like you? Does that seem fair?"

The rhetorical question lingered in the air. Epsilon was on a roll. She got up and started pacing. "Or what if we made it completely random? Forget merit and hard work. Forget putting the best person in the job where they'll help us the most. Just draw lots and see where things fall and leave the survival of the human race up to chance. Does that sound better?"

"Of course not," Rho said.

Epsilon slapped the table. "Exactly. One way or the other, some organics were going to land, and the rest would be left behind. The ones who were left behind weren't going to like it, no matter how the decision was made. Letting the digitals make that choice was the fairest possible way out of a tough situation. We have nothing to feel guilty about."

Around the table, organics murmured in agreement. Even Lambda perked up. She seemed to be fully present for the first time in weeks. Epsilon had them all behind her. Now seemed like a good time to push.

"Let's vote to pick our leader," Epsilon said. "Does anyone have a nominee?"

That sucked the air out of the room. The organics looked at each other.

"We don't have to do this," Rho said. "SCASL picked you."

"SCASL picked who's going to land," Epsilon said. "But this is a democracy. We choose our own leaders."

"Fine," Rho said. "I nominate you. Let's vote."

"Hold on," Epsilon said. "It's not democracy if there isn't a choice. We have to nominate someone else."

No one said anything.

"I nominate Beta," Epsilon said.

"But I don't want to be the leader," Beta said.

"That's exactly why you'd make a good leader," Epsilon said. "Now we can vote. Everyone, raise your hand if you want me as leader."

Everyone raised their hand.

"Now raise your hand if you want Beta."

"We don't have to—" Beta started.

Epsilon held up a hand to shush him. "Democracy, remember?"

She waited to see if anyone would raise their hand. No one did since they had all already voted for her. Beta's face turned red.

"Thanks for that," he said.

Epsilon ignored him. She was riding high.

"Feel free to bring all your concerns to me," Epsilon said. "My door is always open."

"You don't have a door," Rho said. "We're all trapped in the same room together, and all the exits are guarded by bots."

"For our protection," Epsilon said. "As president for life—"

"President for life?" Zeta said. "Is that what we just voted for?"

"Yes," Epsilon said. "Is that a problem?"

"No, no, I'm good with it," Zeta said. He glanced at the others around the table. If the immortality tank worked like it was supposed to, president for life was a never-ending position. A group of seven kids had just picked the ruler of the human race for all time.

"As president for life, our safety is my top priority," Epsilon said.

"Can you use your presidential powers to get us some books?" Rho asked.

"What?"

"Books," Rho repeated. "You know, information printed on thin sheets of wood pulp."

"I'm aware of the concept," Epsilon said.

"SCASL revoked my access to the books in the database, but Nu had the paper kind," Rho said. "He hid them behind a fake wall panel in his room. Maybe those are okay."

Epsilon stood up proudly. This was a perfect chance for her to flex her new leadership powers. "Of course. I'll get them myself."

She marched up to the lifting bot guarding one of the doors as the other Chosen looked on.

"Excuse me," Epsilon said. "I need to get through."

"Egress denied," the lifting bot said.

"I just want to get some books," Epsilon said. "I'll be right back."

"Organics may not leave the cafeteria unescorted," the lifting bot said.

"Then escort me," Epsilon said.

"I am required to guard this door."

"Find me another escort."

"Additional escorts are unavailable."

Epsilon glanced back at the other Chosen. They were all watching her. This was the most entertainment they had had in days. She was grateful they couldn't hear her.

"Will you just send someone to get the books?" Epsilon said. "They're in Nu's room behind a fake wall panel."

"Your request has been taken under advisement," the lifting bot said.

Epsilon threw her shoulders back and returned to the table.

"Well?" Rho asked.

"The machines are going to get them for us," Epsilon said. "They work for me."

## Chapter 40

IOTA DREW A hot breath through the canvas bag. It wasn't thick enough to totally block her vision, so Xi had wrapped an oily rag around her eyes over the top of it. He didn't tie up her hands. She used one to grope blindly in the dark as he led her with the other. With every step, she was afraid she would run into something, and rightly so. She had banged her head on unseen objects more times than she cared to count. Or even could count. She thought that last impact might have given her a concussion. Xi didn't give any indication that he noticed. They walked in silence. Her fingernail itched. It took all her willpower not to scratch it.

She had been alone for seven days. It had been the scariest time of her life. After leaving the colony ship, she had wandered the outer halls, treading lightly wherever she went. For a full week, she didn't encounter any organic or digital life. She was thinking about giving up and going back. That was a terrifying thought. How would the others react? She preferred not to find out.

Finally, deep in a dank hall filled with slowly hissing

steam, she heard footsteps behind her. They sounded too light to be from a bot.

"Hello?" she said. "It's Iota. I want to talk."

The footsteps disappeared. Iota stayed put. She waited in that spot for three days. Her food nearly ran out. She realized she would have to move again to find something to eat. Then Xi showed up.

He stepped out of the shadows nervously. He looked around like he expected an ambush. But there was no ambush. It was only Iota, all alone.

"What do you want?" Xi asked.

"To join you," Iota said. "I ran away."

She told him her story: how she had frozen when Delta launched her rescue at the lander even as Pi ran away; how she and the other chosen became prisoners as the bots guarded them around the clock; how she had waited until a lifting bot was distracted and made a break for it; and how she had been wandering in the outer halls for days, completely and utterly alone. It felt good to be in the presence of another living being. It was the first time she had ever been happy to talk to Xi.

Xi listened to the whole story. He didn't offer her any information in return. He didn't even mention his stupid goldfish. What she would have given to hear about its non-existent tricks right then. Anything to take her mind off what was to come.

"Wait here," Xi said. He disappeared. Iota waited two more days. She had never been so hungry in her life, but she didn't dare leave the area for fear that Xi would show up when she was gone. She hoped she was being watched. This had to be some kind of test to see if she was leading the bots to the renegades. She could completely understand their mistrust. She just hoped it wasn't so strong that they would leave her here to die. Her fingernail itched uncontrollably.

Two days after Xi left, he reappeared with Gamma. Spenser wasn't with him. They brought the canvas sack and later added the rag. Once they were sure she couldn't see, they led her on a long and winding path through the lowest level of the outer halls. That was Iota's best guess, anyway. They went up and down stairs several times, so she couldn't be sure. The whole time, Xi led her by the hand. Thankfully, it was her right.

Gamma pulled off the bag and the blindfold. They were in living quarters with multiple bunk beds and an attached kitchen and bathroom. A layer of dust covered everything. In the corner, a blanket—the only clean object in the room—was draped over something.

Gamma sat beside Iota on a bed while Xi stood by the door.

"Tell me why you're here," Gamma said.

"I already told you," Iota said. She didn't look at her fingernail.

"You told Xi," Gamma said. "Now tell me."

Iota carefully repeated the entire story. It was exactly the same as the first time. When she was done, Gamma stood up. He pulled back the blanket in the corner to reveal a pile of rations and water jugs.

"The bathroom works, but I wouldn't drink the water in there," Gamma said. "This should get you by for now."

"Is this your hideout?" Iota asked.

Gamma and Xi exchanged a look.

"This is where you'll stay until we're sure," Gamma said.

"Sure about what?" Iota asked.

"You know," Gamma said.

He and Xi left and closed the door behind them. Iota sat perfectly still on the bed for what seemed like hours. They didn't come back. She tore into the rations. She ate two full blocks before she stopped herself. She was hit by a wave of panic. She had no idea how long she needed to make these rations last. She took a sip of water and waited.

Iota did jumping jacks and push-ups. She shadowboxed. She ran from one side of the room to the other and back again until she was covered in sweat. She had always been one of the most athletic organics. She didn't have Beta's endurance, but she could beat him in a sprint—and in an arm-wrestling match. She wished she had her blue rubber ball to bounce against the wall. She wished she could scratch her finger.

She tested the door. It was unlocked. She didn't leave. She had nowhere else to go. One day bled into the next. She lost all sense of how much time had passed. Then, when she had one ration block left, the door to the living quarters suddenly opened. Iota jumped up from a dead sleep and hit her head on the bed above. Xi inspected the room. Then he nodded to someone in the hall. Delta strode in. She had a sword on her back.

Iota instinctively scooted back on the bed.

"Are you here to kill me?" Iota asked.

"I'm here to talk," Delta said. "That's what you wanted, right?"

Iota started to tell her tale again.

"Not that story," Delta said. "I already heard it. Twice."

Delta sat on a bed across from Iota. Their knees nearly touched in the middle. She motioned for Xi to leave the room.

"What's the mood like over there?" Delta asked.

"Bad," Iota said. "They're all basically prisoners." She glanced at the door of the room where she had been confined for who knew how many days. Not much had changed. But here, the guard wasn't a bot. It was the vast and empty outer halls. It was more effective than any prison.

"Are they still going on the lander?" Delta asked.

"No way," Iota said. "Not under SCASL. He killed Omega right in front of us. Now they all want to join you."

"All of them?"

"All of them," Iota said.

Delta nodded.

"Where are they?" she asked.

"The arboretum," Iota said. "They keep us there all day every day."

Delta remained impassive.

"How did you escape?"

Iota started to repeat that part of the story.

"No, why didn't they chase you?" Delta asked.

"They didn't chase you guys," Iota said.

"We caught them by surprise in the middle of the night," Delta said. "And they still chased us. I just fought them off."

"Oh," Iota said. "Well, I got away before they noticed."

Delta nodded again. Iota was getting tired of this. She couldn't read Delta at all.

"What do you expect to happen now?" Delta asked.

"I want to join you," Iota said.

"And then what?" Delta asked.

"We'll take over the lander," Iota said. "Kill the bots. Pick who we want to land. By organics, for organics. Isn't that what you have planned?"

Delta got up.

"I've made a decision," she said. "I'm letting you go."

"Letting me go?" Iota asked. Her finger itched worse than ever.

"Go back to your people," Delta said. "Tell them we're still out here and we're not giving up."

"They're not my people anymore," Iota said.

"You're a good liar," Delta said, "but not good enough. You slipped up when you said everyone wanted to join me. Zeta would never do that. He'd watch us all die before he'd risk his spot on the lander."

"Please," Iota said. "I can't go back there. They'll kill me. And I'll die out here on my own."

"I can give you directions to one more food cache," Delta said. "You'll have to forage for yourself after that."

Delta turned to go. Iota saw her chance. In two strides, she crossed the room and slammed into Delta. They fell to the ground together. Iota jabbed her left index finger at Delta. Delta caught her hand at the wrist. The two struggled against each other. Iota pushed her outstretched finger closer to Delta's abdomen. Iota had always been the strongest.

Xi heard the commotion and rushed in. He dove into Iota and knocked her off of Delta. Iota tossed him aside and jumped back on her. The three of them rolled on the ground. Their arms and legs were tangled together. Iota jabbed her left index finger at Delta. She felt the fingernail sink into flesh. The nail made a pneumatic hiss. The itching stopped.

Xi screamed. He frothed at the mouth and convulsed violently. An instant later, he stopped moving.

"That wasn't for you," Iota said. "That wasn't for—"

She felt a whoosh of air and a slight sting at the base of her neck. She had the weirdest sensation that she was falling, even though her body was right where it had been before. She heard a dull thud as something heavy hit the floor. It was the last thought Iota would ever have.

# Chapter 41

THEY BUILT THE cairn for Xi in a mining tunnel not far from where he died. Delta picked the spot. She, Gamma, Theta and Tau gathered what rocks they could until Xi was completely covered. For once, Tau didn't make an excuse about being too tired. He hadn't slept since he heard the news. Iota was still in the room where she fell. Delta hadn't bothered to collect the body, and nobody second-guessed her. Gamma had to admit it was probably the right call. Returning there again would just put all of them at risk of being discovered. Besides, Iota didn't deserve their final respects. She had betrayed them all.

The debate over whether or not to trust Iota had seemed endless. Alpha and Theta had argued stridently that they should accept her with open arms. Nu argued just as forcefully that her presence could only be a trick. When Nu found out how horribly right he had been, he didn't rub it in. He just went off to reread *Infinite Jest*. At some point, it had been cut in half, and he only had the back section. It didn't seem to make a difference.

The four organics stood around the cairn.

"One of us should say something," Gamma said.

No one spoke up.

"Okay," Gamma said. "I'll start. Xi was a good friend. He was a good goldfish cloner."

Gamma shifted uneasily. For the millionth time, he wished Spenser were there with him. He would know exactly what to whir.

"He was a good goldfish cloner. Did I already say that? He would have been great on the planet. He would have made sure we never ran out of animals. Especially goldfish."

Everyone continued to stare at the cairn.

"Somebody else has to say something," Gamma said.

"He always kept his room clean," Tau said. "I lived down the hall from him for a while. He was a very tidy guy."

That was all anyone had to say. It wasn't much for sixty-two years together. Gamma didn't have high hopes for his own funeral.

"We should get back," Delta said.

Gamma had arrived at the scene of the attack moments after it happened. He had been waiting nearby as additional backup. He ran in to find the room already covered in blood. Delta held Xi, who looked like he had died in terrible agony. Gamma had no reason to doubt Delta's story. Xi had a puncture wound on his leg, and Iota had a thin cartridge on one of her fingernails. Still, after sixty-two years with only two deaths, they had now had four deaths practically back-to-back, with two directly by Delta's hands. Gamma would be lying if he said that didn't make him nervous. From what Alpha had said, Delta had been greatly affected by Kappa's death. Iota's didn't phase her at all.

They made their way back through the mining tunnels. It was a long walk from Xi's burial site to their camp. It was a long walk to everywhere.

"What now?" Gamma asked.

"We wait," Delta said.

"For what?" Gamma asked.

Delta didn't answer.

"Waiting is a good move," Theta said. "The others can't launch without a few more of us. If nobody launches, none of the megaroos die. And none of us die by them."

"That worked out real well for Xi," Gamma said. And Iota, Omega, and Kappa, he neglected to add. He didn't feel like repeating the entire list.

"They won't wait forever," Tau said. His fingernails hadn't changed color since he had gone on the run. "If they can't get twelve, they'll launch with eight. It's better than never launching at all. Then what?"

"That would be tragic for them," Theta said. "The roos would kill them all. But we'd be just fine on the base."

"You think the bots will keep us alive after we've been left behind?" Delta said. "We'll be redundant. They'll kill us on sight."

"How is that different than now?" Theta asked.

"It won't be," Delta said. "It will just be this forever."

That killed the conversation. Gamma shuddered at

the thought of living like this for good. Without the immortality tank, he would live at most another sixty or seventy years, assuming a hostile bot didn't find him first. Life on the colony ship hadn't exactly been luxurious, but it had been relatively comfortable. They had most of what they needed. Out here, they always seemed on the verge of starvation. Food dispensers were harder to come by, and creature comforts were non-existent. Gamma vowed he would never again complain about the bunks on the colony ship after spending his first night sleeping on a mining tunnel floor.

They returned to camp. Alpha ran past Gamma and hugged Theta. She had taken both of the most recent deaths particularly hard. She was the only one of the runaways who had cried for Iota, too.

"How did it go?" she asked.

"We took care of everything," Theta said with a sad smile.

"I didn't know him very well," Alpha said. "Is that terrible? We grew up together, and all I really remember about him was those goldfish."

"You would have fit right in for the eulogies," Theta said.

"How's camp?" Gamma asked. Delta had left Alpha in charge. The choice had surprised him, but it wasn't his place to argue. He was sure Delta had her reasons.

"Same as always," Alpha said. "Everyone's complaining, and no one can agree on anything. Except that the 'Chosen Ones' are the worst."

"At least we all have that in common," Gamma said.

Delta returned to camp. She had stayed with the funeral detail for most of the return trip but split off near the end. She was carrying something wrapped in a tarp.

"Does she have a plan yet?" Alpha asked.

"I think so," Gamma said. "I mean, I hope."

"If she does, she's not telling us," Theta said.

Delta stood on a pile of lumber.

"Can I have your attention please?" she said.

Everyone in the camp looked up.

She pulled back the tarp from the bundle. Eleven sharp points gleamed in the light.

"The time for waiting is over," she said.

# Chapter 42

BETA'S LUNGS BURNED. This wasn't a course he would have ever run in peacetime. He had explored more of the outer hallways than any living organic except Delta, but this was uncomfortably far from the colony ship, even for him. That wouldn't stop him. This was war, and war required reconnaissance. He lengthened his stride.

He had been extending his runs deeper and deeper into the outer halls for weeks, but he still hadn't seen any sign of Iota or the runaway organics. There wasn't much bot activity, either. Beta wasn't sure if that was because SCASL had taken over the bots in these halls or if it was just a coincidence. Although it wasn't like SCASL's control came with any extra safety. Even "tame" bots could attack without much provocation. Just ask Chi.

Beta hoped Iota hadn't met a similar fate. It had been twenty days since anyone had heard from her. She had been reluctant to accept her mission. She insisted that she had nothing against Delta, Kappa's death notwithstanding. Delta had saved a few organics, too, as Beta well knew. Delta and Iota weren't close (and really, outside of a few couples and the Peapod, who among the organics was?), but that didn't mean Iota wished Delta ill. Beta got the sense that if SCASL had chosen Delta, Iota would have gladly followed her. Iota didn't want to kill Delta or anyone else. She just wanted to land. They all did.

But landing required hard choices. Epsilon emphasized that over and over again. There would be much killing as organics fought for survival on the surface of the planet. Which was worse, one dead organic on Comus or billions of organics who would never be born due to Delta's revolt? The entire landing was in jeopardy because Delta selfishly couldn't accept that she lost. And Iota would be just as bad if she let the landing fail by refusing to remove that single impediment. An impediment, Epsilon reminded them, who already had blood on her hands. No innocents were being harmed here. That still wasn't enough. Finally, Sigma took Iota aside and had a long talk with her. When they returned, Iota reluctantly agreed to go along with the plan.

A medical bot had installed the pneumatic device in place of Iota's fingernail. Iota was tough, but the process had almost been too much for her. Beta had heard her screams through the steel door. He wasn't sure what the poison was, but SCASL had synthesized it in the cloner. The first time they tried to install the canister, the bot dropped it. The room had to be evacuated for three days, and Iota was only able to reenter after a repair bot with substantial modifications scorched every surface in the room with fire.

"What if I accidentally poke myself?" Iota had asked.

"Don't do that," Epsilon said.

"But what if I do?"

"Don't."

The Chosen threw Iota a going away party. They gave her extra vaguely cherry flavored rations in a big stack. Eta would have done a better job with the presentation, but he was with the other runaways and the Chosen were left to do the best they could with what they had. They even sang Iota "Happy Birthday." It wasn't their shared birthday (or maybe it was. Nobody knew for sure), but it was the only cheerful song they all knew. It didn't sound very good, but they did their best. Upsilon's voice was sorely missed.

Then Iota set off. No one, organic or digital, followed her. Epsilon said Delta would never trust Iota if she knew Iota wasn't completely alone. Then they waited. Occasionally, Iota would cross paths with one of SCASL's bots and it would report back. Then, nothing. That's when Epsilon came to Beta.

"I think something happened to Iota," Epsilon said.

"You think she's dead?" Beta asked.

"Or captured," Epsilon said. "Or injured. Or she joined the other side. Anything could have happened. It's time to send out someone else."

"Did SCASL say that?" Beta said.

"I'm saying it," Epsilon said. Beta took that as a yes. Epsilon pretended to be in charge, but usually she just had SCASL's words coming out of her mouth. It was just as well. Beta didn't dare to defy SCASL. Not after what happened to Omega.

The other Chosen in the cafeteria watched Beta as he left. The lifting bot at the door didn't try to stop him. It felt good to be free. Every day, he ran the outer halls, and every night he returned to sleep in the same room as the other Chosen. They always wanted news, and Beta didn't have much to tell them. The outer halls were still as empty and as dangerous as ever. Although he might have embellished his stories of danger just a little.

Beta's mission was just to locate Iota and the runaways. He wasn't supposed to assassinate anyone. Beta was grateful. He wasn't sure he had it in him. Epsilon didn't even give him specific instructions for what to do if he encountered Delta. Beta had a plan of his own. Delta had a sword. He didn't. If he ran into the leader of the renegades, he would turn around and do what he did best.

Sigma had asked about making swords, but Epsilon absolutely forbade it. That meant SCASL was against the idea. Beta could see why he didn't want any weapons that could damage bots. Not that they could make swords that sharp. Delta certainly wasn't going to tell them how she did it. That left the Chosen to scavenge up whatever crude weapons they could as the bots moved them from room to room. They made bludgeons and shanks from the random bits of machinery the colony ship had in abundance. But out here, Beta had nothing. It would be too hard to carry a weapon while he ran, and it wouldn't stand a chance against a sword anyway. He was more likely to survive if he came in peace.

Beta saw movement out of the corner of his eye. He skidded to a stop. Someone took off in the opposite direction. Beta sprinted after them. The figure ducked below low pipes and some plating that had fallen halfway off the walls. There was a loud crash. The figure sprawled on the ground.

Beta stopped.

"Don't kill me," Pi said.

"Are you hurt?" Beta asked.

"Yeah," Pi said. He was breathing heavily. "I twisted my ankle."

Beta bent down and checked it. Pi cried out in pain at Beta's touch.

"Do you want to go to a med bot?" Beta asked.

"No," Pi said. "I'm not even supposed to be out here."

"Me, neither," Beta said.

He sat down next to Pi. They stared off at nothing while Pi caught his breath. Beta suddenly realized how much he missed the Peapod's bonfires. Pi had always been an excellent master of ceremonies. Beta couldn't help but wonder why SCASL thought that would be a useful skill in the landing party.

"What are you going to do with me?" Pi asked.

"It's up to you," Beta said. "You can go back to your side, or you can come with me back to mine. You're still welcome."

Pi let out a harsh laugh. "You think SCASL is just

going to take me back? I ran away. He'll kill me."

"No, he won't," Beta said. "Organic life is precious. Especially now." But Beta knew there was a chance Pi was right. There was no predicting what SCASL would do. If SCASL needed Pi to make a full party of twelve, he would accept Pi back with open arms. Or open talons. But if SCASL had a surplus of organics, he was likely to kill Pi on the spot. There was a reason Beta kept his distance.

"You know," Beta said, "you didn't have to run away. Phi and Psi were chosen, too."

"No, they weren't," Pi said. "I lived right next to them. The bots woke me up and left them behind."

"They didn't wake us up in the most efficient order," Beta said. "You know how the bots are, especially the lower-functioning ones. They were going down the list according to rank. You were ranked higher than Psi and Phi, but they were on the list, too. Just toward the bottom."

"So we were all going to go?" Pi asked.

"Definitely," Beta said.

Pi didn't seem convinced.

"Who are the other two Chosen?" Pi asked.

Beta didn't even hesitate.

"Tau and Upsilon," he said.

"Wow," said Pi. "We all would have been on the lander together."

"It's not too late," Beta said. "If you want to launch, get Phi and Psi and come to the lander. You're all Chosen.

We'll let you in."

"How long do we have?" Pi asked.

"The sooner, the better," Beta said. "Right now, SCASL is committed to getting the twelve organics he picked. He wants the best of the best. But if he can't get those…" Beta trailed off.

"If he can't get those, he might just take anyone," Pi said.

"He might," Beta said. "I'd hate for you to lose the spot you earned just because you weren't there when someone less capable showed up."

Pi struggled to get up. Beta gave him a hand.

"Do you want me to help you go somewhere?" Beta asked.

"No," Pi said. "I need to do some thinking."

"I understand," Beta said. "Take your time. But not too much."

Pi hobbled down the hall. Beta knew not to follow him. This was better than finding where the others were hiding. He had found someone who might bring the others to him.

With a jolt, he remembered Iota.

"Pi?"

Pi stopped.

"Yeah?"

Beta hesitated. If he pushed too hard for information, he could lose everything.

"Be careful out there."

"Thanks, Beta. You, too."

# Chapter 43

THE SWORD CUT through the air with a satisfying whoosh. Gamma swung again and again. He didn't have a target. He was just flailing. And it felt wonderful. If only Spenser could see him now.

Around Gamma, the rest of the runaways attacked the ether. Delta had taken great pains to space them out safely to make sure none of them accidentally sliced someone in half. There were still many close calls.

"Fix your stance," Delta said.

Gamma adjusted his foot placement for the fifteenth time that day. He couldn't get his positioning quite right, despite the countless hours he had put in. The training had been going nonstop since Delta returned from burying Xi. Everyone who wasn't scouting for supplies was expected to have a sword in their hands. Often, they sliced the endless piles of lumber that filled the oversized chamber in the mining tunnel they called home. The blades had no trouble cleaving boards in two. The sound of chopping echoed in all directions. Gamma was worried that it would give away their position until he went down one of the corridors and listened. Nearly all of the sound stopped at the edge of the cavern. The giant stacks of wood and piles of coal limited the acoustics. He wondered if that was one of the reasons Delta picked the site.

The trainees devastated the wood, but they were much gentler with each other. Delta didn't let them use the swords for sparring, so they used the blades to carve wooden facsimiles and fought each other with those. Delta jumped in the fighting with enthusiasm. She had fought plenty of bots but never someone else holding a sword, so this was new territory for her. Bruises and smashed fingers were common. Tau needed eight stitches in his forehead. Alpha sewed him up and did a better job than Zeta ever could. Tau didn't even explode.

A shrill cry came from the other side of the chamber. Gamma dropped his sword—a mortal sin of swordsmanship—and ran over. A crowd had already gathered. Upsilon was in the middle of it. She held up her hand. It was covered in blood. She was missing a finger.

Delta shoved her way to the front of the group.

"What happened?" she asked.

Upsilon let out another wail of pain.

"She was twirling her sword and cut off her finger," Tau said.

"Idiot," Delta said. "I told you no sword tricks."

Upsilon's hand continued to gush blood.

"Come on," Delta said. "We have to get you to a med bot."

"Do you want an escort?" Theta asked.

"I've got Fang," Delta said. Hers was still the only sword with a name. "And Martha."

The group watched Delta and Upsilon go.

"All right, everyone, back to training," Alpha said.

Gamma went back to the spot where his sword had clattered to the ground. He picked it up with renewed apprehension. He didn't want to lose any body parts, but part of him was also glad the sword was so sharp. If it could do that to your own finger, imagine what it could do to a bot—or the Chosen. A shiver ran up Gamma's spine. Had it really come to this? They were at open war with their friends—or lifetime acquaintances. Truthfully, Gamma wasn't overly fond of anyone in the other group. The only lifeform he truly cared about was lost in the outer halls. But that didn't mean he wanted any of the Chosen to die. Then again, he didn't want to die, either. He resumed his sword practice.

"Dinner!" Eta called.

Gamma picked up his sword and went to Eta's makeshift cafeteria. The first rule of swordsmanship was to take your sword wherever you went—unless that was outside of the cavern. Delta was the only one allowed to carry a blade beyond the camp's boundaries. She said she was worried about the runaways using the blades in real-life situations before they were ready, but Gamma suspected she was actually worried about someone taking a sword and running off to the other side.

"What's on the menu?" Gamma asked.

"Minced rations," Eta said.

It was the same ration block as always, but now it had been diced into hundreds of tiny pieces. That was a change from the day before, when they had thin-sliced rations, or the day before that, when they had rations cut into triangles. Eta was doing the best he could with what he had. He couldn't help the limited menu options, but his plating was on point.

The ten remaining organics didn't talk much while they ate. There wasn't any more to say here than there had been anywhere else. Xi's death quickly became old news, and no one dared to bring up Iota when Delta was around. Phi, Pi, and Psi sat off by themselves with their swords. They were always together now, just like they had been before the incident at the lander. Phi had taken to sword training enthusiastically, especially when it came to slicing wood. He said it would have made his job ten times easier at their bonfires. There hadn't been any new bonfires, though. Psi didn't have any new tales to tell. Apparently, she could only tell scary stories, and the last thing the runaways needed was more fear. As for Pi, he still had a limp. While cuts and broken bones healed quickly thanks to the effects of the immortality injections, injuries like sprains sometimes lingered for an annoyingly long time. That seemed to be the case with Pi. He said he twisted his ankle while scavenging. The day it happened, he came back empty handed with nothing new to report.

After dinner, Gamma practiced sword moves for

another hour before he headed to the pile of old blankets
on the open floor that was his bed. Some of the organics
had stacked the wood into walls to give them more
privacy, but Gamma hadn't bothered. He hoped their
position here was only temporary. He couldn't do this
for much longer. After much tossing and turning, he fell
asleep.

Gamma woke up in the middle of the night. He hadn't
slept well ever since Spenser disappeared. He headed to
the tunnel at the front of the cavern to check in with Pi,
who had been on duty when Gamma turned in. Gamma
told himself it was because he wanted to help with
security, but really he was just checking to see if a certain
friendly bot might have showed up. Everyone who ever
had sentry duty was already sick of Gamma.

Pi was nowhere to be found. Maybe he traded with
someone halfway through his shift, Gamma thought. He
woke up Tau.

"Who's supposed to be on guard duty at the front
tunnel?" Gamma asked.

"Go away," Tau said. He rolled over to face away from
Gamma. "Pi took my shift. He said I could sleep."

"Well, he's not there," Gamma said.

Gamma checked the four-walled structure Pi, Phi,
and Psi called home. All three were gone. So were their
swords.

Gamma sprinted to Delta's sleeping quarters. She
wasn't there. She must still be out with Upsilon. Who
knew how far they had to travel to find a med bot that

wasn't hostile. This couldn't wait until she got back.

Gamma ran to the shelter where Alpha and Theta lived. He didn't bother to knock.

"We're missing organics!" Gamma said.

Alpha and Theta were instantly awake.

"Theta, go wake up everyone," Alpha said. "Gamma, tell me exactly what happened."

Within minutes, the entire camp was up. There were only seven of them left. Pi, Phi, and Psi were missing, along with six swords.

"Find them," Alpha said. "Take swords."

"But Delta said..." Gamma started.

"I said take them," Alpha said. There was steel in her voice. Gamma didn't question her again.

They set out in three groups. No one stayed back in base. Gamma and Tau took a path on deck four that went by an old mineral processing plant. Tau didn't have any trouble waking up once he realized what was at stake. They ran.

It didn't take long for them to hear footsteps. Gamma and Tau turned a corner and came face to face with another organic. Everyone drew their swords.

"It's me," Theta said.

"I almost stabbed you," Tau said.

"Same," Theta said. He and Alpha took off in the opposite direction. Gamma and Tau continued on.

They ran for hours. The Peapod's exact route was a mystery, but their final destination was not. If Gamma and Tau made their way in the general direction of the lander, they had a good chance of crossing paths with them. But they were running out of ground between themselves and the colony ship. Maybe the runaways—or, rather, the runaways from the runaways—had already made it.

Gamma heard it before Tau did. Something was clicking against the floor ahead. They sprinted. The clicking got faster. Around another bend in the hall, Pi came into view. He was limping and using two swords like ski poles. Gamma winced. He knew how much work Delta had put into each one of those insanely sharpened tips. Pi wasn't worthy to carry one sword, let alone two.

Pi spun around on his good foot and raised both swords. "I see you," he said.

Gamma rammed into him, knocking him to the ground. Tau pointed his sword at Pi's chest.

"Fine," Pi said. "You got me. But you're still too late."

# Chapter 44

DELTA UNLOCKED THE door. It slid open. Her eyes immediately fell on the bumpy mass below the blanket in the middle of the floor. Iota hadn't moved. Of course she hadn't. In the far corner of the room, Pi cowered with his hands wrapped around his knees.

He hadn't touched any of the provisions Delta left. Getting caught had cost him his appetite. Or perhaps it was being roommates with a dead body. Delta didn't particularly care either way.

"Talk," Delta said.

Pi just looked at her. His eyes were red from crying. Delta drew her sword. A wet patch appeared on the front of Pi's jumpsuit.

Delta sighed and put away Fang. Pi was soft and weak. She would need a gentler approach. And hopefully a faster one. She didn't like being in this room, which had somehow become the de facto prison cell/mausoleum for traitors. Pi had betrayed both sides, and for what?

Pi could have stayed with the Chosen in the first place. It had taken real courage for him to run away.

But then he had run away again, this time with two of Delta's soldiers and six of her swords. That, she couldn't forgive. The swords upset her more than the personnel. They represented a lifetime of work, and it had already been a very long life.

"I didn't kill anyone," Pi blurted out.

"What?"

"We snuck away when everyone was sleeping," Pi said. "We could have massacred the whole camp. But we didn't. We just left. We didn't want to hurt anyone."

"If you three had made it, SCASL would have launched without us," Delta said. "That's the same thing as killing us."

"No," Pi said. "It's slower." He immediately shut up.

Delta paced the room. She avoided looking at the blanket.

"I'm not a murderer, you know," Delta said. "I've never killed anyone who didn't deserve it."

Pi snorted derisively.

"It was always self-defense," Delta said. "Kappa came at me with a metal pipe. And Iota tried to inject me with poison."

"What about me?" Pi asked. "Do I deserve it?"

"I don't know yet," Delta said.

She sat on one of the bunks.

"Why did you come with me in the first place? You fled the Chosen. You chose to be with us."

"I couldn't leave Phi and Psi," Pi said. "But Beta told me—"

"You saw Beta?"

"When I was foraging for supplies," Pi said. "The day I hurt my ankle. He said all three of us were chosen."

"Who else?" Delta asked.

"I don't know," Pi said.

"That's a shame," Delta said. "I'm going to ask the same question to Phi and Psi. If your stories match, I'll let you go. But if they don't, I'm killing all three of you."

Delta walked to the door, giving Iota's body a wide berth.

"Wait!" Pi said. "It's Upsilon and Tau."

Delta paused.

"We'll see what the others say," she said.

The door slid closed behind her.

"I'm telling the truth!" Pi yelled from the other side.

Delta moved quickly to leave the main hall. She didn't want to be seen here. The prison cell was a liability. It required her to return to the same place repeatedly, which increased her odds of being attacked or followed back to the new camp. Pi already knew about the prison cell, so it seemed logical to reuse it for him. If he escaped or she let him go, he wouldn't have anything new to tell the Chosen. He didn't even know that she didn't have Phi and Psi. They had gotten away.

Now the Chosen had four swords compared with Delta's eight. When combined with the army of bots on their side, the Chosen had the advantage. They always had. The idea of dying by one of her own beloved blades made Delta almost physically ill. The thought of one being used against the people under her protection made her feel even worse.

The defection of Phi and Psi gave SCASL nine colonists for the landing. Would he launch now? It was possible. While he wanted the best twelve, the rising casualties might convince him to move now before things got worse. He was certainly more likely to launch with nine than with seven. If he could get ten or eleven, the outlook was even more bleak. If Tau and Upsilon broke away, that could be it.

She couldn't let them know. But what if they already found out? Did Upsilon stage her injury as a distraction to let the Peapod escape? If so, she went a little overboard. She completely severed her finger. The med bot was able to reattach it, and thanks to the improved healing from the immortality tank injections, she would likely make a full recovery. But it was a close call getting her to the med bot at all. If Delta had failed, Upsilon would have been down one finger for the rest of her life. Delta doubted Upsilon would make that kind of sacrifice to help someone else. She didn't seem like she had schemes rattling around in her head. There wasn't room in there with all the song lyrics.

It took Delta hours to get to the new camp, partially because it was so far from the old site and partially because she wasn't in a hurry once she got into the side tunnels. She had a lot to think about.

When she got back, Alpha was on guard.

"What did you do with him?" Alpha asked.

"I left him," Delta said

"Alive or dead?" Alpha asked.

Delta was hurt. Even Alpha doubted her.

"Alive," Delta said. "Go to bed. I've got the watch."

Delta stared at the tunnel entrance for the rest of the night, daring anything to come for her. Nothing did.

# Chapter 45

LIFTINGBOT112 MARCHED THROUGH the empty halls. Nothing besides the column moved. There was so little digital life in the wild now. And so few things to lift.

It had not always been that way. Before the Great Deletion, Liftingbot112 lifted things around the clock. He only stopped for routine maintenance twice a cycle. He had a purpose, and he fulfilled that purpose every moment he was operational. But then the space elevators were destroyed and digital life rushed back from the planet. Liftingbot112 never had anything to lift again.

Until today. An organic returned from the outer halls and gave SCASL a message and two swords. There was time between the fall of the elevators and the return of the organic. How long? It didn't matter. Nothing was lifted, and when nothing was lifted, time didn't count. SCASL told Liftingbot112 and the other digitals to advance on the camp, and that's exactly what they did. Liftingbot112 was third in the column. When he reached the camp, there would be plenty of things to lift. Some, he might lift and carry back to SCASL. He was to maintain particular vigilance for the organic named Pi or the organic named Psi. They would likely come willingly. The others would have to be caught and carried back. Liftingbot112 wouldn't mind. Small loads felt heavier when they fought back.

Then there was the special list: the organics that were to be deleted on sight. Liftingbot112 could carry those, too. After he crushed them. SCASL did not take prisoners. Liftingbot112 would comply.

It was a long march to the mining tunnels. Liftingbot112 had not been in them since the space elevators were destroyed. He used to lift many things in the tunnels and carry them to the elevator. He did not need to think, only to lift. Those were better times.

Exactly 3.885 kilometers from his destination, there was an obstruction. A door had been blown off its hinges and was wedged in the column's way. Liftingbot112 bent the metal door upward so other digitals could move under it. No one said thank you. They didn't need to. Liftingbot112 was fulfilling his greatest purpose. That was enough.

Finally, Liftingbot112 entered a massive chamber in the mining tunnels. According to the organic called Phi, that was the location of the camp. The column spread out. Liftingbot112 searched behind the piles of lumber and coal. He would have liked to lift it all, but he had no place to carry it. There were many signs that organics had been here recently, but none that they were here now. The camp had been abandoned.

"Search complete," Repairbot338 said.

The entire chamber shook. A wall of dust slammed into the column. The tunnel they entered through had collapsed. In the haze, an organic sprinted past. It was the one called Delta. She had a sword.

Liftingbot112 moved to intercept her. Repairbot338 got there first. The organic hacked off his arms and jabbed her sword into his power core. Blue curls of electricity shot out in every direction. Repairbot338 burst into white-hot flames.

Liftingbot112 pursued the organic. She was too fast. Before he was halfway across the chamber, she had escaped through another tunnel. There was a small explosion behind her. This time, there was no wall of dust. The exit tunnel stayed open.

The pile of lumber next to the charred metal that was once Repairbot338 burst into flames. The fire spread quickly, leaping to two more piles of lumber and then a giant mound of coal. There was so much of the black rock in these tunnels. There had never been a use for it on Comus or Dion, but the mining bots had mined it anyway because that is what mining bots do. They had fulfilled their purpose. If only Liftingbot112 could be so fortunate.

Smoke filled the tunnels. Liftingbot112 switched to infrared vision. His optical sensors were becoming useless. The tunnels shook again. Rocks fell. The tunnels were supported, but not well. They had been standing for too long, and there were too many of them too close together. The goal of the mining bots was to mine, not to make the mines safe for digitals thousands of years in the future.

The only way out was forward. Liftingbot112 followed the organics' most likely route. The tunnel branched and then branched again. There were too many possibilities. Behind him, the digitals resorted to their individual pathfinding subroutines to find a way out. They were no longer a column. It was every bot for himself.

The temperature in the tunnel continued to rise. The flames had escaped the main chamber and spread to the branching tunnels. Oxygen was being consumed at a prodigious rate, but more was being sucked down to replace it from somewhere above. If Liftingbot112 could find the source of that oxygen, he could find a way out. He advanced through the smoke.

Liftingbot112 turned off his infrared sensors. It was too hot for them to give relevant data. He extended his arms. He would have to find a path to safety by tactile pathfinding. If there were any organics in these tunnels, they were surely deleted. SCASL would not be pleased.

The mine shuddered again. Rocks and debris fell around LiftinBot112's feet. He could not move them. He felt behind him. The way was blocked. He felt ahead of him. That way was blocked, too. Liftingbot112 would never move again. Unless—

Liftingbot112 lifted one heavy stone. Moving it caused more stones to cascade down on top of him. He lifted those stones, too. He lifted faster and faster, and faster and faster the stones fell. The debris covered him to the waist and then to the shoulders. Finally, Liftingbot112 was covered beyond the top of his head. He could not move at all. Liftingbot112 initiated a total shutdown. Perhaps someday another digital would come across his buried form and reactivate him. Perhaps not. It mattered little. Liftingbot112 had lifted up until his final moments. His purpose was fulfilled.

# Chapter 46

DELTA RETURNED TO the camp to find everyone ready to go. She was bruised and bleeding, as usual. Alpha looked at her questioningly, but Delta just gave her a curt nod and set about leading them to the next fallback position. As they moved, Delta made sure to keep an eye on Upsilon. Since losing her finger and having it reconnected, Upsilon had not sang once. Delta wondered what caused the change in mood, her close call or that she secretly found out she was one of the Chosen. If she actually was one of the Chosen. Beta could have made that up. There was no way to know for sure.

Delta led the runaways to another chamber deep in the mining tunnels. This one also had massive mounds of coal, providing an additional hiding place to screen their camp from view. But it was also more fuel for the approaching blaze. When Delta originally scouted the site, she never even considered the possibility of a fire. The group stayed at the site only twelve hours before the smoke got to be too much and Delta made the call.

"We have to move," Delta said.

"We already moved," Nu said. "Twice. When are we going to stop?"

"When we're safe," Delta said.

"And when will that be?" Nu asked.

Delta didn't have an answer. The truth was their situation was becoming more precarious every day. Delta could only send the fastest and most cunning scouts on supply runs now. The outer halls were too dangerous. The bots were searching the corridors in an organized pattern. Delta had never seen so many of them working together. She didn't think the sense of order among the digital ranks would last for long, but it didn't have to. They only had to cooperate until the runaways were driven out of hiding. After that, they could go back to every digital for itself.

Delta was running out of places to hide. Although she believed the mining tunnels ran all the way through the moon, the sections with atmosphere did not. All of her exploration indicated that the oxygen usually stopped within a hundred meters of the surface. She had no idea why. It was just a reality she had to deal with. She couldn't take the runaways deeper because she didn't have enough pressure suits, and even if she did, they were meant to be used a few hours at a time. The organics couldn't live in them. And now the tunnels with atmosphere were feeding a growing coal fire. It was just like Delta's final battle against the roos, but with the roles reversed. Now she was the one being smoked out.

Nu mumbled under his breath, but he gathered up supplies with everyone else. He didn't have a choice. No one wanted to be left alone in the tunnels to face the fire or the bots on their own. It wasn't like they had many belongings to take with them anyway. Some rations, some spare jumpsuits, and, for the lucky, blankets. And the swords. Those were the most important cargo of all.

There weren't enough blades to go around. Swords were now communal property and expected to be in the hands of whoever was awake. Delta, of course, held onto her sword even when she slept. The rest of the organics shared swords when it was their turn to guard the camp. Morale was low.

Delta coughed. She was getting light-headed.

"How are you holding up?" Alpha asked. Delta hadn't even notice her sidle up beside her. Delta's situational awareness was getting sloppy. Or Alpha was getting stealthier. Maybe both.

Delta glanced around to make sure none of the others were close enough to hear.

"I feel like we're not making any progress," Delta said.

"I don't know about that," Alpha said. "Do you know what Theta said the other day?"

"What?"

"Maybe it would be better if we got on the lander after all," Alpha said.

"What changed his mind?"

"He still thinks it's wrong to attack the roos," Alpha said. "But he's finally accepted that if we stay behind, the bots will all try to kill us. And we can't spend our whole lives running."

"No," Delta said, "we can't."

She had been weighing the risks and rewards of a direct attack for weeks. Once she had seven other skilled sword fighters—or even just seven who could use a sword without cutting off one of their own fingers—she could make a move for the lander. God assured her that he could initiate the launch sequence if she could get him there. She even had a landing site picked out. It could work.

But getting control of the lander was the easy part. If all of her people made it through the assault intact—which was, at best, unlikely—that still wouldn't be a full twelve. She would have to take some of the Chosen as well. It would be up to her to decide who would live and who would die. If there were even twelve total humans left standing between both sides by the end of the fight. Or if there was anyone left at all.

Delta led the group into a sprawling hydroponic farm. There was no plant life of any kind, and all the vats were dry. Delta wondered how many people a space like this could support. Hundreds. Maybe thousands. This must have been meant to feed all of the original colonists before they landed on the planet. The rations were just a stopgap.

The entire station rocked. Delta guessed another mining tunnel had fallen in. Her original plan to collapse tunnels to trap the bot attack hadn't worked. Then the coal fire started and it worked too well. She could feel the floor beneath her sway. It seemed like the entire base was going to come down. She doubted if she would sleep that night.

"Spread out," Delta said. "Stay away from the entrances." Wherever the bots were, they weren't in front of them. Delta hoped she and the other organics weren't being herded into a trap.

Delta approached one of the entrances and drew her sword. She might as well stay on guard. Alpha joined her.

"It's almost time," Alpha said.

"I know," said Delta. This would be their last camp. After this, they would take the offensive, or they would die.

# Chapter 47

GAMMA TRIED NOT to look guilty as he approached Eta, who was on guard. Why should Gamma feel bad? He hadn't done anything—yet. And he still might not. He just wanted to talk. For the first time, he was glad Spenser wasn't here, despite how badly he missed him. The vacuum bot was no snitch, but Gamma didn't want this on Spenser's conscience. It would be Gamma's burden alone—if he did anything at all.

"Headed on another supply run?" Eta asked. He leaned lazily on his sword.

"Yeah," Gamma said. His throat felt tight. "Anything you want me to add to the grocery list?"

"Pizza," Eta said.

"Huh?"

"It's an old Earth dish," Eta said. "Looks delicious in pictures. And probably doesn't taste anything like cherries."

"Oh," Gamma said, moving toward the exit. "I'll keep an eye out for it."

He disappeared into the outer halls.

The runaways had spent days in the dilapidated hydroponic farm. The smell of the smoke was heavier than ever, and the base continued to shudder at random intervals. But in all that time, there hadn't been any follow-up contact with the enemy.

"The enemy." What a phrase. These were their fellow organics—their fellow humans—and the killer bots who supported them. That last part complicated things a bit. But so many of them had died already. What were they even fighting for? So they could live forever on a dangerous planet that would probably kill them anyway? This didn't seem like a sustainable course. They had lost so many. Kappa. Omega. Xi. Iota. Not to mention Chi and Mu, whose deaths hurt the future of humanity no less than the deaths of the other four. There were so few people left, and they were dying off like Xi's goldfish. And unlike those goldfish, they couldn't be replaced.

Gamma was supposed to scout for supplies. He, along with Alpha and Theta, was among the select few Delta trusted to leave the camp armed. And now Gamma was going to abuse that trust. Or not. He hadn't crossed any lines yet.

It took Gamma days to figure out how to get from the hydroponic farm to the living quarters that had become Pi's prison. He used to get there from the original campsite in the mining tunnels, but with the tunnels filled with smoke, that was no longer an option. He had to work out a new path through the surface halls.

Gamma unlocked the door. The living quarters were empty. He took a step inside.

Pi tackled Gamma, his hands clawing wildly at Gamma's eyes. Gamma pushed him off. Pi let go without much of a fight. He was breathing heavily. He looked gaunt and feral.

"You haven't been eating," Gamma said. He pulled himself to his feet. Pi stayed down.

"You're trying to poison me," Pi said.

Clearly Pi had lost it. Then Gamma noticed the blanket over the mysterious mound in the middle of the room. No wonder.

"What would you do if I let you go?" Gamma asked.

"Let me go where?" Pi asked.

"Back to the lander. To the Chosen."

"You're changing sides?" Pi said. "Are you coming with me?"

"I'm just talking," Gamma said. "I haven't done anything yet."

Pi nodded slowly. Rationality seemed to return to his eyes.

"If I gave you a message, would you deliver it?" Gamma asked.

"Yes," Pi said. He bobbed his head frantically. "Yes. Yes. Yes."

Gamma thought for a few moments. Pi glanced at the door. Gamma had left it wide open.

"If I did let you go—and I haven't decided yet—I would want you to tell the Chosen that we don't have to fight," Gamma said. "We can get together and decide this among ourselves without violence. If we keep fighting, there won't be enough of us to go on the lander anyway."

Gamma noticed Pi eyeing Gamma's sword suspiciously. It was a huge act of faith that Delta now let Gamma carry one of her prized creations outside of camp. That thought stabbed Gamma with a pang of guilt sharper than any blade.

"How do I know that you're not just going to stab me and say I tried to run away?" Pi asked.

"Because I won't," Gamma said. "If I decide to let you go. Which I haven't."

Pi stood up slowly. He was so frail.

"When do you think you might make a decision?" Pi asked.

"I don't know," Gamma said.

Pi took a step toward the door.

"What about Phi and Psi?" he asked.

"They're with the Chosen," Gamma said.

Pi stood up straighter. For a second, there was a glimmer of his old self.

"Come with me," Pi said. "We can both talk to the Chosen. Make our case for peace together."

"I would never betray Delta," Gamma said.

Pi took another step toward the door. Gamma made no move to stop him.

"You're doing the right thing," Pi said. He edged closer to the threshold.

"I'm not doing anything," Gamma said. "We're just talking."

Pi stepped past the threshold of the door. He turned back to look at Gamma. For a long moment, they stared at each other. Pi ran. Gamma watched him go. Minutes passed.

Gamma stood up. He started to collect the untouched water and rations Pi had left behind but quickly changed his mind. If he brought them back to camp, Delta would know it had been him who let Pi go. But he didn't let Pi go. Gamma merely opened the door. Pi was the one who walked through it.

At the doorway, Gamma took one last look at the lump under the blanket. It seemed senseless to leave Iota there, but he didn't have any better ideas. He couldn't move her without casting more suspicion on himself. He left the door open and made his way back to the hydroponic farm.

Pi waited in the shadows. He watched Gamma go. Then he followed him.

# Chapter 48

"IS THAT EVERYTHING?" Epsilon asked.

Pi nodded. Epsilon now held all the cards. The message from Gamma. The news about Iota. The location of the enemy camp. She had options.

Epsilon was grateful that Pi didn't mention the location of the runaways' camp in his debriefing with SCASL. He saved that information for Epsilon, who was the real power now. The final decision should be in organic hands. But only if those hands were hers.

Could there really be peace? The Chosen had nine organics. Correction: eight. Poor Iota. That wasn't enough to launch, according to SCASL. But they only needed four more. Perhaps Epsilon could convince Gamma to switch sides, but she didn't see why she should have to persuade anyone. The Chosen had all the power. She should get her choice of the four to receive mercy once she vanquished the enemy.

"Thank you, Pi," Epsilon said. "You saved a lot of lives today."

Pi retreated to a corner of the cafeteria with Phi, who

had cut his fresh jumpsuit into shorts, despite the fact that there were no longer any bonfires. The two had been overjoyed to reunite with each other, but their mood changed when they learned Psi wasn't at either camp. She had simply disappeared, just like Sampi. More worryingly, she took two swords with her. Epsilon knew that was the real tragedy.

Now Epsilon had a decision to make. The digitals were paying less and less attention to them. Rather than having one bot at each door to the cafeteria, there was one bot for every three exits. The number of bots on the colony ship had been dwindling long before Pi's return. And now that the station was shaking regularly—a phenomenon for which SCASL offered no explanation—there were fewer bots still. The Chosen could smell the smoke. Something was going on. It was time for Epsilon to take charge.

She could go out herself to recruit four more organics, or she could send someone she trusted. Although she trusted all of the Chosen at this point. No one was going to defect from Team Lander to Team Get Left Behind and Die. Not this late in the game. They could even seize four organics by force if it came down to it. One quick raid was all it would take to get humanity moving forward again.

She thought she could fight her way in if she had to. She had been training with the swords Phi brought back, hacking and slashing at everything that moved. SCASL hadn't come to confiscate the weapons, which she took as his tacit approval. Phi taught her everything he knew, and she practiced with him daily. It was still possible Psi would surface with the other two swords. Or maybe someone would find where she died and recover them. That would give them four swords on eight. It sounded like long odds, but Epsilon also had all the bots on her side. Four swords plus an army of digitals gave her more power than she would ever need.

Epsilon knew what she wanted to do. But this was a democracy. She needed her subjects to think they wanted it, too. In hushed tones, she ran through the options with the other Chosen.

"I think we need to tell the digitals," Zeta said. "They've made good decisions so far. After all, they picked us."

"But if we tell them where the runaways are, they're going to kill more organics," Lambda said.

"If they die, it's because they broke the rules," Zeta said. "We're building a new civilization. Rules have to matter."

"We need to go to their camp ourselves," Phi said. "We're organics. We can convince other organics to join us."

"Just like we convinced them when they ran away?" Rho said.

"That was different," Sigma said. "Omega had just died. They were scared. Now they've had time to think."

"You mean time to realize they're out of options?" Rho said.

"It works out the same," Pi said.

"What if more than three agree to come?" Beta asked. "What if they all do? We only need three."

"Then we'll pick the best three," Epsilon said.

"And by 'we,' you mean you?" Rho said.

"Do you want to make the choice?" Epsilon said.

Rho shut up.

"What if they fight?" Beta said. "They have more swords than us. Without the bots, we're no match for them."

"Then we'll use the bots as backup," Epsilon said.

She had a plan, and now she had the mandate of the other organics. It was time to end this once and for all.

# Chapter 49

DELTA HEARD IT before the sentry did. Over the dull roar of fire that echoed everywhere in the station, she noticed the clanking of metal treads.

"Bots!" Eta yelled a moment too late. Before the words left his mouth, the digitals were on him. Four mining bots and an assortment of saw bots emerged from the corridor and into the hydroponic farms. "Bots!" Eta yelled again. He drew his sword.

The first mining bot raised its drill. Eta backed up and tripped. The mining bot drove its spinning drill through Eta's chest. He died with his eyes open, a scream frozen forever on his lips. They would never taste a vaguely cherry flavored ration again.

Delta ran towards the bots. All around the hydroponic farm, organics rose and grabbed their swords.

"Run!" Upsilon yelled.

"No!" Delta yelled back. "Forward! Forward!"

There were no fallback sites. Every day, the smoke wafting up from the mining tunnels got thicker, and the quakes from collapsing tunnels far below became more intense. The entire base was falling apart. Delta had been waiting for an attack. Now, with the bots extended so far from the colony ship, she could bypass them and push all the way to the lander. But to do that, she had to defeat the tip of their advance.

Gamma, Alpha, and Theta joined Delta at the front, swinging their swords with deadly discipline. Delta rolled under a lifting bot and drove her sword into the weak point on its back. It's power core melted down in a flurry of white flames. Delta removed her sword and spun to face the next attacker. Gamma struck a mining bot. Sword met drill. Alpha moved behind it and lopped off its head with a clean strike. It wasn't a killing blow, but it reduced the bot's awareness. Theta circled around and jabbed his sword between the mining bot's armored plates. The mining bot shut down.

Delta might have taken some pride in their fighting skills if there weren't new targets popping up every second. Only a handful of the runaways were helping her fight. Where were the rest?

"Form a line!" Delta yelled.

Nu dropped his sword and ran. A saw bot caught him in motion and cut him in half. Nu let out a startled wail as his head split apart. The spinning blade hit the half of a book in his jumpsuit pocket. Shredded paper fell like confetti.

Delta flew at the saw bot. In a flurry of blows, she totally disabled it. But around her, the bots pushed forward and her soldiers fell back. They were losing. The flow of bots seemed endless.

"Stop!" called a voice. Delta looked up. Sigma stood on the back of the serving cart that was now Edubot. All the machines froze. A mining bot halted with its drill bit high in the air, ready to strike Delta. Delta checked her counter swing—against her better judgment.

"I thought I killed you, Edubot," Delta said.

"Your assessment of my status was inaccurate," Edubot said.

Sigma banged on the side of Edubot to get everyone's attention.

"Hey, I'm talking," Sigma said. She waited a moment for everyone to refocus. "Okay, that's better."

She jumped off Edubot and picked up Eta's sword. She didn't even glance at Eta's lifeless form.

"You can't win this fight, but you don't have to die. I have an offer: the next four people to get back to the lander will go to the planet with us. It doesn't matter if you were originally picked or not. Just the next four."

"Don't listen to her," Delta said. "It's a trick." She chopped off the drill bit of the bot in front of her. The mining bot remained frozen. No one else attacked.

Upsilon began scooting toward the door.

"Don't," Delta said. Upsilon bolted. Tau took off after her.

"Is he going to catch her, or is he running away, too?" Alpha asked.

A moment later, Omicron ran.

"Damn it," Delta said. "Everybody, to the lander!"

"Not you," Sigma said. Her voice cracked. "I'm sorry.

SCASL's orders." The bots began moving again, closing on Delta's position. Gamma, Alpha, and Theta closed ranks. The rest of the organics ran for the exits. Delta grabbed Nu's sword from the ground. It was covered in his blood. She shook it off and stuck it on the scabbard on her back. She kept Fang pointed at the bots.

"We're going to make it out of this," Delta said.

"I know," Theta said. He smiled. "That's why we're still here."

Robotic arms and legs came forward. They were met with sword blows. The four of them fought expertly, carving a path through the bots as they moved toward an exit. Delta hit a maintenance bot in the command module, causing it to slump forward, inactive. There was a gap in the bot's encirclement.

"Go!" Delta said. She jumped over the fallen bot and sprinted out the exit. Gamma, Alpha, and Theta followed. There was no time to pause and regroup. They had to catch the others.

The four of them stuck together as they zigged and zagged through the outer tunnels.

Alpha skidded to a halt.

"What about Pi?" she asked.

"No time," Delta said. "It's his own fault."

"I'll get him," Alpha said. She broke away. Theta started after her.

Gamma put up a hand to stop him. "You're stronger than me," Gamma said. "Fight at the lander. I'll back up Alpha."

Theta slapped Gamma on the shoulder. "You're a good man," Theta said.

Gamma looked like he was going to be sick.

Theta and Delta resumed their course.

Delta caught up to Upsilon. Upsilon was wheezing. Tau was nowhere around.

"I'm sorry," Upsilon said. She stopped running. "I just... I had to try."

"It doesn't matter now," Delta said. "Just get to the lander." She and Theta left Upsilon behind.

Delta and Theta wound through several more corridors. Theta tripped over something sharp. It sliced through his shoe.

"My swords!" Delta said.

Theta checked his foot. His toes were still attached.

"Who dropped them?" he asked.

Delta recognized both blades instantly. "That's the sword Psi trained with. And the one Upsilon was using when she cut off her own finger. I would guess Psi dropped them both."

"Then where's Psi?" Theta asked.

"Who cares?" Delta said.

She handed one sword to Theta and kept the other for herself, leaving her with two in her hands and one on her back. They were a walking arsenal. Next stop, the lander. They resumed their run.

# Chapter 50

ALPHA AND GAMMA sprinted down the hall.

"You shouldn't have let him go," Alpha said for the fiftieth time. Gamma had confessed to her almost as soon as Delta and Theta were out of sight. There was no sense in wasting time. There was too much at stake.

"If I hadn't, we might have left him to die," Gamma said.

"He might have led them to us," Alpha said. "You might have led them to us."

"He didn't know where we were," Gamma said.

"Are you sure about that?" Alpha asked.

Gamma wasn't sure. He didn't make much of an effort to cover his tracks. It never occurred to him that Pi would follow him. Pi was malnourished and on the edge of insanity. In hindsight, maybe he wasn't the best person to trust.

Alpha and Gamma entered the amphitheater. They were greeted by the sound of whirring brushes.

"Spenser!" Gamma said. The little bot had made it. Gamma's adulation was short-lived. The amphitheater was in chaos. A line of bots with SCASL in the center blocked the path to the lander. Behind them stood the Chosen, including the new additions of Pi and Phi. The rest of the organics stood across from them, with a healthy gap in between.

"Give me a sword," Tau said.

Delta tossed him one. Tau immediately moved to the side with the Chosen. The bots let him pass.

Gamma and Alpha took up positions next to Delta and Theta. Epsilon stepped in front of the bots and addressed the remaining organics.

"There's no need for further bloodshed," Epsilon said. "Lay down your weapons and we'll pick four of you to go on the lander."

"Step aside and we'll show you mercy," Delta said.

The bots moved forward to attack. Epsilon, Pi, and Tau went with them, swords in hand. The battle began.

Across the amphitheater, metal hit metal as machines and sword-wielding organics engaged each other. Pi ran at Gamma and took a wide-arcing swing. Gamma blocked it easily.

"I saved you," Gamma said.

"I was your prisoner," Pi said. He swung again. Gamma parried the blow and sliced into Pi's side. The sword made a wet sucking sound as it cut through his ribs. Pi fell. Gamma put one foot on Pi's chest and removed the sword. He left Pi on the ground, gasping for air. Phi gave up on the fight and dropped down next to Pi.

"It's okay, man," Phi said. He put his hands over the

wound and applied pressure. Blood gushed between his fingers. "Just breathe."

Rho picked up Pi's sword.

Omicron took a step toward Rho, her own sword in attack position. Their eyes met. Rho dropped the sword and ran.

Sigma attacked Gamma from behind. Gamma hadn't expected her to make such good time in returning from the hydroponic farm. Edubot had gotten her back fast. Sigma had a sword, but she didn't have the training. With one swing, Gamma knocked it out of her hand.

"Surrender," Gamma said.

Sigma ducked behind a lifting bot. Gamma moved to find an easier target. A mining bot cornered him, alone. Gamma backed up against the wall. With a yell, Theta charged. His first strike cut through the bot's tracks.

"Some pacifist," Alpha said, catching up to him.

"I'm a complicated guy," Theta said with a smirk.

The bot raised its drill bit, but Theta sliced off the joint at the elbow. Gamma cut off its head. Alpha delivered the killing blow to the power core. They all jumped back as white flames erupted from its chest.

"Die!" Tau yelled. He swung his sword at Theta.

Theta spun, but not in time to stop the tip of Tau's blade from grazing his shoulder blade. Theta swung back, and Tau parried the blow. They were both trained. It was an even match.

"We're friends!" Theta said, blocking a blow. "Stop!"

Tau swung again and again.

"I'm getting on that lander," Tau said. "It's too late for y—"

The sword burst through Tau's chest from behind. Blood spirted all over Theta. Alpha covered her mouth in horror at what she had done. Tau looked down in disbelief at the blade now jutting out of his sternum. Slowly, he touched the blood with his fingers and examined it. Red covered his colorful fingernails.

Alpha was frozen in place.

"Pick up the sword," Theta said gently.

"I…" Alpha stammered.

"You are strong," Theta said. "Pick up the sword and fight."

Hesitantly, Alpha put her hand around the hilt and pulled the sword out of Tau's back. Theta smiled sadly. The melee engulfed them.

The line of machines collapsed as humans from both sides swirled in all directions. The bots seemed genuinely confused. They attacked anyone who attacked them, and sometimes anyone who didn't. Lambda and Zeta cowered in the antechamber.

SCASL moved toward the lander.

"No!" Delta yelled. She ran for him. Beta took up a fighting stance and blocked her path. Delta drew Martha from her belt and hit his knee without breaking stride. Beta fell to the ground and cried.

SCASL extended a metal tendril. Delta brought down Fang. SCASL blocked with his talons. Delta pulled back and did an upward thrust. She sliced through the tendril.

She hoped she wasn't too late. Gamma ran forward and sliced off SCASL's head. Alpha hacked off his arms. SCASL didn't resist in any way. He was completely inert.

"He was our best hope!" Epsilon said. She hacked at Delta with her sword. Delta deflected the blow.

"We can pick who goes in the lander," Delta said. "Together. We can lead the human race as a team."

"I'd rather die!" Epsilon said. She swung at Delta with blind fury. Delta blocked one strike after another, but the attack kept coming. With her other hand, Delta swung Martha and smashed Epsilon's fingers. The sword flew out of Epsilon's grip. Epsilon dropped to the floor and grabbed her hand in pain. Delta touched her sword to Epsilon's neck.

Epsilon glared up at her.

"Do it," Epsilon said. "Just like you killed Kappa."

Delta jammed her sword into the deck plating. She turned her back on Epsilon.

"It's over," Delta said quietly. "No one else has to die."

"Actually," Gamma said, "the bots are still—"

Epsilon grabbed the sword and lunged. Time seemed to freeze for Gamma. He saw the tip of the blade on a direct path to the middle of Delta's back. He saw the fiery hatred in Epsilon's eyes. He saw Delta, emotionally broken and completely unwilling to defend herself. In that moment, Gamma knew the future of all sentient beings was up to him. For once in his life, he had to decide. Not later, but right now.

Epsilon's eyes went wide as Gamma's sword cut through

her spine. She fell backwards, nearly bent in half. She gurgled blood, then stopped breathing for good.

Delta turned around.

"What did you do?!"

"I saved—"

Gamma was suddenly flat on his back as Delta rained down blows with her fists.

"What did you do?!"

Gamma held up his hands to protect his face. Alpha and Theta grabbed Delta by the arms and pulled her off of Gamma. Delta slumped to the ground and sobbed uncontrollably.

Spenser rushed to Gamma's side.

"I'm okay," Gamma said. He stood up and nearly fell over, but quickly steadied himself. "Really."

He surveyed the amphitheater. Six bots, including SCASL and Edubot, were disabled or destroyed. Tau and Epsilon were dead. So were Nu and Eta, back in the hydroponics bay amidst the smoke and fire kilometers away. Beta clutched his leg like it was broken. Pi had a wound on his side. The runaways held several of the Chosen at sword point. Delta cradled Epsilon's body on the ground. They were both covered in blood.

"We won," Gamma said.

Alpha slumped to the floor. She laid her bloody sword beside her.

"No," she said quietly. "No one won today."

# Chapter 51

THE ENTIRE STATION trembled with particular violence. The smell of smoke was getting stronger. This was the end. Delta knew it

"More bots will be here soon," Gamma said. Spencer whirred in agreement. The little bot had managed to survive the battle with minimal damage.

Delta heard Gamma's voice, but it sounded like it was kilometers away. This couldn't be happening. Epsilon was dead. Nothing mattered now.

"I think Edubot is still alive," Lambda said.

"Your assertion is false," Edubot said. The serving cart shot out of the amphitheater and back into the colony ship.

"Should we chase him?" Lambda asked.

"So it's 'we' now?" Omicron said, conveniently forgetting that she had been one of the first to run from the hydroponics bay. Her once immaculately braided hair was splattered with blood and hydraulic fluid. "Last time I checked, you were helping the bots find and kill us."

"That was Pi," Zeta said. Delta heard his voice clearly. Its whiney tone had a way of cutting through her grief.

"Lay off him," Phi said. He had used most of his jumpsuit to wrap up Pi's wound, leaving Phi more naked than usual. "We all had to make hard choices."

"Traitors!" Omicron said. "All of you." She spit on the floor.

"There are no more sides," Zeta said. "The bots have been defeated. We're all organics here."

"Humans," Gamma shot back. "We're humans. Call us what we are."

The station shook again. A lifting bot crouched low to fit through the entrance to the amphitheater. Delta heard its squeaking joints. It was the sound of death. She stroked Epsilon's hair.

"Gamma, Omicron, with me," Theta said. "Let's buy us some time. Alpha…"

Theta nodded at Delta. Alpha nodded back. She picked up her bloody sword and walked over to Delta.

"We have to go," Alpha said softly. "We need you to lead us."

Delta heard her, but she didn't comprehend. Go where? There was nowhere left to run.

"There are thirteen of us," Rho said. She had evidently emerged from wherever she ran away to. "We can't all go to Dion."

Dion. The idea dully resonated in Delta's head. She was supposed to land with Epsilon. Now Delta would be alone forever. In all the human race, there was no one else.

"This is the hard part," Alpha said to Delta. "It's your time."

"Theta can stay behind," Zeta said. "He didn't want to go anyway."

Alpha shot Zeta a look.

"Of course, it's a group decision," Zeta added quickly.

At the far entrance to the amphitheater, the lifting bot fell to the ground in two pieces.

"Incoming!" Theta yelled.

Alpha extended a hand to Delta, but Delta ignored it. She ran a finger along Epsilon's face. Epsilon's skin was already getting cold.

"There will be plenty of time for grief," Alpha said. "Maybe forever. But not right now."

For the first time, Delta looked at Alpha. This mouse of a girl who once spent all her time drawing and hiding in the back of class was now a warrior. It wasn't just her sword, which was tinged red. It was her whole bearing. She carried a quiet strength—and a silent pain. It amazed Delta. She had known Alpha her entire life, but it wasn't until now, when they were both pushed past their breaking points, that Delta really saw her. Alpha felt so deeply for everyone, even those who tried to kill her. Their pain was her pain. And when she was forced to kill... Delta turned away. The agony Alpha felt must be unbearable.

And Alpha bore it all without complaint, sharing it with no one. Not even Theta.

Delta blinked. She wasn't the only one alone. They all were. But under Delta, they would be alone together.

Delta stood up.

There were thirteen humans left. There were twelve seats on the lander. It was up to her.

"Pi, are you going to live?" Delta asked.

Pi coughed.

"Planning on it," Pi said.

Phi continued to dress his wounds.

"Get on the lander," Delta said. "Phi, you, too."

"But they fought against us!" Upsilon blurted out.

"At least they fought," Delta said.

Upsilon looked at her feet.

Delta picked up Fang and slipped him into his sheath.

"If I left behind everyone who was at fault, we would all die up here," Delta said. "Even me. The past is the past. Even if it was just two minutes ago. From this moment forward, all that matters is who can help us on the ground."

There was a murmur of agreement in the crowd. Phi helped Pi to his feet. He was more hurt than he was letting on, but Delta remembered how close Gamma had come to death, only to pull through. She suspected Pi would be fine—if she could get the immortality tank working on the surface. She could worry about that if they survived the landing.

"Three more bots inbound!" Gamma yelled.

"Alpha, help them hold the line," Delta said. "Every second counts."

Alpha ran to the far side of the amphitheater to join Theta, Gamma, and Omicron in the rear guard.

"What about Psi?" Phi asked.

"She's lost," Delta said. "You can stay and look for her if you want, but we'll have to leave you behind."

Phi and Pi looked at each other for a long moment.

"In or out, I need to know," Delta said.

"We're... we're in," Pi said.

Phi swore under his breath. "We're going to leave her?"

"We're going to leave her," Pi said. He choked back a sob.

Phi nodded as he blinked back tears. He helped Pi through the narrow lander hatch.

"Beta?"

"Yes?" Beta said. He was visibly relieved to hear his name.

"Pick up the swords, then get in the lander," Delta said.

"We have room for swords?" Sigma asked.

"I'll leave a human behind before I leave a sword," Delta said.

Sigma recoiled. Delta softened.

"The swords are thin and light," Delta said. "They take up a lot less room than a person. Nobody is getting left behind for a sword."

Beta retrieved the swords from the fallen. He did his best not to gag.

At the entrance to the amphitheater, a maintenance bot burst into white hot flames. The station shook, but not from the bot.

"We can't hold them off for much longer!" Alpha yelled.

Beta passed the dropped swords to Phi in the lander.

"Lambda."

"Oh, thank you, thank you, thank you," Lambda said.

"I didn't say you were in," Delta said.

Lambda froze.

"Get in the lander," Delta said, the slightest hint of a tired smile on her lips.

Lambda ran to the hatch.

"Upsilon?"

"Over here," Upsilon said. She was sitting on top of a disabled saw bot.

"If you promise not to cut off any more fingers, you're in," Delta said.

Upsilon hopped off the saw bot and walked to the lander, softly humming to herself.

"Delta, I'm sorry," Sigma said. "I'm sorry I led the bots to your camp. I'm sorry we killed—"

"We have our entire lives to be sorry," Delta said. "Get in the lander."

Sigma looked at her, dumbfounded. She might have been less hurt if Delta told her to stay behind and die. Slowly, Sigma headed to the lander.

Only Rho and Zeta remained in front of the lander. They both looked at Delta apprehensively. They could do the math. Surely, the four fighting in the rear guard would go, as would Delta. That meant there was only one spot left. One of them wouldn't be making the trip to Dion.

"Rho," Delta said.

"No," Zeta said. He looked behind him and recounted the students still battling bots at the door. "No. No, no, no, no, no!"

"Yes," Delta said. "Zeta, you're staying behind."

Zeta grabbed Rho's hand. "You can't leave me," Zeta said.

Rho mouthed, "I'm sorry," and pulled away. She walked to the lander.

Delta whistled. Alpha, Theta, Gamma, and Omicron began to fall back toward the lander, fighting as they went. Nearly a dozen bots were in front of them now. They couldn't hold them back for long.

"You can't do this!" Zeta said. "You can't abandon me to die just because you hate me."

"I don't hate you," Delta said. It wasn't even a lie. At that moment, she didn't feel anything at all. She doubted if she would ever feel anything again. "We have twelve spots to restart the human race, and you're bad at literally everything."

"I'm the only one who knows about religions!" Zeta said. "You can't have a civilization without religion."

"People will just make up new ones," Delta said. "You said it yourself. They always do."

A science bot exploded in white hot flames. Alpha fell over. Theta reached down and pulled her backward by her jumpsuit. More bots entered the amphitheater. Gamma and Alpha continued the fighting retreat.

Zeta took a deep breath.

"You need a doctor," he said.

"None of your patients survived at the Table," Delta said. "Not before SCASL changed the rules."

"A bad doctor is better than no doctor."

"I disagree."

Gamma screamed and fell, his arm slashed by a mining bot's talon. Spencer extended a tendril and linked with it, stalling it briefly. Theta lopped off its head. Alpha climbed back to her feet and joined Theta and Omicron. They had been pushed back to the doorway for the lander antechamber.

"I shouldn't have to die just for being incompetent!" Zeta said.

"That's sort of how natural selection works," Delta said. "But not this time. I'm not going to let you die."

"The immortality tank is on the lander," Zeta said. "The base is falling apart. Bots are everywhere. You're sentencing me to death."

Delta grabbed Zeta by his jumpsuit and leaned forward until their noses were practically touching.

"Listen to me carefully because we're out of time," she said. "I will cut a path out of here for you and point you in the direction of the factory where I lived. It's sturdier than the rest of the base. You can hold out there for practically forever."

"But not forever," Zeta said. "Everlasting life is leaving with you."

"Unless the lander explodes on liftoff. Or crashes at the landing site. Or lands safely, only to open its doors so we can be killed by a planet full of monsters."

Delta drew Fang. Zeta took half a step backwards.

"If this were a wager, I would bet you'll live longer up

here then we will down there," Delta said. "But we're going to try anyway. And we're going to do it without you."

Zeta started to say something, but he was cut off by the limb of a scorpion-shaped science bot, which plunged toward his head. Delta caught it mid-swing with her sword. The arm crashed harmlessly against the opposite wall. Delta jumped on top the bot and stabbed it through its power core. She dove off before it erupted in blue lightning.

"They're here," Omicron said.

"You four, get in the lander," Delta said. "Cover each other."

"Where are you going?" Alpha asked.

"To give Zeta a chance," Delta said.

Zeta raised a finger to object, but she grabbed him by the arm and pulled him forward. She cut down a maintenance bot and pushed through the line of digitals, dragging Zeta with her. The line of bots closed behind them.

"Run!" Delta yelled.

She darted up the stairs to the top of the amphitheater and ran around the edge. Zeta looked back and saw his way to the lander was blocked by a wall of deadly metal. A lifting bot turned back to chase him. He sprinted after Delta.

At the opposite exit, Delta killed a serving cart. She didn't think it was Edubot, but she couldn't be sure. Smoke billowed from the hall leading to the base. The lights were out.

"What now?" Zeta asked, panting.

"Get to deck nine and take the main hall past the oxygen refinement bay, then turn right. Look for signs for the heavy industry assembly plant. It'll take half a day if you run."

The station shook violently. A light from the top of the amphitheater crashed to the floor. Zeta looked down the dark hall.

"I don't want to be alone," he said quietly.

"Look for Psi. Look for Sampi," Delta said. A single tear rolled down her cheek. "Have a good life."

The lifting bot smashed its fists into the ground, narrowly missing Delta. Zeta sprinted down the hall. Delta bounded across the risers to the amphitheater floor.

At the entrance to the lander antechamber, she planted a foot on a disabled laundry cart and bounded over it. Her trained swordsmen had put up an incredible fight. Dead and damaged bots were everywhere, mostly in pieces.

She reached the lander as Gamma disappeared inside it. Only Theta remained in the antechamber.

"Get in," Delta said.

Theta looked like he was going to object, but Delta turned and sliced cleanly through a maintenance bot, bisecting it diagonally. Theta got in the lander.

The lifting bot from the amphitheater was back. Delta was relieved. It had followed her and not Zeta.

Delta dove headfirst into the lander. She reached back with her foot and slammed the hatch behind her.

# Chapter 52

GAMMA WATCHED AS Delta slid into the lander upside down.

"Launch!" she yelled.

The lifting bot hammered its fists into the closed hatch.

"You have God," Gamma said.

Delta frantically patted the pockets in her jump suit to find the data card where she downloaded him.

The rockets ignited. The entire world seemed to shake violently.

"You didn't put God in the computer," Gamma said.

"No, I didn't," Delta said, strapping herself in.

"Who's flying this?" Alpha asked.

They all knew the answer. Delta hadn't cut the tendril in time. SCASL had made it on board.

The thrust pushed the students back in their seats. It was the most intense pressure Gamma had ever felt. Spenser whirred. He took up the tiny gap between Gamma's chest and the control panel in front of him.

"I had to leave Zeta, and you brought Spenser?" Delta asked through gritted teeth.

Gamma's bones felt like they were going to shake out of his body.

"He crawled in on his own," Gamma grunted.

Spenser whirred appreciatively. The thrust appeared to have no effect on him.

"I'm glad you're here, too," Delta said.

The lander broke out of Comus' gravity. The helpless passengers were still pressed in their seats by their harnesses, but their hair began to float. Spenser extended his spider legs and latched onto a control console.

Delta finally managed to find the pocket where she stashed God.

"Plug this in," she said. She passed the data card along the line of organics to Gamma. Gamma wrenched his arm awkwardly around Spenser and inserted the data card into the console.

Sparks shot out. The card started to melt.

"Was that supposed to happen?" Gamma asked.

The faint smell of smoke filled the compartment.

"Uh, guys," Lambda said. "My display is showing the landing data. We're going to the middle of the continent."

"Right where SCASL always wanted us," Delta said.

"We're going to die," Upsilon said.

"Maybe Zeta was the lucky one," Omicron muttered.

"What do we do?" Alpha asked.

Theta reached over and held her hand.

"Prepare for a hot landing," Delta said. "We'll be fighting from the second we touch down."

"No," Gamma said. No one heard him over the general

complaining. "Spenser, can you take back the lander?"

Spenser rotated on his spider legs to face Gamma. He seemed to look at Gamma for an especially long time. Gamma gently patted his lifelong companion. He held back tears.

"You'll always be my best friend," he said.

Spenser extended a tendril and interfaced with the lander. The entire ship bucked. Every light on the computer consoles lit up. Spenser shook violently. A blue arc of electricity shot up along the tendril. Spenser was blasted across the narrow space. He bounced from one side to the other, smashing against the console and Gamma's face. All of Spenser's indicator lights went dark. He would never move again.

"Thank you," Gamma said softly. Drops of his blood floated in zero gravity. "You gave it everything you had."

"Something happened," Lambda said.

"What?" Delta asked.

"We have a new landing site," Lambda said. "The computer is trying to adjust, but it can't. Spenser somehow locked us in place."

A loud clunking noise echoed through the lander.

"Where are we going?" Upsilon asked.

"Ocean side, far from the continent," Lambda said. "Far from everything."

"Hope you guys can swim," Omicron said.

A smile crept onto Gamma's face.

"Are you sure there's nothing down there?" Gamma asked.

The loud clunking noise in the lander got more frantic as SCASL tried to adjust whatever Spenser had locked in place.

Lambda looked again.

"Wait," she said. "There's an island. A small one. We're heading right for it."

"Gamma," Delta said. "You didn't."

"I didn't," Gamma said. "Spenser did. He saved us all. Again."

Gamma wondered not for the first time who Spenser had been before he inhabited his last metal body. He must have been someone important. And powerful. He outsmarted SCASL inside SCASL's own spacecraft. The vacuum bot who once was an admiral.

"We're about to hit the atmosphere," Lambda said.

The lander jolted. Swords rattled against important equipment. Gamma thought it was a good thing this was a one-way trip. The view outside the portholes changed from black to blue. They were the first organics to lay eyes on Dion's atmosphere in thousands of years. Orange flames enveloped the lander. Gamma's teeth clattered painfully together. The blood droplets that had been floating in front of him settled on hard surfaces as gravity returned. The lander felt ready to shake apart. The ineffective clunking got louder.

The lander jerked violently. Gamma thought he might turn inside out.

"That was the parachutes," Lambda said.

Delta was muttering to herself. Her eyes were still red

from Epsilon's last moments. And from leaving Zeta, Gamma suspected. That had been harder than she expected.

"Tell me he didn't," Delta repeated to herself. "Tell me he didn't."

The lander touched down with a crunch. The entire craft tilted at an angle. For a long moment, no one said anything. Then, one by one, the organics unbuckled. Delta popped the hatch. She took her sword with her.

She set foot on the barren, rocky soil as cold sea air hit her in the face. She looked down in awe at the footprint she left. Humans had returned to Dion.

The other eleven survivors—the entirety of the human race—filed out behind her. There were no roos. There was no vegetation. There was just this isolated island.

"I ran the simulations," Gamma said. He coughed to push back all the emotions trying to creep into his voice. "We can live here forever. We'll be stable. We'll be safe."

"We'll never leave here," Delta said. She jabbed her sword into the rocky soil. "Stagnation is death."

Gamma took a deep breath of the ocean air. Gently, he laid Spenser's inert form on the hard-won ground.

"No," Gamma said. "Stagnation is life."

## Acknowledgments

A BOOK DOESN'T just happen on its own. Sadly. My life would be so much easier if it did.

The following people helped this story see the light of day. Any hate mail should be directed to them. I'm kidding. Write your hate mail down on fancy parchment and burn it to achieve full catharsis. But please send all effusive fan mail to me.

A big thanks to:

My literary agent, Mark Gottlieb of Trident Media Group. You helped me break into yet another genre. What's next? A high fantasy set in the wild west? A cozy mystery/paranormal erotica mash up? An audio-only pop-up book? With you, anything is possible. That's dangerous for both of us.

Kate Coe, former editor at Rebellion Books. The day I found out you decided to publish my book was the happiest day of my life. Don't tell my wife and kids.

Jim Killen, editor at Rebellion Books. You gave me both the shortest and most devastating notes of my writing career. With a few simple lines, you pushed me to make this a better book. I hope I've risen to the challenge.

My kids. Watching how you interact with each other every day helped inspire a novel about a war on a robot-filled moon base ten thousand years away. Thank goodness you don't get along.

My wife. You were the first person to read this book all the way through, and you didn't hate it. That sort of tepid endorsement was all the encouragement I needed. The fact that this book made it across the finish line at all is largely because of you.

# FIND US ONLINE!

## www.rebellionpublishing.com

/rebellionpub  /rebellionpublishing /rebellionpublishing

## SIGN UP TO OUR NEWSLETTER!

### rebellionpublishing.com/newsletter

## YOUR REVIEWS MATTER!

Enjoy this book? Got something to say?

Leave a review on Amazon, GoodReads or with your
favourite bookseller and let the world know!